Praise for *Love Drunk Cowboy*

First in Carolyn Brown's new Spikes & Spurs series

"Delightful romance."

—*RT Book Reviews*

"Brown revitalizes the Western romance with this fresh, funny, and sexy tale filled with likable, down-to-earth characters."

—*Booklist*

"An absolutely adorable story... Tender and passionate love scenes and endearing and quirky characters... I found myself with a big smile on my face at the end of this book."

—*The Romance Studio*

"Well written, fun, and interesting... I could not put it down."

—*PonyTails Book Reviews*

"Peopled with quirky characters and full of sassy fun, this book will leave readers smiling."

—*BookPage*

Also by Carolyn Brown

Red's Hot Cowboy

Carolyn Brown

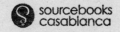

sourcebooks
casablanca

Published by Sourcebooks Casablanca, an imprint of Sourcebooks, Inc.
P.O. Box 4410, Naperville, Illinois 60567-4410
(630) 961-3900
FAX: (630) 961-2168
www.sourcebooks.com

Printed and bound in the United States of America
QW 10 9 8 7 6 5 4 3 2 1

To my wonderful publisher,
Dominique Raccah!

Chapter 1

THE LIGHTS WENT OUT IN HENRIETTA, TEXAS.

Everything west of the bridge into town was black: no streetlights and very few humming generators. But the flashing neon sign advertising the Longhorn Inn motel still flickered on and off, showing a bowlegged old cowboy wearing six guns, a ten-gallon hat, and a big smile as he pointed toward the VACANCY sign at his feet.

Santa Claus and a cold north wind kept everyone inside that Christmas Eve night and there were no customers, which was fine with the new owner, Pearl Richland. She could cuss, stomp, and pout about operating a damn motel in north Texas rather than spending the holiday in Savannah with her southern relatives, and no one would hear a thing. Not even her mother, who had told her she was making the biggest mistake of her life when she quit her banking job in Durant, Oklahoma, and moved to Henrietta, Texas.

"Entrepreneur! Running a fifty-year-old motel and cleaning rooms is not an entrepreneur. You are ruining your life, Katy Pearl Richland," her mother had said.

But Pearl had always loved the time she spent at the motel when she was a kid, and after sitting at the loan officer's desk in a bank, she had a hankering to be on the other side. The one where she was the person with a new business and bright, fresh ideas as to how to improve it.

Now she was, but it did have a price to pay. Pearl, the party girl, was now an entrepreneur and had more work than she could keep up with and hadn't been out on a date in months. Hard work, she didn't mind. Long hours, she didn't mind. Online classes with research projects that took a chunk of her days, she didn't mind. Not dating—that she minded a helluva lot.

Pearl put the finishing touches on the assignments for the two online motel hospitality classes she was taking out of Midwestern University in Wichita Falls. One needed a few tweaks, but she'd have it done by New Year's, and then she'd enroll in more courses, which would begin the middle of January.

She was on her way to the kitchen to see if Santa Claus had left something wonderful like double fudge brownies in her cabinet when all hell broke loose. She thought about that guy in the poem about the night before Christmas as she ran to the window and peeked out at all the vehicles crunching gravel under their wheels—cars, vans, trucks. She wouldn't have been surprised to see a fat feller dressed in red with tiny reindeer stopping an oversized sleigh in amongst all those vehicles.

She hustled back to the check-in counter and put on her best smile as she looked at the crowd pushing their way toward the door. The tiny lobby of the twenty-five-unit 1950s-style motel didn't offer breakfast, not even donuts and coffee. That was something on her list for the future, right along with a major overhaul when she decided whether she wanted to go modern or rustic. It didn't have a crystal chandelier or a plasma television. It did have two brown leather recliners with a small table between them. In addition to the recliners, it was now

packed with people all talking so loudly that it overpowered the whistling wind of the Texas blue norther that
had hit an hour earlier.

She was reminded of Toby Keith's song "I Love This
Bar." He sang about hookers, lookers, and bikers. Well,
if he'd loved her motel instead of a bar he could have
added a bride and groom, a pissed off granny who was
trying to corral a bunch of bored teenage grandchildren,
and sure enough there was Santa Claus over there in
the corner. Pearl didn't see anyone offering to sit on his
chubby knees, but maybe that was because he'd taken
off his hat and his fake beard. He was bald except for
a rim of curly gray hair that ended, of all things, in a
ponytail about three inches long at his neck.

Pearl raised her voice. "Who was here first?"

The door opened and four more people crowded into
the room, letting in a blast of freezing air that made
everyone shiver.

A young man in a tuxedo stepped up to the tall desk
separating the lobby from the office. "That would be us."

"Fill out this card. Rooms are all alike. Two double
beds, microfridge, and free wireless Internet," Pearl said.

A girl in a long white velvet dress hugged up to his
side. "We sure aren't interested in Internet or a microwave oven tonight. This is so quaint and very romantic,
and it's got all we need... a bed!"

The man took time out from the card to kiss her.

Quaint and romantic? Pearl thought. *It's more like
the motel in that old movie* Psycho. *But I do like the
idea of quaint and romantic. Hadn't thought of that, but
it has a nice ring for a black-and-white brochure. Visit
the quaint and romantic inn... I like it.*

Built in a low spot on the east side of town more than half a century before, it had a rough, weathered wood exterior that had turned gray with wind, rain, sleet, and pure old Texas heat; wind-out windows that used to work before air conditioning had been installed (now they'd been painted shut); a covered walkway all the way around the U-shaped building; and a gravel parking lot.

Pearl had twenty-five units and it was beginning to look like it really could be a full house. That meant she'd be cleaning a hell of a lot of rooms on Christmas Day because Rosa, the lady who'd helped her Aunt Pearlita for the past twenty years, decided to retire when Pearlita passed away in the fall.

While Mrs. Bride whispered love words in Mr. Bridegroom's ear, Pearl looked out over the impatient crowd. Santa good-naturedly waited his turn, but the lady behind him with six teenagers in tow looked like she could chew up railroad spikes and spit out ten penny nails.

Maybe Pearl needed to sit on Santa's lap and ask if he'd send his elves to help clean the rooms the next day. Cleaning hadn't been a problem because renting five or six units a night was the norm up until that moment. The east side of the motel had ten units along with Pearl's apartment. The bottom of the U had five units and a laundry room, and the west side had ten units. There was parking for one vehicle per room with extra parking for big trucks behind the laundry room. Part of her last online assignment was designing charts to make a few more spots in the wide middle. Even if she implemented the idea, it couldn't happen until spring. Winter, even in Texas, wasn't the right season to pour concrete.

The motel area had been carved out of a stand of mesquite trees fifty-plus years before, and every few years Pearlita had ordered a couple of truckloads of new gravel for the center lot and the drive around the outside edge. She'd declared that concrete was hot and that it made the place too modern, but Pearl figured she couldn't afford the concrete. When she saw the savings account her aunt left in her name, she changed her mind. Aunt Pearlita was just plain tight.

The bridegroom didn't care that the crowd behind him was getting impatient. He'd write a letter or two and then kiss his new little wife. Pearl tapped her foot and wished he'd take it on to his room and out of her lobby. After eternity plus three days, he finally finished filling out the motel card. She picked an old-fashioned key from the pegboard behind her. It was a real honest-to-god key on a chain with a big 2 engraved into the plastic fob. The back was printed with a message that read, *If found please place in any mailbox* and had the address for the Longhorn Inn. Pearl wondered how many times Aunt Pearlita had been called to the post office to pay for the postage on a key. What the place needed was those new modern card keys that all the motels were using.

Pearl could almost hear her aunt getting on the soapbox: *Keys have opened doors for thousands of years, so why use those newfangled idiot credit card looking keys? No telling what a locksmith would charge to come fix one of those if a kid dripped his ice cream in it. Besides, why fix something that ain't broken? Now stop your bellyachin' and think about how much money you're rakin' in tonight. Besides, a plastic credit card lookin' key doesn't say quaint and romantic to me.*

Pearl set the card aside and laid another one on the counter for the next customer. "That's room two, second room from here. Parking is in front of the room. Next?"

Number one was next to her apartment with only two layers of sheetrock and very little insulation between the motel room and her bedroom. If she was going to clean rooms from dawn to dark the next day then she sure didn't want to be kept awake by noisy newlyweds all night.

Mrs. Claus deferred to the older lady with six kids. "You go on, deary. Me and Santa Claus can wait until you get those kids in a room."

She stepped up to the counter. "I need three rooms, connected if possible."

Pearl shook her head. "I'm sorry, ma'am. I can put you in three side-by-side rooms, but none of them have inside connecting doors."

She laid a Visa card on the counter. "That will be fine if that's the best you can do. Each room has two beds, right?"

Pearl nodded and handed her a card to fill out. When the transaction was finished she handed the woman keys to rooms three, four, and five and looked up at the next customer.

Santa Claus stepped up to the counter. "Thank God you've got electricity. I wasn't looking forward to driving all the way back to Dallas tonight. Whole town is black. Hospital is working on generators, and I guess a few people have them in their homes from the dim lights we saw when we left the motel on the other end of town. I just need one room for two adults. No pets. Me and Momma were at a senior citizens' party when the electricity went out. I was Santa Claus and giving out presents. Do you take AARP?"

"Yes, I do. Ten percent discount," Pearl answered.

An hour later twenty-four rooms were filled, the parking lot was full, and the lobby empty. The north wind still howled across the flat land with nothing but a barbed wire fence to slow it down between Henrietta and Houston. Delilah, Pearl's yellow cat, peeked out around the door from the office into the living room of the apartment.

"Come on out, girl. The coast is clear and we've only got one empty room. I'm going to turn on the NO VACANCY light and we're going to get a good night's sleep. We'll need it tomorrow when we start stripping beds and doing laundry," Pearl said.

Delilah leaped up on the counter and flopped down on her chubby belly, long yellow hair fluffing out like a halo around her body. She was seven years old and spoiled to that fancy cat food in the little cans. If she'd had her way it would have been served up on crystal, but Pearl figured making her eat from a plastic cat dish kept her from getting too egotistical.

Pearl pushed all the guest cards to one side and rubbed Delilah's soft fur. "The worst of it is over until tomorrow when we have to clean all those rooms."

The rumble of a pickup truck overpowered the noise of the north wind slinging sleet pellets against the glass door. It came to a halt right outside the lobby door, the lights glowing through the glass window.

Pearl pulled out a guest card and laid it on the counter beside Delilah. "Hope they don't mind newlyweds in the next room, and I damn sure hope they aren't noisy since they'll be right next to us."

One of Aunt Pearlita's favorite sayings was, "Life is faith, hope, and chaos." The chaos factor had taken center stage when the lights went out in Henrietta. It really put on a show when the lobby door opened and a Catahoula cow dog rushed inside. Delilah was on her feet growling, every long yellow hair bristled and every claw ready for battle. She'd put up with a lot but not a dog in her territory, and no slobbering dog had rights in her lobby.

The dog took one look at the cat, raised up on the counter, and bayed like he'd treed a raccoon. Delilah reached out and swiped a claw across his nose, which set him into a barking frenzy. That's when she jumped on his back, all claws bared. Her yowls matched his howls, and the two of them set out on an earsplitting war. The dog threw his head around and tried to bite the varmint tattooing his back with its vicious claws, but the cat hung on with tenacity and fierce anger.

Pearl plowed into the melee, grabbed at Delilah, and missed every time. The dog howled like it was dying. The cat sent out high-pitched wails that would rival a fire siren. Pearl yelled, but neither animal paid a bit of attention to her. They just kept on running in circles and creating enough noise to make the dead raise up out of their graves in preparation for the rapture. She caught a blur of cowboy boots and jeans and heard a man's deep drawl, loud and clear, when he yelled at her to get her damn cat off his dog.

"What?" she yelled.

"I said for you to get your damn cat off Digger!"

Pearl reached for Delilah again, only to miss in the flurry of noise and fur. "Get your damn dog out of here!"

Delilah chose that minute to bail off the dog, bounce across the counter, and shoot through the door into the apartment. The dog followed in leaping bounds with Pearl right beside him. She slammed the door so quickly that the dog's nose took a hit and it howled one more time.

The man grabbed the dog and hauled back on his collar. "What in the hell happened?"

"That your dog?" she asked breathlessly.

He was panting from the fuss of trying to get his dog under control and ending the commotion. "I opened the door and the wind blew it shut before I could get inside. Next thing I knew fur was flying and it sounded like poor old Digger was dying. Why did your cat attack him? He lives with cats out at the ranch. He wouldn't hurt one."

"Tell that to Delilah, and you are on the wrong side of the counter, cowboy," Pearl snapped. The adrenaline rush over, she looked at more than boot heels and jeans. The cowboy had a scowl on his face, jet-black hair all tousled from the cat and dog fight, and brown eyes with flecks of pure gold floating in them like a bottle of good schnapps. The whole effect sang "Bad boy. Bad boy. Whatcha goin' do?" in Pearl's ears. She shook her head to get the chanting to stop, but it didn't do a bit of good.

The cowboy took two steps and pushed through the swinging doors at the end of the counter. "All I want is a room, Red."

"You call me Red again, Mister, and you won't need

one. What you'll need is a pine box and a preacher to read about you lyin' down in green pastures," she said.

He smiled and suddenly there was a whole orchestra behind the singer chanting about bad boys in Pearl's head. He was bundled up in a worn leather bomber jacket with fleece lining that made his broad shoulders even wider and ended at a narrow waist, faded jeans that hugged a right fine butt that would've had her drooling if she hadn't been so damn mad, and scuffed boots that made him a real cowboy and not the drugstore variety that was all hat and no cattle. His dog was sitting obediently beside him, looking up pitifully as if tattling on that abominable creature that had attacked him.

"Who in the hell is Delilah anyway, and what's she got to do with all this commotion?" he asked in a deep Texas drawl.

"Delilah is my cat," Pearl said.

"That *is* a good name for a she-devil like that thing. You got any rooms left for tonight? It looks like the parking lot is full, but the sign is still on."

If only he could have had a high squeaky voice, but no, he had to be the complete bad boy package with that Texas drawl. And Pearl had run from bad boys ever since she was seventeen. Her mother had been right about Vince Knightly. He'd been a double dose of rebellious bad news riding a motorcycle.

Pearl picked up the card that had fallen on the floor in the middle of the cat and dog fight and laid it on the counter. "I've got one room."

"You got a problem with Digger stayin' in the room?"

"Not if he's housebroke," she said. "He makes a mess, I'll charge your credit card triple for the room."

"Digger's a good dog. He wouldn't make a mess on carpet if he exploded. I should've gone on up to my friend Rye's in Terral, but I've got chores in the morning. I would've if I'd known me and Digger would have to fight our way through hell to get a room."

"Rye O'Donnell?" Pearl asked.

"That'd be the one. Know him?"

"He married my friend."

"Luck of the Irish," the cowboy said as he filled out the card.

"What?" Pearl asked.

He pulled the card across the countertop toward him and laid down a bill. "I don't use credit cards. If Digger makes a mess in your precious room, I'll pay for it in cash. I said the luck of the Irish, and I was talkin' about Rye. Man had to be lucky to get a woman like that."

Her cell phone rang and she grabbed it.

"Hello?"

"Hey, darlin'. I'm at Kayla's party and I don't see you here. I miss you. Are you sick?" Tyler asked.

She shut her eyes briefly and saw him... tall, blond, dimples, and damn, but he could kiss good. She sighed as she rang up the money.

"I'm working. I've moved to Henrietta and I'm running a motel. No party for me tonight," she said.

"Ah, sugar, that stinks," he said. "I'll call later in the week. Maybe we can meet up in Dallas for a weekend?"

"Don't hold your breath. Tell Kayla hello for me." Pearl handed the cowboy a key to room one and a nickel in change and watched him fill out the card. His sexier-than-hell eyes were topped with black brows and set off by ultra-thick black lashes. His high cheek-bones and black shaggy hair left no doubt that there was some Native American blood in his gene pool. His angular face was softened by a lopsided dimple on the left side when he took time away from the card to smile at his dog.

Yes, the whole bad boy package down to the smile, which reminded her too damn much of Vince, and that was one place she was not going on Christmas Eve.

A man who likes dogs can't be all bad, and dammit he's hot, her heart said.

His dimple deepened. "So you got to work instead of play. Too bad. You look like someone who'd rather be at a party."

"That's called eavesdropping," she said.

"I wasn't listening in on your conversation. Couldn't help but hear a man who's yelling above the crowd when he talks."

She shot him a go-to-hell look, which worked the reverse when she realized just how sexy his eyes were.

What in the hell is the matter with me? Probably the fact that I haven't had a date in weeks, haven't been to dinner or a movie. Hell, I haven't even been to the ice cream store with a man in forever. No one told me being an entrepreneur in a little bitty town took away every chance for a date. I want a date with a hot cowboy that looks like this for my Christmas present. The thought startled her so bad that she almost blushed.

"You stay away from that man," her mother's voice said so close that Pearl looked over her shoulder to see if she'd snuck into the lobby through the back door.

She willed herself to think about all the cleaning

she'd have to do the next day to get the thoughts and her mother's voice out of her head.

"So when did Pearlita hire you? Last time I was here she was still runnin' the place by herself," the cowboy asked as he signed his name to the bottom of the card.

"Pearlita was my aunt. She passed away and I inherited the place," Pearl said.

"I'm sorry, ma'am," he said softly.

"Thank you," she said as she reached under the counter and flipped the light switch to add the word NO to VACANCY. "Sleep well. I'll lock up behind you."

"Good night, Red," he said with a wicked grin as she shut the door.

She shook her fist and gave him her best drop-graveyard-dead look.

"Who is he anyway?" she asked as she made her way back to the counter and picked up the card.

Wil Marshall. One *l* on the first name, two on the second.

"Wil Marshall." The name rolled off her tongue and created a warm spot low in her belly. "Hell, it even sounds like a bad boy name, and I'm not getting tangled up with another bad boy. I learned my lesson the first time, and as bad as I hate to admit it, Momma was right about bad boys."

His address was a rural route, phone number still out of Henrietta. He drove a spanking new Chevrolet Silverado truck with Texas plates. And he had a grin that was part sexy and the other part pure wicked.

"Wil Marshall, you sleep well and then get the hell out of my motel. I don't need the heat that sexy grin of yours brings on," she said.

She slipped through the door into her living quarters and found Delilah sitting on the coffee table licking her paws as if cleaning all that horrid dog smell from her claws.

"Poor baby," Pearl crooned as she stroked the cat's long fur. "Guess you showed that miserable slobbering dog who was boss, didn't you? If his master ever calls me Red again I will turn you loose to show him he's not the boss either."

She slumped down into the sofa, glad that she'd decided to keep the comfortable old furniture. She'd started to donate all of it to a charity but then decided at the last minute to put hers in storage until she could figure out just what improvements she intended to make to the motel. The gold velvet sofa was ugly as sin on Sunday morning but comfortable; the old chrome dining room table and four red padded chairs to match were old as God but serviceable; the bedroom suite that had belonged to Pearlita's mother and an oak desk bought at an estate auction the year the motel opened were still usable. When she was a little girl, Pearl had wondered whether Moses or Noah had built that desk. Now she knew it predated both of them.

It was her first night to be truly full since she'd re-opened after being closed a week when her great-aunt died a month before. Pearlita's lawyer read her the will that left everything to her—the motel and all the that. Pearl jumped on the opportunity, used her vacation time as notice, and became a businesswoman overnight.

She and her long-time friend, Austin, had had a memorial for Pearlita on the Texas side of the Red River across the bridge from Terral. Austin said it was the same setup as she'd had for her grandmother back around Easter time, and that's where Pearlita had gotten the idea of a no-nonsense send-off.

She and Austin had stood on the river that foggy day, dumped her aunt's ashes into the river, waited until they floated away in the cold clay-colored water, and then went to lunch at the Peach Orchard over in Terral. It didn't seem right or proper to watch something as vital as Aunt Pearlita get washed down the river. She wasn't even sure it was legal and hoped her aunt didn't wind up in the belly of an Angus bull that drank from the river.

That evening Pearl had gone to the Longhorn Inn and set up business. Five rooms a night was a busy night. Once she had seven customers and she and Delilah had shared a bottle of beer in celebration. But slow business had allowed her time to work on a couple of online hospitality courses, and she'd already written down dozens of new ideas that she'd gleaned from the courses. She was just about ready to take on the remodeling job but first she had to decide exactly what she wanted the place to look like and what kind of feel she wanted it to have.

Quaint and romantic. The new phrase ran though her mind as she stroked the cat's fur, and she liked it better than all the modern ideas she'd come up with. In the spring she'd make a final decision, but right then she tried to come up with a sign to replace old doofus cowboy with his bowlegs and flashing neon sign.

"Hell, girl, tomorrow after we clean all the rooms, we may break out a whole six-pack of Coors." Pearl pulled her kinky red hair up into a ponytail in preparation for a shower. "You get all those nasty old dog germs off you and I'll go get my shower. We'll get a good night's sleep, and as soon as they all check out we'll start cleaning in the morning."

A long mournful howl stopped her in her tracks as she made her way from the living room toward the bathroom. She'd only heard noises like that in scary movies when a dog was sitting on top of a grave. Mercy, this was Christmas Eve and not Halloween. Was the motel haunted? Was Aunt Pearlita punishing her for all the hell she'd given her through the years?

"Damn dog!" She swore when she realized it was Digger in room one and not a ghost dog sent by her late aunt.

The phone rang. She hurried to the bedroom where the second line from the motel lobby was located. She grabbed it on the third ring and started to carry it back to the living room, but the whole phone came crashing down from the end table. Aunt Pearlita hadn't seen the need to invest in a cordless when the old blue desk type phone worked just fine.

"Longhorn Inn, may I help you?"

Wil Marshall's deep drawl answered. "Would you please ask those folks in the next room to lighten up on the noise? The headboard is banging against the wall, and she's wailing and moaning like a banshee. Sounds like his Christmas present is a helluva lot better than mine."

"They are newlyweds. And they were here before you," she said through gritted teeth.

"They're upsetting Digger and if I can hear them, then you can probably hear him," Wil said.

"I can." She heard another mournful howl loud and clear. "I'll tell them to keep it down."

"Thank you!"

She could've sworn she heard him whisper "Red" at the end of the last sentence, but it could have been something he said to his dog. Still it aggravated her enough to set her off in a swearing tirade that lasted all of thirty seconds before the phone rang again.

"I told you I'd call," she said shortly.

"Call who? This is Allie Green in room three and that's no way for you to answer your business phone, young lady. There's a terrible fight going on in the room next door and I think they've got a dog in there because every so often I hear something howling like a dog. I don't cotton to people beating dogs or women. You need to tell them to keep down the noise," she said.

"They are newlyweds," Pearl said.

"Dear God, I'm glad I didn't put my grandchildren in this room. Their sweet innocent ears sure don't need to hear such goings on. Make them be quiet. I can hear them above the television set. Did I hear you say there would be breakfast in the lobby in the morning?"

"No, ma'am. We do not serve breakfast."

That was something on her list for the new updated motel; maybe starting with coffee, juice, and an assortment of donuts, but even that was going to take some major remodeling.

"Well, that's a shame. A few donuts and a cup of coffee wouldn't break you. This ain't much of a room anyway. Not having breakfast sure doesn't make up for it."

"But it does have electricity and heat," Pearl said.

"Don't argue with me. You take care of those people in room two. People shouldn't carry on like that even if it is their honeymoon. What is this world comin' to? I swear, sex on television, sex in ads, sex in magazines, and now I have to listen to it next door in a motel. It's disgraceful, I tell you. Do something about it right now."

"I'll take care of it. Good-bye," Pearl said.

Chaos!

Aunt Pearlita had been a prophet!

She pushed the number for the newlywed's room and on the fifth ring a woman answered with a breathless giggle.

"I'm sorry to call you on your honeymoon, but I've got complaints about the noise on both sides of you," Pearl said.

"We'll hold it down," the girl giggled. "Would you please call whoever is in room one and tell them to shut that howling dog up? He's making more noise than we are. And the old lady in room three has been pounding on the wall with something. You're probably going to find holes in the sheetrock tomorrow morning."

"Thank you," Pearl said.

She sighed as she hung up. Did all those business-people with bright shining eyes who sat across from her loan desk in the bank have days and nights like this? If they did, it was a wonder they didn't throw in the towel and tell her to foreclose on their businesses. The dog set up another bone chilling howl. Delilah shot behind the sofa like a lightning streak and the phone rang again.

"Front desk," she said.

"This is room five. My grandmother rented three rooms, remember. We've only got four towels and there are three of us in here and we all have to wash our hair and we need more towels," a teenage girl said.

"Come on down to the lobby and I'll get some more ready," Pearl said.

"Oh, no! We can't leave the room or Granny will get really mad. She looked out the window and saw that cowboy going into room one and said if we left our room we'd be sorry. Besides, we are already undressed and in our pajamas and it is freezing out there. You bring them to us," she said.

"I'll be right down." Pearl sighed.

She gathered up half a dozen towels in case the girls all needed to primp again the next morning, put on her jacket, and braced against the bitter sting of sleet when it hit her face. Digger barked from the other side of the door in room one. Giggles and laughter came from room two. In the next room she heard nagging tones with a bit of pure old bitching thrown in. By the time she got to room five her nose was frozen and there was a fine layer of sleet on top of the stack of towels.

She knocked on the door, yelled "room service," and grumbled as she waited a full minute before kicking the door with her boot and yelling again.

A teenage girl swung open the door. "It's the towels," she singsonged to her cousins.

The oldest one looked up from the middle of the bed and then went back to texting on her cell phone. "Well, shit! I thought it might be that cowboy!"

Pearl laid the towels on the bed. "I brought a few extra in case you need them in the morning."

"Thanks," the older one said without taking her eyes from her cell phone where her thumbs were working so fast they were a blur.

"Good night, ladies." Pearl backed out of the room.

She kept her head down against the blowing sleet and hurried back toward the lobby. If she had to go out again that night she was putting on a heavier jacket, for sure. She didn't see the boots until she was face-to-face with the cowboy from room one. She came to a halt so fast that it made her woozy. When she looked up into his eyes, she just got dizzier.

"You need to watch where you are going. You came close to plowin' right into me," he said.

"You could have stepped to one side and let me keep going rather than stopping me in the middle of a sleet storm," she snapped.

"I tried calling the office but you weren't answering. I was on my way to beat on the door. Those little girls in four are calling my room every five minutes. They're giggling and saying that they think cowboys are sexy. They said if I'd bring beer we'd have a party," he growled.

"You got a cell phone?" she asked gruffly. Christmas Eve was supposed to be fun and magical, not crazy.

He nodded.

"Then simply unplug the motel phone from the wall and no one can pester you," she said.

He folded his arms across his chest. The woman was pretty with the sleet sticking to her red hair, but she looked like she had one of them hot tempers to go with her red hair.

The wind was chilling to the bone and the tank top he wore with his flannel pajama bottoms did little to keep out the cold, but he wasn't about to lose the battle of the stare-down with the pretty motel owner.

"People ought to keep a better handle on their kids. That's the way trouble starts."

"You'd better get back inside before you get frost-bite." She let her eyes roam over his broad chest and hunky biceps.

You are one to talk about trouble, cowboy. It oozes out of your pores like sweat on a hot summer day.

He dropped his arms but didn't look away from her eyes. "I don't need you to tell me what to do. I can take care of myself."

Pearl popped her hands on her hips. "Don't look like you're doin' too good a job to me. You're going to have pneumonia in the morning if you don't get inside where it's warm. Even your stupid dog has enough sense to stay in out of this weather and he's got a fur coat."

He stepped into his room and slammed the door with a loud bang.

The phone was ringing when she opened the lobby door. Delilah was sitting on the sofa staring at it as if with her evil yellow-eyed glare she could send the noisy thing into room one with that other horrible creature who'd barked at her.

Pearl grabbed it and said, "Longhorn Inn, may I help you?"

"This is Georgiana over in room twenty-three. There's a spider in my bathroom and I'm terrified of spiders. Send someone to kill it," she whimpered.

Pearl rolled her eyes and wondered if old Digger would be interested in killing a big, mean spider. "I'll be there in a minute."

"The door is unlocked. I'm standing in the middle of the bed. I won't get down until that thing is dead, so come on in," Georgiana said.

"Yes, ma'am," Pearl said and hung up.

Pearl picked up a can of bug spray and a flyswat and grumbled the whole way across the parking lot as she made her way between cars and trucks. The sleet had gotten serious. A thin layer covered the parking lot and stuck to the vehicle windshields. She knocked on the door, announced herself as pest control, and opened it to find Georgiana right where she said she'd be.

The woman had to top six feet because her head was almost touching the ceiling when she stood in the middle of the bed hugging a pillow like a shield. She wore a flimsy red lace teddy and shivered like she'd been snow skiing in that getup. She had a shoulder span that would rival a Dallas Cowboy linebacker and hair so big they'd have had to order her a special helmet if she'd played for them. "You've got to kill it and flush it down the potty because I'm afraid of dead ones too. I thought you'd send your husband to do this kind of work."

For a split second Pearl wondered if the red teddy and the fear was in hopes that a man would rush to her aid and she'd repay him for his chivalry in ways that would blow the bottom out of that commandment about adultery.

"No husband. Just me, but I'm armed and dangerous." Pearl held up the bug spray and the swat.

And chaos truly does rule tonight, Pearl thought on her way to the bathroom. *It's a good thing I'm not afraid of spiders. A mouse would be a different thing altogether. If it had been one of those varmints you'd be standing on the bed until you starved to death or until you talked Santa Claus into chasin' it down for you.*

It wasn't a spider but a stinging scorpion. A nice big

one with its tail crooked up over its back and a threatening look in its beady little eyes. She gave him a healthy dose of bug spray but it barely slowed him down. The fly swat showed him who was boss, and Pearl picked up what was left of him with toilet paper and flushed his remains down the toilet.

"It's dead and buried," she told Georgiana. "You can get off the bed now."

Georgiana scanned the whole room before she stepped off the bed. "I'm just not comfortable in these little motels. I like a big old chain hotel like a Motel Six or a Holiday Inn or preferably a Hyatt."

"But they are all out of electricity, right?" Pearl said.

"That's the only reason I'm here. Spiders are like dogs. They know I'm scared of them so they follow me," she whined.

"Well, it's a dead bug now."

A team of wild, longhorn bulls wouldn't make Pearl admit to a customer that what she'd killed was deadlier than a common house spider. Next week she'd call the exterminator. It wouldn't stop the problem but it would slow it down. Scorpions were as native to Texas as sexy cowboys and rodeos, and when it got cold they went looking for a warm place to hole up. The woman trying to walk six inches above the floor wasn't a native of Texas or she'd know the difference between a spider and a scorpion.

"Thank you." Georgiana's voice didn't match her size. She could be a Dial-Up-Sex woman with that sweet little girl voice. "I'm sorry I said that about your motel. God, I can't wait to get home to Buffalo, New York."

Pearl had her hand on the doorknob but stopped in

her tracks. "What in the hell are you doing in Texas on Christmas?"

"I was maid of honor for that married couple. She was my roommate in college and he's my second cousin. I introduced them. I flew into Dallas and I'm flying out tomorrow. I'll be back home by late tomorrow night, and it won't be a minute too soon," Georgiana said.

"Well, the bug is dead. Sleep well and be careful on the trip to Dallas. Roads might be slippery." Pearl eased out the door.

The door to room one opened when she reached that side of the motel. Jesus, Mary, Joseph, and all the wise men, did she have to run into him every damn time she went on a room service call? Digger pranced at the end of a bright red leash and Wil had enough sense to put on his jacket.

She pointed toward the road. "There's a doggy section over there."

He nodded. "That's where we're headed."

She was about to open the lobby door when she caught a movement in her peripheral vision. The texting grand-daughter had slipped out of room five and was headed straight for Wil. She wore high-heeled boots, a denim miniskirt, and a bright red halter top that didn't have enough fabric in it to sag a clothesline much less keep her from frostbite if she stayed outside very long. When she walked under the porch light of Wil's room, Pearl could see too much makeup and shoulder-length blond hair that had had a recent session with a curling iron.

Wil didn't even know that trouble was headed his way in the form of cute little jailbait. He was watching Digger sniff every frozen blade of grass in the small area.

Pearl sighed. She should let Wil take care of himself. He was a big boy and could most likely set that little bit of fluff straight with a stern look and a few words. She didn't owe him protection with the $49.95 room rate. But she couldn't let her motel get a bad reputation. It might be old and antiquated, but it did have a reputation for being clean, cheap, and quiet.

"Hey, Wil, darlin', you think you could get that dog to hurry up?" she yelled.

He jumped like he'd been shot and turned so quick that he almost dropped the leash. "What did you say?"

"I asked if you could get that dog to do his business any faster. It's cold out here and there's a warm bed waiting," she said.

Wil looked back and waved at Pearl. "I'll be right there," he yelled. "Soon as Digger does his business. Open up a beer for me."

The room five girl popped her hands on her hips and almost fell when she spun around. When she passed Pearl she gave her a look that would have turned the devil's pitchfork blue.

Digger melted the sleet on a section of grass and then pulled at Wil to take him back to a warmer place. Pearl waited until the girl was in the room and the door shut before she reached for the lobby door. The wind continued to blow hard enough to slap the sleet against the windows with little pinging noises like a whole army of terrorists attacking the Longhorn Inn with BB guns.

Wil reached the door at the same time Pearl did and he reached out and opened it for her. He wiggled a dark eyebrow. "You serious about that warm bed?"

"It was the only way I could keep that little hussy

from knocking on your door later tonight. Don't read anything into it, cowboy." Yep, he was definitely a bad boy. Damn fine looking but a bad boy and everyone knew that even though Pearl loved to date and was the life of most parties, she did not have time for bad boys.

"Thanks. I didn't even know she was there until you hollered."

"You are welcome. I'm just glad she didn't slip on the ice. Her grandmother would've sued me and owned my motel by sundown tomorrow night." She slipped past him, her bare hand brushing his on the way, and smoldering heat shot through her lower gut for the second time. It had been too damn long since she'd had a date, been to a movie, or even talked to a guy other than to check him in and out of her motel.

She melted into one of the recliners to catch her breath, but the phone rang again. She hopped up, grabbed it on the fourth ring, and looked at the clock. One in the morning. "Merry damn Christmas to me," she grouched as she picked up the receiver.

"Longhorn Inn. Front desk," she said as cheerfully as she could.

"This is Albert Blass in six. Those kids next door still have the television turned up to the last notch, and they're listenin' to that music that sounds like a truckload of wild hogs got hit by another truck carryin' crystal dishes. It's a hell of a noise. Me and Momma ain't slept a wink yet and we got to drive all the way to Sherman in the mornin' for our grandkids' Christmas party."

"I'll take care of it, Mister Blass."

"Thank you. We ain't ones to complain. We wouldn't

even be here but our generator plumb played out and I ain't bought a new one. Word has it that our kids are goin' to give us money towards one for Christmas. Okay, okay, Momma, I don't know that for sure, but Bubba Joe said his daddy was talkin' about it," he fussed with his wife and talked to Pearl at the same time.

"I'll take care of your problem, Mister Blass." She hung up and dialed room three and waited through four rings before someone picked up.

"Hello," a groggy voice said.

"This is the front desk. Your grandchildren in room five have the television turned up so loud that the elderly couple next door to them can't sleep. Would you like to take care of that or should I?" Pearl said.

"Henry, wake up and go take care of those boys. I told you to sleep down there with them. You go on and stay down there and next year when you get a wild-ass notion to take them all six on a trip you remember tonight. God, what a mess. We'll take care of them kids. Don't you be worryin' none about it."

"Thank you." Pearl hung up the phone and rolled her green eyes toward the ceiling. "Lord, what was I thinkin'? Entrepreneur, my ass."

She slumped down into the sofa, leaned her head back, and fell asleep. Fifteen minutes later she sat up with a start. It was two o'clock when she finally crawled between the sheets, only to be awakened at three by Digger's howls and Wil's sleepy voice threatening to throw him out into the cold if he didn't hush. She slammed a pillow over her head and went back to sleep until four minutes past four when Digger must've held it as long as he could and Wil's tone said he wasn't

real happy about having to put on his boots and take the
dog outside.

"Thank God I don't have a dog. I'd kill it," she declared.

Chapter 2

AT FIVE THIRTY HER ALARM WENT OFF. SHE STUMBLED INTO the kitchen, made coffee, and jerked on a pair of jeans and a red sweatshirt screen-printed with Rudolph on the front. It was a far cry from the suits and spike heeled shoes she used to wear to work during the holidays or the cute little green velvet dress she would have worn to Christmas dinner in Savannah. She poured a cup of coffee before it finished perking and took a sip. If she'd have had the energy she would have shuddered at the bitterness, but she didn't have that much spunk and the second sip didn't taste half bad. Lord, even a night of partying until daylight had never knocked the energy out of her like running a full motel.

The lobby door opened at six o'clock. The grandmother handed Pearl a handful of keys and asked where the nearest place to get breakfast might be.

"This is Christmas so I really don't know what might be open," Pearl answered.

The grandmother sighed. "Six half-grown, half-awake kids who are starving and one idiot husband and no place to feed them. Next time my husband comes up with a harebrained idea like this I'm going to have him committed."

Pearl smiled.

The door opened again and she expected to see the couple who would be either getting a generator or else a dose of disappointment that morning, but it was two uniformed policemen from Wichita Falls.

"What can I do for you?" she asked.

"You got a customer by the name of Wil Marshall?"

She nodded. "Unless he left real early this morning, he and his dog, Digger, are in room one right next door. What's going on here?"

"Just stay in the lobby. We'll take care of it," the shorter, thinner one of the two answered.

They drew their guns and the bigger one was talking softly to the radio on his shoulder when they started toward the first room past the lobby. Pearl did not take to any man, not even one with a badge and a radio attached to his shirt collar, telling her what to do, so she stepped out and leaned against the wall. Short Man gave her a dirty look, but Big Man was busy pounding on the door and announcing he was Wichita Falls police.

Wil crammed a pillow over his head. He didn't care if the newlyweds next door had robbed a bank or a jewelry store; he just wanted a couple of hours of uninterrupted sleep.

"Wil Marshall, open this door or we will kick it down," a booming voice said.

He sat straight up, eyes wide open.

Digger let out a mournful howl.

"You kick that door down and you'll be replacing it!" the red-haired motel owner said loudly. "I'll unlock it, but don't you dare kick it down. This ain't the damned *NCIS* on television!"

Why would the police be threatening to kick down his door? Was he dreaming?

Digger howled again.

A key turned the lock and the door opened. Two policemen rushed in with guns as big as cannons, drawn and pointed at him. That's when he decided he wasn't dreaming and he was in trouble.

"Wil Marshall, you are under arrest for the murder of Starla Matthews. You have the right to remain silent. Anything…" The short man read him his rights as the taller one slapped cuffs on his wrists.

"Hey, man, I'm barefoot," Wil said.

Short Man looked across the room at Big Man who shrugged and removed the cuffs. Wil stomped his feet down into his boots and grabbed his jacket.

"What about this dog?" Pearl asked.

"Call animal control," Short Man said.

"Call Rye. He'll take him to my ranch," Wil said. "This is all a misunderstanding. I don't know anyone named Starla."

Digger bounded out of the room and started toward the car.

Wil yelled, "Stay! Sit."

The dog stopped on the slick sidewalk and sat down. He didn't move a muscle as the car backed out on the slippery sleet-covered concrete and drove away.

"Now what do I do?" Pearl asked.

Digger looked up at her.

She reached out cautiously and hooked her fingers around his collar. "If you bite me, I'll call animal control, and believe me, they are not going to be happy about coming after you on Christmas morning."

The dog obediently let her lead him back into the motel room, but when she shut the door behind him he set up a howl that made the hair on her neck stand straight up. She trotted back to the lobby and called Rye. It took him an hour to get there, by which time Delilah was matching Digger's high-pitched yowls with deep-throated howls.

Rye grinned when he opened the lobby door. He was a dark-haired, green-eyed cowboy, built like Wil Marshall, only not nearly as sexy to Pearl's way of thinking. He wore a denim jacket lined in red plaid flannel, a black Stetson, creased jeans, and dress boots. "Guess Digger ain't none too happy."

"Just take the dog and tell Austin I'm sorry I stole her husband on their first Christmas morning," Pearl said.

Austin poked her head in the door and crossed the lobby in a few long strides. She hugged Pearl tightly and said, "Merry Christmas! Tell me what and who stole my husband."

Austin was a tall brunette with blue eyes, several inches taller than Pearl, which meant she had to bend to hug her friend that morning. She'd inherited her grand-mother's watermelon farm the previous spring and had every intention of selling it until she fell in love with the cowboy that lived across the road.

On one hand Pearl was jealous as hell that her friend had found "the one" and was walking on the honeymoon clouds. But on the other, Pearl wasn't ready to settle down with one man. To give up the dating scene and look at one man the rest of her life was downright scary. The one time she'd thought she might be ready to do that it had all gone south anyway, leaving another scar on her heart.

Pearl smiled at Austin. "It's the Christmas from hell and it ain't shapin' up to get any better. I was telling Rye to tell you that I was sorry I had to steal him away from you on your first Christmas together. Digger is in room one. Door is open."

"I'll get him, darlin', and meet you back at the truck," Rye said.

Austin watched Rye swagger out the door. "Ain't nobody stealing that handsome hunk away from me. If he goes to Wil's ranch then I go with him. I brought you a bottle of Lanier Wine." She set it on the cabinet. "It's still Granny's makings. Mine won't be ready to taste until springtime, but it's going to be just as good as this is. Everything went perfect when I was making it. What did you think about Wil? Ain't he the hottest cowboy you've ever seen?"

"Thank you! I may drink the whole thing in one setting! And I thought your new husband, Rye, was the hottest cowboy in the world. And Wil just got hauled to the jailhouse for murder. That definitely seals the part about him being a bad boy, doesn't it?"

"Rye is the hottest, but Wil comes in a close second, and honey, Wil didn't kill anyone. He might have a little bit of bad boy in him, but he wouldn't hurt a woman. That much I know. It's a big mistake and he'll be home by noon. Come on over to Ringgold with us and spend the day with Rye's folks. There's food and music and presents," Austin said.

"I can't. I've got laundry and cleaning for the whole motel. Electricity went out in Henrietta last night. Every single room was full. Thanks anyway."

"You haven't replaced Rosa?" Austin asked.

"Didn't need to until now. Another night or two like last night and I'll have to hire two cleaning women."

Austin patted her shoulder. "Well, if you get it all

done by supper, come on over. I hate for you to spend the whole holiday alone."

"After last night, alone is very, very good."

"I can't believe words like that are coming out of your mouth. You still got the crown for being the biggest party girl in Texas, don't you?"

"Yeah, but here lately it's getting pretty tarnished. I haven't been to a party or even out on a date since I inherited this place." Pearl sighed.

Wil waited in an interrogation room with his right wrist cuffed to a ring in the table. They insisted he knew some woman by the name of Starla, but he had no idea who they were talking about. His dark brows knit together above shut brown eyes. Surely, if he thought long and hard, he'd remember the woman. Was she a rodeo groupie that he'd met in passing? Or did she work at the Dairy Queen in Henrietta at one time?

He was deep in thought when a detective slapped a file on the table and pulled up a chair across from him. He opened up an ink pad and motioned for Wil to put his fingers on it. Wil gritted his teeth and shook his head.

"My prints are on file. Have been since I turned pro at bull riding, and besides, I've got an alibi. I was at the Longhorn Inn all night. I don't know who got killed or who you think I am, but I did not do it."

"Can you verify without a doubt that you were in that motel then? Was someone with you? It's less than half an hour to Wichita Falls. You could have easily snuck out and back in."

"Call the motel owner."

"You sleep with her."

"Call her or give me a phone and I'll call my lawyer. I'm innocent and we can save a lot of time and money if you'll just call the motel."

The detective got up slowly and meandered out of the room as if he had all day. Wil was running on no sleep, no breakfast, and his patience had played out a long time before. He fumed and waited. His stomach growled and he waited. He laid his head down on his forearms and shut his eyes, but sleep wouldn't come no matter how tired he was so he waited some more.

Finally, when he thought he'd go stark raving mad sitting cooped up in a room barely bigger than a two-hole outhouse, the detective poked his head back in the door. "Ready to talk?"

Wil shot him a dirty look and the detective shut the door.

Two hours later the door opened again and the detective opened the cuff from the ring in the table. "Our apologies. We made a big mistake. You are Wilson Marshall. We were looking for William Marshall. You both go by Wil with one *l* so…" He shrugged.

"Am I free to go?" Wil's tone was as cold as the walls of the room.

"Yes, there's a red-haired woman out there by the name of Pearl Richland who said there was no doubt you were in the motel all night. Besides, your truck has four flat tires this morning, and the forensic team that went over the room and your truck says that it was sitting right there all night from the sleet that's piled up around those flat tires. Too bad we didn't catch the mistake. We wasted several hours of time at the motel."

"Not to mention several hours of my time. Did Red bring me some clothes?"

The detective nodded toward the window and a female officer brought his duffel bag into the room.

"My cell phone?"

"In the bag."

Wil opened the bag and took out jeans, a shirt, and his boots. He was so tickled to see his jeans that he vowed to sleep in them the rest of his life.

"You know a William Marshall? About your age. Dark hair and eyes."

Wil shook his head.

"He's from over in your area and he's a cowboy," the officer went on.

"Don't know him. Never met him. Never want to meet him. Don't know a woman named Starla. Can I get dressed now?"

The detective nodded. "There's a men's room right outside in the hallway. When you are ready I'll escort you to the front door. Your billfold and everything the team found in the motel is in your bag there."

Wil left the jumpsuit on the floor when he changed into his own familiar clothing. He shoved his cell phone down into his shirt pocket. Four flat tires? How in the devil had that happened? Who would have flattened his tires?

Those little girls you didn't play house with, his conscience said bluntly. *Little hussies snuck out and let the air out of the tires. Betcha anything all you have to do is air them up and they'll be fine.*

"Women! Young or old!" he said to the haggard reflection in the mirror.

"Ready?" the man asked when he was out in the hallway again.

"I am."

He led the way down one hall to the end and through another, finally ending in an almost empty room where Pearl Richland sat in a folding chair against the wall.

"What are you doing here?" he asked.

"Well, I'm damn sure not here by choice. I had to leave my job to come convince these people that there wasn't any way you left the motel last night. I'll take you back with me or you can walk. I don't give a damn what you do."

Chapter 3

"WHICH WAY TO YOUR CAR OR TRUCK OR HORSE AND buggy?" Wil asked when they were finally outside the police station.

"Follow me."

She led him to a 1959 Caddy Eldorado Seville. The light brown and ecru two-tone paint job looked like it had just rolled off the factory floor. She used a key to unlock the door and then reached across the white leather seats and undid the passenger's door.

Wil had the urge to pinch himself to see if he was in the middle of a nightmare. First getting accused of murder and now being escorted home by a gorgeous redhead driving a vintage car. His world was upside down and inside out, but the cold door handle said he wasn't dreaming.

"Where did you get this thing?" he asked.

"It was Aunt Pearlita's. I've loved this old boat of a car since I was a little girl. Pretty, ain't it?"

"Pretty? This thing is priceless. It should be in a showroom, not on the street."

She fired up the engine and turned on the heater. "Aunt Pearlita said things weren't worth shit if you didn't use them. She took care of it but she used it. That's what I'm going to do."

It was an old boat of a car compared to modern vehicles and drank gas like it still cost less than fifty cents a gallon. It had tail fins sporting two extra taillights that looked like alien's eyes. The backseat was wide enough to haul around half a dozen kids or four adults. And it was the first car Wil had ever sat in that he didn't have to kiss his knees.

Pearl's curiosity got the best of her when they were out of town and headed east toward Henrietta. "Why did they think you'd murdered that woman, and who is she?"

"It was a big mistaken identity. William Marshall is the one they are looking for. My name just happened to be close to his. Damn, this is a comfortable car. You want to sell it?"

"Honey, there ain't enough money in the world or dirt in Texas to buy this car," Pearl said.

"Well, if you ever change your mind, I want first bid on it. Did Rye come get my dog?"

Pearl nodded. "He's back on your ranch, chasin' rabbits or layin' up on the porch waitin' on you or whatever it is that dogs do on Christmas Day, and I won't change my mind about the car."

He stole a long glance at her. Damn she was pretty, but he'd always been a sucker for red hair. Those freckles across her nose begged to be kissed, and he could swim in her green eyes. "I'd buy you breakfast to say thanks for getting me out of this mess if there was a place open."

"You hungry?" she asked.

Just sitting beside him sent off a string of electrical jolts that she had only felt one time before. She and Vince had gotten together after he'd dived into his rebellious stage. He had a motorcycle, tattoos, and a diamond earring as big as a butter bean. Her mother said he had been a good boy his whole life until his senior year in high school. And then he'd done a three-sixty and was nothing but trouble.

And that was one time Tess Richland had been totally right.

After graduation night, they'd spent a night in a motel celebrating being real adults. They'd both lost their virginity that night and she had visions of a diamond ring after a couple of years of college, followed by a white wedding dress. But he kissed her good night at the door and she never saw him again. Last she heard he was in Africa. She'd cried for a week and her mother didn't even gloat, bless her heart.

She shook the memory out of her head and glanced over at Wil.

Oh, shit! This ain't fair! Even with scruff on his face and dressed in yesterday's jeans and shirt, he was sexy as hell and made her hot as... *What was it that Mark Chestnut said in that song about being hot? Oh, yeah, hot as two rats in heat inside an old wool sock. Well, those two varmints don't have any idea about heat.*

He yawned. "Pardon me. I'm starved. They brought me a bottle of water, but no one offered breakfast."

"The Valero station in Jolly is open. I saw folks going in and out on my way over to Wichita Falls. You can get a donut and some coffee, and it's the next exit," she said.

"Thank you."

"Did that hurt?" she asked.

"What?"

"Sayin' thank you to me?"

"Yes, it did, but I do appreciate what you've done."

"Good. I want it to hurt because I'm wasting my time. I had a full house last night and every room has to be cleaned. Don't look like that. I really, really want to lay a guilt trip on you."

"Well, Red, you're doin' a fine job of that. I am sorry that I'm taking you away from your job."

She shook her finger under his nose. "I told you not to call me Red! I hate that nickname."

He grabbed her hand and put it back on the steering wheel. "It takes both hands to drive a car like this. I bet it doesn't even have power steering."

The touch of his callused hand wrapped around hers made her suck air. "You don't know jack squat about my ability to drive or this car, and you better not call me Red again or you are going to be using the old boot leather express to get your sorry ass the rest of the way home."

"Whew! You got a temper to go with that hair, don't you?" He chuckled to cover up the sizzle bouncing around in the car. He had the sudden desire to grab her hand again just to see what kind of reaction he'd get.

"And don't you forget it!"

She was careful to keep both her hands on the steering wheel. She'd left all three washers and dryers loaded and running, but it wasn't a deep desire to fold sheets and towels that made her threaten to throw him out on the side of the road. And calling her Red wasn't the reason either. It was the visual she got when he crawled into her vintage Caddy, with his dark hair tousled back with a fingertip combing, scruff on his sexy face, and those damn tight fittin' jeans. She'd had to blink away the urge to reach across the front seat and run her fingers through his hair and to see up close and personal just how hot those lips were. His touch on her hand did not throw ice water on the vision but took it to the next level.

She made herself erase that picture from her mind and think about the motel. Six rooms had been cleaned and were ready to rent. That left nineteen to do and she'd lost two hours driving to Wichita Falls, swearing on Jesus, Mary, and Joseph as well as her great-aunt Pearlita's good name, that there was no way in hell that Wil had gone to Wichita Falls the night before.

The sun had come out and the roads were wet and slushy instead of slippery. In the median and off to the sides, grass still sparkled with sleet in shady places but the rest was melting fast. Texas might have ice or even snow on occasion but it didn't last long, and for that Pearl was grateful. The few times she'd had to drive on icy roads gave her an acute case of the hives, but it wasn't driving in hazardous conditions that made her jumpy; it was the steaming hot cowboy in the seat beside her.

She pulled off at the next exit and nosed her car into a prime parking space right in front of the store. Her stomach growled and she bit back a string of cuss words that would have scalded the paint off her Caddy. If she'd have listened to her mother, she would have been in Savannah, Georgia, that day with the rest of her family at her grandma's place. She would have been eating turkey and dressing, candied yams, baked beans, and her grandma's famous hot rolls. Afterwards she would have gone out and had a long walk in the gardens behind the old plantation house, and if the sun was out, she might have even stretched out on a blanket and read one of those sinfully thick romance books for a couple of hours.

"Can I get you something? Coffee? Coke? Candy bar?" He reached across the seat and laid a hand on her arm, unconsciously making lazy circles with his thumb.

How in the devil could a single square inch of skin build such a big old bonfire in her gut? If his thumb on her arm could make her tingle, then what would it feel like to... she quickly shook the notion from her head.

He swallowed hard and said, "I'll only be gone a minute."

If he was gone much longer than that she intended to leave him at the station. He could thumb a ride the rest of the way home. He'd already kept her up half the night with his dog and problems with young girls. But when he shook his jeans down over his boot tops and swaggered toward the door, she forgot all about the dog, the girls, and even Georgiana's spider. Her pulse kicked into a higher gear when she looked at his backside. He filled out his jeans very well, and his broad shoulders left no doubt that it was hard muscles filling up that jean jacket and not air. The wind whipped his hair into his face and he pushed it back away from his eyes.

"The devil has brown eyes like that," she mumbled as he disappeared into the store. "And probably wears blue jeans and boots just like that too. And I bet he's got a thumb with pure fire in it too!"

Wil bought a dozen Krispy Kreme donuts in a box, two cups of coffee, and a bag of potato chips. If he'd had to wait in line he might have purchased a few candy bars and a couple of packages of peanut butter crackers too. Everything he looked at made his mouth water.

"Not a very fancy Christmas dinner," the lady checker said.

"Looks like the food of the gods to me this morning," he said.

She winked. "Wife done threw you out?"

"Something like that."

She smiled and flirted. "Well, I get off at one. You want to hang around I'll take you home and make you a proper Christmas dinner."

He handed her a bill and she made change. "Thanks but I got someone waiting in the car."

"No wonder your wife throwed you out in the yard if you been cheatin' on her."

"Stuff happens," he threw over his shoulder as he picked up his purchases and made his escape.

"You must be hungry," Pearl said when he'd settled back in the Caddy.

He handed her a cup of coffee and brushed her fingertips on purpose in the transfer. "It's hot. Be careful."

She sipped the coffee gingerly. "Thank you."

"I bought plenty. Help yourself to a couple of donuts."

Her cell phone set up a ringtone with Zac Brown Band singing about having his toes in the water and his ass in the sand. She fished it out of her purse, smiled when she saw the name, and said, "Hello."

Wil wasn't two feet from her so there was nothing to do but eavesdrop. The man on the other end was talking so loud that he could even hear that end of the conversation if he paid close attention… which he did.

"My sweet Pearl. Where were you last night? I went to Emily's Christmas party and you weren't there. Damn thing fell flat without our Pearl to make us laugh. Were you slow makin' the rounds? You always end up at Em's party last. Tell me where in the hell have you run off to?"

"Brett, darlin', I'm in Henrietta runnin' a motel and I couldn't leave. I missed all you guys. I'm glad y'all missed me too," she said.

"Well, if you're in town over the holidays, call me. We'll run down to Dallas and maybe catch a play," he said.

"I won't be this year. Just got things up and going. If you're ever over here give me a call," she answered.

"You got it but don't hold your breath. Merry Christmas, sweet Pearl," he said.

"Old boyfriend?" Wil asked.

She shook her head. "Just an old friend that I date sometimes."

"With benefits, sweet Pearl?"

"None of your business."

"Want a donut?" He chuckled.

"The coffee is enough. And to think, I could have been in Savannah for dinner." She wished she could reach out in the air, grab the words, and put them back in her mouth. She had no intentions of spilling her guts to this man, whether he was a killer or not.

"Savannah, Georgia?"

She nodded.

"Who lives there?"

"My grandmother. Where are you going for Christmas dinner?" She steered the conversation away from herself. She might be pouting but she was bound, damned, and determined to prove her mother wrong about the motel and her decision to leave her cushy bank job.

Wil ate a donut in three bites and took a sip of coffee.

Pearl Richland was one of those fast women who lived for the next good time. Not surprising with her looks, build, and sass.

"I had the big dinner thing yesterday down in Bowie with my family. I got sisters older than me with enough kids to outfit two or three orphanages. My momma and daddy are retired and live down south of Bowie. My sisters live in Chico so they're all close. We all go home on Christmas Eve and do the big traditional thing with food and presents. Then on Christmas they can do whatever with their own families and Momma and Daddy usually go to my grandma's place down in Decatur. She's ninety years old but she still expects her only child to come see her on Christmas. They load up the leftovers and have dinner with her."

"She lives alone?"

"Yes, ma'am. Ain't a nursing home that would have her, she's so cantankerous." He polished off a second donut and licked his sticky fingertips. "Sure you don't want one? I'll feed it to you while you drive."

"No thank you." Pearl shivered at the thought of him putting his fingers anywhere near her mouth.

"Granny still runs a few head of cattle. Says she'll retire when she's a hundred. Us Marshalls have a long life. My grandpa was just shy of a hundred when he passed last year. Kind of like your Aunt Pearlita."

Pearl giggled. "She'd roll over in her grave if she heard you say such a thing. I'm not sure you could get into heaven after such vile words spew forth from your mouth. She was eighty-three and always claimed to be ten years younger than that."

"She did have spunk. I only knew her the few times

my electricity blew and I had to come into town for either heat or air conditioning, but I could tell she was full of spit and vinegar."

A helluva lot like you! he thought. *Did anyone ever tell you that you are cute as a button when you smile and those green eyes light up?*

"Yes, she was. You want me to take you to your ranch or back to the motel?" she asked as they neared the outskirts of Henrietta.

"Ranch please. I'll bring a truck with extra tires and an air pump later and get my vehicle out of your parking lot. I'll have to get someone to ride along with me to bring my truck home. I gave my foreman a couple of days off to spend with his family so it could be until he comes back."

She glanced at the donut box and wished she had one, but there was no way that she'd let him feed her, not when the touch of his thumb turned her inside out. "Tell me when to turn."

"My ranch is north of Henrietta, going toward Petrolia. So turn left at the Petrolia sign."

She slowed down and looked at each sign closely, making the turn while he was tearing into the bag of chips. He held them toward her and she shook her head.

"I know you took a chunk out of your day to help me. Could I take you to dinner to repay you for it?" One little dinner date to pay for the favor and then he'd be out of Miss Richland's life so fast it would tilt the world off its axis.

"Hell, no!"

He dropped the chip bag in his lap. "That was pretty damn quick."

"Quick and honest. Dinner wouldn't come close to repaying me for the time I lost."

He'd never had a woman turn him down flat before. Looking back, he'd never had a woman turn him down at all. "Make a right at the next section line."

She turned into the lane and saw the two-story house at the end of the lane. It was painted white with a wide front porch that would offer shade in the summer. Digger gave a few yips and bounded down the three steps and ran around Wil's legs when he got out of the car.

"Thanks again," Wil said as he leaned into the car's backseat to retrieve his duffel bag. "You ever change your mind about that dinner, you just call and I'll be glad to take you out."

"You really want to repay me, drive down to the Longhorn Inn and help me clean rooms all afternoon."

Pearl couldn't believe she was turning down a date. It didn't have to be a lifetime commitment and he did owe her, but something told her to steer clear of Wil Marshall. He was one of those wolves running around in sheep's clothing. A bad boy in good guy Wranglers.

He grinned and waved over his shoulder.

Just what I thought. He's not about to clean rooms, but oh my! He does fill out those blue jeans just right! She backed out of his driveway and headed home to an afternoon of laundry and cleaning.

Lunch was a peanut butter sandwich eaten standing up in front of the dryer as she waited on a load of towels to finish. She reached the last room she'd cleaned, slung open the door, and picked up four white bath towels and an equal number of washcloths and hand towels from her maid's cart. She stacked the towels on the rack above the toilet, set out complimentary bottles of shampoo, conditioner, and lotion, and put tiny motel soaps on the edge of the tub and beside the sink.

She stacked the sheets and comforter on the desk top and set to making beds, but her thoughts went to the cowboy on the other side of the truck. With those tight-fitting jeans and those devil-may-care eyes, he could run James Dean some competition. Slick back his dark hair, roll up the sleeves of a white T-shirt, and dangle a cigarette from those sexy lips and... she drew her thoughts up short with a sigh. Bad boys! She had to stop thinking about them in general and Wil Marshall in particular.

She shook out the bottom sheet on the first bed and stretched it over the mattress. But her thoughts wouldn't be still. She could still visualize Wil with a pack of cigarettes rolled up in his shirt sleeve, sitting on the fender of her vintage Caddy and pushing back a lock of dark hair that kept falling on his forehead. Her fingers itched to see if his hair was as soft as it looked. And did he have a fine sprinkling of chest hair that she could nuzzle down into after a hot bout of...

"Shit! What has gotten into me? It's because I've stagnated for so long—but then when and where would I meet a man in a town this size? And besides, I'm tied to the motel seven nights a week. Now I understand the real look of all those young entrepreneurs who wanted loans. It wasn't because they were fired up and eager to set the world on fire. It was loss of sleep and social life."

She shut her eyes and a picture of her last boyfriend, Marlin, appeared. He'd been the closest thing to a lasting relationship she'd ever had and she'd thought she was ready to settle down, to really forget about Vince.

Marlin Johnson was a preppie with blond hair styled weekly to feather back perfectly. He wore three-pieced suits tailor made to fit his lanky frame, red power ties, and loafers with tassels. His cologne was expensive and subtle. And her mother loved him, so he had to be the right man for her. Right?

Wrong! With all capital letters and shouted from the backside of a bullhorn.

They'd dated nine months a couple of years ago and she really thought she had found the right man, but it all came to a screeching halt one evening over dinner. He'd found the love of his life in the form of a grad student who'd taken one of his classes. She had long blond hair, big fake boobs, and a high squeaky voice.

A spider scampered across the motel room floor and Pearl stomped it. Felt right good, it did! Almost as good as if she could have put a pin in Miss Big Boob's silicone implants.

Texas is the buggiest state in the union and has more bugs than all other forty-nine states combined. I've probably put the damn exterminator's kids through medical school, but I won't have anyone saying I run a nasty business. So make sure the crickets, ants, and scorpions are all dead and vacuumed. Aunt Pearlita's words were as real as if she'd been standing right behind Pearl.

She forgot about Marlin and threw the top sheet out over the bed, letting it come to a rest and then adjusting the sides to a uniform distance. She placed the ecrucolored blanket on the bed and made hospital corners on the end of the mattress. She finished up by putting on the light brown comforter that matched the Western motif in the wallpaper border around the top of the room. Pistols, longhorn cattle, horseshoes, and mesquite: Pearlita had found the border on sale about thirty years before and bought up enough to last until eternity dawned. Pearl couldn't remember a time when the border hadn't been in the rooms and she'd been coming to Henrietta since she was five. But come spring when she decided on what she wanted to change to, it was all going out the door. She could see soft shades of blue with Amish quilts instead of bedspreads, or maybe vintage chenille if she went with the quaint and romantic theme.

She scanned the room: vacuum marks on the floor attesting to the fact that it had been cleaned; towels and toiletries in the right places; a tiny note pad and a pen with the Longhorn Inn logo on each nightstand; remote on top of the television. Everything looked good so it was on to the next room. Maybe she'd build onto the back of the lobby and put in a cozy little dining room and make a modified bed and breakfast place. But first things first, and she had to get the rooms cleaned.

If only one word could be engraved under Pearl's name on her tombstone it would be organized. Despite the chaos that so often ruled in her life, she could organize and compartmentalize. In a week's time she'd found a dozen ways to cut corners while cleaning rooms.

The next thing on her super-duper organized list was to remove all the sheets and towels from the next three rooms, take the dirty linens down to the laundry room, and reload the cart. While that washed she'd clean those three rooms, redo them, and then strip down the next three rooms. The washers would be finished so she'd move laundry to the dryer, start three more loads, reload her cart, and start all over. She opened the door to room eleven and rounded up the towels from the bathroom floor.

"Why do they always pitch them on the floor? There's a rack, the top of the shower rod, and even the edge of the tub. Why the floor?"

"Who knows?" a deep voice said from the doorway.

She jumped and spun around in one fluid movement to find Wil leaning against the jamb. Her heart was pounding so hard it felt like it might crack a rib. Flight or fight had taken hold and she wanted to do both: fly into his arms for protection and then beat him senseless for scaring the bejesus out of her.

Second thought: fly into him and push him back on one of the freshly made beds.

"Are your tires fixed?" she asked breathlessly.

"Didn't come to fix tires but I did check them. Someone just let the air out of them. They're not ruined. The towels and sheets from the rest of the rooms are in the laundry room in piles ready to be washed. I took out what was in the dryers, folded it, and stacked it up on the racks; put what was in the washers over in the dryers; and started another load. Now what do you want me to do? Start vacuuming from the other end or scrubbing bathrooms?"

She was totally and utterly speechless. Surely he was teasing.

Wil grinned. She was pretty damn cute standing there in tight-fitting jeans, no makeup, and sweat beading up below her nose. He stood to one side and she brushed against him as she closed the door. It stretched his supply of willpower almighty thin to keep from planting a kiss on those soft-looking lips right then. The heat from her breasts ever so slightly touching his abs was enough to start a wildfire right there in gravel parking lot.

"You clean?" she asked.

Dammit! I didn't realize how tall he is. What would it be like to... whoa, hoss! Yes, he's hot. Yes, he turns me on. No, I will not think about it.

"I have a house. Cleaning rooms couldn't be that much different. You scrub the bathroom, vacuum the floor, and do some dusting."

"Why?"

"Because my house gets dirty."

"No, why are you here?"

"I don't like to owe people. You won't let me take you to dinner so I'm here to help clean rooms."

She blinked three times and he didn't disappear, but surely she'd heard him wrong. Men did not offer to clean. In her experience it took an act of God to get them to pick up their dirty socks and actually put them inside the hamper instead of tossing them at it. And forget about them ever offering to scrub a bathroom. There was no way Wil had just offered to scrub bathrooms. Not with his looks and sex appeal. It wasn't possible.

"So?" he asked impatiently.

"I'm thinking. Don't rush me."

"You really ought to hire some help. If you had a cleaning lady you could be catching a nap after that horrible night you just had."

"I don't need your advice but I will take your help."

He nodded. "Fair enough. What next?"

Did those cute freckles taste sweet? Would she claw him like a cat if he bent down and kissed those sexy full lips?

She took a deep breath and exhaled slowly. "Vacuum and dust. Start the next room and work your way around to the end. I'll come in behind you, clean the bathrooms, make the beds, and put out fresh towels. I'll check the laundry each time I go back to reload the cart and keep that going."

"Sounds like a plan to me. When I get done with the vacuuming, I'll fold laundry. When we get finished Rye says for us to come on over to his momma's place for supper. They put out a big spread at dinner and then eat on it all day. We can get in on the leftovers."

She was shocked all over again. Sexy as hell; cleaned and scrubbed bathrooms; and was comfortable enough in his own skin to tell his buddy! "Rye knows you are here?"

"Yep, I called him to thank him for taking care of Digger. It would have cost me a wad of money to spring Digger from the dog pound. He asked me to come on to Christmas dinner, but I told him I'd just downed a dozen donuts and was coming over here to repay you for all the time you lost. Then he asked us both to drop by for supper. I saw the vacuum in the laundry room. I'll get busy so we don't miss Christmas dinner. Rye's momma is a great cook and I can already taste her pecan pie."

He said the last few words as he was walking away and she barely caught them. Suddenly, the day didn't look so long with the promise of more than a glorified TV dinner for supper. Maybe it hadn't been such a bad idea to spend those two hours getting Wil out of jail after all. And on one hand it wouldn't count as a date, so her mother wouldn't have to pitch a southern hissy at her going out with a sexy cowboy that made James Dean look as tame as a kitten. On the other, she could feel like she was finally back in the dating game if she went with him. And what would one little date hurt?

―――∾∿∾―――

Wil hated to dust but he made sure every surface was cleaned of fingerprints, spilled milk and soda pop, potato chip grease, and all the other things that motel renters leave behind in their wake. Then he sprayed the mirrors in both the bedroom and bathroom with cleaner and wiped them streak free. After that he vacuumed and finished scrubbing out the bathroom. She'd said she would do that but it was already two in the afternoon. He really did look forward to supper with Rye and Ace. Both had been his friends since they were kids as well as Dewar and Raylen, Rye's younger brothers.

He picked up a plastic tote of cleansers and started out of the room at the same time Pearl grabbed the door and plowed into it behind a stack of towels. She ran into him and they both grabbed for the falling towels at the same time.

When they untangled their tingling arms and started to straighten up, with the towels on the sidewalk between them, his eyes locked with hers. He leaned in and she rolled up on her tiptoes. She knew she was playing with bad boy fire, but when the tip of his tongue moistened his lips, she couldn't stop.

He shut his eyes and leaned in for the kiss, barely connecting to her lips and sending a heat wave over the whole state when her damn cell phone caused her to jump backwards. She blushed and fished it out of her hip pocket, touched a button that quieted the country music ringtone, and said, "Hello!"

"Merry Christmas!" A deep voice made at least a dozen syllables out of each word.

"Hello, Matt," she said. Weeks and weeks she'd gone without a call and the holiday season brought them out of the woodwork like scorpions in the wintertime.

She looked at Wil, who was busy picking up the towels and taking them to the laundry. The way he swaggered made her wish she'd left her phone in the lobby. That was a fine beginning of a kiss. She felt cheated that it hadn't gone on to the full power, but it would have been pure danger if it had.

"There's a New Year's party we're cookin' up at our house. Jasmine said you needed to get out or you were going to stagnate?" Matt said.

"I'm sorry. I'm going to have to pass. Tell everyone hello for me."

"Will do, but if you change your mind, get in touch with Jasmine and she'll tell you a time and who all is going to be here. And we miss you over in our part of the world. Holiday parties aren't the same without you." The line went dead and Pearl went to the next room.

She sniffed the air. "Is that window cleaner I smell?"

Wil was close enough behind her that his breath was warm on her neck. "And bathroom cleanser."

"Well, hot damn!" she said.

They passed again in the doorway and even though she wanted to look up at his eyes and lips she was careful not to do so as she hurried on outside. *Holy shit! I can't be kissing this man. Just because he knows his way around a bathroom and knows how to operate a vacuum doesn't mean jack shit. What is the matter*

with me? I'm jittery as a damn teenager and my palms
are sweating in freezing weather. I haven't felt like this
since Vince.

She let her mind wander back to her first love. The
boy on the ranch next to theirs who had stolen her heart
that summer before they started their senior year of high
school. Vince Knightly. Her knightly-in-shining-armor,
as she'd said. It sounded corny now but when she was
seventeen just saying the words almost put her in a
swoon. That and the fact that he was just the baddest
boy in the whole state that summer.

Thinking about the way she felt back then just
brought back the heartache that had almost killed her
when Vince was gone. At least she'd figured out early in
life that no one was ever going to hurt her like that again.

———

Wil really felt cheated. He'd wanted to devour those
lips, not just nibble at the edge. *Hell's bells! I don't need*
a spitfire like her in my life. After I get through helping
her out today I'm going to keep a mile between us. I'm
going to pretend there is a restraining order that says I
can't get within a thousand feet of her.

She could hear him vacuuming in the next unit when
she finished the beds and towels, amazed the whole
time at the immaculate job he did. "Wonder if he'd be
available on a stand-by notice?" she mused aloud as she
braced against the cold when she opened the door and
moved her cart down the sidewalk.

She carried towels into the next unit, straight to the
bathroom, and racked them up, set out complimentary
toiletries, and went back for bed linens. He moved on

without passing her in the doorway, vacuumed, cleaned
the bathroom, and was pushing the vacuum down
the sidewalk when she went in to put the room back
together. They fell into the routine and at exactly five
o'clock they finished the last room. He wound the cord
around the vacuum, picked it up with one hand and the
cleaning caddy with the other, and carried both back to
the laundry room where he'd found them. She pushed
her maid's cart behind him and enjoyed the view of
those tight-fitting jeans.

Stop it! she commanded, but her eyes wouldn't listen.
She looked at the only two trucks in the parking lot, at
the white winter clouds dotting a blue sky, at the windows as she passed one room after another, but it didn't
work. She still kept sneaking peeks at the way he filled
out those Wranglers.

"How long will it take you to get ready to go to Rye's
momma's place?" he yelled over his shoulder.

"I didn't say I was going."

He set the caddy down and opened the door, held it
for her, and then followed her into the steamy hot laundry room. "Why wouldn't you? It's Christmas. Austin
was your friend. Rye is my friend."

"I'm tired. I'm cranky. I thawed out my own
Christmas supper."

"That isn't a decent excuse."

He was right. It wasn't even a bad excuse, and the
only reason she didn't want to go was she didn't want
Austin, who was still in the first bloom of marriage, to
get any wrong ideas. Austin was already on the verge
of driving Pearl to alcoholism with her sly attempts at
matchmaking. Bless her heart, she was happy as a toad

on a lily pad and wanted all women in the world to find a sexy Texan, especially Pearl.

"Come on, you've worked like a slave all afternoon. You deserve a good dinner, and Rye's momma is the best cook in the county. Don't tell my momma I said that." He grinned.

"I'm tired."

"So am I but I'm going. You don't have to get all dressed up. It's just leftovers, even if they are better than a five-star restaurant's food." He threw an arm around her shoulders and squeezed her up next to his side. "They'll think I did something wrong and hang me from an old pecan tree with a nasty rope if you don't go with me."

"Okay. Okay! I'll go eat leftover Christmas turkey," she said. She was surprised she could utter a sane sentence in the heat waves radiating out from her body.

"Good!" He lingered a minute before he dropped his arm and started toward the door. "You've saved my life again this day."

She rolled her eyes at his evident flirting but had to give him credit for a few new and fresh come-on lines. "Give me half an hour to get cleaned up. Tell Austin I'll be along."

"Ain't no sense in you getting out a vehicle when mine is going that way and coming right back past the motel. I'll pick you up in an hour."

She wiped sweat from her forehead with the back of her sweatshirt sleeve and picked a sheet out of the dryer. "I can't stay very long. I'll need to be back by eight or so to rent rooms."

"That's doable." He reached out to touch her shoulder.

"No, I don't want to make you leave early. I'll meet you there in an hour." She dropped the sheet on the folding table and looked up but stopped at his lips.

"Sounds fine to me, but don't back out. You know the way?"

She nodded.

"Turn south on 81 when you get to Ringgold. About two miles down the road you'll see a sign that says McDonnell Horses, make a right and you'll see the house from the road. Big white two-story with a porch that wraps around three sides. Lots of pecan trees."

"I know how to get there."

"Well, I was just repeating whatever directions Austin gave you. Women never get it right."

"Be careful, cowboy. You might find yourself eating those words."

He disappeared out into the cold air. She picked up another sheet but tossed it back on the table. There would be plenty of time to finish folding the next day. The rooms were ready; the laundry done except for one last load in the dryer and two loads of folding piled up on the table. And suddenly, Pearl wanted to be pretty when she arrived at the O'Donnells' for supper.

She'd never gone so long in the fourteen years she'd been dating without some kind of social connection and felt plumb giddy at the idea of mingling among people her age, eating good food, and conversation about something other than the price of a hotel room.

~m~

Wil would have liked to race back to his ranch but as luck would have it a Henrietta policeman pulled out from the Dollar Store parking lot and fell in behind him. The squad car followed him all the way through town and even turned north when Wil did. He slapped the steering wheel, watched his speed, and kept an eye on the rearview mirror.

"Shit! I need to get home and get a shower if Red's coming to the O'Donnells'. Raylen and Dewar and even Ace will be there all spiffed up and they'll be sidling up next to Red the minute she walks in the door. Hell, I haven't had a shower or shaved since yesterday and I look like the devil," he fussed, but the policeman stayed two cars behind him.

When he turned right into his lane the policeman did a three-point turnaround and headed back to town. He pushed down on the gas pedal and raced to his ranch. He parked the truck in front of the house, ran inside and up the steps, ignoring poor old Digger. He shed his shirt on the way up the stairs and took the quickest shower in his history. When he finished running an electric razor over two days of black stubble, he splashed on shaving lotion and used a real comb on his hair.

He chose a pair of black jeans fresh from the cleaners and a black Western shirt: his Johnny Cash look. If only he could sing like Rye and play the guitar like Raylen, he'd really impress Red. What was it she said her name was anyway? Oh, yeah… Pearl! Hell, that name didn't fit her. She was too full of piss and vinegar to have a name that feminine.

She took a quick shower, semi-dried her red hair with a dryer and scrunched mousse into it, applied makeup,

and stood in front of her closet in her underpants and
bra trying to decide what to wear. There was last year's
Christmas dress: a lovely green velvet that hugged every
curve. She picked up the high-heeled velvet shoes em-
bellished with red and white sparkling stones set across
the toe. After moving all the hangers from one end to the
other and back again, she decided on black dress slacks,
a pair of high-heeled dress boots, and a red sweater de-
signed with a Christmas tree on the front. Sequins and
beads decorated the tree and velvet ribbons tied up the
packages under it. She checked her reflection in the mirror and decided to change the boots for a pair of red high
heels. After all, it was Christmas and she had a pseudo-
date. She topped the ensemble off with a chunky silver
bead necklace with a silver pendant of angel wings with
crossed pistols. The pistol grips were black onyx and the
angel wings were covered in pave diamonds. It had been
a gift from her father the previous Christmas.

Even if Wil was a total bad boy and the date was leftovers at a friend's house, she was calling it a real honest-
to-god date. She picked up a small cut crystal vase that
she wrapped for a co-worker two months before—back
when she thought she'd be exchanging presents with the
bank employees.

It would make a lovely hostess gift for Maddie
O'Donnell. She loved flowers and Pearl could see red
roses in the crystal vase or maybe a big bouquet of wild-
flowers in the spring. She set the gift down long enough
to pull on her coat and pick up her purse. Hopefully, she
wouldn't lose too much business in the two hours she
planned to be gone from the Longhorn. She made sure
the lobby door was locked and went out the back way

to the garage. She pushed a button on the garage door opener and backed the Caddy out of the garage, closed the door, and pulled out onto the highway. The wind whipped the bare mesquite tree branches around but the roads were clear. That's the way it was in Texas. Ice storm in the night, melt off by noon, and sunshine the next day. But the wind always blew. At least until July Fourth, and then a person couldn't buy, beg, or cuss up a breeze until after Labor Day weekend. That was according to Aunt Pearlita, who was only second to God in knowing everything about everything.

"Damn good thing it don't blow during that time of year," Aunt Pearlita had told her repeatedly in the summer. "If it did it would cook the flesh right off our bones. Hell is cool compared to Texas in July and August."

Pearl giggled at her aunt's description and turned south in Ringgold toward Bowie. A couple of miles down the highway she turned into a long lane and drove slowly, feeling more than a little nervous at being in the same social setting with Wil. If she could have turned the big yacht of a car around she might have, but it wasn't possible on the narrow lane between rows of dormant pecan trees. The yard was full of vehicles so she parked at the end of a long row of trucks, pulled down the visor mirror and checked her hair and makeup one more time, picked up the present, and slung open the car door. Her heart did a flutter or two when she reached the porch. It was just a pretend date but it felt so good that she took a long, deep breath before she pushed the doorbell.

Maddie O'Donnell yelled from the other side of the living room, "Hey, Wil, get that door, will you? You're the closest one to it."

"Sure thing," he said. He expected to see Pearl on the other side but he didn't think she'd be all dolled up and fancy. His mouth went as dry as if he'd just brushed his teeth with Red River sand.

"Hello, Wil," she said.

He stood to one side. "You look lovely."

"Well, thank you, so do you," she said and wished she could undo the words.

"Lovely?" The gold flecks in his eyes twinkled.

"You know what the hell I mean. You look sexy as hell in black."

He grinned so big that she could have slapped him silly. Instead, she deliberately brushed against him on the way through the door. Yep, there it was again. That sizzling jolt of electricity that tied her tongue into knots and made her wish she'd tossed a couple of extra pairs of panties in her purse before she left. Why did he have to be so handsome and so nice? The two shouldn't go together. Bad boys on this side of the fence. Good guys on that side. Now take your pick, ladies. It wasn't fair to have bad boy sex appeal and good guy sensitivity. And it damn sure wasn't fair for him to look that sexy and smell so good. And one more thing while she was bemoaning the fact that she was so drawn to him—how had he cleaned up so fast?

The quick graze of her against Wil created a quiver that he had to get under control fast or else he'd have to make an excuse to untuck his shirttail.

Austin crossed the room to hug her. "Pearl, I'm so glad you came."

"Wil talked me into it. He made me feel guilty," Pearl whispered.

"Be careful. He'll talk you into a whole lot more than that," Austin whispered back. She looped her arm through Pearl's and led her into the living room. "Everyone, meet my friend Pearl. She's inherited the Longhorn Inn over in Henrietta. Her great-aunt, Pearlita Richland, and my Granny Lanier were best friends most of their lives. Now they are telling God how to run heaven, I'm sure. Pearl, these are my sisters-in-law."

Pearl finished for her. "Gemma and Colleen and brothers-in-law, Raylen and Dewar. Hi, everyone. Colleen and I are friends from way back. I've been here before."

Wil crossed his arms over his chest and glared. "That was mean. And when were you here and how come I never saw you?"

"You didn't ask me if I knew these folks; you asked me if I knew how to get here and then disagreed with me when I said I did."

"You could have been up-front and honest," he said.

Ace came from across the room and grabbed her hand, bringing it to his lips for a long lingering kiss on each fingertip. "I'm Ace Riley. Don't pay any attention to him getting even. Can I take you to dinner next week?"

Wil wanted to shoot his best friend.

Ace had lovely blue eyes and blond curly hair. Just exactly what Pearl had always been attracted to; however, not one tingling sensation traveled from his lips through her fingertips to set her on fire. It did not affect her nearly as much as a single brush in the doorway with Wil.

Austin laughed. "Come on in the kitchen and have

some supper. Wil said he'd wait for you and he's been bitchin' and moanin' like a little girl about being hungry."

"Come on now! I wasn't that bad." Wil moved across the room and put a hand on Pearl's back to lead her to the kitchen.

Gemma and Colleen followed them. Gemma was the shorter of the two sisters. She had black hair cut in short layers that framed an oval face, deep green eyes beneath arched dark eyebrows and heavy lashes, and a wide mouth. She took care of her short height with a pair of three-inch spike heels. She wore an olive green velvet skirt with three tiers and a white velvet peasant top with olive green edging.

Colleen's hair was that strange burgundy color that usually comes out of a bottle. Her face was a little rounder than Gemma's and her lips a wee bit wider. She was a little taller than her sister but Gemma's high heels equaled the difference. Her cute designer jeans, Western cut denim shirt with red velvet trim, and red boots said she was definitely a cowgirl.

"How is it that all the times you were here you never met Wil?" Colleen asked.

"God was protecting me against that renegade," Pearl answered.

And why hasn't Wil made a play for one of Rye's sisters? They're both beautiful and have the same ranching background.

"More like He was protecting me." Wil didn't take his hand away from her back until they were in the kitchen.

"Are you children arguing?" Maddie joined them and set out the cranberry salad and other dishes that had been put back in the refrigerator.

Pearl handed Maddie the present. "This is for you."

"You shouldn't have and mustn't do it again. At least not until next year," Maddie talked as she tore into it. "Oh, I love it. You remembered how much I love cut flowers, didn't you? Now get busy and make a plate. If Wil doesn't eat soon I swear the boy is going to turn into an old bear. O'Donnells and Marshalls are both cranky as hell when they get hungry. And I hear that you worked him pretty hard all afternoon."

"He owed me big-time. I saved his neck from the noose this morning," Pearl said.

Maddie patted her arm. "I heard. I'm glad the electricity went out and he came to your motel."

Austin picked up a dessert plate with poinsettias printed on it. "I'll have another piece of pecan pie. If I don't get one soon, Gemma is going to eat it all up from me."

"I'll have a beer with y'all while you eat," Colleen said.

"When did you and Colleen meet?" Austin asked.

Colleen grinned. "We go back to when we were about eighteen. Pearl came to see her aunt and we wound up... well, we won't talk about where we met or those two handsome cowboys that were there, will we? But I will say that this girl can out-party anyone I ever knew."

"That's all muddy water under the bridge, isn't it?" Pearl smiled.

Wil had only known the woman a day and yet Colleen's comment turned him green with jealousy. He picked up an oversized paper plate and began loading it full of turkey and dressing, candied yams, baked beans, and cranberry salad. "You hang back, you starve."

Pearl picked up a plate and got in line behind him.

"As long as I get a piece of pecan pie, I'm fine. How good is that pie?" Pearl asked Austin as she set her plate down across the table from Wil.

"Best this side of heaven," Austin said. "I swear I've gained ten pounds since I married into this family. And I'm supposed to have Granny Lanier's DNA and that means I don't gain weight. But Maddie can sure test their powers."

Pearl picked up her fork. "That better not be the last slice or I may fight you for it."

"There's one more in the pan." Austin smiled.

One bite of the corn bread dressing and Pearl forgot about good guys, bad boys, and even motel rooms. Two bites made her forget everything but how good the food was. Three and she would have fought a full-grown coyote away from her plate with nothing but a long-handled teaspoon.

Austin, a tall brunette with eyes the color of a summer sky, grinned. The girl Austin had known as a child was brazen and foolhardy; the woman hadn't changed a lot. She'd quit her job as a bank executive but took a firm hold on that old motel and ran it single-handedly without so much as a backward glance.

Pearl's cell phone sent up a ringtone and Wil looked at Colleen.

"Don't be lookin' at me. Mine plays 'Hello Darlin'.'"

"And mine plays 'Sweet Home Alabama,'" Austin said.

"It's mine," Pearl said. "They'll call back."

Two minutes and three bites later, it rang again. She sighed and reached for her purse.

"Hello," she said.

"Hi, darlin'. Thought I'd call early and invite you to

the New Year's Eve party at Billy Bob's. Bunch of us are going down early and staying the whole weekend. I'll pick you up at five," Trent said.

Pearl smiled. "Can't, sweetheart. I'd love to but I've got a motel to run. Maybe next year I'll have things ironed out and some help. Don't give up on me."

Wil was sitting close enough he could hear every word of the conversation. Just how many men did she know, anyway?

"We'll miss you. Party won't be the same without you there."

"Jasmine will take up the slack." Pearl laughed.

"No way that's possible. It's a shame you have to work so hard, darlin'. Sure I can't talk you into shutting down the motel for a couple of days?"

"I'm sure, Trent. Got to run, honey. Enjoy the party and think of me." She smacked him a kiss over the phone and snapped it shut.

Austin giggled. "So the tribe misses the queen bee of the party girls, does it? How in the world are you surviving without a social life?" Austin asked.

Gemma pulled out a chair and sat down beside Austin. "Y'all hadn't seen each other in a long time? Why? Sounds like you were good friends when you were kids."

Pearl explained between bites. "My father sent me to Aunt Pearlita for two weeks every summer because she didn't have any kids and she adored my daddy. Aunt Pearlita and Granny Lanier were best friends so they always had a few play days for us since Austin visited the same weeks I did. When we were about sixteen we got summer jobs so our trips ended and we drifted apart. We did see each other last spring at a rodeo down, remember? Besides, it was probably for the best that we drifted apart. She got me in trouble every time we were together."

Austin pointed her fork at Pearl. "Me! You were born a hellion and grew up to be the party gal. I was the good kid who studied hard and never did a thing wrong. Someday I'll tell you stories about what a daredevil she was."

Wil finished eating and went back to the kitchen for dessert. He grabbed the last piece of pecan pie and carried it to the table. "I believe you, Austin. Ever since I met this woman I've been in trouble."

"You!" Pearl exclaimed. "I was minding my own business running a motel when you showed up. Cops had never come around beating on my door at the Longhorn until you rented a room. Don't blame me."

Austin turned her fork toward him. "I do believe that my friend had dibs on that piece of pie."

Pearl shot a look that would have had a seasoned convict whimpering in his tracks and crossing his legs to keep from putting a wet stain on his orange jumpsuit. "I got you out of jail, drove you home, and you steal my pie. Is that the thanks I get?"

Wil had the audacity to shrug as if the look didn't affect him one bit. "I cleaned rooms in your motel all afternoon to pay off that debt, so don't use the old you-owe-me card. I don't owe you jack shit and this don't have your name on it, does it?"

Before he could blink she reached across the table, picked up the saucer, and licked the pie from crust to tip.

"It's got my slobbers on it so I guess it's mine."

"I can't believe you did that." Austin knew flirting when she saw it. Had Pearl set her cap for Wil? God help the man! But then, Austin wasn't even sure God had that much power.

Pearl shrugged. "A woman has got to protect her rights and I already said that pie was mine."

Wil popped a piece in his mouth. "Darlin', that's just sugar on the top."

"Ewww," Gemma groaned.

"What?" Wil asked while he chewed.

"That's gross."

"Would it be gross if I'd kissed her?"

"That's different?"

"Don't get your hopes up, cowboy," Pearl said.

"Darlin', don't you get your hopes up either," Wil said.

Austin, Gemma, and Colleen burst out laughing.

Pearl gave them all an evil look.

Chapter 4

SLEET STILL HID IN THE SHADED AREAS ON THE NORTH SIDE of Highway 82 from Ringgold to Henrietta, but the roads were dry and clear. Stars twinkled around a full moon but Pearl didn't see any of it. She couldn't get away from how handsome Wil was in that black shirt. And just thinking about his hand on her back on the way to the kitchen gave her a warm, oozy feeling all over again. She was glad she'd gone to the O'Donnells' for a few hours and really felt as if she'd had an outing. She deserved it after a whole month of work and classes. Wil was just the icing on the cupcake, and knowing those were his headlights right behind her put a warm glow all over her body.

When she turned off at the motel she expected him to honk but he followed her, parking the truck between the garage and the back door that led into her apartment. By the time she got the Caddy situated and the garage doors down he was out of his truck and leaning on the fender.

"After last night and today, I figured you'd be eager to get home," Pearl said.

"I told Austin I'd get you home safely." Wil grinned.

"Austin worries too much. Who saw to it she got home safe last spring?"

"Hey, Rye was right across the road the whole time. From the time he first laid eyes on her that man was love drunk as hell."

"Love drunk?" Pearl asked.

"Yeah, he was besotted with that woman. How come you weren't at their reception? I'd have remembered you if you'd been there."

"I had to be out of state for a training seminar for the bank."

"You going to invite me in for a cup of coffee?" he asked.

"No, I am not. I'm going to open the lobby and get ready for customers," she answered.

"Then I'll walk you around the motel and make sure you get inside all right."

"Wil, I'm a big girl. I'm not afraid of the dark. I can take care of myself." She talked as she walked.

He fell into step right beside her.

She unlocked the door, didn't look back as she went straight for the counter, and flipped on the cowboy neons. If she decided to go with quaint and romantic the old cowboy was going to have to retire his bowlegged stance to the garage. Or she'd sell him on eBay... could be that he'd bring a fortune since he was getting right up there close to being a bona fide antique.

Last night she'd had a full house; tonight she probably wouldn't have one customer. It was Christmas! No one, not even Santa Claus, was out on Christmas. She hoped he was tired to the bone and sick of cookies and milk. It would serve him right for not bringing her a nice quiet night like she'd wanted. Hell's bells, she hadn't been a bad child that year but he'd damn sure treated her like her name was right up there on the top of his shit list when he dumped all those people in her lobby at one time.

Wil stopped on the lobby side of the counter and leaned on it. "Austin tells me you were a big-shot banker. What happened?"

"I quit because I wanted to be my own boss and Aunt Pearlita left me the motel. Mother said I was making the biggest mistake of my life. My friend, Jasmine, said she was jealous of my spunk. Austin encouraged me to move here, but I got to admit sometimes I wonder if I bit off more than I can chew." She talked fast and kept her eyes away from his lips. She stepped out around the counter and straightened the few magazines on the table between the two recliners. If it had been a real date he would have kissed her good night at the door. She turned around to find him right behind her.

Already in motion with a step forward, she couldn't stop and ran right into his chest. His arms wrapped firmly around her and she looked up. One second she was sinking into his dreamy eyes, the next she was melting into a steamy kiss that sent waves of liquid desire shooting through her body.

He broke away but kept her in his embrace for several seconds. "Well, good night, Red. Thanks for being my date for the night."

"Date?"

"Yep. It felt like a date. You looked like a date. And a good night kiss sealed it. It was a date. I'll call you later." He walked across the floor and out the door. She had to lean on the counter to keep her jelly-filled knees from collapsing, but she watched that sexy strut until it disappeared into the darkness.

"Dammit, Austin! You started this whole thing when you moved to Terral. I figured if you could make a drastic change then I damn sure could," she muttered as she rounded the end of the counter and sat down at her computer. But she couldn't keep her mind on her work. She kept thinking of how much fun she'd had at the party and how she'd missed flirting and dating and kissing and the whole nine yards.

Home? Even though she owned the motel and had moved into the apartment it still didn't feel like home. Austin had said that when she had first inherited the watermelon farm she had thought of it as Granny's place until she'd made up her mind to keep the farm, plant and harvest watermelon crops, and make watermelon wine. After that she felt like she was going home every time she started toward Terral from Tulsa and that she was leaving a part of her heart when she had to leave Terral.

Pearl had one advantage over Austin, who'd been thrown in the middle of Small Town, USA, like a chicken in a coyote pen. Austin hadn't known anyone. She had no friends other than Pearl's Aunt Pearlita. Pearl had Austin and the O'Donnells and in a pinch she could call on Rosa if she needed anything. She couldn't remember when Rosa hadn't been a fixture at the Longhorn Inn. She had tried to talk Rosa into staying on when she took over, but Rosa told her that she had only worked the past five years because of Pearlita, and it was time for her to retire.

Thank God for Austin, Rosa, and the O'Donnell family or she'd have been out in the cold just like Austin had been. The O'Donnells were 100 percent Irish on both sides of the family. They loved and fought with passion and if they were your friends, nobody messed with you and got away with it. She had no doubt the whole bunch would come to her aid if she needed them.

Her thoughts went to the O'Donnell brothers.

Dewar was shorter than Rye but just as handsome. His face was more angular and he had a scar across his cheek, a gift from busting a bronc when he was a teenager. He'd flirted with Pearl a few times, but nothing he'd ever said made her giddy like a wink from Wil Marshall.

Raylen was the pretty boy. Cash said that God made it up to him because he was the shortest one of the lot. He had dark hair that turned chestnut red when he got out in the sun and the prettiest blue eyes this side of heaven. His voice was deep and resonant and eyelashes so long and sexy that one wink would cause a virgin's underpants to slide down toward her ankles. But he'd never caused Pearl to need to change her underpants, not like Wil Marshall had done.

"It's what I get for letting that man get under my skin," she said as she kicked off her shoes and heard a vehicle motor at the same time. She looked up half hoping that Wil had remembered something else and she'd get one more look at him or maybe another searing kiss. But it wasn't Wil and the car didn't stay. It backed up in the parking lot and the red taillights disappeared out onto the highway. Then a woman slipped inside the lobby and stopped midway across the floor.

"May I help you?" Pearl asked.

"The lady that brought me here said you might be needin' help," the woman said softly. She wore a stained gray hooded sweatshirt with the hood up, shading most of her face. Her jeans were white at the knees and not in a fashionable way. They hung on her slim hips like a flapping towel out on the clothesline.

"Who brought you here?" Pearl asked.

"Rosa. She said that I was to come in here and tell you that I'm lookin' for work," she said in a deep southern accent. Pearl was very familiar with a Georgia accent since her mother was born and raised there and Texas had not taken a bit of it away from her in the past thirty-three years. But this skinny woman sounded more like she came from backwoods Tennessee.

She pushed the hood away from her face and Pearl gasped. It was a motley green and purple mess of bruises. One eye had started to heal, but it was still sporting a mouse under it half the size of Pearl's fist. Her crystal clear blue eyes looked everywhere but at Pearl. Her limp brown hair was pulled back in a ponytail at the nape of her neck. Her delicate face looked like an amateur artist's dirty palette.

"It don't hurt like it did at first," the woman said. "I just need a job. I'll do anything, ma'am."

"Who are you?"

"My name is Lucy Fontaine. I come from up in the Kentucky hills. Little bitty town you wouldn't even know. I used every dime I had to get this far away from there and my husband. I got a ride from Gainesville with a nice lady. She said you might be needin' some help because she used to work here."

"What happened to you?"

"Husband whooped me for the last time. I been savin' for five years and figured if I didn't leave, the next time he'd plumb kill me. I can clean rooms for a place to stay and some food."

"Have you eaten lately?" Pearl asked. She couldn't turn anyone away on Christmas.

"I ain't here for a handout. I got some crackers left in my purse. What I need is a job."

The phone rang before Pearl could tell her that a frozen dinner was going to waste in the kitchen. "Longhorn Inn. May I help you?"

"This is Rosa. I dumped a stray puppy on your doorstep. Hire her. You need help. She needs a place to heal and work."

"But what if—" Pearl started to argue valid points.

"She's broke. If you are anything like your aunt, you'll help fix her."

"You sure?" Pearl asked.

"Yes, I'm sure. Put her on for a month. She'll work hard and heal slow. Check the books. You're going to have a very busy season during duck hunting season. You can't run it by yourself. If Wil Marshall hadn't got his ass in a bind, you'd have still been cleaning rooms tonight, and you'd have missed out on Maddie O'Donnell's Christmas supper."

Pearl gasped. "How'd you know about that?"

"Honey, whatever happens in Henrietta is all over town before the clock strikes the next hour. So?"

"Okay, okay!"

"Feed her too. She's been living on crackers for three days. Call me sometimes and let me know how she's doin'."

Pearl set the phone down and looked up to see Lucy munching on a saltine cracker that she'd taken from her purse. "Is your husband going to chase you down and cause trouble?"

"My husband thinks I'm dead. I fixed it that way. I took his truck and left him a note." She looked Pearl straight in the eye and didn't blink.

"Okay, do you have a social security card?"

"Yes, ma'am, I do. It's still in my name, Lucinda Fontaine. I never changed it because he wouldn't let me do no work outside of the house. He lived by the old ways that said a man was the head of the house and the woman obeyed him. It was the way we was both raised up."

"What was your married name?"

"Molly Brooks."

Pearl frowned.

"My name is Molly Lucinda Fontaine Brooks. He wouldn't call me Lucy because he hated them old television reruns with Lucy and Desi." She swallowed hard and went on, "I'm makin' a clean start so I want to be Lucy, not Molly. I ain't never again goin' to be Molly."

"Okay then, Lucy Fontaine, have you ever done any work at a motel?"

"No, ma'am. All I did was some waitress work and a little cooking for the café when the fry cook called in sick. And that was twelve years ago when I was just sixteen. But I can learn right fast. You show me one time how you want it done and I'll learn it."

Hire her right now before she changes her mind. You can date if someone is here to watch the lobby. And having someone help cleaning rooms would be an added bonus. You just won the lottery. Don't tear up the check.

Pearl didn't even argue with the voice in her head. "Here's the deal I can offer. I'll pay you minimum wage and give you a room to live in as long as you want it. After thirty days we'll sit down and decide if you want to stay. If we are both happy, I'll give you a raise. I got one question. Are you sure your husband thinks you are dead?"

"Cleet ain't too smart but I fixed it so there wasn't no doubt. I waited 'til a day when he rode with his daddy to work and took his truck to the river in the middle of the mornin'. I left it in the middle of the river bridge with my good purse settin' on the seat. I left my best shoes and my coat on the bridge. I ate a candy bar and was so nervous that I puked it up, but I was careful to do that over the side of the bridge. Then I crawled up on the railin' with my messy hands so there'd be fingerprints."

She hesitated and then went on. "Then I walked five miles to the next town. Bus comes through there once a week after the station closes. You got to buy your ticket ahead of time but I begged the driver to let me buy one from him to Memphis. If he hadn't of done it I'd have kept on walkin' but he did. I reckon he put the money in his pocket but I really don't care. When I got to Memphis I counted out what I had left and got another ticket to Little Rock. From there I made it to Dallas, but I was almost out of money so I asked the man how far I could get on what I had left. That took me to Gainesville and I started walkin' west and that lady picked me up on the side of the road right outside of town. That's a lot of words but I reckon if you're goin' to hire me then you oughta have the whole thing."

Pearl was amazed. "Why didn't you leave sooner if he beat you?"

"Wife is supposed to be good. Momma said that if I was good I wouldn't get them whoopin's. Took me five years to save the money and to figure out that some men is just plain mean and it don't matter how good a woman is they're goin' to beat on them. Savin' the money had to be slow or he'd have found out and he had to think I was dead so he wouldn't come after me so I had to plan it down to the last thing."

Pearl opened the gate at the end of the counter. "Get your things and I'll take you to your room."

Lucy looked down at her sweatshirt and jeans. "This is my things. I bought 'em at a garage sale and didn't tell him. If he goes through my stuff he won't find a thing missin'."

"Okay, then. I've got a frozen dinner in my apartment that you are going to take to your room and heat up in the microwave. The room has a small refrigerator with a microwave on top." Pearl headed through the back door when the crunch of gravel took her attention to the parking lot.

Headlights lit up the lobby and in a minute a young man rushed inside out of the cold. He removed his cowboy hat and looked from Lucy to Pearl and back again. "You go on. You were here first."

"We've already gotten her taken care of. What can I do for you?" Pearl said.

"I need three rooms," he said. He wore his jeans right. His eyes were a soft brown and he held his black Stetson in his hand as he talked. An evening shadow of a beard gave him a rakishly handsome look, and his dark hair was just a little too long. So why didn't he jack Pearl's blood pressure up like Wil Marshall did? Why didn't she have the sudden impulse to drag him off to bed? He was a cowboy, wasn't he?

Nothing made a lick of sense.

Pearl watched him fill out the card. "Each room has two double beds."

"I know. Me and the guys stay here every Christmas. We ought to make reservations but there's always room. But them other two snore and there ain't no way I'm stayin' in the same room with either of them so we get our own rooms. And if you can I'd just as soon there was an empty room between me and them. Where's that other lady? She knew what we liked."

Pearl pulled out three cards. "That was my aunt and she passed away back in the fall."

He nodded his head reverently. "Sorry to hear that, ma'am. She was a sweet old gal."

"Thank you. Got a preference on rooms?"

"Over on that other side. It's quieter."

Pearl handed him the keys. "Okay, then here's twenty-four, twenty-two, and twenty. If it doesn't fill up tonight like last night there'll be a space between all of you."

The cowboy grinned. "Great!"

He put his hat back on and tipped it at Lucy before he left. The headlights lit up the lobby again and the noise of the truck moving slowly let them know that the men had turned around and parked in front of one of the rooms on the other side of the gravel lot.

"I'll grab that dinner and take you up to your room," Pearl said.

"Thank you," Lucy told her. She would have been grateful for a bologna sandwich right then. Soul and body was about to split up from hunger and she'd just eaten the last of her crackers. But she was a long, long way from Cleet and his anger spells and she'd starve plumb to death before she went back.

Pearl put the TV dinner, a two-liter bottle of Coke, a package of Oreos, a banana, orange, and apple into a plastic grocery bag. She added a fork, knife, and spoon from her silverware drawer, a plate, cup, and saucer from the cabinet.

Lucy was still standing in the middle of the floor when she went back out.

"You could have sat down," Pearl said.

"I didn't know what to do."

Pearl set the food bag on the counter. "I forgot something. Go on and sit down and if anyone comes in tell them I'll be right back."

She grabbed another bag on her way through the apartment and carried it to her bedroom. She put in two sweat suits and followed that with a nightshirt and a lined denim jacket, a couple of pairs of socks, and she hesitated for a long moment but then shoved in three pairs of underpants. There was no way that Lucy could wear one of her bras so she'd just have to keep hers washed until they could make a run to a store.

Lucy sunk down into one of the comfortable recliners. She thought of Cleet sitting in his chair in front of the television, yelling at her to bring him a beer or a piece of cake or pie. Always yelling at her and yet being so nice to everyone else. She'd tried to be good. Where had she gone wrong?

Lucy was sitting very still when Pearl returned to the lobby. For a second she thought the girl had sat down in a recliner and died, but then she noticed that Lucy was breathing. Pearl picked up the key to the room and the extra bag and said, "Let's get you settled into the room."

Her voice startled Lucy and she curled forward in a ball around her worn tote bag.

Pearl touched her shoulder. "Hey, I'm sorry."

Lucy flinched.

"Lucy, no one is going to hurt you again. If they do I'll beat the shit out of them."

Lucy looked up. "I'm sorry. It just happens."

Pearl put the room key in her hand. "No need to be sorry. You'll get over it. It'll just take time. Now follow me and we'll get you settled in for the night. I bet you'd like a warm bath after all that travel."

Lucy nodded. She couldn't begin to imagine a long hot bath with no fear. She usually took very quick showers, careful not to use an ounce of extra hot water or Cleet would be furious when he took his shower. If the hot water ran out before he was finished she was in for a beating. If he wanted chocolate cake and she had peach cobbler he'd jerk off his belt. To take her mind off that wide brown belt she looked up at the Texas sky. A person could see from here all the way to the end of the world. It was so different than back in the mountains of Kentucky. She'd miss her momma and her youngest sister, but if she never saw a mountain again she'd be happy. All they'd brought was pain and misery.

Pearl stood to one side while Lucy opened the door. "It's not much but it'll do until you can get on your feet. It's got beds, a television, phone, bathroom, and I've got a few things here for you. Tomorrow I've got to go buy groceries. I'll give you an advance on your first week's salary so you can get whatever you like."

"I'm obliged for it all," she said, her accent even

thicker since she'd started to relax. "What time do I start to work in the mornin'?"

"Checkout is at eleven but most folks get up and gone by eight or nine."

"I'm used to havin' breakfast on the table at six o'clock so I get up right early." Lucy couldn't keep from looking at everything in the room. All that luxury was more than she could take in with a single scan. Later, when she was alone it might sink in but right then it looked like a big slice of heaven.

"When we've got a couple of rooms empty, I'll give you a call. The laundry room is next door. Use the machines to wash your clothes and there are towels and linens stacked up on racks. Change your bed whenever you want and help yourself to the towels. I'll see you in the morning." Pearl backed out of the room and shut the door.

She picked up the pace when two trucks pulled into the lot and beat the first customer to the lobby. It was an elderly lady wearing a cute little blue sweat suit decorated with rhinestones and pearls. "Honey, me and the husband out there in the truck need us a room with two beds for tonight. We're on our way home from Christmas with the kids and I can't see worth a damn when it gets dark and the husband has beginnin' Alzheimer's so I can't trust him to make the right turns."

"I've got just what you need." Pearl picked the number two key from the wall and handed her a card to fill out.

She was getting computerized even if it caused Pearlita Richland's ashes to reconnect, swim upstream from the Red River, and haunt her. Lucy was there to

clean rooms so she would have the time to install the
programs and talk to several people about key card
locks. She could afford it and it would make things so
much simpler.

"Thank you, darlin'," the lady said after she'd filled
out the card.

Pearl could have sworn she had heard and seen two
trucks. She looked out the glass windows and sure
enough there was another vehicle sitting there. She
sucked in a lung full of air and prayed that old Cleet
hadn't found his way to her hotel. The truck door swung
open and Wil stepped out, leaned in and picked something up, and carried it toward the motel lobby.

She cocked her head to one side and waited. Maybe his
electricity had blown again. She raised an eyebrow when
he pushed inside and laid a card on the counter. "Is the
whole town out of electricity or just your ranch again?"

He set a whole pecan pie on the counter. "You can put
that card away. I'm just taking care of a guilty conscience."

Pearl's eyes widened.

"It was in the kitchen the whole time and I let you
think I got the last piece. I really did get the last one out
of that pie pan, but Austin fussed at me when she found
this one and I got to feelin' so guilty that I brought it to
you. But I forgot about it in the truck until I got all the
way back to the ranch. So merry Christmas, Red."

"Thank you for the pie but if you call me that again,
I intend to shoot you and feed your dead carcass to the
coyotes," she said around the lump in her throat.

*It's got to be Lucy's sad life that's making me so emo-
tional. God knows it can't be a pecan pie. Nothing is
so damn good that it would make me go all mushy and*

weepy. I swore off that after I cried for two weeks when Vince left.

He waited for her to say something else but she just stared at the pie. She looked up and he saw the pain in her eyes. He took two steps forward and wrapped her into his arms again. "What is it?"

"Post holiday blues," she mumbled.

Using his knuckles, he tipped her chin up and lips met lips again in another clash of heat. He teased her lips apart with the tip of his tongue and deepened the kiss. She wrapped her arms around his neck and rolled up on her tiptoes to get the full effect of the scorching hot kisses.

Finally, he broke away but looked down at her face. Soft, sexy desire had replaced the pain. Another kiss or two or another minute of gazing into her mesmerizing eyes and he'd be acting like Rye did when he met Austin. He quickly took a couple of steps backwards and said, "I'll be goin' now. Christmas is about over and it will be work as usual tomorrow. Oh, before I forget, Austin said to tell you that she's having a New Year's Eve party up in Terral and you are invited. She'll be callin' in the next couple of days, I'm sure. Good night and enjoy the pie. I didn't even lick it."

"I wouldn't care if you did. I'd eat it anyway. I'm not squeamish," she said.

He gave her his over-the-shoulder wave as he pushed out into the night air.

———

Lucy slowly circled the room, lightly touching the comforter on the beds and the recliner in the corner. She was afraid to shut her eyes for fear it would all disappear before she could open them again. When she was sure it wasn't a dream and she really had a place to stay and a job, she opened the sacks Pearl had set inside the door. She hugged the clean clothing to her face and wept over them. She carefully placed them inside the dresser drawer, leaving it ajar so she could keep them in sight as she opened the next bag.

"Ohhh!" She grabbed up an apple and bit into it while she read the instructions on the dinner. She polished off the whole apple, leaving nothing but a very slim core and the stem, while the turkey and dressing meal cooked. While she waited for the microwave to ding she set the tiny table in the corner with her very own fork, knife, and spoon. When it finished, she sat down, bowed her head with no fear of being slapped when she finished saying grace, and ate slowly, savoring each bite.

Afterwards she ran a bath, washed her hair with the cute little bottle of shampoo on the counter, and leaned back, letting the warm water soak away the aches and pains all over her body. That last beating had been the worst ever. Cleet had gotten tired of using the belt and had thrown it at the wall and finished the job with his fists. That's why her face was such a mess. She ran a hand down her side. No broken ribs but they were sore as the devil. When the water had turned lukewarm, she got out, dried on a wonderful soft towel, and dressed in the clean nightshirt and underpants. She washed her bra in the bathroom sink and hung it over the shower rod to dry.

"Merry Christmas, Lucy Fontaine," she said as she crawled in between clean sheets and shut her eyes.

—◦◦◦—

Wil twisted the lid off a bottle of beer, settled into his favorite chair, and surfed through dozens of television channels. Nothing kept his attention very long. He kept thinking about Red. She was full of spit and vinegar. He liked that in a woman, but dammit but her kisses made him want more and more and more.

"I've gone and let her get under my skin, and I'm not sure it was the right thing to do," he told Digger, who was curled up on the floor beside him.

Digger rolled his eyes upward but didn't stir a muscle.

—◦◦◦—

Even though she was full, Pearl cut a small slice of pecan pie and nibbled on it as she rented out six more rooms. In between bites and guests she let her thoughts go to Wil. She touched her mouth and was surprised that it didn't burn her fingertips. She shut her eyes and got a picture of him standing right beside her. She wrapped her arms around her body and imagined they were his.

The vision of his broad shoulders raised the heat factor another notch or two. And the thought of his eyes flamed the fires even more. She could never remember any man affecting her like that. She'd been in love with Marlin and he hadn't made her need an icy shower in the middle of the winter like Wil did.

Why now? Why him? I've been looking for someone to share my life with for years and dated dozens of men and not a single one of them made me go all hot and mushy just thinking about them. None of this makes a

blasted bit of sense, not even if he is as sexy as hell...
even with a dust rag in his hand.

"If I don't stop right now Lucy's first job will be calling the Henrietta Fire Department to put out the fire in the lobby," she mumbled.

She was grateful for the next guests who arrived to take her mind off Wil. A young couple with two little children who were tired and cranky so she put them at the end of the south wing close to the breezeway with the ice machine. The next were two middle-aged sisters that she gave the key to number three.

"Eleven rooms. Damn, I'm glad I hired Lucy," she said as she turned on the NO VACANCY sign and went to her apartment.

She showered, put on a pair of flannel pajamas printed with Christmas trees, and sunk down on the sofa with Delilah. "Well, girl, I had an interesting day. Downright exciting, really. I sprung Wil Marshall out of jail, cleaned rooms with him all afternoon, and had dinner over at the O'Donnells' place. Food was wonderful as usual and they've got cats all over the porch. You'd love it there. Wil kissed me three times today. The first one barely counts but it was hot as hell. The next two... well, let's say I'm having trouble shutting my eyes without seeing him, feeling his lips, and needing to change my panties. Oh, and I hired us some help. Her name is Lucy and I think you'll like her."

Delilah purred and snuggled up to Pearl's side.

Pearl picked up the remote and flipped through several channels. There was a rerun of a two-year-old Christmas special on CMT and she fell asleep watching it. A loud commercial, advertising kitchen knives for only $19.95, awoke her. She turned the television off, picked up Delilah, and carried her back to the bedroom.

It was past midnight when she set the alarm and went back to sleep, only to dream of Wil Marshall. He was in a jail like they built in the old west—a small stone structure with barely enough room for an outer office and one cell. She awoke in a cold sweat, sitting straight up in bed and clutching her pillow to her breast as she wept.

"Dammit! It was just a dream. It wasn't real so why am I still carrying on like this?" she asked Delilah, who was sleeping like a queen on her throne on the extra pillow.

The cat opened both eyes and then closed them again.

"You're no help at all. If it wasn't so late I'd call Austin or maybe even Lucy, just to talk to someone about that stupid dream."

Chapter 5

THAT ANTSY FEELING CREATED BY THE NIGHTMARE STILL
lingered in Pearl's half-sleep the next morning. She
blinked a couple of times but the feeling that someone
was in the room with her didn't disappear. Finally she
opened her eyes full awake, screamed, and jumped out
of bed all in one fell swoop. When she realized it was
Delilah's eyes not an inch from her pillow she stopped
hopping around like a frog in a hot skillet and sat on the
edge of the bed, her heart thumping so hard her ribs hurt.
Delilah looked at her like she'd done lost her fool mind,
sniffed the air, and headed for the living room.

"So chaos starts the day!" she gasped.

When her weak knees stiffened she headed to the
kitchen to make coffee. The guests would be checking
out before long and if she was going to greet them with
open eyes after a restless night then caffeine wasn't a
luxury; it was a necessity. She poured four cups of water
into the back of the pot, added extra grounds to the basket, and flipped the switch. While it dripped, she went
back to the bedroom and dressed in jeans and a bright
pink sweatshirt. She washed her face and pulled her
frizzy hair back into a ponytail, twisting it around the
base into a loose bun and securing it with a wide clasp.

She carried a cup of coffee to the lobby, set it on the
counter to cool, and unlocked the door. She'd barely
made it back to the counter when Lucy arrived. The

bruises were still shades of green and yellow like a tie-dyed T-shirt but they didn't look as horrendous as they had the night before. Her light brown hair was shiny clean and a thick ponytail swung almost to her shoulders. Her eyes had more life in them that morning and her wide smile lit up the whole lobby.

"Good morning. I been watching out the window to see when the lights would come on in the lobby so I'd be here on time. What do I do first?"

"First thing you do is get a cup of coffee. Through that door in the kitchen. Help yourself. Donuts are on the counter if you want one. Then you sit down in one of those recliners and wait. The customers will start checking out soon but they can stay until eleven if they want to."

"I already used that little coffee pot in my room and had coffee and some cookies for my breakfast but I'd like another cup."

Pearl pointed. "Help yourself. Cups are in the cabinet right above the pot."

"Oh, a cat!" Lucy squealed when she saw Delilah. "Can I pet it?"

"If she'll let you. She's temperamental."

Lucy reached down and picked up Delilah, hugged her to her chest and forgot all about the coffee. She carried her to the recliner and sat down, holding her like a baby in her arms and petting her between the ears. "I love cats. I had one when we got married but Cleet hated it. He said if it got in the house one more time he was goin' to shoot it so I took it to Momma. Daddy, he didn't mind cats in the house. I could sit right here all day but there's got to be something I can be doing while we wait."

"The dryers are full of sheets," Pearl said with a yawn.

Lucy promptly stood up and laid Delilah in the chair. "Is that room open?"

"You got your key ring with you?"

Lucy fished it out of the pocket of her sweat bottoms and laid it on the counter. She was so disappointed that she could've cried. She'd thought the key was hers to keep all the time, not collect at night and give back in the day.

Pearl added two keys and laid the ring back on the counter. "I'll put the laundry room key on it and the storage room back behind it too. If you want to do your laundry at night or if you wake up early and want to finish folding a load out of the dryer, you'll have the keys."

Lucy picked up the ring. She'd been trusted with the keys to the laundry and the storage room. She felt like a princess. "I'll go on and take care of the folding. And I was wondering, could we take one of those beds out of my room? I only need the one."

"Sure. We'll put the extra out in the garage. There's plenty of room. So you like the room all right?"

"I slept better than I have in years. Thank you for all the food. It was so good that I ate that whole dinner before I went to bed. I'll see to it I work some extra hours to pay you back for everything."

"No, you won't. That would've gone to waste if you hadn't eaten it, and the clothes were on their way to the Goodwill store. We've got a little while before they start checking out. Want to go move that bed right now?" Pearl asked.

Lucy's eyes lit up. "Yes, I would and then I'll get on that folding job."

The sun was peeking through the naked outstretched arms of the mesquite and scrub oak trees on the east and west sides of the motel. The north wind whipped through the limbs making them dance gracefully. Lucy took it all in as they walked under the awning covering the sidewalk in front of the room doors.

Pearl yawned again. "Pardon me. I didn't sleep so well last night."

Lucy opened the door into her room. "I'm sorry. I slept better than I have since I married Cleet. I didn't even dream and when I woke up I felt like Sleeping Beauty did in that storybook."

The place was as spotless as it had been when she let Lucy inside the night before. Everything, including the remote control, was in its place.

"Which one do you want to move out?" Pearl asked.

"Might as well take the one closest to the door. I slept on the other one already. We could just fold up those covers and put them away. Besides, it'll be easier to tote out the door. I might put my little table over there where it is and maybe someday I'll find me one of them little sofas. That is if it would be all right with you for me to put it in here."

"It's your room, apartment, or house. Whatever you want to call it. You can do whatever you like to the place. Rosa lived here when I was a little girl back before she remarried and moved into a house. She had a sofa and end tables and a bookcase on that wall. I remember because I was a little girl and she used to read to me. Then when I got older we'd watch movies together sometimes and she'd make popcorn for us. Back then she used the refrigerator and old cookstove hooked up in the storage room behind the laundry. You're welcome to use those any time you want to, Lucy."

Lucy melted into the recliner, put her head in her hands, and sobbed.

"Lucy, what's the matter? Did I say something wrong?" Pearl asked.

She shook her head. "It's more'n I hoped for when I left Kentucky. I can't believe I'm this lucky."

"You'll think lucky when you have to clean rooms. Sometimes they leave them in a mess."

She wiped her eyes and stood up with a ramrod straight back. "Enough of that bellyachin'. You didn't hire me to listen to me whine around like a kitten took away from its momma. Let's get this bed outta here and then go to work."

Together they removed the comforter, folded it, then the blanket and linens. When they were done, they carried the mattress out to the breezeway, leaned it against the wall, and went back inside for the box springs. Before they could pick it up Wil had parked his truck in front of Lucy's room.

He hurried out of the truck and into the room. "Saw y'all moving a bed out when I was passin' by so I turned around and come back to help. Here, let me do that for you."

"What are you doing out this early?" Pearl asked.

"Darlin', it is almost seven o'clock. I done been up long enough to feed the cows, horses, pigs, and chickens and me and Digger had a big breakfast. I'm on my way over to Rye's to break a couple of young horses. Me and Raylen said we'd be there before eight but I got time to haul that stuff wherever you want it took."

"It's just a bed and we are takin' it to the garage," Pearl said.

His eyes lingered on hers a few seconds longer than necessary. "Okay, then. Stand back and I'll put it on the truck and take it around there."

He brushed past her and his touch slapped every single sane thought from her head. She did have enough sense to step back and let him into the room but it took a second before she regained her composure.

"I was trying to think about where we would put this in the garage. There's a couple of places," she said to cover her blush. "Lucy, this is Wil. And Wil, this is Lucy, my new hired help. She's going to live in this room. That's the reason we're moving the bed out."

Wil noticed the bruises and the way the woman kept her eyes downcast. It didn't take a high-powered psychologist to figure out that she'd been abused. He hoped Pearl knew what she was doing hiring a woman with trouble riding on her tail end. When her husband or boyfriend or loan shark caught up to her, Pearl would try to cut them into bite-sized pieces with the edge of her sharp tongue. Boyfriends, she might get away with it. Husband, probably not. Loan shark? No way in hell.

"It's a pleasure to meet you, Miss Lucy. I'll get this out of your road," he said. He picked up the heavy box spring like it was a feather pillow and carefully carried it outside. Then he loaded the mattress just as easily and went back for the bed frame.

"Thank you," Pearl said.

"No thanks necessary. Neighbors help neighbors. Now if you'll ride with me and show me where to put this thing I'll unload it and be on my way."

Pearl crawled inside his old work truck. They passed his new Silverado with four flat tires still sitting in front of room one on the way though the parking lot. He pulled around the west end of the motel and backed his truck up to the garage door.

"I'd be glad to drive one of these trucks back to your place if you want to air up those tires this evening," she said.

"See! Neighbors helping neighbors. Thank you, Red. I'll take you up on that offer. Want to have dinner with me when we get done?"

He wanted to slap himself right in the forehead. He'd cleaned rooms to pay off his debt so why did he keep asking the woman out? He didn't owe her anything and she had enough boyfriends to go out with a different one every day of the week. Maybe she had them tattooed with the days of the week on their arms, like those little undershorts his mother bought him when he was a kid. Superman on Monday; Mighty Mouse on Tuesday and so on.

"You cleaned rooms. Your debt is paid in full and I've warned you about calling me Red. You are skating on some mighty thin ice."

"I'm a good skater." He grinned.

She bailed out of the truck, entered the garage from the door at the end, and hit a button to roll the big doors up. He already had the mattress in the garage and was going back for the box springs before she had time to jog past the Caddy, around her truck, and back to his vehicle.

"What's her story?" he asked when he had the bed stacked at the far corner of the garage.

"Wife abuse. Comes from Kentucky. Got an accent you couldn't cut with a sharp knife."

"You trust her? She could be feeding you a line just to have a place to hide from a loan shark."

"I do and Wil, she's not lyin'. I'm a pretty damn good judge of character. What time you reckon you'll need me to drive a truck for you?"

He leaned on the back fender of his truck. "Long about suppertime if that's a good time for you."

"That'll be fine. Lucy is here now. She can watch the lobby while I drive your truck home." She started around him but he reached out and drew her tight against his chest. He'd tipped her chin up with his fist and landed a hard, passionate kiss on her lips.

Everything about her said that she had to end the kisses but her heart and lips begged for more. She melted against his rock hard chest and pressed against him even tighter.

Wil hadn't planned to kiss her. It just happened. And it glued the soles of his boots to the gravel and erased every sane thought from his head. Damn that woman had some fine lips and she fit right into his arms. He teased her lips open and tasted her morning coffee and something sweet like a donut.

When the kiss finally broke, she took a step backwards. She started to say something, but he brushed a sweet quick kiss across her lips and abruptly turned around and started for the front of the truck. He left her standing there with bee-stung lips and a silly grin. He pulled out onto the highway and was completely out of sight before she could make her feet take a step.

She went around the motel and into the lobby, into

her apartment, and poured a cup of coffee and picked up her second donut. Neither tasted as good as the bacon and maple syrup on his lips. She'd only taken one bite when the bell on the lobby door rang, so she laid it on the cabinet and went to check someone out or else see what Lucy wanted.

I probably need to suck on a lemon to get this shit-eatin' smile off my face. Lord, the way that man can kiss it's a wonder someone hasn't already lassoed and branded him.

It was the sisters who'd arrived fairly late the night before. She gave them a receipt and then checked out the three guys who'd been her first customers. She waited a few minutes but no one else showed up so she walked toward the laundry room, rubbing her lips several times along the way. They felt cold on the outside, but thinking about that kiss generated enough heat to keep her warm all day.

Lucy was folding sheets and singing something by Patsy Cline as she worked. A burst of steam flowed outside when Pearl opened the door and the singing stopped.

"Did you get it took care of? I moved the little table over and now it looks like a little apartment. That was one fine lookin' man. Is he your boyfriend?" Lucy said.

Pearl tried to change the subject. "You were singing."

"I was, wasn't I? I hadn't done that in a long time. Is he?"

"Is who what?"

"Is that Wil feller your boyfriend?" Lucy asked again.

"No!"

"Then why does he look at you like he could eat you

plumb up? And why are you smilin' so big like you'd let him do it?" Lucy asked.

Pearl needed to talk and Lucy needed a friend. "I'll tell you about the last couple of days while we clean a room. First of all we load up this maid's cart. It saves a lot of work and runnin'."

Lucy watched every move and followed Pearl to the first room. "On Christmas Eve every room was full because the lights went out in Henrietta." She went on to tell her what had happened. Lucy laughed at the story of the spider and the big woman standing in the middle of the bed, but she clucked her tongue when Pearl told her about the young girls flirting with Wil.

"He's a good man. And those girls were lucky. They could've got in big trouble," Lucy said as she helped make up the two beds.

Pearl went on to tell her about the policemen and Wil helping clean rooms. She didn't tell her about the kisses.

Lucy giggled. "A man who can clean, looks like he does, and who has kind eyes. You can tell if a man is mean by his eyes, you know. There's something in them that's kind of dead lookin' if they're mean. If you got any idea that you want a man in your life, you'd better be chasin' after that Wil. I can do the next room all by myself," Lucy said.

Pearl nodded.

"I didn't mean to be tellin' you what to do. Maybe you don't want to get tangled up with a man. I was just sayin' what I saw," she said.

Pearl laid a gentle hand on Lucy's shoulder. "If we're goin' to live this close to each other and work together every day, let's be honest and say what we think."

Lucy smiled. "I'd like that."

"I see some folks ready to check out. I'll see you in a bit." Pearl left her alone.

It was an hour before she got back to check on Lucy. She was in the third room by then and singing again. Pearl found her standing on a kitchen chair dusting the tops of the door frames.

"Good grief, woman! You're liable to fall. There's a step ladder in the laundry room if you need to crawl up on something."

Lucy laughed. "I'll use it next time. There was dust up here and spider webs behind the pictures above the beds."

Pearl was amazed. "I hired a perfectionist."

"Whatever that is, I hope it's a good thing."

"It is. I'm going to go on back to another job. Watch the clock and come on to the lobby at noon. We'll grab a sandwich in my apartment."

Lucy smiled again and the bruises didn't look nearly so horrid. "Thank you," she whispered.

Wil found Raylen sitting on the top rail of the round pen where Rye penned up his horses to break them. He wore a snug-fitting denim jacket just like Wil, but he already had his chaps and spurs on. Wil pulled his from the back of the truck, belted on the chaps, and snapped on the spurs.

"You been here long?" Wil asked.

"Just got settled on the fence. Rye's on his way. Had to kiss on the pretty wife. That's the way of it, you know."

Wil leaned on the fence. The icy wind found its way through the thick denim jacket and chilled him to the bone. Later when he was roping and breaking one of those horses in the corral next to the pen, he'd work up a sweat and wouldn't even feel the cold, but right then he wished for some of the heat that had flowed between him and the red-haired motel owner when they'd been tight against each other.

"So what would you do if you found a woman you'd rather kiss than break a horse?" Wil asked.

"Drop down on my knees and beg her to marry me." Raylen grinned. "There's Rye. Look at that smile on his face. I'm goin' to get me one of them one of these days." Raylen hopped down and got ready to lasso a horse.

———

The sun was drifting toward the horizon when Lucy and Pearl came out of the grocery store that evening. Lucy had been frugal, buying necessities and very little luxuries.

"Is there a library in town?" Lucy asked when they left the grocery store.

"Sure is. I'm not sure if it's open after the holiday, but we can check. You like to read?"

"When I get a chance."

"Well, let's go check it out."

The librarian was the only person in the small brick building a block off the main street through town. She had asked the board of directors to close the library for Christmas and the day after since no one would be interested in books. They'd disagreed but she'd been right. Up until Lucy and Pearl arrived, she hadn't had a single customer so she'd spent the day arranging books and getting completely caught up on overdue notices.

"Good afternoon, ladies. We'll be open another fifteen minutes."

"I guess the first thing we need is library cards. I'm Pearl Richland. I run the Longhorn Inn out east of town. This is Lucy Fontaine. She works for me."

"I'll fix you right up." The librarian raised an eyebrow at Lucy before she handed both women a card and looked at the clock.

"Point me in the general direction of where J. A. Jance and Sue Grafton will be," Pearl said.

Lucy was like a kid in a candy store with a hundred-dollar bill in her pocket. She'd choose a book and put it back, pick up another and read the fly and put it back, all the time watching the clock's second hand speeding around the numbers.

"You know you can have as many as you want long as you bring them back in two weeks," the librarian finally said.

"The library back in my hometown was so little we only got one book at a time. How can you let them go for two whole weeks?" Lucy began stacking them on the counter.

"I bet you and I'll be seeing a lot of each other." The librarian smiled.

"Yes ma'am, we will." Lucy had seven on the counter when her time was up.

"You are one eclectic reader," the librarian said.

"I'm not sure if that's good or bad. But I do love books," Lucy said.

She had checked out Nora Roberts's Three Sisters

Island trilogy along with *Vows* by LaVyrle Spencer, *Gone With the Wind* by Margaret Mitchell, and two thick mystery books by James Lee Burke.

"You really must like to read," Pearl said.

"Always have. I can't wait to get home. I think I'll start with *Gone With the Wind*. I always wanted to read that but someone stole it from our library."

It was a few minutes past five when they got back to the motel. The parking lot was empty except for Wil's truck. Pearl helped Lucy carry in her supplies and then drove down to her apartment. Wil drove up at the same time she pulled into the parking spot, grabbed two bags with one hand and a case of Coke with the other, and headed for the lobby door.

"Show me where you want this stuff," he said.

He was still wearing chaps and spurs, and his Western cut jean jacket hugged his broad chest. He smelled like cold outdoors, horses, and sweat. There was a shadow of scruff on his face. Pearl had thought he was hot as hell before but this Wil was absolutely scorchin'. She bit back the moan before it escaped her lips. She wanted to kick him down the hall and into her bed.

She led the way into her apartment. "You are handy as a pocket on a shirt and show up at just the right time."

When he unloaded the bags onto the table his arm brushed against hers and the tingles got hotter'n a tin roof in the middle of a Texas summer. The reaction in his jeans let him know that it had been a while since the last woman and that the redhead had soft, kissable lips.

Wil kicked at imaginary dirt, making his spurs jingle. "Ah shucks, ma'am, I ain't that handy. Today was just good timin'. I'll get busy airing up the tires. Should be about done by the time you get your groceries put away."

"Which one are you going to trust me to drive?" Pearl asked quickly.

She didn't want him to leave but couldn't think of a single reason to keep him in her apartment. She wouldn't mind if he'd just stand over there in the corner in that cowboy getup and she could kiss him every time she passed by. That would be enough for a couple of hours and then they'd talk about something more… like seeing just how to get those chaps and spurs off and strewing clothes down the hallway.

She put up a palm between them. *Whoa! Stop it right now!*

"What?" he asked with a smile.

She blushed and lowered her eyes from his lips to the area in front of his jeans the chaps didn't cover. She quickly turned around and busied herself putting Cokes in the refrigerator. The cold fridge air did manage to cool the crimson blush sneaking into her cheeks after that glance at his zipper.

"Nothing. I'll put away the food and be out there in a few minutes."

"Sure thing, and it don't make me no never mind which one you drive back to the ranch." The spurs jingled as he left.

She wished he would have swiped all those groceries off the table and made wild, passionate love to her right there in front of Delilah, Aunt Pearlita's memory, and the Almighty, Himself. When she looked over the fridge door he was gone. She slowly put away the rest of the food, stuck her two books on the bedside table, and went outside to find him airing up the third tire.

For the first time she appreciated the chill of the north wind sweeping down from Oklahoma, across the Red River, and into Henrietta, Texas. It cooled her blistering thoughts and red-hot desires.

Wil loved to break horses; he loved the challenge and the wild ride. But when he saw her walking toward him, he would gladly take a ribbing from the boys waiting at the round pen if he could hold Pearl in his arms and kiss her as much as he wanted.

He looked up from a bent position and said hoarsely, "Didn't take you as long as I figured it would."

She decided that there wasn't a man alive wearing a custom tailored Italian three-piece suit as hot as a cowboy bent over a truck tire in chaps, boots, and spurs. Good guy; bad boy. It didn't matter as long as he looked like Wil Marshall, smelled like Wil Marshall, and set her body on fire like Wil did.

"Don't take long to put up groceries to feed one person for a whole week." Her tone was two notches deeper than usual and sounded gravelly in her ears.

"So Lucy isn't sharing all her meals with you?"

"I've got a feeling Lucy needs some time all alone. She checked out seven books and plans to have them read in two weeks. I get the impression that she's going to enjoy the evenings in her little motel room all alone with no one to answer to."

"How long has she been puttin' up with that stuff?" Wil finished that tire and went on to the next one.

"She told me the short story but I reckon it would be

more than ten years. It took five to save the money to get out of it."

He pulled the long hose stretched from compressor in the bed of the old truck to the last flat tire. "Then I guess she will need some time. One more to go."

She leaned against the front fender of the older truck and watched, her hormones humming and her ears buzzing while she tried in vain to rope in her wild imagination. She shook her head to erase the sexy visions and the hum. She had a motel to run, Lucy to help heal, and two books to read. She damn sure didn't have time for whacked out hormones no matter what pretty tune they were humming or how bad she wanted another one of those steamy kisses. God Almighty, she needed to get back in the dating world. She needed to date lots of men, a different one every weekend.

But what if he's the one? What if Wil Marshall is the very one you have been waiting on all your life, your soul mate?

He tossed the air hose into the back of the truck, flipped a switch to turn off the compressor, and handed the keys to the newer vehicle to her. His thumb lingered on her palm and the steamy heat was still there. "You can take my new truck. This old one has a stick shift and gets cantankerous on second gear. I'll lead the way since you've only been out there one time."

She hopped inside and started up the truck only to have her ear drums rattled by a CD turned up to the highest volume with Blake Shelton singing "Kiss My Country Ass." She quickly twisted the knob to decrease the noise and looked across at Wil who shrugged and smiled.

Ten minutes later they were parked in his front yard. Digger came running from behind the house. Wil bent down and rubbed his ears, said a few words to him, and opened the truck door for him to get inside the truck. He bounded up onto the seat, licked Pearl from jawbone to eyebrow, and then sat down like royalty. Wil got in the passenger's seat beside him and strapped the seat belt across his chest.

She wiped at the dog slobbers and frowned. "Yuck!"

"Look at that, Digger. She don't take to dog slobbers but I had to eat that pie after she'd licked it. Seems like she's more'n a little bit hoity-toity."

"I'm not hoity-toity!" she said quickly.

Wil grinned. It didn't take much to fire her up and he loved the way her eyes flashed when she was angry. "Yeah, you are. You wouldn't go to dinner with me because I'm nothing but a plain old farmer."

She turned the truck around and started back toward town. "You're picking a fight, Wil Marshall, and you know it. I don't give a damn if you are a plain old farmer or richer than Bill Gates. That doesn't have jack shit to do with anything. And why does your name have only one *l* in it instead of two?"

"You are changing the subject but I'll tell you. My name is Wilson, not William, so it had only got one *l* in it. My full name is Jesse Wilson Marshall. Wilson after Momma's maiden name. Jesse after my father. What's the rest of your name?"

"You'll laugh," she said.

He crossed his chest and held up two fingers. "I promise I won't."

"Double dog promise?"

"You got it. Is it all that bad?"

"It is ten times that bad. I was supposed to be a boy so they didn't have a name picked out at all for a girl child. The day they left the hospital they were still in shock that I didn't come with the right plumbing to make me John Tyson Richland Junior. So Momma said she wanted to name me for her favorite aunt, my grandmother's sister in Georgia. That gave Daddy the idea of naming me for his favorite aunt, which was Aunt Pearlita. He'd spent some time over in these parts when he was growing up around her and my great-grandmother."

"I figured that's where they got the Pearl."

She reached Highway 82 and turned east toward the motel. "Mother's favorite aunt was Minnie and she didn't have a middle name. So they named me Minnie Pearl Richland."

He bit the inside of his lip and swallowed hard three times before he got the laughter under control.

She stuck out her lower lip in an exaggerated fake pout. "You are laughing!"

"Am not," he said from between clenched teeth.

"Yes, you are. I can see it in your face. Whatever you are thinking is written all over your face, Wil Marshall. You can't hide a thing."

He bristled. "I can too. I'm part Seminole Indian. I've got a great poker face."

"Yeah, right. Your eyes are laughing so hard they are about to pop right out of your head. And I don't care if you are full-blood Apache. You do not have a poker face. I could whip your cowboy ass in poker any day of the week and twice on Sunday."

"You can't see my eyes."

"Yes, I can. You looked at me to see if I was lying and you were laughing."

He couldn't contain it another second. It exploded and bounced around the cab of the truck like a marble in a glass jar. He tried to stop by clamping his mouth shut but even that didn't work. A vision of the late Minnie Pearl from *Hee Haw* appeared in his mind, only it was Pearl Richland wearing a big straw hat with the price tags hanging from it.

Pearl was grinning when she nosed the truck into the parking spot in front of the motel lobby. "I'm so glad you got such a kick out of that story. Now do you want my real full name or will that one do to entertain you?"

The laughter stopped as suddenly as it started. He drew his dark brows down into a single line and narrowed his eyes. "You lied to me?"

"You broke your promise and laughed at me. I lied. Not much difference."

"What if I hadn't laughed?"

She smiled sweetly. "Then I would have let you think my name was Minnie Pearl for the rest of your life."

"What is your name really?"

"Would you believe Olive Oil Pearl?"

"Come on, Pearl. Tell me the truth. Is it worse than Minnie Pearl?"

She turned to look out the side window so he couldn't see her expression. "Okay, the truth? But you cannot laugh. Just remember that they had to come up with a name or they couldn't take me home. It's Oyster Pearl."

"Now you are being stupid. No one would name their child Oyster."

She pulled the handle to open the door. "Well, that's

my name. Good night, Wil. Don't bother coming to the Longhorn Inn if your electricity goes out because there won't be a room for you even if I have twenty rooms empty."

"Okay, okay. I'm sorry I said that about your name. I won't ever bring it up again."

She stepped out of the truck and slammed the door. He crawled out on his side, told Digger to sit still, and walked to the lobby door with her. She unlocked it and went inside, her ribs aching from pent up laughter. She had to 'fess up so she could laugh or else she was going to explode.

"Wil, my full name is Katy Pearl. Katy Minerva is Momma's favorite aunt. I always thought it would've been a hoot if they'd shortened Minerva to Minnie like they did Pearlita to Pearl. I was just joshing you."

"Okay, Katy Pearl, which is a lovely name, by the way. You have a sense of humor. I like that in a woman."

He followed her almost to the counter before he took two steps to her one and was suddenly in front of her, his arms around her and his lips parted as they came closer and closer. He opened his eyes slightly and saw the tip of her tongue wet her lips and zeroed in for the kiss. He hugged her tightly and made love to her mouth until she was breathless. When he broke the kiss, he buried his face in her hair and inhaled. Cold, sweat, and a faint floral scent mixed together to take his breath away.

"Good night, Red."

She was speechless. He should've been angry at her for lying to him or embarrassed at believing the lie. She should've been madder than hell at him calling her Red again but nothing came to mind so she watched him go with one of those backward waves.

Chapter 6

WIL PUSHED THE NUMBERS FOR THE MOTEL THREE TIMES and hung up before the phone rang. He didn't need a woman in his life who was a female player. Since Rye had found Austin, he and Raylen both had been bitten by the "settle down" bug. And then the lights went out in Henrietta... and the rest was history. The motel number was engraved in his brain after thinking about calling her all evening.

Finally he gave in to the itch and let the phone ring. She picked up on the second ring.

"Front desk. This is Pearl." Pearl groaned. She had ten rooms filled and the last one was a woman who looked like she'd faint at her own shadow. Pearl hoped the woman didn't find a scorpion behind the potty in the bathroom. As exhausted as she looked, she'd faint, bust open her head on the sink, and sue Pearl for the whole motel. When the phone rang, she just knew the woman had found a bug.

"Well, I guess I done got the wrong number. I was calling for this pretty red-haired woman who works there called Red," Wil said.

"I should hang up." She ignored the fact that he called her by that abominable nickname. "What can I do for you, Wil Marshall? Is your electricity out again?"

"No, but I'm lonesome. Come out here and keep me company."

"Too bad, darlin'. I've already turned out the lights and I'm in bed," she said.

"That's a provocative idea," Wil said.

"Want to know what I'm wearing?" she teased.

"A black lacy thing…"

"In your dreams. I've got on flannel pajama bottoms and a thermal knit shirt. Both of them are gray and match my socks," she said.

"Can I come over there and see for myself? I think you are lying to me and you've really got on one of those black lacy things with fishnet hose and a cute little bow at the front right under your—"

"Whoa, cowboy! I don't have phone sex on the first phone call," she said.

"Can't blame a cowboy for trying." He chuckled. "Okay then, what's the rules? Second phone call?"

"Try the twenty-fifth," she said.

"Can I have your cell phone number?"

"Not until the third phone call," she said.

"Okay, hang up and I'll call you back twice," he drawled.

She giggled. "Good night, Wil. Sweet dreams."

"Ah, come on. Talk to me, Red. I'm too wound up to sleep and too tired to do anything else. Did I tell you that Austin and Rye are having a New Year's Eve party Sunday and we're supposed to go?"

"You told me that already."

"What time can I pick you up?"

"I'm going in my car. That way I can leave when I want," she answered.

He chuckled. "Okay, then are you wearing something black, tight, and lacy to the party?"

"First phone call, Wil. I'm not talking about clothes, underpants, or teddies."

"Well, damn. I might as well read my book until I fall asleep. I'm going to Wichita Falls tomorrow for feed. Want to go with me? We could get some lunch and I'll have you back in plenty of time for the guests."

"Got to clean rooms," she said.

"You ain't no fun at all tonight, Red. I think I'll just go on to sleep."

She laughed. Every hormone in her body whined. It would be so easy to tell him to come right on over, especially after those fiery kisses.

"You've got a delicious laugh," he said.

"If it's so delicious, what does it taste like?" she asked.

"Peach cobbler with homemade ice cream. Good night, Red. I'll holler at you tomorrow after I get home from Wichita Falls." He hung up.

So much for steering clear of the woman. He was drawn to her like metal to magnet. There was just something about the electricity between them that kept bringing him back for another dose.

—⁓—

Pearl held the phone for a full minute before she put it back on the base, and it was a very long time before she finally went to sleep.

Tuesday morning she awoke half an hour late and barely made it to the lobby before the first of the guests were ready to check out. She and Lucy cleaned rooms until noon, stopped long enough to run into town to the Dairy Queen for a hamburger, and then finished up the rest of the rooms by three o'clock. Lucy went to her room to read and Pearl cleaned her apartment.

Six rooms were full and another customer coming through the door with two teenage kids in tow when the phone rang that evening. She laid a card on the counter and picked up the phone on the third ring.

"Longhorn Inn. Front desk. Please hold." She laid the phone to the side and turned back to the guest.

"I either need two rooms or one with two beds," the woman said.

"Each room has two beds, but I have vacancies if you want two rooms," Pearl said.

"One room then," she said and filled out the card.

"Thank you for holding. What can I do for you?" she said as she finished the transaction and the woman was on her way outside with the key to room eleven.

"Well, I'd like one of those empty rooms I heard you talking about and you waiting for me in it wearing that black thing you had on last night," Wil said.

"Wil Marshall! I told you I was wearing gray flannel and socks!"

"Not in my mind, but we can't talk about that, can we? This is only our second phone call. It has to be the third? Isn't that right?"

She smiled.

"Are you going to answer or at least let me hear a peach pie giggle?" he asked.

"You are—"

"Tired," he finished for her. "It finally caught up to me this afternoon. I almost fell asleep on the way home from Wichita Falls. If I had and it killed me it would've been your fault. If you'd have come out to the ranch and kept me company I wouldn't have tossed and turned all night."

She couldn't have wiped the grin from her face if it had meant giving up chocolate donuts. "It would not have been my fault. You shouldn't drive when you are that tired. You should be sleeping, not talking to me."

"It's only eight thirty. If I go to sleep now I'll wake up at midnight and won't be able to sleep anymore all night. Let Lucy run the motel and come watch a movie with me. I promise I won't even kiss you."

Pearl laughed so hard that she got the hiccups.

"What's so funny, Red?"

"I'm not a walk-behind-you-three-steps kind of woman, Wil. What if I wanted to kiss you?"

"Well, hell, honey, we could work out some kind of arrangement. That mean you are coming out here?"

"It does not. I don't kiss on the second date."

"I do believe I remember that you've kissed me already. Do those kisses count as one phone call and I get your cell phone tonight?"

"No, you kissed me. When I kiss you, darlin', you will already have my cell number. This is only number two."

It was fun to flirt again after a long, dry spell. She'd always loved dating, loved flirting and the chase, whether it was her doing the running after or the running from, she loved the game. But here lately she'd felt as if she was running toward that special man who loved her so much that when she looked into his eyes she only saw a reflection of herself hiding there.

"Then tomorrow night I get lucky?" Wil asked.

She laughed again. "Lucky as in what?"

"Is your mind in the gutter? I was talking about

getting your cell phone number so I could call anytime I want. What were you thinking about?"

"Giving you my cell phone number. When do I get yours?"

His voice deepened and he whispered, "Miz Red! I'm surprised at you being so forward. I don't give my cell number to anyone on the third date. I'm an old-fashioned guy. I wait until I see you in that little black thing before you get my number."

The laughter stopped and her insides went all soft and mushy at his sexy voice. "Wil, this is goose and gander."

"What?"

"I don't put out until you do."

"And are we still talkin' about phone numbers?"

She bit the inside of her lip to keep from laughing. She couldn't remember the last time she'd had so much fun with anyone. Wil had wit, charm, and downright sex appeal. "What's good for the goose is good for the gander. I don't give out my number until you are willing to share yours."

He sighed. "Well, shit! I figured that's what you meant. Okay, darlin', then tomorrow night we'll both put out at the same time. I hope it's as good for you as it's going to be for me."

"I've got a customer headed for the door. Good night, Wil," Pearl said.

"Dream about me," he said and the phone went dead.

Pearl and Lucy were just finishing up the last room when the florist's van pulled up in front of the lobby.

"Hello!" Pearl yelled, hoping that the flowers in the

lady's hand weren't for Lucy. If her sorry husband had found her and sent flowers to butter her up so she'd come back to Kentucky to wash his clothes, cook his supper, and take whippings, Pearl intended to shoot the sorry bastard herself.

"I'm lookin' for Miz Richland," the woman said.

Lucy pointed. "That'd be her. And thank God! Cleet never did get me no flowers but that give me a scare. If he ever finds me he'll kill me, Pearl. If he sent me them flowers I was goin' to run again. I don't never want to see him again."

Pearl patted her arm. "You won't have to run. I'll shoot him. I don't ever want to lose you, Lucy."

The woman handed Pearl the crystal vase with three roses in it. She carried it to the lobby and set it on the counter. She didn't want them to be from Marlin. Like Lucy, she didn't ever want to hear from her ex again.

"You goin' to open the card?" Lucy asked.

"I'm afraid to. If they are from Marlin, my old boy-friend, then there'll have to be a phone call telling him that I'm not interested in him anymore and I—"

Lucy reached up and grabbed the card, flipped it open, and frowned. "They ain't from anyone. It's a phone number and it's wrote down in red ink." She handed it to Pearl who recognized the area code and smiled.

Lucy giggled. "Wil Marshall. That's who they're from. He called you Red. I told you that cowboy has the hots for you. I betcha he kisses you on New Year's Eve."

"I might not even go to that party."

Lucy crossed her arms over her chest. "Oh, you are goin'. I know how to run this place and you need to go play. You work too hard."

Pearl smelled the roses. Were there three because she said they had to have three phone calls before she would give him her cell phone number?

"Why are you pushin' me so hard?" she asked Lucy.

"This might be your chance at happiness. Don't be slammin' the door before you see what's behind it. And," Lucy took a deep breath and her eyes widened, "if you don't I'm goin' to quit workin' for you."

"What made you a therapist?"

"I'm just tellin' it like it is."

"I thought you were sworn off all men," Pearl argued.

"I am but that don't mean you are. There's some good men out there and you deserve a happy life with one of them. I don't do so good when it comes to pickin' out menfolks. Now 'nuff said. I'm goin' to go finish my book and start another one. Can I steal Delilah to keep me company this afternoon?" She picked the big yellow cat up from one of the recliners.

"Sure." Pearl smiled at Lucy's newly found independent streak. As soon as she and Delilah were outside, Pearl smelled the roses and fished her cell phone out of her pocket. She programmed the new number into the phone and left a text message with her cell number.

At eleven o'clock that night her cell phone rang. She picked it up, checked caller ID, and answered, "Hello, 8725. Thank you for the roses. They are lovely."

"Miz 3407, you sure do have a sexy phone voice. You ever think of applying for a job at one of those 900 numbers?"

"How do you think I made the money to get my degree?" She flipped the lights to old doofus cowboy

off and the NO VACANCY light on, locked the door, and
headed back to her apartment.

"I finally got you!" she said when he didn't answer.

"I was thinkin' maybe that's where I'd heard your
voice before," he said quickly.

"Wil Marshall!"

"Who? I'm 8725. Who is this Wil feller? Someone I
need to be worried about? Did he send you roses today?"

"Hell, no! He's only interested in my body. 8725 sent
me three lovely red roses," Pearl teased as she filled a
glass with ice and poured sweet tea over it.

"Do I hear you getting ice out of the freezer? Do I
make you that hot?" Wil asked.

*Oh, honey, you have no idea just how hot you do
make me but I'm not admitting it to you.*

"I don't even know who you are. You are just a phone
number that came with some roses. You might be eighty
years old, bald, and…"

"And what?"

"And bowlegged," she said quickly. If she'd said
what she'd really been thinking she would have blushed
so badly that the sky would have lit up like daylight.

"That's not what you were thinkin', but just for your
information, Red, when I'm eighty years old, bald, and
bowlegged I will still be damn good in bed. It's in the
Marshall genes. Remember how I told you my grandpa
died when he was a hundred years old? Well, me and
Rye asked him when he was eighty how old a man was
before he couldn't do it no more and Grandpa said we'd
have to go find someone older than him to ask."

"You are horrible! How do you know that's what I
was thinking?"

Wil chuckled.

Pearl wondered how in the devil a man could even have a deep Texas drawl when he laughed. "You didn't know. You were fishin' and I let you catch me."

"Now what do I do with you now that I caught you? Throw you back or keep you?"

"You got to ask, you don't deserve an answer."

"Well, crap!" he said.

"What?" she asked.

"Sorry, darlin', but my dad is callin' on the house phone. He's been to a sale to look at a tractor for me. I'll talk to you tomorrow."

"Good night, Wil."

She held the phone to her chest. Damn, but it was good to have someone to flirt with again.

—◊◊◊—

On Thursday he sent a text message in the morning that said: *8725 has to be in town at lunchtime. DQ at noon?*

She sent one back that said: *3407 says ok.*

The sun was out but it was bitter cold when she finished her deposit at the Legends Bank and walked across the street to the Dairy Queen. Wil met her at the door, threw an arm around her shoulder, and led her to a booth on the west side. "Tell me what you want and I'll order for us before the school kids get here."

"Burger, fries, and chocolate malt," she said. She'd hoped that among all the flirtatious phone calls that she'd built him up to be hotter and sexier than he really was. That when she saw him again, his touch wouldn't turn her insides to hot, whining butter. Hope was only a minor part of Aunt Pearlita's saying about life being faith, hope, and chaos, and it damn sure didn't hold much power that day. If anything his butt was ever sexier as he swaggered toward the counter to put in their order. And his arm around her shoulders had come near to causing a major fire right there in the Dairy Queen.

When he returned he slid into the booth across from her, reached over, and took both her hands in his. "I like looking at your eyes when we talk."

"I bet you say that to all the girls." She wished she'd taken time to at least take her hair down from its working ponytail and maybe smear on a little makeup. His face was freshly shaven and whatever shaving lotion he'd used was about to send her into orbit. His thumb caressed her hand like a lover and his eyes never left hers.

"No, just to the ones who talk dirty to me on the phone."

She blushed and every freckle popped out like stars in a moonless sky.

He laughed. "You are cute when you are embarrassed."

"I'm not—"

He brought her fingertips to his lips and kissed them one by one. "Yes, you are, Red."

The waitress brought their food on a tray and set it down in the middle of the table. "Anything else I can get you?"

How about a room? Pearl thought but she shook her head.

Flirting was okay. Rooms and sex were out of the question no matter how hot he was or how hot he made her.

She pulled her hands back before they scorched all the way to the bones and said, "I did not say one dirty word to you on the phone."

He dipped a fry in ketchup. She barely had time to open her mouth when she realized he was putting it in her mouth. She grabbed his wrist and held it while she licked the ketchup from his fingertips. She'd show him that two could play the flirting game and that she could make him almost as hot as he'd made her. Almost! Nothing could come close to the way he'd made her body hum.

He sucked air when she wrapped her tongue around his finger to remove every smidgen of ketchup.

She smiled when she finally reached up and pulled his finger out of her mouth with a pop. "Good French fries. Better fingers."

"You *are* wicked!"

"Goose and gander, Wil. Don't forget it."

"Okay, okay!" He picked up his burger and bit into it. She did the same.

"Are you really not going to let me take you to the party Sunday night?" he asked between bites.

She shook her head. "I want to have my own car there because Lucy will be minding the store for the first time all alone. If she panics I want to be able to get back to the motel quickly."

"Then I guess you going with me to Waco tomorrow is out of the question?"

"Why are you going to Waco?"

"I bought six cows from a rancher down there. I'm driving down tomorrow and back on Saturday morning with them. If I pay for them before the end of the year it'll be a tax break," he answered.

"I can't. Lucy's only been with me a few days. She's catching on to everything fast but I can't leave her alone that long."

"Then it's back to phone sex?" His eyes twinkled.

"You are crazy!"

"But I'm not boring."

She shook her head while she slurped the malt. "No, Wil, no one could ever say you are boring."

When they finished eating and started outside he reached down and laced his fingers in hers. "I'll walk you to the car."

They crossed the street. He opened the door for her and let her get settled into the big old vintage Caddy before leaning down and cupping her face in his hands. The kiss was soft at first and then deepened into passion. From there it sent flashes of heat from her lips to her ankle bones. She couldn't have stopped him if he'd crawled inside the vehicle and made wild love to her right there in broad daylight.

He finally kissed her closed eyes and said, "That'll have to hold me until Saturday. I'll call you soon as I get home."

"So you aren't calling for two days?"

He smiled. "I've got your number, darlin'. Now I can call anytime day or night."

He waved over his shoulder after he shut the door.

Chapter 7

PEARL WAS COMPLETELY DRESSED AND READY TO GO TO the New Year's Eve party, checked her reflection in the floor-length mirror on the back of the bathroom door, and went back to the bedroom to start all over— six times she did the same thing. The bed was covered with clothes and the floor with high-heeled shoes before she finally threw up her hands and donned the first outfit she'd chosen.

She'd loved dressing up for dates ever since she was sixteen and left the house with Vince to go to a movie. But she'd never wanted to impress anyone as much as she did Wil that night. It had to be because he was the only man she'd flirted with or dated since she left Durant.

She looked in the mirror at the olive green lacy blouse trimmed in darker green velvet around the neckline and the ruffles at her wrists, with a muted floral velvet skirt that skimmed her ankles in the same shade of dark green and a long duster length coat with gold buttons to match. Now what shoes would set it off? She settled on a pair of spike-heeled dress boots in black kid leather. Then she flipped her hair up in a loose French twist, roping it down with a rhinestone clip and leaving the ends to poke out anyway they wanted as long as they gave her some height. She applied a touch of perfume with a name she couldn't pronounce that her mother had given her for her birthday last February.

Wil had called three times on Friday. Once on his way to Waco; once when he was getting out of the truck to talk to the rancher about the cows; and then again that night before he went to sleep. Hearing his deep drawl and sexual innuendos made her pant, but she was able to give tit for tat even though her heart was pounding so hard it was about to bust her boobs right out of her bra.

On Saturday, he'd gotten a late start because of rain, then traffic was held up in Dallas because of a wreck. It was dark when he got home and he and his foreman had to unload the cows into barn stalls because it was raining too hard to do anything else.

He'd been apologetic that he couldn't talk longer. Now it was time to go to the party, and she was more nervous than she'd been on that first date more than ten years before.

The motorcycle made so much noise that Momma fussed and fumed, said she would have never thought little Vince would grow up to be so rebellious. But he did, we were, and then it was over.

"Whooo-weee!" Lucy looked up from the counter.

"Am I overdressed?" Pearl asked. "It's just a house party, not a ball."

"You'd look good at either one. You goin' to tell some poor old lonesome cowboy that your name is Minnie Pearl tonight or are you going to spend all your time with Wil?" Lucy grinned.

Pearl giggled. "I don't know, Lucy, but I intend to have a good time. You sure you can handle the motel?"

Lucy nodded. "I can do this, Pearl. I need to do it. I can rent rooms and listen to folks bellyache. As long as possible I'll leave rooms between customers so that they don't gripe as much. You sure you don't mind me lookin' up a few things on the computer in between?"

"Of course not. Internet is hooked up to wireless. I don't know why Aunt Pearl put that in the rooms but I'm glad she did. It's like she started to modernize then changed her mind. I was goin' to put in card locks but I think I'll just keep the old keys since if I make changes next spring I've decided to go with quaint and romantic," Pearl said.

"I like the keys. Makes it more old timey-like, especially since we… I mean you've decided to go with that idea. But you know what, I like the motel just like it is. When I was on the bus goin' through towns I saw a lot of new hotels and motels but not many like this with an old cowboy up there on the sign, pointing down at the lobby. I think it's kind of quaint and romantic just like it is."

"Lucy, you are a part of this now. It's we, not me," Pearl said.

Lucy blushed and pointed at the door. "And that's enough business for tonight. Go have fun. Kiss Wil at midnight. He's a good guy."

"Who are you goin' to kiss?" Pearl asked.

"I'm done with kissin'. Cleet broke me from suckin' eggs the first week we was married. That kissin' business got me in trouble and I ain't doin' that again. That don't mean you can't though." Lucy's head moved back and forth with each word. "Here comes my first customer drivin' into the lot. Go on and let me do my job. I got the computer, my book, and Delilah says she'll keep me company."

Twenty minutes later Pearl rang the doorbell at Austin and Rye's house.

Austin yelled, "Come in!"

Pearl turned the knob and stepped into the noise and chaos of too many people in too small a space. Small groups were gathered in pockets; eating, drinking and talking, some even managing to gesture with their hands while doing all three.

Austin left her circle and grabbed Pearl by the arm, pulling her past the liquor bar into the kitchen. That's where the food was laid out and if anyone went away hungry that night it was their own fault. Pearl felt like if she put a single miniature taco in her mouth, she'd upchuck.

Austin was a mixture of country and city that night in a stunning black dress with side slits up to mid-thigh, a pair of black eel cowboy boots, and a Western cut lace jacket that was either vintage or else she had a really close relationship to Miranda Lambert or maybe Dolly Parton and had borrowed it from one of them.

"I'm so glad you are here," Austin said. "Take off your coat."

Pearl removed her coat and Austin's eyebrows shot up. "You look plumb sexy. Is it Wil?"

"I don't get to get dressed up anymore and I still like to wear pretty things and no, it's not Wil and dammit, I'm talkin' too much and I didn't realize how much I miss a good party and lookin' at sexy cowboys."

Austin crooked a finger at her husband. "Rye, darlin', take Pearl's coat to the guest bedroom. Thank you, sweetheart."

"I really didn't know what to wear and there's enough clothes thrown around in my bedroom to start a Goodwill store. I must've got dressed six or seven times before I decided," Pearl said.

"It is Wil. I knew it when I saw y'all flirting at Christmas. He looks at you all dreamy. And you said six months ago that you wanted someone who can't see anyone but you and you wouldn't settle for anything else. I think you've found him, girl. Ain't Wil just the hottest thing you've seen?"

Pearl cut her eyes around the room but didn't see him anywhere. "Looks like there's some pretty hot stuff here tonight. Do I have to make up my mind about that 'ever seen' thing right now?"

Austin picked up a plate and loaded it. "You are evading the question so that means I'm right. Now, grab a plate of food. Maddie made these crab cakes and they'll make your mouth water. Get a beer and mingle. Gemma and Colleen are both here. And Raylen and Dewar and Ace, and if you don't know someone, ask Wil; yes, he is here. He'll introduce you if I'm not around."

The living room, dining room, and kitchen were all one big open area with comfortable furniture beckoning to folks to sit and visit. The bar separating the kitchen from the dining room was covered from one end to the other with everything from miniature tacos to barbecue sandwiches. A galvanized washtub filled with ice and beer sat on a fancy cast iron stand. Pearl picked up a longneck Coors from the washtub, twisted the lid off, took a long swig, and came up for air to see Wil standing not two feet from her.

He wore a brown Western cut shirt the same color as his eyes and starched and ironed jeans that stacked just right over his dark brown boots. His black hair was feathered back and he smelled like Stetson aftershave. It wasn't the most expensive aftershave on the market, not by far, but there was something wild and free about it that turned her into mush anytime she got a whiff of it.

I begged Vince to wear that kind but oh, no, he liked Drakkar. That's what he was wearing that night when we both lost our virginity in that motel outside Sherman. We rode up there on his motorcycle, registered as Mr. and Mrs. Waylon Haggard. God, we thought we were being so cute using two country music stars' names. The lady behind the register didn't care if we were Mr. and Mrs. Mickey Mouse as long as Vince put his money on the counter.

Wil held up his empty bottle of Coors and took a step toward her and all the thoughts of that first love vanished. He brushed a quick kiss across her lips and hugged her tightly. "It was a long three days."

"Oh, really?" Her voice sounded normal. That was a big shock. That kiss made her feel as if she'd jogged the whole twenty-something miles from Henrietta, Texas, to Terral, Oklahoma.

"Hello, darlin'." A tall brunette plastered herself to Wil's side. "I didn't know if you'd be here but I was hopin'."

Wil could have put his big hands around Colleen's neck and strangled her until her lips turned blue and her eyes popped out. He had no idea she'd bring her friend from Randlett to the party—the friend he'd dated a couple of times. The one who'd wanted to move in with him after the first date.

"Stormy, meet Pearl. She's—"

Stormy threw her arm around Wil's waist and tucked a thumb in his belt loop. She wore tight skinny-legged jeans, a black knit shirt decorated with flashy multi-colored jewels across her perky silicone breasts, and high-heeled black shoes. Her straight brown hair was cut in a feathered look, probably by Gemma, and her makeup had been applied with an egg turner or a shovel, whichever had been handy at the time. Her eyes were blitzed and her lips slack from too much whiskey.

She giggled and hugged up even closer to Wil. "She's the one who bailed you out of that murder trouble, right? Well, thank you for doin' that for my feller. You did a good thing. Wil, darlin', you are here so that means we got another chance, don't we?"

"You are drunk, Stormy, and the answer would be no, we don't have another chance," Wil said.

Stormy pulled her thumb from his belt and slapped him playfully on the shoulder. "At midnight I'll be right here by the beer tub. You come on over and I'll change your mind."

She did an abrupt turnaround that would have sprawled her out on the floor if Dewar hadn't caught her. "Well, Dewar O'Donnell, if I hadn't already promised my midnight kiss to Wil, I'd give it to you for saving my ass from embarrassment."

"Story of my life. I save the maiden in distress. Another cowboy gets the kiss," Dewar said with a sideways wink at Wil.

"Sorry, darlin'. Little ol' me can just stretch so far and Wil has already spoken for me." Stormy went over to the table and mixed a Long Island iced tea.

Pearl raised an eyebrow.

"She's drunk," Wil said.

"Do you like women with trendy names like Stormy?"

"No, one time I got mixed up with Minnie Pearl."

Pearl grinned. "No kiddin'. The real one from *Hee Haw*?"

"Hell, no! This was a foxy lady from Texas with red hair."

"And what did you think of her?" Pearl asked.

Before he could answer, Stormy stomped past them. "Damn it if I have to take that from someone who says she's my friend. What right has she got to tell me to stop drinking? This is New Year's Eve and by damn, I can drink what I want and kiss who I want and it's none of Colleen's business."

Colleen followed behind her. "Okay, Stormy, I'll take you home. You're in no shape to drive."

"And have you whine around that I ruined your New Year's Eve? I don't think so," she slurred. "I'll drive my own self. I'm free, white, and a damn sight over twenty-one so get away from me."

Colleen looked at Pearl.

Pearl shrugged her shoulders and raised both eyebrows. "She's got a point."

Colleen threw up her hands. "Friends don't let friends drive drunk."

They waited five full minutes for Stormy to return from the bedroom where she'd gone after her coat before Colleen went searching for her.

"She's slipped out. I'd go after her but I don't know which way she went," Colleen said.

Wil patted her on the shoulder. "Hey, you didn't take her to raise."

Colleen dug her cell phone out of her purse and punched in a series of numbers. "Where in the hell are you?"

Pearl tried not to eavesdrop but Colleen was standing on one side of her and Wil was right in front of her. It was either eavesdrop or else stare at him, and listening in on Colleen's conversation was a hell of a lot easier on the hormones than letting her eyes fall to that big silver belt buckle embossed with a bull rider.

Colleen's tone softened. "You are crazy."

Pearl tipped back her beer for a small sip. One beer and one glass of champagne to bring in the New Year was her limit. She'd have rooms to clean the next day. Bending, stooping, and stretching made horrid bed partners with hangovers.

"Promise?" Colleen laughed.

Wil winked and nodded toward the door.

She shook her head.

He raised an eyebrow.

She took another sip of beer.

"Okay, then, if you'll stay right there. Good-bye." Colleen flipped her phone shut. "She drove up to Ryan and is holed up at an old boyfriend's house. She promised she'd stay there until she sobers up."

"Aunt Pearlita always said that life is made up of faith, hope, and…"

"Love?" Wil said. "You are a good friend, Colleen."

Colleen shook her head. "Patience? And mine is running thin."

"No, you are both wrong. It's faith, hope, and chaos," Pearl said.

Colleen smiled. She was a beautiful woman, with that strange burgundy-colored hair and dark green eyes. She had translucent skin that very few redheads get blessed with. She wore tight jeans, an ecru sweater splashed with rhinestones and pearls, and three-inch black spike heels.

Pearl could forgive her every bit of it except the skin. That she was jealous about because when the angels were passing out freckles they dipped heavy in the wine hidden under the altar and had a heyday with Pearl's face. Not even the best makeup in the world could cover them so Pearl had stopped trying years ago. At least until she saw another redhead with beautiful skin and then she felt that old bullfrog green jealousy oozing out her pores and freckles too.

Wil took another drink of his beer. "Chaos, huh! Ain't that the gospel truth?"

It was a wonder that Pearl heard her phone in all the noise, but she fished it out of her purse and flipped it open.

"Darlin', where are you?" Tommy asked.

"I'm at a party in Terral, Oklahoma," she answered.

Wil frowned. Did she know every man this side of the Gulf of Mexico? A jealous streak shot through him. Austin had said she was the queen bee of party girls and all the phone calls he'd been privy to lately were proving that beyond the old shadow of a doubt. Was he wasting his time?

"Okay, tell Jasmine and all the girls hello. Kisses to you too, darlin'," she said and flipped the phone shut.

"You know a lot of guys, huh?"

"*Knew* a lot of guys. In this part of the world, I know you, Raylen, Dewar, and Ace. Oh, and Rye, but I think Austin has him branded pretty solid." She laughed.

Colleen giggled. "*Knew* is right. This lady had more energy than six women. Sometimes she had three dates lined up for one weekend. She'd dance on Friday night, rodeo on Saturday night, and on Sunday afternoon she'd wind down the weekend with a lunch date." She set her empty bottle on the bar and pointed. "There's Hart Avery comin' in the door. I intend to go do some serious flirting. You two don't do anything I wouldn't do."

Pearl laughed. "That gives me a hell of a lot of wiggle room."

Wil grinned. "Can I watch you wiggle?"

"There's not room to wiggle in this house. I wonder why they chose to live on this side of the road?"

"Didn't Austin tell you?" He leaned over and whispered, then brushed a kiss on her earlobe.

Her toenails curled and goose bumps popped up on her arms.

He picked up her hand and ran his thumb over the top. "Let's go outside where it's quieter and I'll tell you."

She shivered just thinking about sitting out in the chilly north wind. "It's cold out there."

"I can fix cold!"

"I bet you can but not on Austin's porch." The picture of just how good he would be at the job of fixing cold put high color in her cheeks.

"Get your mind out of the gutter. I wasn't suggesting that we have sex on the porch swing. See that quilt rack over there in the corner. We can bundle up and stay warm and I can actually hear you speaking. Bring your beer. I'll even be a gentleman and come back inside and get you a drink when you finish that one." He led the way across the room and picked up two quilts from a rack beside the door.

She followed and slipped out the front door right behind him. He held her beer while she wrapped up in one quilt like an oversized shawl. When she was comfortable in one corner of the porch swing, he handed the half-empty beer back to her. He settled in next to her and pulled the second quilt up over both of them like bed covers.

"So why are they living on this side of the road?" she asked.

"Rye says that Granny Lanier's ghost wouldn't let them have sex over at his place. They had a big old king-sized bed over there and... how long has it been since you were in this place?"

"Fifteen years or more," she said.

"Remember what it looked like?"

"She liked stuff. I remember knickknacks sitting around everywhere."

He didn't answer so she looked up. He'd set his beer in the corner of the swing and cupped her face in his big hands. "I really did miss you," he whispered as he claimed her lips.

It felt right and that scared the hell out of Pearl. A week of phone calls, a hamburger lunch, three roses, and a few kisses and she was ready to throw common sense in the nearest trash pile. What if he wasn't the one? What if she fell hard and he left her heart lying on the ground in misery?

All the "what ifs" evaporated into the cold night air when he pulled her in close to his side and she snuggled into his warmth.

"Go on with the story," she said.

"Rye says that the house was so full of stuff that you could barely get around in it, but even among all that nothing happened when they wanted to have sex. But over at his house was a different story. People came by; bulls got out of the pasture. All kinds of things. So Austin said that Granny had manipulated things so that they'd have to live on her side of the road. Austin wanted kids and you got to have sex to get them so that meant they had to live in this house."

"He does still have his land over there, doesn't he?" Pearl asked.

"Yes, he does. Felix, Austin's hired help from Mexico, is getting legal papers to bring his family up here in the spring. They're going to live in that house. The next year they hope to bring another family and put them in this house. By then their new place will be built on up the road half a mile." Wil buried his face in her hair. "You look beautiful tonight, Red. I can see you all curled up in front of my fireplace in that outfit."

"Fireplace? You've got a fireplace?"

"I do." His lips settled on her neck and slowly found their way back to her mouth.

"Then why did you come all the way into town when your electricity went out? You could have started a fire in your living room."

"I might've been warm in the living room but my bedroom is upstairs, and besides, that didn't make enough light to read and it damn sure didn't power up the television."

"You could've slept on your sofa." She needed conversation to keep her mind from drifting toward thoughts of the bed in the motel room and the way he'd looked that morning when the policemen came. Even in flannel pajama bottoms and boots he was sexy as hell.

"I could've done a lot of things, but I'm damn glad I came to town and got a room at your motel right next door to your apartment. You ready for another beer or would you rather have wine or a mixed drink?"

She settled into his shoulder again. Nothing could be wrong that felt so right. "One beer and one small glass of champagne at midnight is my limit."

"Can't hold your liquor, huh?" he teased.

She jerked her head up. Hold her liquor, indeed! Aunt Pearlita had damn sure left her more than a motel. She'd given her the genes to whoop man, woman, or professional at poker and hold her liquor better than any man. And then there was the gene pool on the maternal side of her family that could have put Aunt Pearlita to shame if there'd ever been a contest between the country and the city aunts when it came to drinking.

"I could drink you under the table any day of the week."

Wil pulled her back into his embrace. "I don't think so, darlin'."

She settled in again. "Everyone knows Indians can't hold their liquor. I'm Irish, German, and English. There's no way you can outdo me in shots."

"Is that a challenge?"

Despite what experts said, some small people could definitely hold their liquor better than big people. Aunt Katy said it had to do with the boobs. It all went in there before it hit the brain, so Pearl could hold a hell of a lot more than it looked like she could.

"It is not a challenge. It is a fact. Don't push it and you won't get embarrassed."

Wil chuckled. "It's not a fact until it's proven. You want to prove it?"

"Anytime, cowboy!" She wished she would've eaten the words rather than spit them out.

He finished off his beer and set the empty bottle on the porch floor. "So I get to choose time and place?"

"Like I said, anytime."

"What are you thinkin' about? How to cheat?" he asked.

"I was thinking about Aunt Katy, and I do not cheat. I don't have to. I'm Irish."

"What about Aunt Katy?" he asked.

"How she'd be disappointed in me if I disgraced her name by letting you win. That old girl could drink enough to float the *Titanic*. Then she could whoop all the other southern ladies in Savannah, Georgia, at bridge—and that was playing for dollars on the point— on Sunday afternoon after church services. After which she could gargle with Listerine and make Sunday night services down at the Baptist church without the preacher even knowing that she'd had a drop of anything stronger than lemonade all afternoon. She said she had to have a few drinks to win, and she always tithed on her winnings so the Good Lord turned an eye the other way."

He leaned back and cocked his head to one side. "You won't cheat. It needs to be a fair fight."

"I don't cheat, but I will not let you win so you don't whine around like a pissy little girl. I'd hate to face Aunt Katy if I did."

Using his fist, he tipped her chin up and kissed her again and it still felt right even when they were arguing.

"When are we going to do this?" he asked.

"Like I said, anytime," she murmured breathlessly. One more sizzling kiss and she'd forget about booze and challenge him to a game of strip poker. And she would definitely win. She'd still be dressed and he'd be showing her what was hiding under those jeans.

"Okay, then I choose tonight."

"I'm not getting drunk at Austin's party!"

"You said anytime."

"That does not include Austin's party."

"Okay then, we'll stay here until after the stroke of midnight and then start shots back at your place."

She pushed a hand outside the quilt. "Deal. But not at my apartment. We'll use one of the empty motel rooms. That way when you pass out cold I can leave you in the room and go on back to my own bed."

He shook her hand firmly and then raised it to his lips to plant a kiss on the palm. "What if I'm the last one standing?"

She didn't even know the palm of the hand was on the list of erogenous zones mentioned in the magazines, but it should be. "There are two beds in each room. Don't drive drunk if I pass out before you do, and don't try anything funny."

"I don't take advantage of women, especially drunk ones, and I do not hit them. That latter is just for the record. I'm a grown man, but either one of those things would bring down the wrath of my momma and, darlin', even angels are not brave enough to face off with Momma when she's angry. Now let's change the subject before we get into a real argument. Tell me about that trouble you were always getting Austin in when you were kids."

"You ever been to Vegas?"

He cut his eyes around at her. "I got this belt buckle at the Professional Bull Riders Finals in Vegas. Why are you asking? You are changing the subject to keep from answering me, aren't you? I'll ask again when you are too looped not to give me a straight answer."

"I thought you said that you didn't take advantage of women."

"Let me clarify that. I do not take sexual advantage of women. But if I ask a question and you are too drunk to keep your mouth shut then that's not taking advantage. It's making conversation. Why did you ask about Vegas anyway?"

"Darlin', the sayin' is 'What happens in Vegas stays in Vegas.' What went on when we were kids stays on the banks of the Red River."

Wil's chuckles turned into laughter. Pearl could probably tell a full-grown man to go straight to hell and make him look forward to the trip.

Austin poked her head out the door. "What's so funny out here?"

"Pearl just said that what happened when you two were little girls stayed on the banks of the Red River."

"And that's so funny why?" Austin asked.

Pearl motioned for her to join them on the other end of the swing. "It was one of those you'd-have-had-to-be-here things. Hey, did you ever wonder what kind of trouble we would have gotten into if we'd known about the watermelon wine?"

Austin pulled the last quilt from the rack and wrapped it around her shoulders before shutting the door. She sat down on the porch steps rather than joining them on the swing. "Can you imagine what your aunt and my granny would have done to us if we'd have found that wine? You'd have been cleaning rooms and I'd have been hoeing watermelons until the angels came to take our souls to heaven. It would've been worth every bit of it though, wouldn't it?"

Pearl nodded. "Or else they'd have taken us to church and gotten us saved, sanctified, and dehorned."

"Savin' and sanctifyin' us would have been as likely as St. Peter setting up a snow cone stand inside the front gates of hell. Speakin' of cleanin' rooms, how are things going over at the Longhorn? How's your hired lady working out?"

"Great. She even cleans the doorjambs and the light fixtures. I've never seen anyone who can work as fast and perfect as Lucy. I hope she stays forever."

Austin stood up and headed for the door. "Y'all can stay out here and freeze your butts off if you want to, but I'm going back inside where it's warm."

"Before you go, maybe you could tell this Indian brave that he's about to embarrass himself," Pearl said.

Austin looked down at Wil.

"He thinks he can out-drink me," Pearl said.

Austin frowned. "Whiskey or vodka?"

"Her choice," Wil said.

"Whiskey. Jack Black," Pearl said.

"Shot for shot? Can I watch?" Austin asked.

"Sure. You can be the referee," Pearl said.

"When?"

"Tonight. In one of my motel rooms. That way when he passes out he can sleep it off in a room and I can go on to my bed. Colleen says that friends don't let friends drive drunk."

"Oh, no! I'm not leaving my handsome husband's side to watch you two play king of the shots. Call me tomorrow and tell me how it turns out, and Wil, you have met your match. When it's over, she'll be staggering but you'll be passed out so you won't know what happened. Pearl, promise me that you won't paint his toenails while he's drunk."

Pearl frowned. "Ahh, shit, you ain't supposed to tell what happens if I win."

Austin narrowed her eyes into slits. "Promise."

"Oh, okay. No blushing pink or red devil fingernail polish. Does that mean I can't pluck his eyebrows either?"

Austin nodded. "Or cut his hair or wax your initials in the middle of his chest."

"I promise." Pearl pouted.

Austin slipped inside the door then poked her head out again, "Or dye his hair?"

Pearl sighed. "You really must like Wil a lot. You never made me make promises like that before. I promise I will leave him, his body hair, and his fingernails and toenails alone while he is passed out in my motel."

How in the world had she gotten herself into a pissing contest with Wil Marshall anyway? She was thirty years old, not twenty-one and barely legal. Come to think of it, that was the last time she got slap drunk and even then she didn't pass out. She'd rather spend the whole night cuddled up in Wil's arm under a quilt. Could she change his mind with a few long, sexy kisses?

Probably not, since the gauntlet had been thrown and Austin even knew about it. Thank God for Lucy! She'd clean the rooms the next morning while Pearl ate aspirin like M&Ms and held her aching head. But she wouldn't hurt as badly as Wil, and he'd have to go home to the ranch and feed bawling cows, clucking chickens, and listen to Digger howl.

"You got a bottle of Jack?" he asked.

"I do. How about you?"

"I brought one but Rye had one already opened so I left mine in the truck. We can drink it until it's gone, and if you are still standing then we'll start on yours."

Women who could hold their liquor didn't appeal to him. He put them in the same basket with low-down trailer trash and pure old hookers. Pearl was neither of those. She was a lady just like her Aunt Pearlita, so why was she acting like that? And had she really, really painted some fool's toenails while he was passed out? She sounded like a wild party girl instead of the responsible businesswoman who didn't even want to leave her help in charge of the motel.

"We don't have to do this," he said.

"You doubting me or you?"

Deep down she knew better than to play with fire, but suddenly it was imperative that she not stagnate in a world of numbers, classes, and cleaning rooms. She needed the excitement that night of a pissing contest and Wil was not going to win.

"You think you can win this fight, don't you?" she asked.

"I know my ability, but it's been a long time since I set out to prove that I was better at shots than anyone else, especially a woman. But if you insist on this, I can damn sure show you that I'm the boss," he said.

She might have backed down if he hadn't said "especially a woman." Those words were like kerosene tossed on an open bonfire. The flash could be seen in her green eyes as clearly as if there had been an explosion right there on the porch swing.

"I'm thirty years old and tonight I will prove that 'especially a woman' is going to make you eat crow."

"What in the hell has got your dander up? What did I do wrong?" Wil slid over a few inches. He hadn't meant to make her angry. Hell, they'd been having a wonderful time until the idea of drinking came up. All the flirting and phone calls had said that she was interested in him, like he was her. Now he was getting mixed signals.

"You got my dander up, darlin'," she said sarcastically. *Especially a woman,* indeed!

"Don't call me darlin' in that tone. It sounds downright dirty. And since you've got a burr up your cute little butt, why wait until midnight? Let's go take care of this right now. Hell, I'll be home and asleep when the New Year comes in and you'll be snoring on a bed," Wil said.

"Just let me get my coat."

"Honey, I'll get it for you. The dark green one with the gold buttons, right?"

"Don't call me honey in that tone. It sounds like you are cussin' me."

Chapter 8

THE PARKING LOT WAS TOTALLY EMPTY WHEN PEARL parked in front of the lobby. Wil nosed his truck in beside her Caddy and waited while she went inside to pick up a room key from Lucy. He should wait until they were in the room, call the whole thing off, and see where a few of those steamy hot kisses would lead.

She dreaded the contest, but she'd made her brag and now she'd have to pay the fiddler. She had no doubts that she could out-drink Wil Marshall, but she also held no half-assed notions that it would be an easy feat or that tomorrow morning she wouldn't have a full-fledged head-banging hangover.

"What are you doin' home so early? It's not even nearly midnight yet." Lucy looked up from the computer. "Guess what? They had a memorial service for me. I'm dead. Cleet had a few words to say about how he couldn't understand why I'd commit suicide. My sister said it was because I never got over losin' that baby. Kinda strange, readin' your own funeral thing from the newspaper."

Pearl leaned on the countertop. Whiskey shots could wait a few minutes. "You lost a baby recently?"

"Not recently. Three months after me and Cleet married. I was sixteen and pregnant. He was twenty. He married me and three months later got drunk and beat me so bad I lost the baby. It was a girl and I was glad she didn't have to grow up and get whooped on. I made sure there wasn't no more pregnancies. Cleet didn't know that I went to the health department and got pills."

"You all right?" Pearl asked.

"I left it all behind me. My family, my momma, all of it. I'm not sorry. Never will be. You want to take over or let me finish up until closing time?"

"I got a bet goin' with Wil Marshall. That fool thinks he's better at shots than I am so we're going to have a fact-proving test."

Lucy's brow furrowed and she cocked her head to one side. "What are you goin' to shoot at? Can you do that this close to town? You goin' to use a rifle or a pistol?"

Pearl smiled. "Not that kind of shot. Whiskey shots. I told him I'm Irish and I can drink him under the table any day of the week. So I need the key to room two. That way when I get the job done and come on home to my apartment I won't have to listen to him snoring."

"Room two is already full up. We've got eight customers in all. They've all gone to parties, I guess. They checked in, stayed in their rooms a little while, and then come out and left. I'd take number ten if I was you. It's on the end and there's nobody next to it. You really think you can out-drink a man big as him?"

"I do," Pearl said.

"Well, I wouldn't test your mettle." Lucy took the number ten key from the pegboard and handed it to Pearl. "Still want me to lock it up?"

"Yes, and sleep late tomorrow. I'll help clean rooms since you worked half the night for me."

Lucy smiled. "This ain't work. Cleanin' rooms ain't even work. And you are goin' to have a big headache in the mornin' even if you do win the bet."

Pearl pointed at Lucy. "I'm lucky to have you."

Wil got out of the truck when he saw Pearl coming out of the motel lobby. "I was about to go on home. Figured you'd backed out and was just goin' to leave me sittin' out here for pure spite."

"If I backed out you'd win by default. I was talkin' to Lucy. We're in room ten. You got the Jack?"

He held up a brown paper bag, the top twisted around a square bottle. "Never been opened. If we empty this one and you can still stand on your feet, then you can go get yours."

"Shot glasses?"

He held up his left hand. The shot glasses looked tiny in his big hand. "I borrowed two from Austin."

She held up the key.

"Walkin' or drivin'?" he asked.

"I reckon we can walk that far. We've each only had one beer." The high heel on her boot slipped off the sidewalk onto the gravel and she had to catch herself on a porch post to keep from falling into him.

He reached out and grabbed her arm. "You are already a little tipsy on just one beer. I bet you don't get three shots down before your cute little ass is fried."

"Ah, honey, you've got a hard lesson to learn," she whispered.

All the hair on his neck stood straight up. Her voice was always slightly husky, but when she whispered it was so hot that he wanted to make love to her until dawn rather than drink whiskey with her.

"Okay then, braggy butt, if you don't pass out after number three then I'll take you to dinner next week," he said.

She slung the door to the room open and stood to one side. "If I do?"

"Ladies first."

She stepped into the room, peeled off her coat and tossed it on the bed closest to the door, sat down on the other bed, and removed her boots. He put the brown bag and two shot glasses on the small table in the corner and sat down beside her, close enough that she could smell the remnants of Stetson and beer on his breath. He kicked off his boots, removed his coat, and tossed it across hers.

"If I'm still standing after three shots?" she asked.

He tipped her chin back and kissed her, teasing her mouth open with his tongue. "Then you can take me to dinner next week."

She moved over and sat down in his lap, wrapped her arms around his neck, and cupped a cheek in each hand. She pulled his lips down to hers in another searing kiss. "If I'm still standing you have to cook dinner for me. Nothing frozen or prepared."

"Deal. And if you pass out, you have to cook for me. Nothing frozen. No take-out. From scratch with dessert." He wrapped his arms around her and slipped a hand under her shirt. Her bare skin was soft as satin sheets and warm on his cold hands.

She'd never known rough cold hands could cause her skin to sizzle.

"Deal," she gasped.

"Anymore bets or ground rules or do we spit on our knuckles and begin this war?" he asked.

She kissed him on the cheek as she stood up and straightened her shirt.

Kissing was finished.

Battle was beginning.

She pulled out a chair and sat down at the table. "I'll pour. Only ground rule is that all is fair in chaos and Jack."

Wil grinned and took the other chair. "Then let the contest begin. Are we doing doubles or singles?"

She held up a glass and studied it. "These are made for doubles but let's do singles. To this line"—she pointed to a rim halfway up the glass with the name of a bar written above it—"should be a single shot. So here goes."

She filled the two glasses to the mark and tossed hers back like a gunslinger in an old Western movie. Heat, almost as fiery as what smacked her when she kissed Wil, hit her empty stomach like a blowtorch. The first one was always the hottest. It paved the way for the rest. By the eighth or ninth she wouldn't even feel the fire.

Wil threw his back and swallowed. He had an advantage over Pearl that he hadn't told her. He'd eaten a whole plate full of goodies before she arrived at the party so he was working on a full stomach. Unless she'd eaten half an Angus steer before she left home, she was drinking on an empty stomach. But she'd said all was fair in chaos and Jack so that meant open disclosure wasn't an issue.

She refilled the glasses, giving him a few drops more than she put in hers. All was fair in Jack and chaos. His exact words had been to let the contest begin.

"I'll drink this one but only if I get to pour from now on. You put a little more in my glass," he said.

"All's fair?"

"Whoever wins will do it honestly. No cheating."

She took the clip out of her hair and let her red ringlets free to fall to shoulder length. "Okay, no cheating is rule one, then. But you didn't say that in the beginning."

His fingers itched to get tangled up in her hair, but more of those kisses in a room with two beds would end the drinking contest and she'd say he cheated. "I'm sayin' it now."

"Then I will not cheat. I don't break rules. But if there are no rules then I don't have to follow them. That's the full mark." She pointed.

He nodded and downed his shot. "It's a shame to be drinkin' good whiskey like this. Jack is sippin' whiskey."

"Might as well like the taste."

She sent her second one down and sure enough, the blazes weren't nearly as hot. But like always, whiskey had a way of making other things hot; that warm gushy feeling deep down in her gut sent her imagination into overdrive. No fantasy she'd ever come up with while downing shots compared to the real thing called Wil Marshall.

She poured the third round, making a big show of filling them exactly even, and downed hers before he had time to pick his up. She didn't feel the fire that time, at least not in her stomach. The rest of her body felt like it was one degree away from combustion, and he didn't look like he was feeling the liquor at all. She might have met her match after all.

"Talk to me. Tell me something about yourself. Your momma got red hair like you?" Wil asked.

"Hell, no! Momma is a blonde and a stereotypical southern belle. I got this red hair from a distant great-grandma. There's a connection between my dad and some folks up in northern Oklahoma. Little bitty place called Corn. We went there for a couple of family reunions when I was a kid. Have a distant cousin named Sharlene who has red hair just like mine. Kinky curly and unruly. We shared a great-grandma and we were the only two redheads in the bunch."

"What happened to her?" Wil asked.

"She writes romance books and used to own a bar over around Mingus, Texas. That would be east of Mineral Wells. But she fell in love with a carpenter and moved back to Corn. Last I heard she had a couple of kids of her own. The guy she married had custody of a niece and nephew and she adopted them so she's got a houseful."

"She got a temper like yours?"

"Worse."

Wil chuckled and tossed back the next round.

"Your turn," Pearl said. "Something about you now?"

"I like to dance. Want to go over to Mingus to the Honky Tonk sometime for a beer and a dance?"

"Hey, that's the place Sharlene owned," Pearl said.

"That's why you look familiar. I saw her one time when me and Ace stopped by there for a cold beer one night after we'd been to a rodeo in Abilene."

"Small world," Pearl said.

By the eighth round she was still lucid and Wil was getting sexier by the minute. The room got hotter than a hooker in the front row pew of a holiness tent revival in the middle of July in Texas. She removed her lacy shirt.

He raised an eyebrow.

"I'm not cheatin'. I'm hot," she said.

"Liquor, weather, or otherwise?" he asked with a wicked gleam in his eye.

"All damn three. I think it's close to time for the countdown on television, ain't it?" she slurred.

"Hell, I don't know. All I know is that you are damn beautiful, Red, and I'd rather be doing something else than showing you I can out-drink you. Let's have a pissin' contest that involves sex rather than shots." His words came out slow and deliberate.

She grinned. "You are about to lose it, cowboy. That was as romantic as a trip to the outhouse."

He laughed too loudly. "Never was one much for words."

She pointed her finger at him. "Don't tell me that after all the text messages and phone calls. You *are* getting drunk."

"So are *you,* darlin'. Too bad I don't take advantage of women when they're drunk. Pour us another round. Is this nine or ten?" He moved his chair close enough to hers that their shoulders touched.

"See, you don't even know how much you've had. It's nine and you'll be snoring by ten," she told him.

He grinned and downed the ninth one, set his glass down with a thump, and took off his shirt, revealing a gauze undershirt and showing muscles she'd only dreamed about. Would she give up before the clock struck midnight and a New Year began? He'd never live it down if he let a woman out-drink him.

"Ten more bottles of beer on the wall, ten more bottles of beeeer. Take one down, pass it around…" he sang off-key and out of tune.

It sounded just fine to Pearl. She didn't care if he sounded like a cross between Alvin of the Chipmunks and a big green bullfrog, as long as he didn't put his shirt back on. The room was spinning but she wasn't going to holler calf rope yet. His eyes looked bleary and his head would hit the table before hers did. She eyed the distance to the bathroom and decided she could make it if she was very careful. She'd concentrate on putting one foot ahead of the other and he would not see her stagger. But first they'd have one more round.

She poured and slopped a little out on the table. "You can have that. I don't want it."

He dipped his finger in it and wiped it on her lips, leaned forward, and licked it off.

She opened her mouth and grabbed a fist full of dark hair to keep his lips on hers. She was panting when he pulled back.

He chuckled. "Are you trying to seduce me, lady?"

"Yes, I am. Is it workin'?" She giggled.

"Nope. We've got a contest here and I can't be bought."

"I've got to pee. Is that against the rules?"

"No, but let's do one more round and that'll finish my bottle. You'll have to get yours, but I'm goin' with you."

"Why?"

"To make sure you don't cheat."

She poured the last of the bottle up into the glasses and tossed hers back. There wasn't a bit of fire in her stomach, but she wished she'd brought extra underpants in her purse. Damn, that man got sexier with every single shot.

"I vote we take a ten-minute intermission. You can have first at the bathroom." He slurred, but her ears were buzzing and she understood him perfectly.

She stood up slowly.

His eyes followed her all the way to the bathroom.

She didn't stagger one bit. He'd never met a woman who could match him shot for shot, but that redhead could sure hold her liquor. The numbers on the digital clock beside the bed said it was eleven fifty-something, but they were dancing around like line dancers doing the Cotton-Eyed Joe in a honky tonk.

He stood up slowly and held onto the chair until the walls stopped spinning. He would be standing outside the bathroom door when she came out. He wasn't admitting defeat, not yet.

She put her head between her knees as she sat on the potty and took long, deep breaths. Damn Wil Marshall anyway! Most men folded after round nine. Only twice had she had to go to round ten and that was with her best friend in college. A girl who'd come from a long line of AA members.

Had the ten-minute intermission already passed? Actually only five of it was hers. He would have to use the bathroom too. She sat up, got a fix on the cold water faucet to still the walls, and pulled up her underpants. When she opened the door he was leaning on the jamb.

"Thought you'd passed out in there and I'd won." He grinned.

"Ready for the second bottle?" she asked.

He moved to one side. "I'm ready. How about you, Red?"

She took a step, got off balance on the second one, and the brown carpet was coming up in slow motion to meet her when Wil's strong arms grabbed her around the waist. That motion set him off balance and he fell toward the bed, taking her with him.

"You did that on purpose." She was cuddled up in the crook of his arm with her head on his chest. How in the hell did two people fall on a bed in such a perfect position? Was it fate or just plain dumb luck? And why did it feel so damned natural and good?

"I didn't trip you, darlin'," he whispered.

He buried his face in a mop of red hair. He deserved a kiss for saving her from breaking an arm or worse yet, her cute little nose, with that fall. Besides, the count-down on the television had begun and the announcer yelled nine. He wanted a New Year's kiss and he wanted it to be with Miz Red Richland.

Eight. She pushed her hair out of her face and looked up into the depths of his brown eyes and saw only her own reflection there. Austin would say that she'd found her soul mate. The thought scared her but not enough to wiggle out of his embrace.

Seven. Her eyes looked like warmed-over sin on Sunday morning, but they were searching his face in a way that made him sweat bullets. Why didn't that man count faster?

Six. She pressed her body against his.

Five. He brushed back a cascade of red curls so he could see her face better. Every single freckle should be kissed.

Four. She combed his black hair back with her finger-tips. If he passed out without kissing her, it would be grounds for justifiable homicide.

Three. His lips started coming closer to hers.

Two. She licked her lips and shut her eyes.

One. Boom! They met in a clash of heat and desire hotter than any pepper grown in Texas as the old year faded and the New Year began with the familiar tune playing on the television.

One passionate, hot kiss would not satisfy all those shots. Two stirred the red-hot embers and got a big fire going in her gut. Three fanned the fire so high and hot she tugged his undershirt up out of his jeans and over his head.

With his lips still on hers he pulled her camisole up. He broke the kiss long enough to get it over her head and then his lips settled back on hers.

She undid his belt buckle and unzipped his jeans, then pressed her body so close to his that she could feel his hardness on her belly. His hands were all over her, undoing her bra, tossing it in a blur toward the other bed. She moaned when his fingertips grazed her breast and when he strung kisses from her neck to her belly button.

His fingers were white-hot fire on her skin. She started to tell him that she liked to date, loved to party, adored the chase, but she didn't go to bed with men she only knew a week, but words fled her brain when his tongue found her belly button. She arched her back and gasped at the sensation.

Her hands grazed the tight muscles on his chest, through the soft dark hair that extended from taut nipples to belly button, to that dense soft bed of curls, for his erect penis. She wrapped her cool fingers around it and he gasped.

His hand grazed her inner thigh and she opened up for him. She was ready but he wasn't through playing… not yet… and he liked those little kitten moans when he touched her in the right spots.

She grabbed his hair and pulled him back up for another kiss before she peeled his jeans completely off and threw them across the room. She crawled up his body like a sleek mountain lion and stretched out on top of him.

His rough hands were hot as hell when they skimmed her back and flipped her over under his body. "Is this because we're both drunk or do you really want this?" he asked.

"I. Want. This." She panted.

With a firm thrust he started a nice easy rhythm. She wrapped her arms around his back and raked her nails across his flesh. She'd never felt so uninhibited, so totally into sex as she did right then.

His mouth covered hers in a string of passionate kisses that fanned the flames already sending her up in blazes. She arched her back against him and gave herself to the red-hot fire that only Wil could put out.

Wil felt as if he'd waited his whole life for that night and he didn't want to rush. Besides, as drunk as he was, he might pass out cold when it was done and he wanted to hold her in his arms as long as he could.

Pearl gasped when she climaxed and he brushed a sweet kiss across her lips.

She expertly flipped him over onto his back without missing a stroke and said, "My turn, darlin'."

"Mercy!" he whispered as she started to do the work, bringing him right up the edge of passion and then slowing down, all the while kissing his ears, his eyes, and his lips with so much fire that he wondered if all there would be left in the morning was a pile of ashes in the middle of the motel bed. She put one hand behind her on his tense thigh and the other on his chest and settled down to serious business. When she heard him call out her name in a throaty southern growl, she gave into the desire and buried her face in his neck in a moan. He rolled to one side without letting her out of his arms and held her tightly.

"My God!" she said.

"Nope, just mighty fine Jack Daniel's sex," he said as he ran his hands down the length of her body. "Your skin is as soft as whipped cream. Which reminds me, maybe sometime I'll cover you up in whipped cream and then lick it all off."

She shuddered just thinking of the sensation that would cause.

"Ready for round two?" He kissed that soft spot right below her ear and worked his way down her body, tasting, nibbling, sucking, and licking, causing brand new liquid heat spasms. He kissed her toes one by one, then her ankles and then suddenly he was lying on top of her planting hot, steamy kisses on her lips again.

She'd truly met her match in shots and in sex. She bit the inside of her lip to keep from screaming out and arched against him again.

When he stretched out on top of her, she flipped him over and sat on his chest. "My turn," she said. All was fair in love, war, whiskey shots, and sex, and Wil was about to find out just how hot she could make him.

"But—" he started to argue.

"Shhh." She put a finger over his lips and kissed his eyelids.

His skin quivered when she gently scraped a nipple with her teeth and his breath came out in ragged gasps when she finally got back to his waiting lips.

The kisses that followed weren't soft and sweet; they were demanding and passionate and set loose a desire that she'd never felt before. It went beyond want, further than need, and into a place where she felt if he didn't make love to her that her heart would stop beating and she'd wither up and die.

He did an expert roll, which impressed the hell out of her since they were both still drunk and tired from the first round.

She wrapped her arms around his neck and asked, "We goin' to ride the bull again or just sit in the stands and cheer?"

"At this point we'd better ride the bull, darlin'."

She nibbled his ear and whispered, "You think you can stay on eight seconds?"

"How about eight minutes for every one of those ten shots?"

She tried to do the math in her head but couldn't get past the fact that it added up to more than an hour. She'd concede the battle to him if he could make love to her the second time around for more than an hour with ten shots in him. Hell, she'd get down on her knees and propose to him right there in the Longhorn Inn if he could stay the course for eighty minutes when they were both drunk as rabid skunks.

She ran her hands down his muscular back and tangled her hands in his hair, pulling his lips to hers.

"This feels so right."

"Does, doesn't it?" He wasn't a bit surprised to find her ready again.

Twenty minutes later he collapsed on top of her with a loud moan.

"That wasn't an hour," she said breathlessly. He wasn't getting the crown for only twenty minutes.

"That was the appetizer and the entrée. We'll have dessert in a few minutes. I'm afraid I'm not up to seven courses. Not unless I'm sober."

He rolled to one side and pulled her close to his side burying his face in her neck and starting to fan the fires of the still smoldering embers with his kisses.

She sighed heavily.

"Want me to stop?"

"Hell, no!"

"Three courses it is, then. When we're sober we'll try for the fancy stuff."

Drunk or sober or somewhere in between, Pearl had no doubt that the heat from seven courses would kill them both graveyard dead.

But what a hell of a way to go!

Chapter 9

THUNDER AWOKE HER THE NEXT MORNING. SHE opened her eyes long enough to see that it was eight o'clock, then snapped them shut against the ribbon of gray light sneaking through the slates in the window blinds. It thundered again and she crammed a pillow over her aching head.

Wil snored and she threw the pillow at the wall and sat straight up. Realizing what she'd done the night before put a crimson blush on her cheeks. Knowing that she'd do it again if she had a chance turned it even darker. She pulled the sheet up under her arms and fell back on the pillows with enough force to bounce the bed.

"Mmmm," Wil mumbled in his half-sleep. "God, my head hurts."

"So does mine."

"Did I win?"

"Of course not. You passed out cold."

He propped up on an elbow. "You don't lie worth a damn, Red. I remember everything, including that cute little freckle on your fanny."

Thunder rolled again and hard rain pelted against the window. A truck crunched the gravel as it pulled away from the motel. She snuggled closer to his side and pulled the covers over her head. "Go back to sleep. My head hurts and Lucy said she'd take care of the rooms today."

"Happy New Year," he mumbled and drew her closer into his embrace.

Which was a helluva bad idea. The moment that her soft little naked body touched his, he was aroused and ready. He kissed her on the forehead and she opened one eye. Her clothing was strung all over the room. Bra in one corner. Underpants peeking out from under the bed. Coats on the other bed. Camisole beside the empty bottle of Jack.

Dear God, what have I done?

"You are still beautiful in the morning and I'm sober," he whispered as he pulled the covers over his head and made lazy circles with his tongue on his way down her body.

"Thank you, I think," she mumbled.

Her cell phone ringtone echoed like a screeching night owl and her body was responding to Wil entirely too well. There was a knot of pure desire in her gut that only long, slow morning sex would cure, but the cell phone wouldn't shut up. She reached out from under the sheet with one hand and grabbed it from beside the empty bottle of whiskey.

"'Lo," she muttered.

"Who won?" Austin said.

"You are entirely too cheery for the morning after." Pearl gasped when Wil found one of those erogenous zones.

"Morning after what?" Austin asked.

"I think I'd better call you back when my head stops hurting," Pearl said.

"Sex is good for a headache. Is Wil still there?"

"Good-bye!" Pearl moaned the minute she snapped the phone shut and hoped Austin hadn't heard it.

He flipped the sheet back and smiled. "That was your

wake-up call and I'm not talking about the cell phone. Are you ready for breakfast?"

"As in?" She blinked.

"As in I'm sober and I'm ready to do justice to that seven-course meal. It might take all day but..." He let the sentence hang.

The phone rang again before she could wrap her mind around seven courses of cowboy sex. She ignored it the first three rings but when he reached for it, she grabbed it out of his hand.

"Hello, Momma," she said.

"Happy New Year. Did you have another boring night at that horrid motel?" her mother asked.

Pearl swallowed hard to keep from giggling. Wil nibbled on her ear, whispered that he was going for a shower, and threw the covers off. She was struck speechless at him strutting across the floor in all his naked glory. There wasn't a spare bit of fat on his hard body, which was all muscles and sinewy flesh. Even his sexy butt cheeks were firm and had no wiggle when he swaggered toward the bathroom.

"Are you awake?" Pearl's mother asked gruffly.

"Sorry, Momma, but I'm barely here. I went to a party at Austin's last night and had a late night."

"Well, I'm glad to see you doing something other than sitting in that godforsaken motel and taking those silly online courses. Did you get all dressed up and have a good time?"

"Oh, yeah," Pearl said.

The shower started. Wil began singing an old Willie Nelson song. Pearl fished the remote from under the edge of the bed and quickly turned on the television.

"Who is that I hear?" her mother asked.

"Television. I turned it on to see what the weather is going to be today. Looks like rain all morning. I guess I'd best get up and help Lucy check out the guests. Tell Daddy happy New Year's for me. I've got to run now," Pearl said.

"I'll call later today when you are awake and you can tell me all about the party. We went over to the Kings' place. Jasmine sends her love."

"Tell her hi for me," Pearl said.

When her mother said good-bye and hung up the phone, Pearl kicked the rest of the covers off and padded across the floor to the bathroom. One look at her bloodshot eyes in the mirror said yes, she'd really drank enough to stagger a rodeo bull and yes, she had stayed awake through three courses of fantastic sex. She looked like hell, smelled like sex and Stetson, and her mouth tasted like the remnants of half a big bottle of Jack Daniel's whiskey.

Wil pulled back the shower curtain and crooked his finger at her. "Come on in. The water is fine."

"Let me brush my teeth first. I taste horrible," she said.

"Don't take too long." He winked.

I shouldn't be doing this, she thought as she looked at the woman with smeared mascara and tangled red curls in the mirror. She ran the minty-flavored toothbrush over her teeth and argued that she should wrap up in the blanket and make a hasty retreat to her apartment. When he finished his shower he'd find her gone, get mad, and never call again.

I'm crazy, but there's something different about Wil. There's an excitement I've never known, something deep inside me that feels so right. Am I headed for a heartache?

She threw back the curtain and stepped over the edge of the bathtub. Heartache or not, she needed a shower and Wil had already invited her in.

"So you have a headache?" he asked.

She nodded.

His gaze started at her toes and heat traveled with it all the way to her eyes. He leaned in and kissed her. She tasted toothpaste and wondered briefly if he'd used the same motel complimentary brush that she'd just used. The thought slipped away when he teased her lips open with his tongue and made love to her mouth before running a warm soapy washcloth up her backside and across her shoulders.

He broke the kiss and gently walked her backwards until her hair was under the spray. When it was thoroughly wet, he poured shampoo into his hand and massaged it down to the scalp.

"That'll make it all better," he whispered as he planted wet kisses on her eyelids.

She moaned something but it wasn't words.

He leaned her head back, cradling it in his big hands, and rinsed every smidgen of soap from her tight red curls. Then he began to soap her body using his hands instead of the cloth. It took forever and she'd forgotten all about the headache by the time he finished.

He stepped out of the tub, grabbed a big white towel, and hurriedly wiped the water from his body. Then he wrapped one around her hair and a second one around her body before scooping her up in his arms and carrying her back to bed. He laid her down gently, kissing her passionately before he flipped her over on her stomach.

"A good neck and back massage is good for a headache too," he said softly.

She didn't even know he'd picked up the small bottle of lotion from the vanity until she heard the burp of it leaving the plastic bottle. "If this is the awkward morning after then I vote we have another contest tonight," she said.

"No thank you, Red." He applied the lotion and massaged the knots from her neck and shoulders, working his way down her back, her fanny, and that tight place right under the butt where it meets up with the back of the leg.

"Oh, God, that feels so good," she groaned.

"Now for the heat pad to help the lotion soak in and do its job," he said.

"Heat pad?"

He stretched his warm body out on top of her back and kissed her neck, nibbled on her ear, and unwrapped the towel from her head. Then he dug his fingers into her damp curly hair to massage her scalp.

"Dear God," she said.

"Are we going to pray? I'd rather turn you over and have sex." He chuckled.

"Forget prayers," she mumbled as she felt the hardness against her lower back.

He flipped her over, kissed her lips until they were swollen and her panting matched his, then he began a rhythm that kept time with the fast beat of their hearts.

"Have I told you this morning that you are even cute with wet hair and freckles shining?" he whispered as his fingers laced into hers.

"Have I told you that you are sexy as hell when you are all wet?" she answered back.

"Open your eyes, Red."

"Why?"

"Because I want you to look at me."

Her eyes popped open and stared right into his dreamy eyes as he lowered his lips to hers. He kissed her one more time, his tongue doing a mating dance with hers, then he left her bee-stung lips and worked his way down to her breasts, touching and feeling and tasting.

Before he went on further down her body, she pulled him back up for another kiss.

"I like your lips on mine," she said.

"They fit right together real well, don't they?" he whispered.

"Like all the rest of our bodies." She giggled.

"We're sober now, Red. You sure you want to do this?"

"Yes, I am," she said.

His hands slid down past her breasts to her hips. Just his touch fired her up to the explosion stage. She arched her back against him and the world disappeared in a blink. The delicious ache had returned. She'd never wanted sex more than she did right then, not in her entire life. No one or nothing had ever erased everything from her mind except the primal need to be satisfied.

She ran her fingers through Wil's hair. "Please, Wil, take me now. I'm so hot," she said.

"Your wish," he said as he covered her mouth with his in a searing kiss and entered her with a powerful thrust that made her groan.

She arched her back and tangled her fists in his hair. "I don't need a marathon. I just need release," she whispered.

"Me too this morning," he said as he sped up the motion. He thought he heard her say his name but his ears were ringing so loud that when he collapsed on top of her he wasn't sure what she said.

"Dear…" she gasped.

"God ain't interested in mighty fine sex, only begetting," Wil said.

"Well, I'm not ready for the begetting but that was wonderful," she said between raspy breaths.

"I'm sober."

"What the hell has that got to do with anything?"

"It's better when I'm sober."

"Then you can't ever drink again," she said.

The storm had passed and the sun was sneaking through the slits in the mini blinds. She looked over at the clock and let out a squeak. It was already ten o'clock. Lucy would be frantic, trying to check out customers and worry about getting rooms cleaned at the same time. And Pearl had a research project due in three days for her last hospitality course that had to do with creating a space for a breakfast nook in the lobby. She didn't have time to be lying around in a bed of pure unadulterated 100 percent guaran-damn-teed best sex ever, even if it was where she wanted to be.

"Wil, I've got a million things to do and you've got a ranch to run. It's the middle of the morning. We've got to get up and—"

"Get up! I think I can arrange that at least one more time." He smiled.

She kissed him and bounded out of bed before he could wrap his big arms around her again.

"You are a tease. Talk about getting up and then leave me cold," he said.

She knew better than to look back at him. If she did

she'd be in the motel room until she starved to death or
died from too much sex.

"Time to go, cowboy. I'm going around the end of
the motel and going in through my back door. You leave
however you want. And Wil…"

He winked at her. "I'll call you later today. I'll cook
for you tonight. You can cook later in the week. I think
the whiskey contest was a draw so we'll each pay up."

"Sounds like a deal to me," she said.

———⁓———

Delilah met Pearl at the door, yowling and fussing because she'd had to spend the night alone. Pearl took
time to rub her ears for a few seconds before she unbut-
toned her coat and dropped it on the sofa and headed
straight for the bedroom. She undressed, piling all her
rumpled clothing on a chair to send to the cleaners.
She pulled clean underpants and a bra from a dresser
drawer, jeans and a sweatshirt from her closet, and was
dressed in record time. She was on her way to the living room when she caught sight of herself in the mirror
above her dresser.

She went to the bathroom, took a very quick shower
to get the smell of hot sex off her body, and scrunched
mousse into her hair. She was on the way to the lobby
when the feeling hit her. Austin used to tell her that the
Lanier gut was never wrong. Well, the Richland gut
knew when something or someone was watching. She
turned around slowly. Her gun was stuck between the
mattress and box springs, handle toward the outside so
she could get at it easily. But she was in the living room
and there was no way she'd make it back to the bedroom

if an intruder was hiding over at the end of the sofa or jumped out from the pantry.

The hair on her arms tried to stand up but the sweatshirt and the jacket pushed it back down. The itch was unbelievable. When she'd made the full circle she saw Wil standing just inside the back door into her apartment.

"You forgot this." He pulled her lace bra from the pocket of his jacket and held it out. "Don't know what you are going to tell Lucy, but I didn't want her to find it in the room when she goes to clean it up."

"I'm cleaning that room today. She'd take one look at those sheets and know…" Pearl blushed scarlet.

Wil laughed. "I took all the linens to the laundry room and put them in the washing machine. Threw the whiskey bottle in the big trash can out back and made sure no one would ever know exactly what went on in there. You can tell her whatever you like."

Pearl crossed the room, rolled up on her toes, and kissed him soundly on the lips. "You are a good man, Wil Marshall. Now go home and feed the cows. I've got a helluva lot of work to do."

"Dinner is at six thirty at my house. Bring a tote bag and spend the night?"

"I'm not leaving Lucy with the place two nights in a row." She shook her head.

"Then dinner is at my house tomorrow night at six thirty," he teased.

She kissed him on the cheek. "Tomorrow night then it is. We'll see about bringing a bag."

He waved over his shoulder and disappeared outside. Pearl opened the door into the lobby.

Lucy looked up from the counter. "Good mornin'. I been checkin' out folks and lettin' you sleep. Who won?"

"I think it was a tie," Pearl said.

"How's your head?"

"Not too bad considering I almost got defeated," Pearl said.

"Well, everything went smooth as it could last night. Got two more guests who called to say they'll be out by the check-out time. They sounded like they had big old hangovers. Then I'll get busy on the rooms."

Pearl's cell phone rang before she could tell Lucy that she'd help clean that morning. She expected to hear her mother's voice but it was Wil's deep drawl that answered when she said, "Hello."

"So is it tonight or tomorrow night?"

"Tomorrow."

"We really brought in the New Year in style, didn't we?"

She smiled. "We did."

"Have a wonderful day. I'm going to be whistlin' and singin' all day."

She giggled. "You are…" She looked up to see Lucy grinning from ear to ear.

"Can't think of anything sexy enough to call me, can you?" Wil teased.

"Have a good day, Wil," she said and flipped her phone shut.

Lucy kept grinning.

"What?" Pearl asked.

"First thing is that you got your shirt on wrong side out. Next is that you got that glow all around you. You might've got drunk but you slept with that cowboy, didn't you?"

"Damn sure did," Pearl said. "But that's all I'm sayin' about that."

"Kind of like that *Forrest Gump* movie, huh?"

Pearl nodded. "You got it, Miss Lucy Fontaine."

Chapter 10

ONLY ONCE HAD WIL EVER LET A WOMAN SPEND more than a night at his place, and that had turned out to prove the old adage absolutely correct about fish and visitors stinking in three days. New Year's Eve had been so hot it was a complete wonder they hadn't melted a hole in the motel bed. And now Red was coming to his place for supper. She declared that she wouldn't be staying the night, but that could change.

And that's what bothered Wil that afternoon as he put the steaks in his special marinade sauce. Would she think that because he'd invited her to stay the night that she could take over his kitchen? Would she tell him how to grill the steaks or get all domestic and think she could make better bread than he could?

Everything was right where it needed to be by six o'clock, and he and Digger were watching out the living room window when the lights of the old Caddy came down the lane at six fifteen. She was punctual. The woman who'd tried to take over his kitchen was perpetually late for everything, so maybe it was a good thing that Red was on time.

"I didn't think any woman on the face of the earth could get me this excited," he told Digger as he headed across the living room floor in his bare feet.

He slung open the door before she could knock and

stepped aside. "Come on in. I hope you like steaks. That's what we're having for supper."

"Love steak. What can I do to help?" She wanted to walk right into his arms and have a steamy making out session before supper, but he kept his distance so she did too. She hadn't felt awkward when she woke up next to him naked as a jaybird but she did standing in the middle of the foyer in his house.

"Nice house," she said.

"It's part of the reason I bought the place. Fell in love with it first time the owner gave me a tour. That and the fact that I can see all the way to the Pacific Ocean out my front door and to the Atlantic out the back."

She laughed. "That's stretching the imagination."

"Maybe, but I figure I can see to where the land stops and the sky begins, so that must be where the two oceans are. My father says I need to plant trees in the front and backyards, but it would block my beautiful sunrises and sunsets. There's plenty of shade from those big pecan trees on the north and south ends, and I don't care to look at Canada or the Gulf." Wil helped her out of her coat and hung it on a rack beside the foyer table.

The touch of his big hands on her shoulders came close to giving her a dose of good old southern vapors. She took a deep breath and willed them away. It wouldn't do for her to pass out cold right there on his shiny hardwood floor.

The house reminded her of her Aunt Kate's in Savannah. She'd learned to drink mint juleps sitting in a rocking chair like the one drawn up to the fireplace. She was fifteen and Aunt Kate said that she'd had her first julep at fifteen and it hadn't killed her so Pearl could have one. That had happened in the heat of the summer, not in a Texas winter with a cold north wind whistling through the limbs of ancient pecan trees.

She took a deep breath and got a heat-producing whiff of Wil's aftershave that jacked her hormones up to the unbearable level. He wore soft worn jeans and a three-button red knit shirt with all the buttons undone. She had the urge to slip her hands up under that shirt and snuggle up to his broad chest. But he hadn't made a move toward anything other than her being a guest. No "hello" kiss after a dozen phone calls that bordered on downright pornographic. Had he changed his mind in the course of the last two hours?

She sniffed the air. "Is that homemade yeast bread cooking?"

He nodded. Dammit! He'd wanted to kiss her so bad that he ached from want, but something kept him back. It was that damned kitchen idea from earlier. If he greeted her with a passionate kiss like he wanted, then she'd think she could waltz right in and take over.

What is the matter with me? he thought. *This woman makes me hotter'n than…* he thought for a minute and the lyrics to a country song came to mind… *hotter'n hell in the middle of a Texas summer. Yep, just lookin' at her shoots desire all the way through my body, and I'm acting like her brother instead of a lover.*

"I love hot bread. Where's the bathroom so I can wash up? I was pettin' Delilah before I left."

"I'll show you. I've been meanin' to put one in downstairs but haven't gotten around to it. Especially since there are two upstairs. After you." He motioned toward the staircase.

She started up with him right behind her.

He couldn't keep his eyes from her rounded rear end, which did nothing to help his semi-arousal state. She wore snug-fitting designer jeans with glittery rhinestones on the hip pockets and a tight-fitting dark green sweater that stopped right above the shiny stones. Her high-heeled shoes were the same shade of green as the sweater, and her hair was pulled back with a band of green velvet. For a chance to undress her slowly and then make love to her all night he'd forget all about the steaks and the bread in the oven.

She stopped on the landing and looked at five doors. Two on each side of the hall and one at the end. She pointed at the one at the end.

He shook his head. "That is the linen closet. There are two bedrooms on each side with a bathroom between them. If you'll go through this bedroom"—he slung open a door—"then the bathroom is straight ahead. I wanted this ranch because it's good grazing land, but I also love this old house. The man who sold it to me was eighty years old and had lost his wife. His kids wanted him to retire to Arizona where they both lived so he did. I got the house intact with all the furniture."

"It's beautiful," she whispered.

The dark maple four-poster bed was draped with sheer white fabric that matched the curtains on the window. They looked as if they'd billow in the springtime if the window was left open and the cool night breezes were allowed to flow through the room. A vanity against one wall and the tall chest of drawers matched the bed. A floral carpet covered most of the floor, but shiny hardwood peeked out around the edges.

She turned around to thank him and found his sultry eyes searching her face. He held out his arms; she walked into them and laid her head on his chest. He tipped her head up and bent to kiss her. It wasn't hard and passionate or even hot and sexy but soft and sweet.

"You can do better than that. I've got proof," she mumbled.

He chuckled and picked her up. She wrapped her arms around his neck and the kiss lit up the whole bedroom. When he set her down, her legs felt like they had no bones in them. If he hadn't reached down and taken both her hands in his, she would have melted right there on the floor.

"Wow!" she said.

"Yep, wow! I'll see you in a few minutes for supper." He squeezed her hands and shut the door behind him.

She washed her hands and applied a cold cloth to her neck in an attempt to put out some of the ramped fire inside her gut. She headed back across the room but the bed looked so inviting that she flopped down on it. It was every bit as soft as it looked. She wondered what it would be like to have Wil's strong arms around her in a bed like that after a bout of sex like they'd had in the motel.

"Hey, Red, dinner is on the table. If you don't shake a leg you'll be eating your T-bone cold," Wil yelled up the steps.

She didn't need a second invitation. She followed her nose to the dining room where Wil waited. Wil seated her to his right and then he sat down. She wished she'd taken time to dress up all fancy when she looked around at the table. Plates and flatware were arranged just right; cloth napkins matched the tablecloth; candles were flickering; and a bottle of red wine chilled in a thick glass bucket.

The smell outdid the table setting—grilled T-bones that covered half of each plate, potatoes in a covered casserole dish that looked like they'd been cooked in cheese sauce, a tossed salad in a crystal bowl, hot rolls, and steamed broccoli.

Pearl picked up her knife and cut a bite of steak, popped it in her mouth, and came close to swooning. "God, this is good. Have you got an indoor grill or something?"

"No, but I do have a grill on the back porch which is screened in to keep out the flies and mosquitoes in the summertime. It don't do much to keep out the cold in the winter, but I like a good grilled steak so I brave it," he answered as he passed the rest of the food to her.

"For a steak like this I'll do the cleanup," she said.

"Oh, no! Women are not allowed in my kitchen."

Pearl cut another chunk off and started toward her mouth with it then stopped. "Why can't I go in your kitchen?"

"The last time a woman was allowed in my kitchen she thought she could move in here, rearrange it, and move me out of it."

Pearl narrowed her green eyes into slits. "Well, dar-lin', you don't have a thing to worry about if that's the problem. I don't give a damn how your kitchen is ar-ranged. I'm not one of those clingy little wifey critters."

"And what's that supposed to mean?" Wil asked.

"It means I do not have a problem with you cooking. I can cook but I'm not one of those 'this is my kitchen and I won't ever let a man in it' type of woman," she said.

"You ever think about getting married?" he asked.

"Every woman thinks about it, Wil. Some do more than think. Some don't," she said, evasively stepping around the question. She couldn't tell him that she was a party girl who loved dating—all of it. The anticipation of the chase, the dressing up, sitting across from a good-looking man in a restaurant, holding his hand in the movies, kissing him at the door; every single bit of it. But lately she'd been yearning for more than what the dating scene had to offer. She'd been thinking about waking up in the morning to a man who'd love her when she wasn't all dolled up and on her best behavior. One who'd think she was the greatest thing since ice cream on a stick when her red hair looked like a string mop that had dried all wrong or when she wore gray flannel pajamas to bed.

Whoa! Pull back on those reins, her conscience scolded.

Chapter 11

WIL REFUSED TO LET HER IN THE KITCHEN AFTER SUPPER so she made an excuse to go up to the bathroom again. She was still pondering over whether she was really getting ready to settle down when her foot hit the top step but the back part missed. One minute she was poised with her head held high and one arm on the banister. The next she was tumbling backward, sparkling diamonds on her hip pockets blinking like twinkle lights on a Christmas tree. She grabbed at the banister, at the wall, and even tried to clutch a handful of air to slow her down, but she only went faster and faster until she hit bottom and stopped with a thud and everything went black.

Wil heard her scream and made it to the staircase a split second after she hit bottom. He'd reached for his cell phone attached to his belt and fumbled with the snap, cussing the whole time until his shaking hands could get it out. Only seconds had passed from the time she hit bottom until he dialed 911, but it seemed like hours and hours. The dispatcher told him to stay on the line with the paramedics and keep them updated as they drove from the Henrietta hospital to the ranch.

He sat down beside her, afraid to touch her, dying to pick up her head and lay it in his lap, hold her close to his chest, check the back of her head for blood… something… anything but wait and do nothing.

"Shit!" Pearl opened her eyes.

"Don't move. Whatever you do, don't move," Wil said.

"Why?"

"Paramedics are on the way and you aren't to do anything until they get here."

"But my leg is twisted up under me and going to sleep," she said.

"They're turning down the lane," he said.

"Nothing is hurt but my pride," she argued.

"Red, please be still," Wil begged.

She looked up at the worried expression on his face and forced herself to be as still as possible.

"Wil, honest, nothing hurts. I'm fine," she reassured him.

Wil kept the paramedics informed of everything she said but they told him not to move her at all. By that time they were on the porch and coming through the door with a stretcher, bags of equipment, and an apparatus to stabilize her neck.

"I'm not hurt. I don't want to go to the hospital," she argued.

"Oh, yes, you are going to the hospital. You could have a fracture somewhere or a busted spleen or any of a dozen things. You're going for an MRI and I'm going with you." Wil reached down and laced his fingers in hers.

"But how will we get home?" she asked.

"Sir, it's only a few miles. Drive your vehicle in case she's released later tonight," the paramedic said.

He nodded. "I'll be right behind you."

By the time she was loaded into the ambulance, her head began to hurt and things were slightly blurry, not totally unlike the night they'd had the shot contest. Not really unfocused, yet the edges were soft like one of those pictures where nothing is truly sharp and clear. She drew her eyes together to bring it all into focus, but that didn't work.

"What is your name?" the paramedic asked.

"Pearl Richland."

"Do you know where you are right now?"

"In an ambulance on the way to the hospital."

"Do you hurt anywhere?"

She frowned. "My head is hurting."

"On a scale of one to ten, how bad is your head hurting?"

She giggled but that made it hurt worse and brought on an instant frown. "Nine shots."

"What are you saying, Miss Richland?"

"I'm sayin' it feels like I had nine shots. Kind of big and woozy and blurpy."

"Shots of what, Miss Richland?"

She looked at the man as if he were crazy. "Jack Daniel's."

"I see, so it feels like you have a hangover?"

"No, it feels like I just drank nine shots of Jack. The hangover won't be until tomorrow."

On his way to the hospital Wil called the motel and told Lucy what had happened and asked if she'd please take care of the office that night.

"Oh, my! Was there blood or broken bones?" Lucy asked.

"No, but she fell hard and… we are here. I'll call as soon as they tell me what is going on."

"I'll be right here beside the phone," Lucy said.

Wil was out of his truck and beside the ambulance door by the time the paramedics opened it. He walked beside her into the emergency room where they gave their report to the nurse and doctor who were waiting.

"It's down to five or maybe six," Pearl told the doctor.

"She's measuring her headache by how she feels after whiskey shots. On the way here she said it felt like she'd had nine," the paramedic explained on his way out the door.

Wil grinned.

"Shut up," Pearl said.

"Didn't say a word."

"Yes, you did."

"Well, she appears to be lucid enough to argue with her husband," the nurse said.

"We'll do a scan to be sure, but I think she's got a mild concussion," the doctor said.

"You are in luck. We had a car accident come in to-night and the lady who does scans is still here. I'll call her and we'll get you right on down there."

"Go ahead with blood work and a chest X-ray."

"Then I can go home? And he's not my husband," Pearl said.

The doctor patted her shoulder gently. "Then we'll talk about what we're doing next."

Wil sat down beside her and took her hand in his. "About that headache? You didn't tell me that you had a headache after the shots."

"You took my mind off it." She smiled.

Three hours later after every test result had been read and reread the doctor stuck his head in the door. "You can go home but only if someone wakes you up every hour the rest of the night and you are lucid every time."

"I will take care of her and do whatever you say," Wil told him.

"Everything looks fine except for a slight concussion. I'm not expecting you to have anything but a headache since you are so lucid, however, to be on the safe side, you can either wake her up or I'll keep her here and the nurses can do it."

"I can do that," Wil promised.

"Okay, then I will release you. It's almost midnight. Start waking her at one and then on the hour until nine tomorrow morning. Then you can both get some sleep," he said.

A nurse helped her redress in her clothing and pushed her to the exit door in a wheel chair. Wil picked her up like a bride and carried her to the passenger side of his truck. When she was settled in with the seat belt fastened, he shut the door and rounded the truck.

"Just take me home. I'll be fine," Pearl said when he was inside and had started the engine.

"I'm taking you to the ranch and I'm doing just what the doctor said. No arguments," he said firmly.

"Wil, this is crazy. I have a headache. I'm not dead."

"And you won't be dead on my watch. I called Lucy while they were bringing you out of the hospital. She's of the old school that says you have to stay full awake for at least eight hours. So if you go home, she's going to sit beside you for the next eight hours and poke you with pins if you go to sleep. Your choice."

"Okay, okay, I'll go to the ranch. But I didn't bring a bag because I had no intentions of spending the night."

"I've got a T-shirt that will fit like a nightshirt on you," he said.

"Can I sleep in that big old soft bed?"

"You can sleep anywhere you want." He grinned.

Fifteen minutes later they were back at the ranch where he carried her into the house and up the steps without a single argument. She laid her aching head on his shoulder and shut her eyes. She felt as if she could sleep for a week and still not be rested when she awoke.

He set her in a rocking chair in the corner of the room and pulled the covers back on the bed. She started to stand and he shook his head. She sat back down and waited while he disappeared across the hall. In seconds he was back with one of his T-shirts. He undressed her down to her cute little hot pink underpants, slipped the T-shirt over her head, and carried her to the bed.

"Now, sleep, darlin'. I'll wake you up in an hour." He kissed her gently on the forehead.

"Mmmm," she mumbled, but she was already dozing.

Until the clock showed that it was one o'clock he watched her sleep. Red hair going every which way; lashes resting on her cheeks; mouth barely open as she breathed so softly. He wondered what it would be like to wake up with her beside him every morning.

He touched her shoulder. "Time to wake up."

"I don't want to. Go away," she said.

"What's your name?"

"Minnie Pearl."

Wil chuckled. "Don't be silly. Just answer the questions and you can go back to sleep. Where are you?"

"At Wil's ranch and he's being mean and won't let me sleep."

"How many shots did we both have before we stopped drinking?"

"Hell, I don't remember. Nine or ten or maybe eleven. It was a tie and the sex was fabulous." She didn't open her eyes.

"Okay, that's good enough."

At two o'clock he woke her up and she told him that her name was Red Richland, that she was at his ranch, that she'd fallen down the stairs and never intended to wear high heels again.

By three o'clock he was snoozing in the rocking chair, his feet propped up on the edge of the bed. But each hour he roused both himself and her to ask her questions. And every hour she got sassier. By nine o'clock she swore if he woke her one more time that she'd never sleep with him again.

Chapter 12

A THIN LINE OF ORANGE ON THE EASTERN HORIZON promised a sunny day. The north wind had died down, which was a miracle for the first week of January in north Texas. The wind was hot, cold, or somewhere in between from Labor Day to July Fourth. Then it stopped completely and a breeze couldn't be bought, traded for, cussed up, or prayed for until Labor Day.

Pearl curled up on the end of the sofa with a soft throw over her bare feet. Her headache was nearly gone, but she felt as if she'd been awake for a solid month.

"Want another cup of coffee?" Wil asked. He'd dressed in gray sweat bottoms and a matching shirt with a picture of a bull rider on the front.

"No more coffee. Take me home."

He sat down on the other end of the sofa. "I'm too sleepy to drive. I've called Jack, my foreman, and he's taking care of chores this morning. Let's go back to bed and get some rest. I'll take you home later today."

"I'll sleep right here," she said. Her stomach growled loudly in protest, and she laid a hand on it as if her touch would quiet the grumbling.

"Breakfast first. Just something light and then sleep."

He crossed the foyer to the kitchen and poured two glasses of milk, put two toaster pastries in the toaster, and set out a plate to use when they were ready. "Don't be fallin' asleep before I get there," he yelled through the open doors.

He leaned against the cabinet beside the refrigerator and shut his eyes while he waited. When the toaster popped up the pastries, the noise woke him and he rolled his neck to get the kinks out. He hurriedly removed the hot pastries and dropped them on the plate, balanced it on the top of one of the two glasses of milk, and slowly made his way across the foyer to the living room.

"Are you awake?" he asked.

"I can open my eyes but I'm not so sure that qualifies."

"Eat and we'll take a nap. I'm too tired to do anything but sleep."

"I don't know if I've got the energy to climb back up the stairs. Why don't you sleep up there and let me rest right here?" She wasn't sure even in her tired state that she'd trust herself to get into bed with Wil. One snuggle might cause a heat that he'd have to put out before she could sleep.

"I'll carry you."

She smiled and bit off a chunk of the pastry. He ate fast, polished off the last of his milk, and stood up, scooped her up in his arms yet another time, and started for the staircase.

She looped her arms around his neck and said, "Wil, you are going to break your back carrying me around like this. I can walk. I managed to get down the stairs."

"I know, but that was because I was already down here and didn't know you were awake. Besides, I lift sacks of feed and bales of hay that weigh more than you do."

He wasn't even winded when he reached the landing.

"Put me down now. I can walk to the bathroom. I need a bath before we go to sleep. I feel all sticky and grimy."

"Okay, I'll put a clean shirt on the vanity for you," he said.

She stripped out of the T-shirt and underpants and laid them on the back of the potty before turning on the water in the tub. When she sank down into the warm water, she sighed. She adjusted the water, making it even warmer, and leaned back. Everything was still slightly fuzzy, but her head didn't hurt anymore. She vowed she would never wear high heels again. If she'd been wearing her cowboy boots she wouldn't have fallen.

The tub was extra deep and the water covered her completely when she finally turned off the faucets with her toes. Steam hung in the air like fog on a London wharf, covering the opaque shower doors, the mirrors, and even putting down a layer on the toilet seat.

Being awakened every hour was worse than getting no sleep at all. She grabbed one of the towels on the rack, rolled it into a neck pillow, and leaned back. She only meant to shut her eyes for a minute or two but when she awoke the water was cold, the steam gone, and the prickly feeling on her neck had more to do with someone staring at her than the terry cloth of the towel.

She popped her eyes open and sat up slowly, peeking out around the end of the shower door.

She grabbed the washcloth to cover her breasts. "What are you doing in here?"

"I was waiting for you to wake up so I could take a shower. I was going to give you five more minutes and then I was going crawl in with you. I've seen every bit of you up close and very personal. You can drop the washcloth and stop blushing."

"I'm not blushing," she protested even though her cheeks were blazing.

He didn't move from the potty seat. "I figured you'd be finished by now."

"What time is it?" She didn't make a move toward getting out of the chilly water.

"Almost eleven o'clock."

She popped up out of the water like a fishing bobble and wrapped a towel around her. "I need to call Lucy."

"Already did. Ten guests. They're all checked out and she's cleaning rooms." He ran a hand up her wet thigh.

"But…" she stammered.

"Yes, darlin', you have a nice butt, however, we both need sleep. We'll talk about butts later."

"Oh, hush!" She could hear him chuckling after she'd shut the door. It turned into a roar when she remembered she'd left her clothes in the bathroom, opened the door to retrieve them, and found him standing there in all his naked glory waiting for the tub to drain so he could take a shower.

The sleep she'd gotten in the tub had revived her and she was wide awake. She tried counting backward from a hundred, but that reminded her of that old song about ninety-nine bottles of beer on the wall and then she couldn't get the tune out of her head. She tried making her mind go blank, but that just provided a blank screen for pictures of Wil, most of which involved no clothing and lots of muscles, and that made her pulse race and her blood heat up to the boiling point.

She flipped from one side of the bed to the other; beat the lumps out of her pillow half a dozen times. Did Wil really mean no women were allowed in his kitchen at all, or was it only for cooking and cleanup? She tip-toed down the stairs and carefully made her way to the kitchen. She tried three different cabinet doors before she found where he kept the glasses. Leave it to a man to put them as far from the fridge as he could.

"Still hungry? Want me to cook you a real breakfast?" Wil asked from the deep shadows of the kitchen.

She jumped as if she'd been shot. "Good God Almighty! Just how far do you go to protect this kitchen? Have you got a gun hiding in the knife drawer?"

He grinned. "I'm not protecting my kitchen, Red. I was too wired to sleep so I came down here for a glass of milk so take down two glasses. We would probably sleep better if we snuggled up together. I know I would because I could stop worrying about you."

"It's been nine hours. I'm going to be all right, Wil."

He picked her up and set her on the counter. She wrapped her legs around his waist and pulled him toward her. When their lips met, she groaned.

She tucked her head into his shoulder while he breathed in the scent of her clean, still slightly damp hair.

He laughed and smacked a kiss on her forehead. "I was so worried about you. But we'd better stop makin' out. I'll pour the milk."

He set her back on the floor, poured two glasses of milk, and handed one to her. While she sipped, he turned up his glass and downed half of it. Even the way his Adam's apple bobbed was sexy that morning. She couldn't imagine having a permanent relationship with him. With the heat between them they'd burn out in a week's time and then there they'd be just like other miserable married couples. No fire. Bound together with kids and finances and wishing to hell they were anywhere else in the world but together.

"Whoa!" she said. The *m*-word set her mind going in circles.

"What did I do?"

"You drank milk. That set my mind to thinking of… well, it set me off on a merry-go-round of thoughts. I'm going to bed. I think I can sleep now."

He wiggled his heavy black eyebrows. "Sure you don't want to cuddle up next to me?"

She stood up, rinsed her glass, and put it in the dishwasher. "Too dangerous."

"Then good night." He stretched and yawned.

She refused to let him carry her up the steps and barely even muttered good night to him before tumbling into the bed again. She didn't have to count sheep or count backwards when she slipped between the sheets the second time. She shut her eyes and dreamed of Wil. He was standing in a cemetery with a bouquet of red roses. His face was a study in misery and the tombstone had one word on it… Red.

She sat up gasping for air and shivering to her toes even though she was toasty warm under the down comforter. Was the dream telling her how he would have felt if she'd broken her neck and died in the fall?

"Are you all right?" Wil asked from the bedroom door.

"Bad, bad dream. Must have been the fall messing with my head," she said.

He crossed the room in a few easy strides, sat down on the bed, and wrapped her in his arms. "You scared me when you yelled out like that."

She could hear his heart thumping like the drums in

a country band when she laid her cheek on his broad chest. "I'm fine. It was just a dream, but you can call me Red anytime you want to, and would you just lie down with me for a little while?"

Pearl felt the tenseness leave her body when he slipped beneath the covers and wrapped her up in his arms. She threw one arm over his wide chest and dreamed again of him, but that time he wasn't standing in a cemetery. They were leaning on a corral fence and he was showing her a brand new bull calf born that morning. Spring was everywhere in minty green buds on the pecan trees, yellow daffodils up against the fence row, and purple irises showing off next to the back porch.

She told him that she had to get back in the house because she was canning plum jelly that day and he kissed her long, hard, and passionately. "I'm a lucky man to have you, Red."

And she woke up to the sound of the door into the bedroom opening.

"Good evening, sleepyhead." Wil carried a wooden tray into the room. It was laden with omelets, steaming hot biscuits, bacon, coffee, juice, and even a silk daffodil in a bud vase.

She sat up. "Do you have a harem or is that all for me?"

"It can be, but I thought we'd share and no, there is no harem. One woman, namely you, Red, has brought enough chaos in my life these past few days to scare the hell right out of me." He set the tray over her lap.

Coming out of his mouth, the nickname didn't sound bad at all. She picked up the coffee first and sipped.

He kissed her soundly then crawled up beside her on the bed.

She looked up into his eyes and said, "I don't believe I've got the power to scare the hell out of you, cowboy. Mostly because I don't see any wings or a halo, so you've not got the whole hell scared out of you yet."

"Don't underestimate yourself."

She picked up a piece of bacon, crammed it inside a biscuit, and bit off a chunk. "This tastes like heaven. What time is it?"

He looked toward the window. "Five thirty."

"You are shittin' me."

He swallowed quickly to keep from spewing coffee. He slung an arm around her shoulder and squeezed. "Feelin' better?"

"Yes. Headache is gone and I'm hungry," she answered.

She looked up and their eyes met across the short distance. He leaned and she shifted and their lips locked with so much passion that it staggered Pearl. What amazed her even more was the feeling that she belonged right where she was—in his house, in his bed, and in his arms. Right there on that ranch with him forever.

The kiss deepened and Wil moved the tray to one side. He stretched out beside her, drawing her so close that her body molded to his. He rested his chin on her tousled hair and sighed. "This feels so good."

Wil Marshall was a mystery, soft and gentle, demanding and rough. All the qualities of both a good guy and a bad boy combined to keep a woman guessing. Did he have any idea how complex he was?

She sat up and pulled the T-shirt over her head. He eased her underpants off, the brush of his fingertips on her hips and thighs flaming hot embers that seemed to be ready all the time for his touch.

He jerked his shirt over his head and tossed it toward the door and swiftly removed his sweatpants. They flew through the open door and landed in the hallway. Her skin was like an aphrodisiac to him. Just touching her ribs and brushing the back of his hands over her breasts brought him to full hardness. He was ready.

She liked the gentle sex as much or more than what they'd had at the motel when their hands couldn't touch fast and furious enough. When Wil began a slow rhythm, she looked up into his eyes and got lost in the depths. What would it be like to wake up every morning to sweet love like that?

"What are you thinking?" he whispered.

"That I like this kind of sex as well as the hot stuff," she said.

"It's all hot." He chuckled.

"You got that right." She smiled.

He brought her up to the very edge of a climax then backed off and let her cool down a bit before repeating the performance. When they both reached the apex at the same time, he could see it in her eyes and gave way to the aching desire in his body. With one last thrust they both found a sweet release.

"Wow!" she said when she finally found her voice.

"Yes, ma'am," he whispered hoarsely.

The ringtone on her phone started playing "Georgia on My Mind" and she gasped. "That'll be Momma. I bet she's already called a dozen times."

Wil moved quickly off the bed, found her purse, and brought the phone back to her. She flipped it open to find that it had been her mother calling, that there were eleven text messages from her and two from Aunt Kate and one from Jasmine. That meant the whole family had heard about the unfortunate incident. Pearl pushed the right buttons and called her mother.

Tess didn't even say hello but started in on a tirade. "Pearl Richland, what in the hell is goin' on over there? I told your daddy that you didn't have a bit of business runnin' that motel. And now I find out that you've nearly got yourself killed in a strange man's house. Speak to me! Don't just sit there like a deaf and dumb donkey. I swear if I'd have known your daddy had an aunt like Pearlita I wouldn't have married the man. I could've had a good southern boy but oh, no, that damned Texas drawl and his swagger in those cowboy boots put me in heat. Now I've got to pay for it with a daughter who is just like him and acts like his brazen aunt. You should've been raised in Georgia. You haven't said a word since I picked up this phone. Speak to me, I said." Tess Landry Richland had kept her southern accent even though she'd been in Texas for years, and when she was angry or worried, it surfaced with more power than a class five tornado. Pearl had inherited her short height and her big boobs from her mother, but the rest of Pearl was pure Richland. Tess had blond hair, blue eyes, and at near sixty, a person would have to use a magnifying glass to find more than a few wrinkles. And Tess wouldn't have been caught taking out the trash without her makeup and being dressed to the nines.

"Momma, you haven't shut up long enough to let me work a word in edgewise. I'm fine. I was not hurt. I just tumbled down the stairs and got a couple of bruises on my leg and a minor concussion, which is already gone…"

"And what were you doing in a strange man's house anyway? It's the Texan blood in you. The Landrys are a respectable bunch of southern people. It's the Richlands who are renegades."

Pearl rolled her eyes.

Wil grinned and gathered up his shirt and sweat bottoms.

"Momma, can we do this later? I really need to get dressed and go home now," Pearl said.

"Well, just where are you? And how undressed are you?" Tess demanded.

"I'm at Wil's. We were up most of the night because I wasn't supposed to go to sleep for a few hours and then I took a long nap, then we had wild passionate sex right here in this bed." Pearl figured that was enough to set her mother off into a tirade that would give her enough time to snag another biscuit and another few bites of omelet.

Tess gasped so loud that Pearl was afraid she'd caused her to have an acute cardiac infarction right there in her posh Sherman, Texas, home. "Pearl, that's no way for a lady to talk to her momma. And you know I hate it when you tease about things like that and are crude like the Richlands! Dammit to hell and back! I should have never moved to Texas. I hope Mr. Marshall wasn't where he could hear such talk. Did I tell you that Jasmine has broken up with that fellow she's been keeping company with the past five years? I swear to God, I do hate to be right, but why buy the cow when you can get the milk free? And you remember I said that if you are taking milk right to that cowboy's house! Jasmine has been practically livin' with him for at least two years." Tess changed the subject and went on like she'd never heard a word about S-E-X. "Well, her poor, poor momma is mortified and fit to be tied. And it wasn't even like Jasmine caught him with another woman. She just told her poor momma, bless her heart, that they had grown apart. Now what in the hell does that mean? Tell me, what kind of woman gives that for an excuse when her momma had the whole wedding planned out for more than two years?"

Pearl swallowed quickly. "Eddie Jay has always been an asshole. He was born one and just got bigger with age. I'm glad Jasmine finally woke up. I've been telling her for years that he's a no good sumbitch. She deserves something a hell of a lot better than Eddie Jay Chandler. Got to go, Momma. Got a motel to run and rooms to clean."

"What did I do to deserve this? You're as bad as Jasmine. We should have never let you be friends with that girl," Tess said with a sigh.

"Jasmine is a decent person. She just attracts men that are worse than swamp scum. And the reason you let me be friends with her is because her momma is your very best friend."

"Good-bye, Pearl," Tess said and hung up the phone.

Pearl flipped her phone shut.

"So?" Wil asked.

"Momma says that my friend, Jasmine, has kicked out her slimy boyfriend and that I'm just a notch above causing the ruination of a fine old southern family because I spent the night in your house. I told her we'd had passionate sex but she thought I was teasing. I always have figured if you tell the truth, they'll never believe it. If she did, she'd commit me to a convent."

"That's all? You were on there a long time."

"Momma's from Georgia. Why use five words when you can spit out five hundred?"

Wil chuckled deep in his chest and his brown eyes glittered. "My momma is from Bowie, Texas. Born on a ranch. Married a cowboy and raised one. She's the same way. I think it's a mother thing instead of a regional one."

"You are probably right. Thanks for breakfast and for getting the phone for me. Would you please drive me home now?"

He wiggled his eyebrows. "Naked?"

She playfully slapped him on the arm and got a brand new set of red-hot tingles down in her gut for it. "No, I've got clothes in the bedroom."

He moved across the bed and kissed her on the cheek. Now that they were rested and fed, he was ready to spend the night in bed with her. Whether they had hot passionate sex, sweet sex, or no sex, he'd like to wake up with her beside him the next day.

She slid out of bed, snatched the last piece of bacon, and carried it with her on the way across the landing. When the phone rang again she'd just fastened the last button on her shirt. It wasn't her mother coming up to bat again because it wasn't her ringtone. She sat down on the little velvet and brass stool in front of the vanity.

"Hello," she said cautiously.

"Hi, girl, this is Jasmine. I heard this morning that you tried to fly without wings. I could have told you that you never were an angel. Not a party girl like you. Thought I'd best call and make sure you are all right."

"Momma called," Pearl said.

"Then I guess you know the dirt from this area of the swamp."

"I'm fine and Momma said you finally got rid of Eddie Jay. Good for you. I told you he was a worthless asshole."

"But he is a pretty and rich worthless asshole."

"Pretty and rich ain't so important now is it?"

Jasmine didn't hesitate for a minute. "You got it, girlfriend."

Pearl sat down on the edge of the bed. "Quit your fancy job and move over here close to me. You always wanted to own a café and there's one for sale over in Ringgold. It's even got a little apartment up above it. Come stay in one of my motel rooms and buy a café."

"Momma's already wrung out a dozen hankies with worry over what people might say. I might come over for a few days, but honey, Momma would hide in the cellar and not even go offer up Sunday morning prayers if I was a cook in a café, even if I did own it," Jasmine said.

"Well, at least come see me. I've got twenty-four extra bedrooms. You can take your choice. Are you still working at Texas Instruments?"

"Yes, but I've got some vacation time coming. Is there really a little café for sale over there in your part of the woods?"

"It's called Chicken Fried and it's got an apartment above it. Life's too short to put up with sumbitches in bed or at work."

Wil poked his head in the open door. "Need any help?"

She shook her head and pointed at the phone.

"Who do I hear? Would that be the cowboy who ruined your name last night? It's a damn good thing your momma don't know what I know, isn't it?" Jasmine giggled. "Is he really sexy?"

"All of the above, but it's time for me to go back to my motel mansion so I cannot talk right now."

Wil crossed the floor and kissed her, teased her mouth open, and tasted coffee, bacon, and juice.

"Is that sexy cowboy in the room right now? I swear I can hear you panting," Jasmine teased.

Pearl pushed Wil back and tried to give him a dirty look, but it came out with a giggle. "He is but he's leaving. Talk."

"Your momma called my momma. She called your cell phone and when you didn't answer she called the motel phone. Someone named Lucy said for them not to worry, you were fine and staying at Wil's because you had to be wakened up every hour to make sure the concussion wasn't getting any worse and that you'd probably be home later today. Your momma called the Henrietta hospital and got the whole medical story. You know she could weasel a confession out of the devil's minions. And then she called Momma and they commiserated together about their wayward daughters. And to answer your question quickly, I've really been thinkin' about quittin' my job so if you aren't serious, don't offer me a room in your motel," Jasmine said.

"I'm not telling you about the café or offering to give you a room at my motel lightly. Come on over here to Montague County. I'd love to have you close by."

"When can you talk about the cowboy?"

"Much later."

"Then I'll call much later and if you don't answer I'll call your momma."

"Don't you dare," Pearl said and hung up.

"Relatives again?" Wil asked.

"Better than relatives. That was my best friend from high school, Jasmine."

Wil brushed back his black hair and strolled past her, taking time to stop and brush a soft kiss on her neck. "Either get dressed or I'm going to undress you and make wild passionate love to you all night long. Your choice."

Pearl's better judgment won the battle of choices and she got dressed but she grumbled the whole time.

Chapter 13

THE NO VACANCY SIGN WAS FLASHING BRIGHTLY IN the semi-dusk when Wil pulled into the Longhorn Inn parking lot, but there wasn't a single car or truck in the lot. The lobby lights were on and she could see the top of Lucy's head behind the counter.

Wil was so involved with his own thoughts that he didn't even notice the VACANCY sign. His world had been flipped on its back like a turtle. No amount of waving his legs would get him back on course. He'd realized while he was driving to the motel that Pearl was the only one who could pick him up, turn him over, set him back down, and let him get on with life. And he wasn't sure about her. Not sure at all. The indecision drove him crazy. The idea of not seeing her again wasn't even a possibility.

"You've been pretty quiet since we left your ranch," Pearl said.

"Are you sure you are up to going back to work so soon? That fall was a trauma. Why don't you let Lucy run the motel and spend a couple of days with me?"

"I'm not leaving Lucy in charge. Besides, we haven't even had a date. Lots of good sex but no dates, Wil?"

He reached across the seat and touched her cheek. "You want to date, darlin'?"

"I do." She grinned.

"Well, then we will date. Tonight we will—"

"Oh, no! Not starting tonight. Lucy needs some time

off. This is Wednesday. I could be free tomorrow. What have you got in mind?"

"What's your bowling game like?"

"Oh, honey, I'm as good with a bowling ball as I am with shots."

"I'll pick you up tomorrow night at seven and we'll go bowling, have a beer and a hamburger at the alley, and I'll get Cinderella home by midnight," he said.

She laid a hand on his leg. "I'll be ready, and Wil, thanks for everything. Taking care of me, loaning me a T-shirt, staying up with me all night, all of it."

He leaned across the console and kissed her softly. "Be careful, Red. And call me if you can't sleep. I'll be here as quick as I can... no strings attached."

"I'm fine. Don't get out."

He put a hand on her arm and looked deep into her eyes. The way his eyes went all dreamy she would have stripped down to her bare skin and had wild sex with him right there in the cab of the truck if he'd asked.

"I'll sit right here until you are safely inside the lobby then."

He watched her cute little fanny sashay into the lobby. If she wanted to date, by damn, he'd give her a dating good time. When she was safely inside he backed the truck out of the parking lot and headed west back through town.

Lucy looked up when the door opened and smiled. "I've been lookin' for you all day. Your momma called and I told her what was going on. Are you all right for real? Is anything broke? Did Wil keep you up like I told him to do? You can't be lettin' somebody who cracked their head like that go to sleep."

Pearl nodded. "I'm fine, Lucy. Wil took good care of me. Momma got a hold of me. No vacancy?"

"That's right. We'll have a job tomorrow, won't we? Delilah is down in my apartment. I took her home with me so she wouldn't be lonesome," Lucy said.

"How can we have no vacancies when there are no cars out there?" Pearl asked.

"Reservations. Got a funeral going on in town and that bunch needs ten rooms so I put them all over on the west wing. Got a set of elderly couples on their way home to New Mexico after the holidays, so I put them down in the end rooms. Then there's a busload coming from an abused women's place over in Wichita Falls. They needed ten rooms for one night and wanted to know if I'd give them a discount. I gave them the senior citizen's ten percent. Was that all right?"

"Sure, it's all right. If they've got a tax number, get that and don't charge them taxes either. Why are they coming here?"

"The lady said those ten women had been compromised and they had to get them out of the place in a hurry. Tomorrow there's a place in Sherman that will take them, but they've got to get things squared around. They just needed a place to put them for one night. The bus will bring them in, unload them, and leave. Tomorrow morning the bus from Sherman will come and get them. I feel so sorry for them." Tears brimmed in Lucy's eyes and her lip quivered.

"I'm sorry, Lucy. I'll get some money out of the safe and watch the motel while you drive down to the Diamond Food store before it closes. Take the truck and get a bag of food for each of those ten rooms. Something to make sandwiches with tonight. Chips. A six-pack of Coke or Dr. Pepper. And some cookies in case there are kids coming with mothers. Get a box of donuts for their breakfast and a gallon of milk for each room in case there's kids or babies."

"Bananas or fresh fruit?" Lucy asked.

Pearl nodded. "Fruit would be good, and get whatever else you want to put in each bag. I won't let children go hungry or abused women, either."

"You are a good woman, Pearl," Lucy said.

"That's debatable. Maybe you'll be back in time to put the bags in the rooms before the bus gets here."

Lucy looked at the clock. "They said they'd be here at eight and the Sherman bus would come get them tomorrow morning at ten thirty."

Pearl shut the door into her apartment and opened the safe under the counter. She removed three one-hundred-dollar bills and handed them to Lucy. "Get going. I'll hold down the fort while you are gone. There's our first bunch of tired travelers pulling in now. I'll get them settled into rooms while you are gone."

Lucy put the money in her worn denim purse. "You sure you feel up to it? I can take care of them and then go."

"I'm sure. Get on out of here, and thanks for everything you've done."

Lucy grinned. "Wasn't nothing. Mostly what I did was worry about you."

The motel door swung open. An elderly gentleman held the door for Lucy and then stepped up to the counter. "I've got reservations for ten rooms. I understand each of your rooms has two double beds, a small refrigerator, and a microwave. We have everything from newborn babies to me." He handed her a credit card.

She shoved a card across the table. "I won't make you fill out one for each room."

"Thank goodness. Slow as I write these days we'd be here all night."

"You are all in the rooms over on the west side." She gathered keys from the pegboard behind her.

"Real keys. I like that."

"I was thinking of going with computerized locks and door cards."

"If I owned a motel, I'd never do that. They're just something fancy that will cause you a headache. These old things have worked for centuries and will still be working when all the computers in the world go ka-putz. We'll be out by nine in the morning. Our funeral is at eleven and there's a family breakfast at nine thirty."

"Thanks for letting me know. And Mr. Whitsell, I'm sorry for your loss."

"That's sweet. It was my aunt. The last of the line in that generation. She's been in a nursing home for twenty years but her mind was clear as the day she was born. A delightful old girl and the family will miss her."

He left and the next group arrived five minutes later. This time an older woman with short gray hair, wearing jeans, boots, and a denim jacket came through the door. Her lipstick had vanished but the deep wrinkles around her mouth had soaked up the remnants like Texas dirt after a hard rain in August. She reminded Pearl of Aunt Kate and she made a mental note to call her later in the week when everything settled down.

"Hello. I've got reservations under Leona Teasdale."

"Yes, ma'am, you surely do. On your way home?"

She passed her credit card over the counter to Pearl. "Yes we are. New Mexico. Back to our ranch. Love going to see the family but I'm always glad to go home."

Pearl gave her a handful of keys and a card to fill out.

Back to our ranch... The words played through Pearl's mind like they were on a continuous loop. Back to the ranch! That's where she wanted to be, but she had a motel to run.

"We are early risers. Can I sign everything tonight and leave the keys in the rooms? Pearlita always let me do it that way. I was awful sorry to hear of her passing. We've been staying here at this time of year for over twenty years. We always look forward to seeing that crazy old neon cowboy."

"Thank you. She was my great-aunt. I miss her too. And leaving the keys in the rooms will be fine."

It was a few minutes until eight when Lucy pulled the truck into a parking space in front of number six and trotted down to the lobby. "I'm back and I helped them sort the groceries into bags as we checked it out so there are ten bags out there. Here's your change." She laid a hundred-dollar bill and several coins on the counter. "I bought sale items and cheaper brands so I could stretch it out. I'll get it unloaded." Her eyes were twinkling and red spots dotted her cheeks.

Pearl had never seen her so excited. "I'll help you."

"You might not ought to be liftin' so soon."

"I'm just fine, Lucy. The headache is even gone now and my vision is clear as a bell. It was just a fall, not a major catastrophe."

"Well, Wil sure sounded like he was scared to death," Lucy argued.

"Come on. We've only got a few minutes to get the stuff in the rooms. You need my help."

"Okay, but if you get dizzy or winded you tell me. I figured we'd put the milk, meat, and cheese in the refrigerator. Then we'd just leave the rest in the bag and let them do whatever they want with it. I got a loaf of bread, some bananas, chips, juice boxes for kids, and cookies. I didn't buy Cokes though. Figured the milk would be better for everyone. I also got a box of cereal and some of those cheap Styrofoam cups and plastic spoons. That way they can have breakfast," she said as she led the way to the truck.

"You didn't use your money, did you, Lucy?"

"No. I used what you gave me. The lady at the store asked me what I was doing and I told her it was a charity case. I was afraid to tell that it was abused women for fear it would get them in trouble. She said the bananas were going on sale tomorrow so she let me have them at sale price. Then she looked at the sale bill for tomorrow and the milk was on it so I got it cheaper too. The rest I just got the cheap brands. Oh, I nearly forgot." Lucy dug in the pocket of her sweat bottoms. "Here's the ticket in case you need it to prove anything on your taxes."

Pearl shoved it down into the hip pocket of her jeans. "You did really well, Lucy."

"I'm used to making money go a long way. Cleet never did too well with a job. I thought about tellin' the lady at the store about the women comin' in so she'd feel good about lettin' me have the sale prices, but I was afraid to."

"That was smart. We wouldn't want the women in trouble again."

Lucy nodded. "She didn't charge me tax since it was for charity so that helped too."

The bus pulled into the lot seconds after Lucy and Pearl finished their job. A short man with premature gray in his temples got out and held the lobby door open for them.

"I am Luke Cornell. I believe we have ten rooms reserved."

"Yes, you do. I talked to you," Lucy said.

"And you own this place?"

"No, sir, I just work here. Pearl owns the Longhorn Inn and she's been kind enough to put some food in each room for the women."

"Thank you. They will appreciate it. They had supper but…" The man let the sentence hang.

"I'm sorry," Lucy said.

"These things happen. We had a client who went back to her husband and wasn't very discreet. All of these women have children so they'll be glad to see food in their rooms. I'll get them settled and the Sherman folks will pick them up tomorrow morning. I don't think there'll be any trouble. We got them out the minute we realized which ones had been compromised."

Pearl handed him ten keys and picked up the check, but her heart wouldn't let her put it in the cash drawer. "I'm going to let you have these rooms at half price and you tell any shelters in this area if they need to use this motel as an underground service for abused women that they can have the rooms for half price. I can take it off my taxes. Here's your change for the other half." She put a couple of hundred-dollar bills and a fifty in his hand. "I'll just need you to sign a paper for me."

"Be glad to do that. You are a good person. You been abused?"

"No, I have not. Got too much temper for that."

"Well, God bless you! Too bad you couldn't give some of that to these women and my sister. I tried to get her out of the situation she was in, but she wouldn't have none of it. The last time around she died. I drive the bus for these people as a payback and tell her story for her in hopes that it will wake some of these women up."

"Bless *your* heart," Lucy said.

He left and escorted each woman and her children from the bus to a motel room.

Lucy watched from the window and when the last one stepped out of the bus, tears flooded her cheeks. The woman was barely more than a child, a skinny girl that didn't look to be more than eighteen carrying a baby with a diaper bag thrown over her shoulder and two toddlers struggling to keep up beside her.

"That could've been me," Lucy whispered.

Pearl patted her shoulder and headed back to her apartment. "But you got out of it, Lucy. And you've got a job and your dignity back. They'll have the same. It just might take them a while because they do have children."

"My heart hurts for them, especially that last one."

"I'm leaving. Wanted to thank you one more time," Luke said as he made his way from the door to the counter.

Lucy looked up. "Can you tell me about that last one? We could see a little by the light above the lobby door and she looked so young."

"She looks young but she's twenty. Got pregnant with

those twin boys when she was eighteen. Married the man and he began to beat her after they were born. She says he was good until he lost his job in all this economic mess, then he started layin' around drinkin' because he didn't have anything to do. She got pregnant again and the baby is six months old. The husband got mad last week and slung one of those boys against the wall and beat the hell out of her when she picked the baby up to comfort him. She waited until the husband went to sleep and walked out with nothing but the clothes on her back, a bottle of milk for the baby, and ten dollars. She'd heard of us somehow and walked three miles with those kids to our shelter. She's tough and she's finished taking abuse. Don't worry about her. And thanks again for the food. They were excited to have it. And many thanks for the half price rate."

"You want a cup of coffee before you go back?" Lucy asked.

"That'd be nice," Luke said.

Lucy motioned toward the chairs. "Have a seat over there and I'll get you one."

"Pearl?" she whispered as she eased the apartment door open.

"In the bathroom," Pearl said.

"All right if I get some coffee?"

"Help yourself."

He'd barely sat down before she was back with two mugs in her hand. She handed him one and sat down in the recliner beside him.

"I'm sorry about your sister. I was nearly to that point when I left."

"I could see in your eyes that you had problems

before. You can get out of it, but getting the pain out of you ain't so easy," Luke said.

"You sure got that right. What makes a man like that?"

He sipped the coffee. "Lots of excuses but not one damn good reason for a man to ever treat a woman like anything but a queen."

She nodded.

He set the cup down and stood up. "Thank you, Lucy. Maybe I'll come by sometime when I'm not driving a bus for the shelter. I work at the Department of Human Services over in Wichita Falls. Maybe you'd go get an ice cream cone with me sometime?"

"I'd like that," Lucy said with a bright smile.

"Okay, then, I'll call sometime. I'm in this area once a month, usually on a Wednesday," he said.

Lucy nodded. She wanted to jump up and down and dance, but she kept her cool until Luke was in the bus. Then she hopped up, ran to the apartment door, and knocked on it.

"I see a glow on your face." Pearl smiled as she answered the door.

"His name is Luke and he's a decent man and he asked if I'd go get an ice cream with him some Wednesday when he's in this area and I said I'd never even look at another man and I'm still married and what do I do because I like him?" Lucy said in one breath.

"Lucy, I've got a lawyer friend in Sherman who can take care of that marriage thing in a very quiet way. And what you do if you are attracted to that feller is go eat ice cream with him and tell him your story."

"Really? You'd do that for me?" Lucy asked.

"Oh, yeah! Now I'll take care of the motel. You go on and think about Luke." Pearl laughed.

"Never say never," Lucy mumbled as she rinsed the two cups and put them in the dishwasher. "I'm going on to my room now. Me and Delilah are going to spend a while reading after I feed her. She's a good cat. You ever want to get rid of her I'd sure like to have her as mine."

"Lucy, you are welcome to find a cat or a kitten of your own. There are advertisements in the paper all the time for free kittens."

Lucy's face registered pure joy. "You serious?"

"Yes, I am."

"I want a yellow one just like Delilah. You call me if you need anything. If you feel dizzy or like you are going to faint or anything like that."

"I promise I will," Pearl said.

Lucy nodded seriously and left the door into the lobby open as she left.

⁓

Pearl was alone and it felt strange. "Chaos," she said. She'd barely gotten the word out of her mouth when her phone rang. She fished it out of her purse and hurriedly said, "Hello!"

"Hi, Red. I can't sleep. Are you all right? Talk to me a while," Wil said.

She smiled. "Of course I'm all right. I was about to read until time to turn out the lights. I'm not sleepy either after sleeping all day. But tomorrow is going to be a stinker. We've got a full house."

"Well, I'm too wired to sleep and now I'm thinking

about tomorrow night. We could do something other than bowling if you want."

"I haven't been bowling in months. I'd love to go. And a good old greasy hamburger and a cold beer sounds wonderful," she said.

"Just don't want any other cowboy to come along and offer you something more exciting," he said.

"Honey, I barely have time for one cowboy in my life right now," she said.

He danced a jig right there in the bedroom and Digger looked at him like he had clean lost his human mind.

"I'm glad. I wouldn't want there to be two cowboys in your life," he said.

"Hey, it's all I can do to keep up with the cowboy who puts things that trip me up at the top of his stairs just so I'll spend the night with him."

"Awww, I wouldn't do that to my favorite red-haired lady," he drawled.

Her heart skipped a beat. So she was his favorite red-haired lady, was she? Who was his favorite blonde? A wide band of green jealousy wrapped itself around her heart.

The business phone rang before she could think of a comeback. "Gotta run. Business calls on the other phone."

"Call me if you have a change of heart. I can be there in less than ten minutes."

"I will." She hung up and made a dive for the phone before it went to the fourth ring and the answering machine.

"Longhorn Inn, may I help you?" she said.

"Either I just interrupted the best sex in the world or you are cleaning. Those are the only two things

I can think of that would make you that breathless," Austin said.

"Well, it damned sure wasn't sex or I'd have hung up on you and went back to it. Hell, if it had been that good I wouldn't have even answered the phone."

Austin giggled. "Get a cold beer. Sit down and we'll talk while you take a break."

"That I can do because I wasn't cleanin' or havin' good sex," Pearl said.

"I'm coming to Henrietta tomorrow and I'll either bring hamburgers from the Dairy Queen or we can go there to eat. But I couldn't wait that long to hear the story from the horse's mouth. Ever since you were a kid, trouble has followed you."

"Chaos," Pearl said.

"One and the same. So start talking and only stop when you get a drink of beer."

Pearl laughed. "You'd better bring hamburgers here because Lucy and I've got a full house tonight. We'll be cleanin' rooms all day long tomorrow. Now where do you want me to start and are you planning on getting any sleep tonight?"

"Rye is out coon huntin' with his brothers. If I get sleepy we'll put it on pause and do the rest tomorrow."

Pearl took a long swig of beer and started. "Once upon a time there was a red-haired fairy who—"

Austin laughed so hard. "You, darlin', were never a fairy. You were born with horns that I had to clip when you were a kid. Wings were never your thing so why in the hell did you think you could fly down a flight of stairs?"

"Who's tellin' this story?"

"Okay, red-haired fairy child, go on."

Pearl grinned, settled into the corner of the sofa, and told her story.

―᠁᠁―

Wil surfed through the channels on television but nothing took his attention. He and Digger took a long walk out around the barn, checked on the cattle, the moon, and the stars, and went back inside when Wil's nose was so cold it began to ache.

Digger raised his head and perked up his ears. He looked toward the door and growled deep in his throat.

"I hear it," Wil said.

He hoped that the vehicle they both heard would be Pearl. He was halfway across the floor when the doorbell rang. He peeked out the triangular pane of glass at the top of the door to see the three O'Donnell brothers: Rye, Raylen, and Dewar.

He slung the door open and said, "Come on in. Want a beer?"

"No, we got cold ones in the back of the truck. Thought maybe you'd like to go do some coon huntin' with us. Put on some warm boots and bring old Digger. He'll like the run," Rye said as all three men filed into the foyer.

"Give me five minutes. Y'all make yourselves at home." Wil took the stairs two at a time. Coon hunting took a second seat to an evening with Pearl, but it might get him out of the wide-awake doldrums.

"Man, that wasn't five minutes. If I'd have known you could get ready that fast I wouldn't have even took off my coat," Raylen said when Wil came down the stairs fully dressed carrying his shotgun.

"I slept all day. Spent the night up with Red so she wouldn't fall asleep, and then we slept all day and now I'm wide awake. I'm glad y'all showed up," he said.

Raylen slipped his arms back into his buff-colored work coat and grinned. "You slept with Pearl?"

"Yep, I did, as in shut your eyes and go to sleep." Wil whistled for Digger and headed for the truck. "How we going to do this?"

"We got Blue, Amos, and Moses in the pens in the back. Last time Digger didn't have a problem with old Moses. We could put him in there with him or he can sit up between you and Raylen in the backseat," Rye said.

"Throw him in with Moses," Wil said.

Rye opened the tailgate and Digger hopped up on it. He unfastened the cage that housed Moses and Digger ducked his head and went straight inside. He and Moses touched noses and sat down beside each other.

"Looks like they're goin' to get along fine," Raylen said.

All four men got into the truck and Rye drove around back of the house, down the tractor path, behind the barn, and to the very edge of Wil's land. Back where it hadn't been cleared off and the pecans, oaks, and mesquite created thickets of trees that attracted coons, coyotes, and possums.

They unloaded and turned the dogs loose. Moses gave a mournful old howl and led the pack into the woods. Men followed dogs in a trot. The dogs stopped at the base of a pecan tree that was all of thirty feet tall. A possum hung on a low limb from its tail, his beady little eyes tormenting the dogs.

"Digger, you know that's not a coon. Nose like yours can't be fooled by a stupid possum. Go on," Wil said.

Digger put his nose to the ground and took off with the rest of the dogs behind him.

"You got a thing for Pearl Richland?" Raylen asked.

Wil removed his cap and raked his fingers through his hair. "Hell, I don't know. It started out on Christmas Eve and has been something wild goin' on ever since. Might just be adrenaline."

Raylen clapped a hand on his older brother Rye's shoulder. "Remember when you first saw Austin? Wasn't no doubts there. You was plumb in love from day one. Colleen didn't think Austin would convert from city girl to country girl but she did. Hard to believe they can give up them high-heeled shoes, ain't it? Maybe you done stood too close to Rye and got yourself a case of lovesick blues like he had, Wil. Only one way to cure them kind of blues and that's to marry the girl."

"I wasn't that bad from day one. It took at least to day two." Rye laughed. "Moses is baying. They've got one treed."

"What's your plans with Pearl?" Dewar took off in a slow jog.

"I don't know. It's complex and confusin'. Why are you askin'?" Wil followed.

"If you was in love, I wouldn't want to get in your way. I might've got in Rye's way with Austin, but we could all see from the first that they belonged together. But if you ain't sure, then I might be interested myself. Always did have a thing for redheads and I liked her the first time Colleen brought her to the house. Just been draggin' my feet."

Jealousy flared up in Wil's soul. Instant, red-hot

jealousy that he'd never felt before. "I'd appreciate a little time, Dewar. Maybe a month or two."

"You got it. How about if you ain't sure by Valentine's Day then I'm free to take her dancing," Dewar said.

"Sounds more than fair to me."

"I don't know. Maybe I ought to give ol' Wil some more time. He's kind of slow. Now if it was Ace who had her marked for his territory, it would be a different story. I saw him checkin' her out at the New Year's Eve party, but he already had a woman hanging on him and he couldn't do anything about it," Dewar said.

Wil slapped him on the shoulder. "Don't be callin' me slow, partner. I ain't the only one that's still single. Now that Rye's married, you are next in line. You better hurry up or else Gemma is going to find a wife for you."

Dewar grinned. "I like a girl with some spunk and a little temper. Makes for an interesting life. I wouldn't want a woman who walks behind me and puts up with my bullshit. I want one that'll stand up for herself and back me up. I see that in Pearl."

"Y'all tryin' to railroad me into something?"

"Naw, man, we just visitin' while we're out huntin' come coons. There goes Moses again. We'd best find what he's got treed," Rye said.

Austin grilled Pearl for details about who won the shot challenge, but all she got was that they both passed out after the exact same amount of liquor. She wouldn't be pinned down to whether or not she and Wil had done anything more than sleep in the same room that night.

Finally, at midnight, Austin yawned and said that she

was hanging up but that she expected more details at lunch the next day. She'd bring hamburgers for Lucy, Pearl, and herself, along with chocolate malts and French fries. According to Austin, calories and fat grams melted away to nothing when women were in the middle of a gossip fest.

Pearl barely hung up when the phone rang again. She checked the caller ID and flipped the phone open. "Hello, Jasmine."

"How'd you know it was me?"

"Caller ID. It still comes up E&J. So it had to be you or Eddie Jay, and if it was that sumbitch and I said your name, he'd hang up on me which would be fine. He never was good enough for you and I knew it from the beginning, but you wouldn't listen, no sir," Pearl said.

"Who died and made you a prophet?" Jasmine asked.

Pearl giggled. "Dammit! I didn't know that when someone died I got to be a prophet and got my own keys to the pearly gates. I thought those keys come in the mail. I been checkin' every day for my whole life and now you tell me someone has to die. Well, hell's bells!"

Jasmine's laughter was so loud that Pearl wondered if the young mother in room one right next door heard it.

"You are so damn good for me. I may move to Henrietta or where was that other place? Ringgold?" Jasmine said between the hiccups that the laughter had left behind.

"Come right on, darlin'. If you ever get the itch for another man, I know a couple of sexy-as-hell cowboys named Raylen and Dewar who are yummy."

"What about that cowboy who you spent the night with? Is he yummy?" Jasmine asked.

"Yes, he is, but we slept all day. Together, yes. Sex, no."

"Fallin' down a flight of stairs scared you, did it? You was afraid to do any more sinnin' because you're afraid that you done sinned enough for a whole month?" Jasmine asked.

"Something like that."

"So you had sex with him after you slept with him all day? You can't beat around the bush with me, girlfriend. I'm the queen of that art!"

"How in the world did you find out so quick about my accident? Oh, I forgot that Momma..."

"Yep, that's right. Your momma told my momma all about it."

"God bless! That woman can find out more in two phone calls than a detective could in six months. They ought to give her a badge and a gun. She'd clean up the whole state of Texas."

"She's a mother. They're naturally nosy," Jasmine said.

"Okay, enough about me. Tell me the dirt. Why did you really decide to kick Eddie Jay out? Come on, girl, 'fess up."

"Jadeen Jones."

"No shit!"

"Yep, and I think it's been goin' on for about a year now that I've seen that son of hers. He's just a baby but he's the spittin' image of Eddie Jay. Blond hair and blue eyes. And guess what else? Kid's name is Jay Edward. Crazy thing is he kept telling me we weren't ready to get married and have kids. Guess that part of his life was saved for Jadeen and I was just the fool who kept house for him, cooked for him, and picked up his clothes at the dry cleaners. Can't you just see his mother if he marries

Jadeen after all the things she's said about her since we were kids?"

Pearl opened another beer and sat down at the kitchen table. "Sorry, darlin'."

"Thank you. Crazy thing is I hope he does marry Jadeen. Kid shouldn't be raised up without a father, even if he is a worthless sack of shit like Eddie Jay."

Pearl remembered the women in ten rooms of her motel that night. She wouldn't wish Eddie Jay Chandler on a single one of them or Jadeen either. No woman deserved to be physically abused. Or mentally, and Eddie Jay was a pro at the latter. Jasmine was a helluva lot better off without the fool.

Chapter 14

PEARL OVERSLEPT THE NEXT MORNING. WHEN SHE AWOKE Lucy had checked everyone out of the motel and was busy cleaning rooms. She dressed in a hurry and rushed out to room four where she and Lucy fell into their normal routine. But the song in her heart that kept playing over and over was that she had a date with Wil that night. A real date with just the two of them and she was giddy just thinking about it.

"What are you thinking about?" Lucy asked.

"Why?"

"You've got a smile, but you are blushing."

"It's the rushin' around that got me all flustered," Pearl said.

"You sure it's not your head?" Lucy narrowed her eyes.

"I'm sure, Lucy. Positive sure. Other than a bruise on my leg and one on my shoulder, nothing is wrong. Wil asked me out on a real date tonight. We need to talk about how many nights a week you want to work in addition to the cleaning duties."

"All of them," Lucy said.

"That's not right. How about you work Monday and Tuesday, take Wednesday off in case Luke ever calls, and then work Thursday and Friday. And we'll split the weekend according to whoever has plans. I'd like to have Saturday night this weekend if that's all right with you and you can take off on Sunday night."

"That sounds more than good to me. I love working the desk, Pearl. It makes me feel like I'm somebody," Lucy said.

Pearl touched Lucy on the shoulder and she didn't flinch. "You are very important, Lucy Fontaine. Don't you ever forget it."

Lucy nodded and pushed the cart to the next room where she'd strip beds, vacuum, and clean the bathroom. Pearl would come in behind her to make the beds and restock towels and toiletries.

Pearl was putting out towels in the room Lucy had just left when her phone vibrated in her pocket. She grabbed it and read the text message: *Miss me?*

She typed back: *Yes.*

Lunch in an hour?

Instead of or in addition to bowling?

The phone rang before she could type in another message.

"Hello?"

"Do you really miss me? You sound all sexy. Did I ever tell you that I like the gravel in your voice? It turns me on," he said.

"Wil!"

"Well, it does. I was teasing about lunch. I've got too much to do today to get away. I'll pick you up this evening."

"I'll be ready."

He chuckled and hung up the phone. He'd never met anyone like her and that scared the devil out of him. The sex was fabulous. She was witty and fun. But what if all she wanted was a good time? That could be a heartache in the making because he wanted so much more.

———~~~———

Pearl dressed in jeans and a dark green sweater. She wore her cowboy boots and picked up a bag with her shoes and bowling ball in it. She'd never dated until Vince came into her life that summer. She and Jasmine talked about boys until they came close to fraying the subject at the corners, but neither of them ever found a boy that really took their eye.

Then Vince changed her life when he asked her if she'd like a ride home on his big Harley motorcycle. He'd lived next door to her their entire lives. They'd played together as children, but he'd been too perfect for Pearl with his blond hair and pretty blue eyes. He seldom ever said a word to anyone, and he made perfect grades in school and never, ever got into trouble. Then it all changed. He let his hair grow long and although he kept up his grades he was constantly into trouble.

She had crawled on the back of his cycle and that had started it. She was in love. There was lots of heated making out sessions but they waited until graduation night for the big event. Her folks thought she was at Jasmine's so she had the night covered. His were waiting up when he got home at dawn. They knew which motel he'd been in and that Pearl had been with him. If he went away to his grandmother's in Wyoming, they wouldn't bring the Richlands in on the knowledge.

They took his cycle, his cell phone, and his credit cards. He wrote her two letters, which she still had tied with a ribbon in her keepsake box on the attic. The first told her what had happened and that he'd write every day.

She waited every day for the letters that never came. Until a month later the second one showed up in the mailbox. It was the most difficult letter he'd ever had to write but he had to do it. He'd been acting out, fighting the true calling in his life. The next day he was dedicating his life to God and planned to become a priest. In time, he would go to Africa and do mission work. He was sorry that he'd gotten her tangled up in his rebellion and he'd love her always but his first and true love was God.

And that's when Pearl Richland's heart broke into a million pieces. She declared she'd never give her heart to another man to be shattered again. She'd date. She'd have fun. But serious relationships weren't for her. Then Marlin came along and proved it all over again.

She looked into the mirror.

"And that brings me to today. Have I changed my mind?" she asked.

"Pearl, you alone back here?" Lucy called out.

"Come on in. I'm just getting ready. Is Wil out there yet?"

"He just now drove up."

Those five words erased every single thought of Vince and her first dates. By the time Wil was in the lobby she couldn't have remembered a single date during the last twelve years. She only had eyes for Wil.

"Well, look at this; you've got your own bag and shoes. I'm impressed." Wil took the bag from her and slipped the other arm around her shoulders.

"It's not my first time," she teased.

"Aha, and I thought I was going to show you up," he said.

"I don't think so, cowboy." She giggled.

"Y'all have a good time and don't hurry home. I'll turn out the lights at eleven," Lucy said.

"Thanks, Lucy," Pearl said over her shoulder as Wil steered her out to the truck.

Wil opened the door for her, leaned in to give her a scorching hot kiss, and then whistled "Hello Darlin'" by Conway Twitty as he rounded the front of the truck and crawled into the driver's seat.

"You look gorgeous tonight," he said as he started the engine.

"And you look sexy as hell." She slid across the bench seat to sit close to him.

After all, it was a date!

Chapter 15

IF SHE HADN'T GOTTEN DISTRACTED BY THOSE TIGHT jeans stretched across his damn fine butt she might not have rolled that gutter ball. And if she hadn't then she would have beat him, but when the tally was done, he had four more points than she did.

"You're pretty good," he said as he removed his shoes and slipped his feet back into his boots.

"Looks like you're a little better than pretty good." She sat down in his lap and planted a kiss on his lips right there in the bowling alley.

"Hell, I'd gladly let you win for a few more of those. Look at that team over there. They are all jealous!" he whispered.

"Poor babies. Let's get a hamburger and a beer and check into that motel next door," she said.

"Are you serious?"

"Oh, yeah. You know what watching you stretch out like that does to a woman's hormones? That women's team over there is ready for drooling bibs."

He chuckled.

She stood up and picked up her bag.

"You were joking, right?" he asked.

She winked.

They ordered burgers and beers and ate slowly with Wil wondering if she was teasing. Pearl kept wondering if she should tell him that this wasn't her normal dating life. She liked to go out, but she did not fall into bed with every man who took her to a rodeo or a movie.

On the way out of the bowling alley, he slung an arm around her shoulder and drew her close to his side. Things got so hot in the truck cab that Pearl opened one eye to see if the windows were steamed up. It surprised her that the stars were twinkling brightly and there was no fog on the windows.

He pulled back and untucked his shirt. "Dammit! We're going to have to quit or get a room for sure."

She laid a hand on his zipper and grinned. "I vote for a room."

"Are you sure?"

"I am," she said.

He drove to the Hampton Inn and parked. She was out of the truck by the time he was and grabbed his hand, lacing her fingers in his. The memory of the only other time she'd checked into a motel surfaced but only for a minute. That night she'd been nervous and unsure about what she was about to do. With Wil, she was absolutely confident and wanting what was about to happen.

He paid cash for a room, signed in as Mr. and Mrs. Wil Marshall, and told the lady one key would be enough. When they were in the elevator he pushed the button for the second floor and turned to kiss her. She hopped up into his arms, wrapped her legs around his body and her arms around his neck. When the doors opened they were so deep into the making out session that neither of them realized it until the doors closed and they started back down.

He chuckled and pressed the button for the second floor again. That time he paid attention and carried her, wrapped around him, to the room with the picture of the Adirondack chair beside the door. He slid the key down the slot, opened the door and carried her inside the room, kicked it shut with his boot heel, and they tumbled onto the king-sized bed together.

A flurry of clothes being tossed across the room was followed by heated kisses, moans and groans, and steamy hot sex. Her hands were cold as snow, hot as a branding iron, and smooth as satin when they guided him inside her. Her last thought before she gave herself over to the rocking motion of him making love to her was that she should tell him that she wasn't really that kind of woman. But she couldn't utter a word other than, "Oh, Wil!"

He found the faint taste of hamburger and beer to be a heady combination, and the way she shivered when he nibbled on her earlobe made him smile. Red was hot as hell in and out of the bedroom.

"You are so beautiful and so soft," he mumbled.

"And you are making me so, so hot," she said.

It wasn't Wil's most stellar moment in the bedroom and didn't last nearly long enough to suit him, but when it was over Red curled up in his arms and asked him if he could feel the afterglow.

"I always thought that was a bunch of hogwash until you," he said as he pulled her close enough that her head rested on his shoulder.

"Me too," she said.

He felt like he was walking on water. So among all those other boyfriends she'd had, at least he'd given her the afterglow.

He walked her to the lobby door at four thirty the

next morning, after a second helping of steaming hot sex and breakfast at Denny's restaurant. He circled his arms around her and held her tightly to his chest.

"Damn fine date," she said.

"Not as good as tomorrow night's will be," he told her. "We're going to Mingus, Texas, to do some Honky Tonk dancin'."

"You are kiddin' me," she said.

"Not in the least, darlin'. You said you wanted to date. Well, we are going to date. Get some rest, sweetheart." He brushed a kiss across her lips.

He was in the lobby at five thirty the next evening and they drove to Mingus. Before they went to the Honky Tonk, Wil stopped at the Smokestack Restaurant and they had chicken fried steaks for supper.

"No wonder Sharlene liked this place. This would run the Chicken Fried some competition," she said.

Wil grinned. He'd show her that he could come up with fine ideas to date, by damn. By the time a week was over, she wouldn't even think about those fellows who kept calling.

It was a night of two-stepping to country music by the old artists that Pearl loved and drinking beer from Mason jars. And Wil could dance! From the time he wrapped his arms around her and two-stepped her around the dance floor, she was floating on air. Good country music. Dancing with the sexiest cowboy in the place and four beers turned her on hotter'n a fox in a forest fire.

They didn't leave until the place shut down at two o'clock, and when they got back to Henrietta she spent the rest of the night at the ranch house with him. The sex was great and she slept like the dead when it was over. It was full daylight when they awoke and Lucy was already cleaning rooms when Wil took her home.

"Tomorrow is Lucy's day off so we can't go anywhere." She yawned.

"I'll pick you up at three for banana splits at the Dairy Queen and then we'll play in the kiddy park. You ever been swinging in the wintertime?"

She shook her head.

"Well, darlin', think about wrapping your legs around my waist and kissing me while the swing is going as high as my legs can pump," he whispered.

She shivered.

"Yep, and then we'll have an hour or two before you have to check in guests. Your place or mine?"

"I'll have an empty room, I'm sure," she said.

On Monday he came by and they went to the movies and he didn't even complain when she wanted to watch a chick flick. They got home early that night and fell into bed together in room twenty-five.

While she slept in her afterglow state, he propped up on an elbow. It had been fun. Hell, it had been great. But was this what he really wanted? A party every night?

No, I want a woman to settle down with. I want stability, not just insane sex.

She opened her eyes and saw doubt in his. "What's the matter?"

"Nothing, darlin'. I'm played out. I'm going to get dressed and go on home."

"Okay," she mumbled. "I'll see you tomorrow then."

He kissed her on the forehead and she was asleep by the time he locked the door behind him.

—⁓—

On Tuesday he woke up with an excellent idea for a cowboy date. She'd had the city boy dates. Bowling, movies, dancing… well, the Honky Tonk couldn't really be considered city boy but it was dancing.

He called Pearl the minute he was awake. "I'll pick you up at five tonight," he said.

"Where are we going?" she asked. Dammit! But she was tired. She wouldn't mind staying in and watching a movie on television or just cuddling on the sofa.

"It's a surprise. Wear jeans."

"You are one sneaky devil." She grinned.

"Yes, I am so be ready."

At noon while she and Lucy were cleaning rooms her phone rang. Hoping it was Wil telling her more about the secret date, she answered without looking at the caller ID and said, "Hello!"

"That sounds like a come-hither voice rather than a BFF voice." Austin laughed.

"I thought you were Wil. He's been winin' and dinin' me until I'm exhausted and tonight we are going out and he won't tell me where we are going but to wear jeans," she said.

Austin laughed. "Sounds like you and Wil are getting along pretty damn good."

"We are right now but it could all be adrenaline. When the adrenaline has settled there might not be anything there. Remember what that old country song said about there is nothing as cold as ashes after the fire is gone," Pearl said.

Austin laughed. "Yep, but if the fire don't go out, what a helluva life, girlfriend."

"He said for me to wear jeans. Got any ideas?"

"Not a one. Rye and I had an amazing date one night on the banks of the Red River. The cowboys in this area are very imaginative when it comes to wooing women." Austin giggled. "Have fun and I'll expect to hear from you tomorrow."

Wooing women stuck in Pearl's mind and she grinned all afternoon. Whether she was ready to be wooed or not, it might prove to be an interesting evening. No one had ever taken her to the river for a date.

Lucy ran back and forth from lobby to apartment while Pearl put on her makeup and fixed her hair.

"I told you that Wil Marshall had that look in his eye," Lucy said.

"What if he turns out like Cleet?"

"It won't happen. Give him a chance. He looks at you all soft-eyed and he's one hot cowboy." Lucy giggled.

Pearl scrunched up her hair with gel and let it hang in natural curls. "I don't know about the soft-eyed stuff, but you got that hot cowboy right."

Lucy was behind the desk when Wil arrived. He wore a pair of faded Wranglers and well-worn boots. His denim jacket fit tight, but to Lucy's way of thinking he should have been wearing a sports jacket and carrying a rose in his hands. Her friend and boss deserved the best and she was getting far less.

"Evenin', Lucy. Is Red...?"

"Right here." Pearl stepped out of the apartment. She

wore designer jeans, boots, and a Western cut shirt with pearl snaps.

His eyes started at the tips of her boots and slowly made their way up to her beautiful red curls. "Well, you look almighty fetchin' tonight, Miz Red."

"Thank you," she said. She'd had men undress her with their eyes, but one had never made love to her with his eyes. From toe to eyebrows, every one of her nerve endings tingled at the way he looked at her.

She pushed through the swinging door at the end of the counter and he took her hand in his.

"Good night, Lucy," she called as he led her across the floor.

"Don't wait up," Wil threw over his shoulder.

"Can I take Delilah home with me?" Lucy hollered at the last minute before they were out the door.

"Yes, you can," Pearl said.

He opened the passenger door to his truck for her, but before she hopped up into the seat he wrapped her up in his arms and kissed her hard as if they'd been apart for the whole week instead of just a day.

All day she'd tried to weigh pros and cons. To think about how badly she'd wanted off the ranch when she was in high school, especially after Vince had left her to chase after his true calling. But that feeling of Wil's ranch being right where she belonged hovered overhead like a big white fluffy cloud and no amount of thinking could make it disappear.

Then Wil walked through the door, smelling all yummy and looking like one of those old commercials for Marlboro cigarettes; she wondered why she even fought with herself. He wasn't a bad boy once she'd gotten to know him. He was a great person, a wonderful caring man, so why was she fighting against her heart?

She'd figured they were going to a steak house in Wichita Falls for dinner. When they turned north toward Petrolia she thought maybe he'd forgotten something at the ranch. She looked over at him but he was tapping his thumb against the steering wheel to a Blake Shelton tune on the radio.

"Are we going to Wichita Falls?" she asked.

"Nope."

She adjusted her dinner plans to something in Petrolia. She'd never been there so she didn't know if the town was the size of Ringgold, Henrietta, or Wichita Falls. She'd always thought it was a little place like Ringgold or maybe Terral, but Austin had said the cowboys in this area were inventive so maybe it had a world-class barbecue café. Smoked ribs with extra sauce and coleslaw on the side sounded pretty damn good.

He turned down the lane to his house and kept going down a path toward a barn sitting back in the distance. Forget the barbecue or the steak unless he was grilling out behind the barn.

"Where *are* we going?" she asked.

"To dinner." He grinned and stopped the truck in front of the barn.

She had her seat belt undone and the door open by the time he circled the truck.

"Oh, no you don't." He swept her up in his arms. "Tonight you are the princess, Red."

"What?"

"You heard me. You are the princess and I'll take care of you."

"Role-playing?" she asked.

"No, statin' facts, ma'am. I don't role-play. I'm a cowboy to the core, but tonight you are my princess or hostage or maybe just my cowgirl in tight-fittin' jeans." He strolled into the barn like he was carrying a feather pillow.

"I'm afraid I'll have to ask you to climb the ladder, though. It's too narrow for both of us," he said.

Austin had been right. These cowboys did have an imagination. He set her down gently and motioned for her to go first. When she was on the fourth rung, he kissed her fanny and started up behind her. The sight at the top staggered her.

"Oh, my!" she gasped.

"You sit here." He motioned toward a quilt on the floor.

Her green eyes were big as silver dollars as she sat down. Small bales of hay lined the walls and candles in pint jars flickered light even in the darkest shadows. A short table in the middle of the quilt was spread with all kinds of finger delicacies. Cubed cheese and ham, crackers, fancy little sandwiches, and a cascade of fresh fruit. She reached out for a grape and he picked up her hand.

"No, my lady. You cannot feed yourself tonight. That is this old cowboy's privilege." He kissed her fingertips and then traveled up her arm to her neck to her ear and to her lips.

When she was ready for more than kisses, he stopped and put a grape between his teeth and leaned forward. She had no idea that a grape kiss could be so damn sensuous. In four bites she'd be ready to throw the dinner out the loft window and forget about food.

He put a piece of cheddar cheese in her mouth and licked her lips.

She moaned.

"Good cheese?" He grinned.

"Damn fine cheese," she said when she'd swallowed.

"Ham?"

She nodded.

He fed her the ham and while she chewed he brushed her hair away from her neck and planted long, slow, lingering kisses from shoulder to cheek without ever touching her lips.

She picked up a piece of cheese and he shook his head. With a grin she touched his lips with it and he opened his mouth. She pulled it back and kissed him before she let him have the nugget.

He grabbed her wrist and kissed her fingertips.

While he chewed he reached around to a crystal punch bowl filled with ice and six bottles of beer. He popped the top off one and held it up to her lips. She took a sip, amazed that it tasted so good after cheese. Then he drank from the same bottle and sat it on the table.

He picked up her hand and looked into her eyes. "You are lovely with the moonlight on your hair."

She inhaled sharply when his thumb grazed her palm ever so gently, back and forth like butterfly wings. Her toes curled inside her boots as he fed her bites of fruit, kissed her lips, her fingers, and her neck in between bites. The rest of her body encased in clothes and a denim coat begged to be released so he could spend time with them.

And then he stopped and pointed. "There it is, darlin'."

"What?"

Lord, she didn't know whether to expect dancing elephants or real fairies sprinkling shiny dust on the whole barn. What she looked out the loft door and saw was the most beautiful sunset she'd ever seen. Wil's ranch was located on a stretch of flat land that stretched from the barn to the end of the world. And right there close to where the Pacific Ocean should be a big orange ball was falling slowly like the globe on the New Year's countdown in New York City.

"Oh, my!" she whispered. "It's so awesome."

He put an arm around her shoulders and drew her tightly against his side. "It is, isn't it? I love the sunrises and sunsets." He stopped himself before he said, "almost as much as I love you." It was too early to tell her that. He had a lot of courting to do before he could say the words.

There wasn't a steak dinner or a movie in the whole world as wonderful and sensual as what Pearl shared that evening on the Bar M Ranch with Wil Marshall.

She didn't know how long it took from beginning to end; five minutes or eternity. It didn't matter. She rested her head on his shoulder and he buried his cheek in her hair, but other than that neither of them moved or said a word.

When twilight ended and darkness set in he tipped her chin back and kissed her. In that moment she fully trusted Wil with her heart and soul.

He very slowly removed her coat, boots, shirt, and jeans, then picked up a soft fluffy blanket and wrapped her in it when she shivered. His hands moved under the warmth of the blanket and took off her socks, underpants, and bra.

"My turn." She shivered.

"No, darlin', tonight is about you. You'd get cold if you came out from under the covers." He quickly removed his shirt, boots, jeans, and socks. She gasped when she saw that he wasn't wearing underwear and that he was fully ready to make love to her.

He set the food table to one side and quickly pulled the blanket off her before lying down beside her on the quilt, and then he wrapped the blanket around both of them so quickly that she didn't have time to chill.

She snuggled up next to his warm body and ran her hands over his rock hard muscles. His hands roamed over her body while kisses covered her mouth, neck, and eyelids. It might be crazy but she let go of every fear as he stretched out on top of her and made sweet love to her like no one had ever done before. Not even the wild night in the motel after the shot challenge or the one in Wichita Falls after bowling was as sensual as making love with candles glowing all around them and the stars glittering like diamonds in the sky above them.

When they both reached the top at the same time and he groaned "Red!" in that deep Texas drawl, she wanted to scream from the top of the clouds that she was in love with Wil Marshall. But that was crazy as hell. She'd known him less than a month.

It was eleven o'clock when she awoke. He was propped up beside her on his elbow, a grin on his face. He reached over his head and picked up a wedge of mango and put it in her mouth.

"You are lovely when you sleep. I wanted to kiss every single freckle, but I didn't want to wake you. Warm enough?"

"Still pretty damn hot," she said.

He bent down and brushed a soft kiss across her lips. "I can put that fire out."

"I bet you can," she said as she wrapped her arms around his neck and rolled over on top of him.

He pulled the blanket up over them and rubbed her back.

She gasped. "That's making it hotter. Not putting it out."

"That's the plan, sweetheart."

Chapter 16

SHE WAS ANTSY ALL DAY WHILE SHE AND LUCY CLEANED rooms. She'd made it home at two o'clock in the morning, slept four hours, and was wide awake, ready to check guests out and clean rooms. She was humming when Lucy opened the lobby door and came in out of the cold.

"So where did you go last night? Was it all fancy, with candles?" Lucy asked.

"It had candles." Pearl giggled and told her that they'd eaten at the farm, up in a hayloft.

Lucy looked disappointed.

But Pearl couldn't even tell Lucy about it. Words could tell a story. Words could talk about emotions. Words could not describe what had happened the night before.

She had the phone in her hand to call him when it rang in the middle of the afternoon.

"Hello, great minds must think alike. I was about to call you," she said.

"I meant to call before now but the battery was dead on my cell phone and I've been in the field all day. Can I pick you up and we can grab some fast food at Sonic?"

After the enchanting night before, Sonic sounded like slumming.

"Do you have to be somewhere or doing something afterwards?" Pearl asked.

"No, what do you have in mind?"

"Interested in Italian? I've got leftover lasagna. It's not homemade. It's one of those frozen things but there's plenty for both of us."

"What time?"

"Six, and wear—"

"A toga." He laughed.

"I was thinkin' far less," she teased.

"You're going to kill me graveyard dead, Red."

"Don't die before supper or I'll have to find another cowboy to eat all the leftovers."

He knocked at five minutes until six. When she opened the door he handed her half a dozen red roses wrapped in tissue paper and kissed her hard as he kicked the door shut with his boot heel.

"They are beautiful. I'll get a vase and put them in water," she muttered between kisses.

"Not as beautiful as you are."

"Flattery will get you—"

"Darlin', that's fact, not flattery," he said.

He released her reluctantly with one more kiss and followed her to the kitchen. "This place smells wonderful. What can I do to help?"

"Stay out of my kitchen," she said.

"Wow! We're too much alike." He removed his jacket and hung it over the back of a kitchen chair.

The table was set with heavy off-white stoneware; the stainless flatware was good quality but simple; and the napkins looked big and soft. She lit three tapered red candles in mismatched brass holders clumped together in the middle of the table. She pulled a bottle of red wine from an ice bucket, poured two glasses, and set them beside the plates. The timer on the oven dinged and she removed a foil pan half full of lasagna that she had grated fresh cheese on top of. She set it on the table. Then she pulled two bowls of chilled salad from the fridge and set one at each plate.

He circled her waist with a big hand and pulled her to him. She wore jeans, a plain green knit shirt, her hair was up in a ponytail, and the bibbed apron had red stains on it. And she'd never looked lovelier to him.

"I really like lasagna," he said.

"I'm not surprised. You make love like an Italian man. So you must love that kind of food." She giggled. "Let's eat while we can. I might be interrupted by customers."

He raised an eyebrow as he took his place at the table.

She removed her apron and sat down beside him. "I'm watching the front desk. Salad already has dressing on it. I make my own Italian."

He put a forkful of salad into his mouth. "Got any customers yet?"

"Six rooms are full. All older folk so maybe they'll be happy and won't call."

"Damn, this is good. You can cook for me anytime you want, Red."

She smiled and passed him the bread sticks.

He took one and bit the end off, rolled his eyes, and looked at her with a new respect. "Did you make these from scratch?"

"Sure I did." She laughed. "Aunt Kate taught me to make them. You buy this frozen dough at the grocery store, lay it out on a cookie sheet, sprinkle some garlic salt on it, and brush it with butter. Then viola! Bread sticks."

"What else did she teach you?"

"To play poker."

He laughed. "I'm not ever playing with you."

They finished and were washing dishes side-by-side when she heard someone in the lobby. She eased out the door and rented two rooms to a family of eight: grand-parents, parents, and four small children. When she gave them their keys and slipped back into her apartment, the dishes were done and Wil was dozing on the sofa. She sat down in a rocking chair and watched him for half an hour until the bell on the lobby door rang again. She rented one room to a couple who couldn't keep their hands off each other. The man signed the card as Mr. and Mrs. Franklin Jones. She wondered if she ran the tags on the brand new Cadillac if she'd find that wasn't the right name.

Wil roused when she went back to the apartment. "Got anymore of that wine? That had to be Granny Lanier's watermelon wine."

She poured two more glasses and carried them to the sofa. He pulled her down in his lap, clinked glasses with hers, and said, "To us."

"To us," she whispered.

He tossed back the wine like he'd done the whiskey on New Year's Eve and set the glass down on an end table and slowly began to slip Pearl's shirt up over her head. The lobby bell rang and she jumped up.

"Dammit!" he swore. He should steal her away to the ranch and take her to the hayloft. No one disturbed them up there.

"Good evening," Pearl said.

"Hi there. I'm Mrs. Franklin Burbanks and that's my Caddy out there. My husband is staying in your motel tonight. I just wanted you to know that I'm driving my car out of here. I'm not stealing it. In the morning when he comes in here screaming that his car has been stolen, please give him this." She handed a manila envelope to Pearl.

"Yes, ma'am," Pearl said.

The woman walked outside, said something to a lady in another vehicle, and unlocked the Caddy door with a remote device. She drove it out of the lot and Pearl laid the envelope on the desk.

"That's enough for one night," Pearl said. She put the neon cowboy to bed for the night and turned on the NO VACANCY lights.

"One got caught," she said as she settled herself into Wil's lap.

"What?"

She told him the story and asked, "Would you ever do that?"

"Hell, no! To begin with I'm not a cheater. When I'm in a relationship it's one hundred percent. When I want out I'm up-front and honest." He wrapped his arms around her.

He yawned and leaned his head back on the sofa. "You've worn me out, Red."

She laughed and snuggled up beside him.

He traced the outline of her lips with his fingertip. "Don't freak out, Red, but Momma wants to meet you so she's having a little Sunday dinner for the family this weekend. My sisters and their families will be there. Not a big crowd but they all think you saved my life and want to thank you."

"I *did* alibi you out of a murder charge," she told him.

She'd never been any good at meeting "the mother."
The mother could always tell if some brazen hussy
woman had been sleeping with her precious son. And
who's to say she wouldn't talk him into donning a collar and going to Africa? Pearl wasn't ready to give
God another man, so she squirmed at the thought of
meeting Momma.

"Yes, you did, darlin'. Of course, it was a case of
mistaken identity and they let me go because they were
lookin' for William Marshall, not Wilson Marshall. But
it's a moot point. You were willing to drive over there
and get me out of the cell. Will you go? I can pick you
up about eleven. Your guests should be gone by then and
it's just my family."

Just his family! Yeah, right!

"What's your favorite Sunday dinner?" he asked as
he ran his finger around her eyes, tickling her lashes.
"Momma wants to know."

The meal was going to be planned around her wishes
and whims... and she didn't have to worry about it
because it was just his family? Did he have cow shit
for brains?

"Fried chicken, mashed potatoes, hot biscuits, green
beans with bacon in them, and candied sweet potatoes.
But if you don't stop touching me like that I'm going to
ask for oysters on the half shell. Keeping up with you is
a tough job."

"Momma can do that kind of meal standing on her
head and cross-eyed. She was afraid you'd ask for something fancy like oysters on the half shell." He chuckled
and traced her ears with his fingertips.

"Fried chicken is fancy."

"What's plain?"

"Tomato soup from a can and bologna sandwiches."

"Well, my family can do a little better than that."

Turnabout was fair play, according to Aunt Pearlita. So if she had to go to dinner at his mother's place then, well, turnabout was indeed fair play.

"Our mothers think alike. Momma has been bugging me all week to bring you to Sherman so she can thank you for staying up with me all night. So this Sunday at your momma's; the next at mine?"

Wil's dark brows drew downward, forming a single line. "You said you are an only child, right?"

"Yes, I am. But you aren't getting off so lucky. Granny will be visiting from Savannah and she's bringing her sister, Aunt Kate, with her. It'll be a Sunday evening dinner. Cocktails at six. Dinner in the formal dining room at seven. You can have coffee in the library with Daddy after dinner and we'll talk about you while we have mint juleps in the parlor."

Wil squirmed. "I suppose I can do that."

"Good, then it's a deal. I'll be ready at eleven this Sunday, January…" she thought about what day it was and whether midnight had come and gone while they were making love, "January 17. And January 24 in Sherman. Lunch on the seventeenth and we'll leave at four thirty on the twenty-fourth. I'll either pick you up in the Caddy or if you want to do the manly thing and drive, you can pick me up at the motel in your truck."

He swallowed and his eyes opened up very, very wide. "Just how formal is this dinner?"

"Knock the cow shit off your boots. Crease your

jeans and iron your shirt and you should be fine," she said. "Daddy wears jeans and boots all the time and Momma fusses but she does like cowboys."

"Well, that sounds good." He played with a strand of hair. "Just touching your hair makes me hot as hell."

"Then I reckon we'd better put that fire out, hadn't we?" She giggled and snuggled up so close that she could tell he wasn't lying.

She awoke the next morning and reached over to touch Wil, only to find a pillow instead of a warm body. There was a note on the nightstand that said, "Leaving at four o'clock. Didn't want Lucy to demand you make an honest man of me. Will call later."

She held the note to her bare breast then sat up quickly and reached for the phone and dialed her mother's number.

"Hello, Pearl. Is everything all right?" Tess's voice came through the line.

"Everything is fine. I just wanted to call before Lucy and I start cleaning rooms. You got plans for dinner a week from Sunday?"

"Nothing that can't be changed if you want to come home. Your grandmother and Aunt Kate would be tickled to have you for a few days, and God knows it would take some pressure off me to have someone here to entertain them."

"It's just for Sunday evening dinner. I'm bringing Wil Marshall with me and—"

That's as far as she got.

"Oh, that's wonderful. I'll plan cocktails at six and dinner at seven. What's his favorite dessert?"

"Hell, I don't know, Momma! Slow down. I'm not

going to marry the man. I just thought it would be nice for you to meet him."

"Of course it will. We'll invite the Casseys and the Wiltons. Oh, the Wiltons will have to bring their son because he's home from that last job he did in Iraq so maybe you could bring Jasmine for him. That will make everything even."

"No, Momma. Keep it family. Let's don't scare him to death on his first run out of the chute."

Tess barely hesitated. "I suppose that'll be all right but I hate it when you talk rodeo like that. Can't you try to be more southern belle and less brazen?"

"No, I can't. I'm just a brazen redhead with a temper," Pearl said.

"Well, try to be a lady when you bring this fellow home for us to meet. I'm so excited! Is he pretty?"

"Thanks, Momma. We'll be there a little before six, then. And no, he looks like shit."

"Katy Pearl Richland!"

"Well, he's not pretty! He's so handsome he'll take your breath away and he's hot as hell."

———————

Wil called his mother the minute he awoke the next morning.

"That you, Wil?" she answered.

"It is. Y'all got plans for Sunday?"

"Not this Sunday. We're leaving on Tuesday for a couple of days. Goin' down to Austin to see about a bull your dad is interested in buying. Want to go with us?"

"No, but I'd like to bring Red... I mean Pearl... to the house for Sunday dinner. Kind of like a thank you for standing up for me even though it was a mistaken identity thing."

"I think that's a wonderful idea. I'll call your sisters and invite them to come. Dinner at twelve?"

"Yes, and I've been craving fried chicken, mashed potatoes, and gravy and biscuits," he said slyly.

"Corn on the cob?"

"No, green beans with bacon and candied sweet potatoes."

"That doesn't sound like you. Never knew you to eat yams," his mother said.

"Guess my taste is changing."

"It's about time." She laughed.

"Then I'll see you on Sunday. I'll bring dessert."

"You just bring that young lady. We'll take care of the rest."

Chapter 17

LUCY SAT CROSS-LEGGED ON PEARL'S BED AND BRUSHED Delilah's long yellow hair while Pearl stood in front of her closet and swore as she shoved hangers from one side of the closet to the other. Lucy's bruises had healed and she'd stopped looking at the ground every time someone glanced at her. She still hadn't found a cat, but Pearl had assured her that kittens were most usually born in the spring of the year and she'd have her pick of dozens in a few weeks.

Lucy's smile lit up her eyes. She was a pretty woman now that the bruises were healed. She kept her brown hair shiny and she'd bought two pair of jeans, three shirts, and a new bra last week at the Dollar General Store. She looked less like a waif and more like a woman since she'd been eating regularly and sleeping at night with no fear.

"Did you shave your legs?" Lucy asked.

Pearl propped one on the side of the bed and ran a hand down it.

"Then you could wear a dress. I know he said that it was informal but that don't have to mean jeans, does it?"

"It's just dinner with his folks so they can meet the woman who kept their pretty-boy son out of prison."

Lucy giggled.

Pearl put her foot on the floor and sat on the bed. "What's so funny?"

"Woman shaves her legs, puts on perfume, gets her hair all fancied up, and then fusses and fumes over what to wear. You ain't foolin' me none. If it purrs like a cat, catches mice like a cat, and runs from a dog like a cat, chances are pretty dang good that it's a cat."

"Kind of like the duck thing?"

"What duck thing?"

"Walks like a duck, quacks like a duck, it's a duck," Pearl answered.

"I like the cat one better. Never did like them loud-mouthed ducks and never did like eating 'em, neither."

"It's just dinner at his momma's place," Pearl argued with herself more than with Lucy.

And she's goin' to take one look at you and know that you've been beddin' her son every chance you get and think you are a slut, her conscience chided.

"In my part of the world when a man takes a girl home to meet Momma, it's more'n a date. It's the thing before the weddin'. Cleet's momma didn't like me a bit. Said I'd never make him a proper wife but that since I was pregnant she guessed she'd have to live with him takin' the wrong woman. She thought it was good enough for me when he'd get mad and hit me because I didn't have no business gettin' pregnant in the first place."

It was the first time Lucy had mentioned Cleet in a while. Pearl didn't say anything but waited.

"She always thought that baby wasn't Cleet's but it was. There wasn't no other man before him or after, neither. I hope I get my kitten soon," she changed the subject abruptly. "I been lookin' at all those cute little cat toys in the store."

"What color cat did you say you wanted?"

"It changes every day. One day I want a yellow one like Delilah. The next I think a black one would be nice but then maybe a calico. I don't think it would matter, long as I had something to hold and love that... well, that would love me back," she said. "But this day ain't about me. It's about your date."

"I told you, it's a family dinner."

A date is a night in a hayloft watching the sunset while Wil feeds me cheese and ham and grapes and we make love like there is no tomorrow.

"Claws like a cat." Lucy laughed. "Wear that right there. That pretty green sweater with that plaid skirt and some of them high-heeled boots. You'll look like you walked right out of one of them fashion books."

"I should be staying here and helping you clean rooms."

"We got six. I can do that many long before check-in starts up. And don't hurry. Me and Delilah will take care of the guests until you get home. Enjoy the day."

Pearl pulled the emerald green sweater and the matching plaid skirt from her closet and laid them on the bed. She might as well follow Lucy's advice.

She dressed, redid the hair damage the sweater created when she jerked it over her head, put on her boots, and looked at her reflection in the mirror.

"See. You look just like one of the magazine models," Lucy said. "Now that we've got that settled, I'm off to clean then straighten up the laundry room."

"Lucy, you don't have to do that today."

"Yes, I do. I'll go crazy if I don't have something to keep me busy. Could we go to the library tomorrow? I'm even out of books to read."

"The keys to the truck are on the rack with the room

keys. Come and go when you want. If you want to go to the store or drive somewhere else this afternoon, lock the lobby up and go."

Lucy's smile was brighter than the sun. "You mean it."

"Yes, I do. Buy a book to keep. They sell a few at the Dollar Store. Or drive over to Wichita Falls or down to Bowie."

Lucy shook her head. "I wouldn't be comfortable in a place as big as all that. But I might go on to the grocery store and the Dollar Store this afternoon if you are sure that's all right. And is it all right if I take Delilah back to my place to keep me company?"

Pearl touched Lucy's shoulder and she didn't flinch. She'd come a long way in the weeks she'd been at the Longhorn. Not far enough, but then she might never have the spit and vinegar that Pearl did, not after what she'd endured.

"You use that truck like it was yours and enjoy yourself a little bit. And it's getting to where Delilah is as much yours as mine so, yes, you can take her to your place," Pearl said.

"Thank you." Lucy laid the brush down.

Wil didn't know whether he was supposed to knock on the back door to the apartment or walk right into the lobby and ring the bell on the countertop. He was more nervous than he'd been the first time he went on a date back when he was sixteen.

Unlike Rye, who knew the minute he laid eyes on Austin that she was the woman for him, Wil had had to come to grips with the fact that he'd found his soul mate. He'd always thought that a man met a woman and built a relationship with her, then woke up one day and realized she was the one. He didn't think it would all start when he woke up to policemen, handcuffs, and a walk in the sleet to the squad car. That wasn't the way things were done to his way of thinking, but he'd been dead wrong, because that's exactly the way it started.

"And all because the electricity went out at my place on Christmas Eve," he said as he crawled out of the truck and shook the legs of his Wranglers down over his boot tops.

Pearl and Lucy were sitting in the recliners in the lobby. That big yellow cat of hers lazed on the table between them and they were both rubbing its fur. He wanted to peek through the glass for a long time but Pearl waved him on inside and stood up.

He groaned but it was swallowed up in the roar of the wind sweeping down from the north and headed toward the Gulf with nothing in its way but a few barbed wire fences and a couple of straggly old Longhorns. She looked like she'd just walked off a model runway in that outfit.

"Damn," he mumbled under his breath. He hadn't started out to fall for Red, but it had happened and now he didn't know what to do. She wanted a good time; he wanted a soul mate. How did the two ever meet in the middle?

She threw a plaid shawl around her shoulders and picked up her purse. "You are right on time."

"Yes, ma'am," he drawled. "And you are lookin' stunning today."

"Thank you. You don't look so shabby yourself." She

started at his toes and slowly admired his shiny boots, starched jeans, silver belt buckle, and crisp blue shirt under a denim jacket. She stopped when she got to his chin, careful not to go swimming in his mesmerizing eyes. One trip there and they'd never make it to the dinner.

He felt like he was standing in front of his grandmother's old open-face heater when her eyes hesitated a moment on his belt buckle on her way up to his lips. She blinked before she locked eyes with his, which was probably for the best. If he'd ever sunk down into those green eyes he'd grab a room key and forget about his mother's fried chicken.

"I guess we're ready then," he said hoarsely. He wondered what she'd say or do if he asked for a room, swept her up off her feet like a bride, and carried her down the sidewalk.

"Y'all have a good time and don't hurry back. I can take care of things," Lucy said.

"Thanks, Lucy. Do what I said. Lock it up for a couple of hours and go shopping or driving," Pearl reminded her.

Lucy nodded.

Wil opened the door for Pearl, stood to one side, and settled his Stetson back on his head when they were outside, then rested his hand on the small of her back. Heat spread and glowed and her imagination painted a crimson blush on her cheeks. It didn't cool down one little bit when he helped her into the truck and whistled his way around the hood of the truck to slip into the driver's seat.

They'd never been awkward with each other, not the morning after the first time. Not when they'd made love in the loft; not the morning after the session in her bed; but suddenly there was a big white elephant with the word *awkward* tattooed on his trunk in the truck with them.

"You like Blake Shelton?" he asked.

She nodded.

He touched a button and "Hillbilly Bone" rocked the inside of the truck cab. He quickly adjusted the volume to a lower level.

"So which are you? Blake with his hillbilly bone or the New York City friend?" Pearl asked.

"Oh, I'm Blake for sure. I'm not a city man. Been to the big places with the rodeo rounds. Las Vegas is nice. New York City has its own pulse beat, kind of like that thing about listening to a different drummer, and Los Angeles is the same, different drummer, different beat. But Texas is where my hillbilly bone brought me back to every time I wandered. And I like little towns. They have a heartbeat all of their own," he said. "How about you?"

"I'm a mixture. Momma's from Savannah, Georgia, and I could recite a litany about southern girls for a couple of hours. Maybe even a couple of days. Daddy is pure Texan. He's an executive at Texas Instruments, but he's a rancher on the side. I went to college, got a master's eventually, and worked in a bank over in Durant. Taught a few adjunct classes at the school and liked it, but I still like a rodeo, country music, and beer."

"So what are you going to grow up to be, Red?"

"What makes you think I'm not already grown up?" she said with an edge to her tone. Dammit! He hadn't even kissed her and he kept both hands on the steering wheel.

"I think you are picking a fight with me so you can

tell me to turn around and take you back home. You are afraid to go meet my parents and my poor little momma has fried chickens and made biscuits for you."

She shot him a look meant to leave nothing but bones and a greasy spot on the pickup seat but it just made him grin. She hated it when anyone had the upper hand. She slowly turned her head to stare out the window.

"I'm right, ain't I, Red?"

She held a palm up toward him.

"Don't be giving me the old shut-up hand."

She flipped around. "You infuriate me, but I wouldn't tell you to take me home for all the dirt in Texas or tea in China. Nothing keeps me from home-fried chicken and hot biscuits. Not even you."

Blake finished "Hillbilly Bone" and started singing "Kiss My Country Ass" at that time, and Wil pointed at the CD player.

"Bare it, darlin'," she smarted off.

He slowed down as if he was about to pull off the road.

"Okay, okay, you win. I wouldn't want the taste of your ass on my lips when I meet your momma."

He picked up the speed. "I'm disappointed, Red. I thought my ass would sweeten up your sour mood."

Blake went into the next song on his CD, "You'll Always Be Beautiful," about his lady who forgot on her birthday that she was too small to take in all that alcohol.

"Don't seem to be the case always, does it? You hold your liquor pretty good for a little wisp of a lady."

"It's the Irish. They can hold their liquor no matter how small they are."

Wil nodded and kept time with his thumbs on the steering wheel. Blake sang that his woman would always be beautiful to him. Wil stole a glance at Red. She was beautiful whether it was curled up the morning after a drinking contest with the mother of all hangovers, in the hayloft, eating lasagna at her table, or right then all dolled up and nervous.

He was still thinking about her when the next song came on about a cowboy in his forty-dollar blue jeans next to a beauty queen. He sang about not having anything but a big old truck and a little old place.

Pearl had dated cowboys in their forty-dollar blue jeans who thought she was a beauty queen many times, but she hadn't ever laid on the tailgate of a pickup and looked up at the stars like Blake said in his song. Was watching the sunset from the loft window of a barn the same thing? Blake said he couldn't afford to love her but he couldn't afford not to. Was that where she was with Wil?

The next song was called "Delilah" and she'd never heard it. Blake said that Delilah couldn't blame anyone but herself because there was someone right beside her that would never let her down. When she looked at Wil the soft expression in his brown eyes verified that Blake was singing about them. Wil reached across the space and laced his fingers through hers and squeezed.

"You should've been Delilah."

"That mean you're wearin' forty-dollar jeans?" She finally smiled.

"Yes, ma'am, packed down with hillbilly bones."

The last song played and Wil let the CD start all over again without changing it. When it had played through the second time he'd pulled up in the driveway of a low-slung, long rambling ranch house with a deep front porch across the front.

"They're all here. There's Amelia's red truck and Carleen's black one right beside hers."

"They're both into ranching?"

"Born into it. Married into it. You are about to listen to poor old ranchers talkin' about nothing but cows, horses, and makin' hay. We're pretty down to earth and common."

And you can kiss my country ass, she thought. *The size of that house and those two big dually pickup trucks don't spell poverty to me.*

"Well, I'm not ever going to get a dose of Mayberry sitting here," she said.

"Don't you dare get out of the truck before I can get around there to open the door for you. See those fluttering lace curtains in the window. That means Momma and Daddy are both watching and they'll skin me alive and tack my hide to the outhouse door if I'm not a gentleman." He brought her hand to his lips and kissed the fingertips.

The pickup warmed up considerably and the elephant shrunk in size to nothing more than a stuffed toy.

"Was that for their benefit or to turn me on?" she asked.

His grin deepened the dimple in the side of his cheek. "Both. Did it work?"

She unbuckled her seat belt, leaned across the console, cupped his cheeks in her hands, and pulled his lips to hers in a long scorching kiss that fried every nerve ending in her body.

"Did that work?" she whispered softly into his ear when the kiss ended.

"Yes, ma'am, it did. Want to stay out here long enough to fog the windows so they can't see in? The backseat doesn't have a console. We could get closer back there and see where a few more of those would lead. Or we can get a blanket and go back to the hay barn. We can always buy chicken at KFC."

Pearl had met her match. It wasn't easy to admit because she liked having the brassy, sassy upper hand all the time, but she was wise enough to concede when she'd come up against someone just as headstrong and willful. Maybe that's where his name really came from. Wil from willful, not Wilson. One thing for sure, he would keep her on her toes.

He was glad for the cold wind that cooled him as he walked around the truck. One more kiss and he'd have to untuck his shirttail to cover what it had produced. But he hadn't lost the war yet and before the smoke settled from that battle he'd be back full force. If Red thought she could stay ahead of him, she was in for a big surprise.

He opened to door to his big, black shiny truck, reached inside, circled her waist with his big hands, and brought her out like cowboys did back when they were helping their women down from a wagon. He tipped her chin up and bent to kiss her with just enough passion to make her want more. Then he stepped back, crooked his arm, and waited.

She only hesitated a second before she looped her arm through his and hugged up close to his side, causing a heat wave that stilled the cold winter wind. It followed them into a toasty farmhouse living room where blazes sent out a welcome from the big stone fireplace across the room. It was flanked by filled bookcases from floor to ceiling. A family picture hung above the heavy wooden mantel, showing Wil, his mom and dad, and two sisters back when Wil was a teenager. He'd been plumb cute back then but that was before the promise of a full-fledged cowboy had been fulfilled. Pearl was glad she knew him now instead of then.

Cozy brown furniture with a massive wood coffee table scarcely put a dent in the size of the room. Card tables had been set up at one end and kids of various ages were engrossed in two different games. One looked like Monopoly; the other some kind of card game.

"Hey, Uncle Wil. They're all in the kitchen. Momma said if you didn't get here real soon she was going to start eating without you. They were spying on you out the window. Want me to tell you what Granny said?" a Monopoly player yelled across the room.

"Not right now," Wil said. He removed Pearl's shawl and laid it on one of the sofas along with his denim jacket.

Pearl had let go of his arm when they came into the house so he laced his fingers in hers and led her into the massive dining room, kitchen combination. The dining room table for eight and a smaller table for six were both set with white China, crystal goblets, and cloth napkins. Lacy curtains covered the long windows looking outside on the dining room end and out into the backyard on the kitchen end of the room. The cabinets were painted crisp white, and evidently Mrs. Marshall liked roosters because they decorated the whole area. Tiny rooster salt-shakers on the tables, a big life-sized boy with his head thrown back as if he were crowing at daybreak on top of her refrigerator. Rooster planters held cactus plants in the window above the sink, and a set of bright yellow canisters were decorated with paintings of them.

"You must be Pearl Richland. I'm Wil's mother,

Martha Jane. These are his sisters, Amelia and Carleen."
She stepped forward and held out her hand.

In order to shake, Pearl had to untangle her fingers
from Wil's. She hoped that her hand wasn't as sweaty
as it felt.

"Hi. I'm Amelia and this is Carleen. We'd be polite
and shake, but Momma has us makin' gravy and whip-
ping potatoes. If either has lumps she'll disown us and
send us off to the orphanage."

Amelia was the taller of the two with dark hair worn
shoulder length and cut in layers that framed her long,
angular face. Her clear complexion and gorgeous brown
eyes were her good features. Her nose wasn't exactly
too big, but it would have kept her off the front page of
a glamour magazine. Carleen, on the other hand, was
short, had dishwater blond hair that she wore in a bob,
light brown eyes, and nothing really outstanding other
than a beautiful impish smile that lit up her face. They
were both dressed in designer jeans with shiny stones
on their hip pockets, tucked in pearl snap shirts…
Carleen's in a whiskey-colored cotton with darker lace
on the collar and Western cut yoke; Amelia's in a rich
coffee brown with an inlay of stones outlining the Texas
Longhorn on the yoke.

Pearl nodded in their direction.

Wil quickly made introductions. "Red, this is my
dad, Jesse. The tall man on his left is Amelia's husband,
Thomas, and the one on his right is Matthew, who belongs to Carleen."

It was easy for Pearl to see where Wil got his looks.
In forty years he'd be the spittin' image of his father.
Jesse was shorter than Wil, had the same thick dark hair

and brown eyes. His shoulders were as wide as Wil's, but evidently too much fried chicken and gravy had taken its toll on his waistline because he was probably six inches bigger in that area than Wil.

Thomas was taller than Wil, built on a lanky frame rather than a solid one. He had thinning brown hair with a receding hairline and hazel eyes and not a single thing that would stand out in a crowd. Matthew had light brown hair, steely blue eyes, and a smile that would draw women from across the room. He was several inches shorter than Thomas and probably twenty pounds heavier. His shoulders weren't as wide as Wil's and his waistline was much larger but he looked friendly.

She smiled her brightest and said, "I'm glad to meet y'all."

Damn! That came out in my mother's Georgia charm voice and I didn't mean for it to.

"Likewise, I'm sure," Martha Jane said. "Dinner is at the final stages. Pull up a chair, Pearl, and we'll visit in the kitchen while the men catch up on cows and ranchin' in the livin' room. Five minutes, tops, darlin', and your chicken will be ready." Martha Jane tiptoed to kiss her son on the cheek.

She doesn't like me. Not that it matters a tiny rat's ass, but I'm about to get a crash course third degree from her and the sisters and my knees are still shaky from that blistering kiss.

She sat down at the end of the kitchen table. The roosters all glared at her with their beady little black eyes and promised that if she didn't answer all the Marshall women's questions honestly, they'd come alive and commence to pecking her to death.

"I can see why he calls you Red," Amelia said.

"He's the only one that can get away with it. I'm Pearl to everyone else."

Damn! They'll think I've already got my dukes up and drawing the lines for a fight with them.

"I think it's cute and so are you," Amelia said. "We are grateful that you were willing to save his sorry hide, even though he would have gotten set free without your word. But you didn't know that and we are glad you drove over there. Besides, he needed a ride home. It's the first time he's been in any kind of real trouble and it probably scalded his pride to have to ask for a woman's help."

"Don't pay any attention to her," Carleen said. "She's always been jealous of him."

"I have not. I'm not jealous of either of you," Amelia argued.

"So he's the baby?" Pearl asked.

"Oh, yes, he sure is. You ever hear that song by Blake Shelton called 'The Baby'? Well, that is our dear little brother. Momma's last chicken and the prized Texas boy child. He can do no wrong. I actually feel sorry for the woman who gets him," Amelia answered.

"That's a bunch of hog shit," Martha Jane said. "I loved you all just alike. He just came along when we'd given up hope of another child or a son and you two were ten and twelve so you were a lot older. I had more time to spend with him."

Carleen stuck a spoon down in the mashed potatoes and carried them to the dining room table. "That's right, Momma. But I have to agree with Amelia on feeling sorry for the woman that gets him."

"Why?" Pearl asked.

"Neither of us can imagine how tough it will be to live up to his momma's standards in cookin', raisin' kids, or cleanin' house. She's perfect and that's what he'll be expectin' from his wife," Carleen said.

Martha Jane picked up a platter piled high with fried chicken and carried it to the table. "I'm not perfect, and Wil wouldn't expect that from a wife. But hush, now. You'll embarrass Pearl."

"You look like you could go toe-to-toe with him and come out a winner," Carleen whispered on her way to the table with a casserole of candied sweet potatoes.

"If I couldn't I wouldn't be here," Pearl whispered back as she stood up and reached for a dish of steamed broccoli to tote to the table.

"Jesse?" Martha Jane said.

"There's the dinner bell," Jesse said. He took his place at the head of the table. Martha Jane sat on his right with Amelia and then her husband next. Carleen's husband took the other end of the table with Carleen to his right. Wil pulled out a chair beside his sister and seated Pearl before taking his customary place to his father's left.

After Martha Jane delivered a very brief grace, Jesse picked up the platter of chicken and passed it to Wil. He took a leg and passed it on to Pearl who forked a leg and sent it on to Carleen who took a piece of white meat and handed it over her shoulder to one of the grandchildren. That kid took a piece and sent it on to the next kid who did the same and gave it back to Carleen's husband.

The system was strange but efficient. Everyone talked at once and before long Pearl's plate was loaded with a true old southern Sunday dinner. She dipped into the candied yams first and watched to see if anyone picked their chicken up with their fingers or if they cut it off the bone with a knife.

"We aren't very formal around here," Wil said as he picked up a chicken leg and bit into it. "Momma, you have outdone yourself."

"Don't thank me. Carleen fried the chicken. I just made the biscuits and the sweet potatoes," Martha Jane said.

Pearl could see which DNA strands had wrapped firmly around each of the Marshall children and decided that Wil had gotten the best from both his parents.

She picked up a leg and bit into the thick end. "My momma is from Georgia. Fried chicken is her specialty, and even she would admit she couldn't compete with this. You done good, Carleen."

"She had a dang good teacher. I've been trying to get her to teach our daughters, Janey and Mesa, to cook," Amelia's husband, Thomas, said.

Amelia shot him a look. "You have decent meals so don't be whining."

"You have a wonderful cook and my belt size testifies to that. I'm not complainin' one bit, darlin'. The work you do on the ranch couldn't be done if you didn't have help." He soothed her ruffled tail feathers with a soft voice and a pat on her shoulder. "But the girls need to know how to cook. They might not find a husband who can hire a cook and a housekeeper."

Matthew blushed but covered it well. Carleen patted his leg under the table. Pearl didn't miss either gesture.

"So I take it you like to cook?" Pearl asked Carleen.

"Love it. It's good that I have three big strapping

boys to eat up all my fun." She nodded toward the other table. "The one on the far end is Tony. He's fifteen."

Tony looked up and waved a hunk of chicken at her. He looked like a younger Wil. Tall and lanky with a bone frame that would take a few extra pounds to look really good, but if that plate of food was any indication of how he ate every day, it wouldn't take him long.

"He's already into the rodeo circuit for junior riders and plays high school football for Chico. And that's Corey next to him."

Corey smiled tightly. He'd just shoveled a forkful of potatoes in his mouth. He was a strange mixture of his parents with brown hair and piercing blue eyes.

"He's thirteen and into baseball and is our brilliant child when it comes to books," Carleen bragged.

"And the one beside him is Ricky."

Ricky nodded. He was a good looking kid. When he grew up his parents had better invest in a few two-by-fours to beat the girls off the porch.

"He's only twelve and he's our computer geek, like his dad. He doesn't like the sports. No girls to teach to cook, although Ricky does help me sometimes if it's something he really, really likes to eat," Carleen said.

"And the other three over there are mine," Amelia said from across the table.

The oldest girl at the other table stood up. "I'm Janey and I'm disgusting. I can't cook and I hate to clean. I go to Texas A&M to study pre-vet. I live on Ramen noodles with peanut butter in them for dessert. And I put catsup in them for pseudo-spaghetti. I'm twenty years old and someday I'm going to marry a rich man who can hire a cook for me."

Pearl winked at her and she smiled back.

The girl next to her stood up. "Welcome to our dysfunctional family, Pearl. Or is it Red? Anyway, my name is Mesa and I'm disgusting too. I'm eighteen years old and I'm a senior at Chico High School and I'm in love with a boy that works on our ranch and we're going to get married next summer. Momma is trying to talk me out of it. Daddy is finding out about it right now, and I picked this time to tell him so everyone will know if Jason dies that Daddy had him killed. I'm going to be a June bride so everyone can mark their calendars and start thinking about a present."

"What the hell?" Thomas's face turned crimson.

"Shhhh." Amelia squeezed his thigh. "It's a passing fancy. Don't worry."

A boy waved. "And I'm the baby like Uncle Wil and I'm the only one who's not disgusting. I'm sixteen and I'm Tye and my sisters say I'm spoiled even worse than Uncle Wil, but I don't believe it because nobody can spoil a boy like Granny. I play football with Tony at Chico, and Daddy, I think Mesa is dead serious so you'd better open up your billfold and dole out the cash for a big wedding."

Thomas cut his eyes across the wide room at Mesa, but she had her head down, concentrating on buttering another biscuit.

"Well, that was enlightening," Martha Jane said in a tight voice.

Pearl could have kissed Mesa for taking the heat off her. Now they'd remember the dinner as the one where Mesa announced her engagement to the family and not the one where Wil brought home the owner of a motel.

"We'll discuss it when we get home," Amelia muttered under her breath.

"Yes, we will, and it's not happening," Thomas mumbled back.

Janey waved and got Pearl's attention. "Tell us about you now."

Pearl wanted to stand up and say that she was disgusting. She'd challenged Marshall's only son to a Jack Daniel's whiskey contest, wound up drunker than Cooter's owl, and then had a wonderful night of wild sex with him, found out he was a helluva lot of fun on a run of dates, had an ultra romantic side in a candlelit hayloft, and could make her body hum no matter where they made love.

She controlled the impulse and said from a seated position, "I'm Pearl Richland. Wil calls me Red and I don't like it but after he stayed up with me all night and woke me up every hour to make sure I wasn't in a coma, I told him he could call me that and I won't go back on my word. But if anyone else thinks they're big enough to call me anything but Pearl, they'd better bring their lunch because the fight is going to last all day. I own the Longhorn Inn because my Aunt Pearlita died almost two months ago and left it to me. I was an executive banker in Durant until I decided to run the motel."

"Is that all?" Carleen asked.

"What else do you want to know?"

"Ever been married?"

Pearl shook her head slowly and shoveled sweet potatoes into her mouth. Maybe that would be the only embarrassing question. She could hope, even if it was a 10 percent chance. After all, it was only a two-minute marriage and that barely qualified as a white lie.

"Engaged?" Amelia asked.

Pearl held up one finger.

"That mean one engagement or wait until I swallow?"

She did swallow and then took a sip of tea. She might as well spit it out even though it wouldn't help Mesa one bit. "It means that I did something very stupid after my senior year on the rebound. I eloped but I'd barely said I do when Momma caught up with us. She took me home and annulled it the next day. The day after that we went to Savannah and I spent the summer with my Aunt Kate."

Wil stiffened beside her.

Get off your high horse, big boy. You can't tell me you never did anything stupid and if you do, remember that I know Rye well enough to ask him, Pearl thought as she sipped sweet tea.

"Did a summer with Aunt Kate convince you your mother was right or make you want to run away with the boy again?" Thomas asked.

"Oh, honey, Aunt Kate did both. Let's just say she is very influential and by the end of the summer, I knew my husband for two minutes was not the boy I thought he was and that he had his eyes on my daddy's bank account. But she didn't convince me Momma was right. Not that summer. It took a couple more before I'd admit it and I still haven't in Momma's presence."

"Can I have your Aunt Kate's address or at least her contacts?" Thomas asked.

Mesa looked up and caught Thomas looking right at her. She narrowed her eyes and said, "Won't do a bit of good, Daddy. I'm not eloping. I want the big wedding and the big cake and all the hoopla, and I want a small house out on the back forty. We'll build on next year when our first baby is born. Don't look so pale. I'm not pregnant but we're having kids right away. Jason is twenty-one and we want to be young parents."

Wil chuckled.

"What's so funny?" Amelia said.

"You'd better send her to Carleen so she'll know how to cook. I don't expect Jason is making enough to hire a cook and housekeeper, is he?"

"She's not getting married this summer. She's going to college with Janey next year. Subject closed," Thomas said from between clenched teeth.

Mesa gave her father a tolerant smile. Pearl recognized it because she'd used the same expression at least a gazillion times when she was eighteen and so much wiser than either of her parents.

He glared back at her. "I mean it."

"I've got a question for Pearl. How do you feel about Uncle Wil?"

"Mesa Joanne! That's plumb rude," Amelia said.

"And asking her about a personal nickname and her marital status isn't?"

Pearl winked at her. "Your Uncle Wil is one helluva cowboy."

Mesa winked back. "A real one like Conway Twitty sings about?"

Pearl knew exactly what she was talking about. Conway Twitty had a song out years and years ago that said not to call him a cowboy 'til you'd seen him ride. Mesa was asking if she'd been to bed with Wil and knew if he was a real cowboy.

"Maybe," she said with a shrug of her shoulders.

"What was that all about?" Wil asked.

"That, darlin', is personal between me and your sweet little niece."

Mesa giggled. "Is it a secret?"

"My lips are sealed."

"What are you two goin' on about?" Wil asked again.

"It's between us and what goes on at a Sunday dinner is confidential, right, Mesa?"

"Hell, yeah!"

"Gretchen Wilson, 'Redneck Woman,'" Pearl said.

Mesa gave her a thumbs-up sign. "That's me. I may leave my Christmas lights up all year just like she says in that song."

Pearl turned back to the adults. Thomas was grumbling to Amelia. Matthew was grinning. Carleen was telling him not to get too smug because he had three boys on the way to the altar in the very distant future. Martha Jane was staring at Pearl.

"So why did you say you quit your job at the bank?"

"I got tired of sitting on the side of the desk that gave out loans to young folks trying to start up businesses. I'd been thinking about doing something that would make me my own boss for a while and then my aunt died and left me the motel. Seemed like an omen."

"I see," Martha said. The tone didn't match the chill in her voice and she could almost hear Lucy's voice over her left shoulder telling her to get the hell out of Bowie and scoot right on back to the Longhorn as fast as she could.

"Hey, Wil, how's that new bull? Is he going to be worth what you paid for him?" Matthew changed the subject abruptly.

"I didn't get him. The man called from California the morning I was leaving and told me the bull, along with several other cattle, had been rustled."

"That's too bad. I was lookin' forward to seeing him," Matthew said.

The conversation went to bulls, buying cattle, and running ranches and Pearl sighed in relief. The warmth in her chair actually dropped from six degrees above hell's hottest recorded temperature down to barely warm as the spotlight faded from her and onto a tractor out in the barn.

Don't think it's over just because you are out of the hot seat, Aunt Pearlita's voice came through loud and clear in her head. *You've still got dessert and visiting to do before you can go back to the motel.*

Wil chose that moment to push his plate back a few inches and throw his arm around the back of her chair. He leaned over and whispered, "Want to take a ride around the property and have dessert later?"

She nodded.

"If y'all will excuse us, I'm going to give Pearl a tour of the ranch. We'll have dessert when we get back."

"But I thought we'd set two more tables and have a canasta play-off," Martha Jane said.

"You've got enough here for that without us. Besides, Pearl is a sorry loser and she'll throw the cards if she doesn't get a good hand."

"Thank you for a lovely dinner. Truth is I really am lousy at card games other than poker, but he's not telling the truth about me throwing them. I usually just hide the bad cards and cheat," she said.

Martha gasped.

Mesa laughed out loud. "Want some company?"

"No, we do not!" Wil said.

The last thing that filtered through the noise as Wil was shutting the door behind them was Mesa saying, "Don't worry about her red hair, Granny. It's not serious."

Chapter 18

THE SUN WAS OUT WHEN THEY STEPPED OUTSIDE. THE sky was that strange shade of blue that only comes in the winter, not robin's egg blue but not the crystal clear blue of a Texas summer sky. A few marshmallow clouds moved across the sky as if they had nowhere to go and a lifetime to get there. A couple of buzzards looked down from the utility poles bringing electricity and phone lines into the house.

Pearl pulled her shawl tightly around her shoulders and settled down into the passenger seat of the truck, wishing she'd brought along a heavier coat. Mesa's comment worried through her mind like a hound dog with a fresh ham bone. She didn't know whether to bury it and dig it up later to gnaw on or to ask Wil what Mesa meant. His answer might open a can of worms, so she kept her mouth shut while he drove around the house and down a road toward the back side of the ranch.

Describing the bumpy path they were on as a road was using the word loosely. It had tire tracks with grass growing up between them and ruts big enough to shake all that greasy fried chicken right down to her thighs. She'd have to run all the way to the last red light in Henrietta that evening to take off as many calories as she'd inhaled.

"My folks' spread is twice as big as mine. I've only got a section of land, six hundred and twenty acres.

They've got two sections. A mile to the back, two miles of road frontage. Mine runs a mile each way but someday when the neighbors get ready to retire I'm hoping to have enough saved back to buy their place and it will double. By then I'll have to have more than one full-time hired hand, though. So how did you like my family?" Wil asked abruptly.

She turned her head slowly. "That came out of nowhere."

"Yep, it did."

"Your family is great. Love Mesa and her independence. Your sisters are very different, but then so are their husbands. And what did Mesa mean by that last remark?"

Wil frowned. "I hoped you didn't hear that."

"I did. What did it mean?"

"It's the hair."

"Mine or yours?"

"Yours."

"What's wrong with my hair? I washed it so it doesn't stink. Hell, I even shaved my legs."

Wil didn't want to spoil the day, but the look on Red's face said that she would have an answer and he might as well spit out the real one as tell a lie that would come back to bite him on the ass later that day. Besides, he'd hated that damned awkwardness in the truck with them before. He wanted everything to be up-front and honest because he was falling fast for Pearl Richland.

"It's red."

"Is that a major sin in the Marshall family? Do they tar and feather red-haired women or stone them to death? That's why your mother kept giving me funny looks across the table, isn't it? I thought I had sweet potatoes on my face and damn near wiped my freckles off with that napkin trying to figure out where the mess was. She looked like she'd been sucking on a lemon."

"I'm sorry." He grinned.

Even his sexy slightly lopsided smile didn't miraculously make everything all right.

"What's wrong with red hair?"

"Who knows? Maybe she had a red-haired cousin she didn't like. Kind of like those cousins that called you Red and you didn't like them. But every time my sisters brought home a new boyfriend she'd start in before he got to the door that she hoped to hell he didn't have red hair."

"I wouldn't want to bring tainted blood into your royal family."

"It's no big deal. She'll get over it when she gets to know you."

"It's a big deal to me. And I don't give a damn if she gets over it because I probably won't ever see her again."

It started as a chuckle and grew into a guffaw that came close to busting out the windows of the truck. "You *are* one ball of fire when you are mad," he said between laughter and catching his breath. "And tell me, red-hot lady, what about this annulment?"

"It was a long time ago. My boyfriend broke my heart and another guy stepped up to the plate. It didn't work and I'm glad. You got any past wives or almost wives?"

"Hell, no!" He laughed. "Not a single one. Never met anyone who could get so fired up as you can, either!"

A grin tickled the corners of her mouth. He even laughed in a Texas drawl and his brown eyes were twinkling, but she'd crawl up on a rusty old poker and ride it to hell before she laughed with him. She pointed her finger at his nose and said, "And don't you forget it."

"How could I forget after all the hot sex we've had?" He turned her finger toward the window and whispered, "Look!"

"Oh!" she gasped, forgetting in an instant that she had abominable red hair. Two fawns stood on spindling legs and romped around close to a doe that was grazing just inside the fence. "They are so cute."

"And over there?" He pointed the other direction where three Angus calves frolicked in the pasture, kicking up their heels and butting heads.

"Black Angus, not red."

Wil choked back a sigh. The day wasn't supposed to be like this. His mother was supposed to take one look at Red and hear wedding bells, not see visions of red-haired grandchildren.

Don't beat an already dead horse. Aunt Pearlita's voice came through so loud that Pearl looked in the rearview mirror to see if her aunt was in the backseat. *Why do you care anyway? Is it because you are falling in love with Wil?*

Pearl crossed her arms over her chest and argued with her aunt's voice inside her head. *Helluva lot of good it would do me if I was falling for him. He's Momma's pretty baby and she hates redheads.*

He stopped the truck and opened his door. She looked up to see a small log cabin nested in a copse of dormant pecan trees. By the time he rounded the front of the truck and opened her door, she had the seat belt undone and was scooting across the seat.

"Who lives here?"

"No one. We use it in deer season. This piece of land goes back several generations. My many-times-great-grandparents built this place as their home. It's kind of like the Marshall historical marker." He laced his fingers through hers and led her up the thick slab wood steps to the porch.

She forgot all about the red hair the minute his hand touched hers.

He opened the door and stood to one side. "We never lock it. No way to get to it except past the house and few people even know it's back here anyway."

She stepped in and pulled her shawl tighter around her shoulders. It was one big square room with a set of bunk beds pushed up against the wall to her left and another set to her right. Straight ahead was the kitchen area with an old black potbellied stove and small dorm-sized refrigerator. Cabinets had no doors and she could see stacks of plates, cups, and saucers as well as grocery staples. Above the sink a squeaky clean window looked out over the naked trees. Crispy white curtains had been pushed to the sides to allow sunlight to flow in the room.

"I'll make a fire to take the chill off," Wil said.

"We can stay that long?"

"You over twenty-one?"

"What's that got to do with anything?"

He grinned. "Are you?"

"You know I am."

He pulled a patchwork quilt from a bottom bunk and wrapped it around her shoulders. "So am I, so I guess we can stay as long as we want, can't we?"

"Thank you," she muttered seconds before his

lips found hers in a scorching kiss. The quilt and kiss knocked the chill right out of her body.

"Cuddle up on that sofa. It's older than Noah but it's comfortable. It makes out into a bed. I've slept on it dozens of times since I got old enough to come back here with Dad and his brothers and all my cousins on hunting trips."

No bad boy, cowboy, or any kind of boy had ever affected her like Wil did. His touches, his kisses, and everything about him was oh so right. She settled into the corner of the sofa, pulling the quilt tighter around her body like a shield against all the emotions and feelings that bombarded her from every side. She couldn't see him building a fire but she could hear every movement and he was whistling "I Can't Help Falling in Love with You," an old Elvis tune.

The door to the old stove shut with a bang and suddenly he was on the sofa right beside her, tugging at the quilt and melting up against her for warmth. "It'll be warm in a few minutes, but right now I believe this place could put icicles on Lucifer's nose."

"That's pretty cold."

He tucked the quilt in, making a cocoon with the two of them in the center. Then one hand slowly snuck out and cupped her chin. "I believe we were in the middle of a making out session when I felt you shiver."

She shut her eyes and braced herself for the zing.

His thumb teased in that soft, sensitive area below her ear and suddenly she could hear a whole orchestra behind Elvis as he sang the song Wil had been whistling. He teased her mouth open and did a flirting dance with her tongue. The room began to warm from the fire but

Pearl didn't need it anymore. She and Wil were generating enough heat that the quilt hit the floor with her shawl soon following it.

Without breaking away from her delicious lips, he picked her up and carried her to the nearest bunk. He meant to lie her down gently but wound up tumbling into the bed with her, their bodies plastered together without enough room for a beam of sunlight between them.

Need took precedence and she forgot all about the argument or the fact that the door didn't have a lock or anything else. She and Wil tore at each other's clothes as if they had to prove that nothing could keep them from each other.

When they were naked, he pulled the quilt from the upper bunk and wrapped it over them as he covered her face in hot kisses and sunk himself inside her to prove that she was still his woman even though they'd argued.

It wasn't like anything they'd shared before. It was furious, fast, hot, and quick with both of them panting when it was over. He rolled to one side and held her tightly.

"I'm sorry," he said hoarsely.

"For what? I wanted it just like that. I had to know right then that you…"

He waited while she struggled with the words. "That I love you. I do, Red. I know it's too soon to tell you that but I do."

She pulled his mouth over to hers and whispered, "It's not too soon. I love you too, but…"

He finished the sentence for her. "But we've got to slow this wagon down or it's going to burn to the ground with the heat."

"Does that mean an encore is out of the question?" she asked.

"Hell, no! Give me a minute to catch my breath," he said.

Chapter 19

Dusk was settling around the motel when Wil walked her to the lobby door and waited while she fished her key chain from her purse.

"Tomorrow night?" he asked.

She wrapped her arms around his neck and rolled up on her toes for a kiss. "No," she said just before their lips met.

When he broke the kiss, he asked, "Why?"

"You said it, Wil. We really do have to slow things down. You aren't going to back out on going with me on Sunday, are you?"

Lucy yelled from the other end of the motel. "I saw you comin' home. I'd run up to my room to get a bite of supper while there was a quiet minute but I kept an eye on the place in case someone needed to check in."

"Hi, Lucy," Wil said and then whispered to Pearl, "I won't back out."

Pearl nodded, but she wasn't convinced. His momma didn't like red hair. In a week's time that could change the whole course of the universe.

Lucy unlocked the door.

Wil dropped a quick kiss on Pearl's forehead and whistled all the way back to the car.

"We had a slow evening but..." Lucy clamped a hand over her mouth. "You went to bed with Wil. I can see it in your eyes. How did you manage to do that at his momma's house?"

"We took a drive and there's a cabin."

"What're you goin' to do now?"

"We're going to dinner at my folks next Sunday, if he doesn't find some excuse not to go."

"But that's a whole week," Lucy said. "When me and Cleet were first in love we couldn't hardly go a whole day without seein' each other."

Pearl had told Wil that she loved him but she wasn't ready to admit it to anyone else. "You don't have to be in love to have sex."

"I agree." Lucy nodded. "After I found out what kind of man Cleet was I had lots of sex with him, but I dang sure wasn't in love no more. Didn't his momma know when you got back to the house? Lord, it's written all over your face."

"We didn't go back. Wil called and said that I had to get back to work and Lucy, she don't like red hair so she's not going to like me."

"Bullshit! She can get over that part, and if she can't then that's her tough luck. You are a wonderful person and don't you forget it. You hungry?"

"Starvin'," Pearl said.

"Why don't you run up to the Sonic and get yourself a hamburger and let me take care of things here? It'll do you good to ride a spell. It did me. Don't bring your supper home. Sit up there and watch the people. Turn on the radio and listen to some good old country music and you'll get out of them blues."

Pearl stood up and picked up her purse from the counter where she'd dropped it. "You're right, and thanks, Lucy. How many guests we got tonight?"

"Three so far. Get on out of here and go get a burger

or one of those steak sandwiches. After what you been doin' you got to be hungry," Lucy said.

"Thanks. I'll be back in a few minutes," Pearl said.

"Hey, take your time," Lucy yelled as Pearl crossed the lobby.

Blake Shelton's voice singing "The Baby" came through the speakers of the old work truck when she fired up the engine. Evidently Lucy liked the country music channels too. She remembered Wil's sisters saying the song had been written about him. As the song played she agreed that it fit him perfectly. He might not have been all those things that Blake mentioned, but there was no doubt he'd always be his momma's baby.

Just like you, her conscience yelled.

"Yes, I am, but I'm not spoiled as bad as he is."

She drove west into town and pulled into a spot at the Sonic. She rolled down the window and pushed the button, ordered a steak sandwich, large fries, and chocolate malt. A tinny voice came through the speakers telling her the amount she owed. She dug around in her purse and brought out two five-dollar bills.

The wind had picked up and swept across her face. She quickly rolled the window up and looked around just in time to see Wil crawling into the passenger's seat. Her eyebrows shot up.

"What are you doin' here?"

He leaned across the seat and kissed her. "I was hungry. Should've asked you if you wanted something before I left you. Sorry about that."

He reached across the seat and laid a hand on her shoulder. If only he could hug her tightly and never let her go, but there was something that scared the holy hell out of him. He'd found his soul mate, but what if she hadn't? What if in a year or two or three, or after a child or four or five, she decided she wanted to party again?

She wanted to undo his shirt, run her fingers over that broad chest, and dig her nails into his back; to nibble on his lip and watch his eyes go soft and dreamy when he looked at her. It felt right. Matter-of-fact, it felt damn good. But what if it really was a flash in the pan and when the heat died out she was left with nothing but a heart full of ashes?

"There's my order. See you on Sunday. Alright if I call you during this wake?" she said.

"What wake?" he asked hoarsely.

"The death-of-an-attraction wake."

"Yes, you can call." He smiled and brushed a soft kiss across her lips. "Good night again, Red."

"Good night, Wil. You really aren't just putting the brakes on so you don't have to go to my folks' place, are you?" she asked.

"I wouldn't do that to you, Red," he said.

He paid for his order and drove away, leaving her sitting there, the only car in the entire parking lot. It was a very lonely place to be, especially when her heart wanted to follow him out to the ranch.

Chapter 20

WIL HIKED A LEG ON THE FENCE AND LOOKED OUT OVER HIS cattle grazing on big round bales of hay that he'd grown on his land the previous spring and summer. The ranch was prospering and there was still a nest egg in the bank from his rodeo days in case of a bad year. He hadn't had to go to the bank for an agricultural loan yet, and as long as the land supported itself he'd be in good shape.

The ranch had been his dream since he'd been big enough to ride a stick horse all over the front yard, but that morning he wanted more than land and cows. The yearning to have someone to share his life with had become so strong in the past few weeks that he felt like poor old Rye had when he'd gone love drunk over Austin.

He heard the rattle of a truck before he could actually see it. He tipped back his hat and watched the truck come into sight. He was disappointed when it was Ace Riley and not Red's little hand-me-down truck.

He and Ace, along with Rye, Dewar, and Raylen O'Donnell, had all lived close together and had grown up at rodeos and ranch sales. Ace crawled out of his truck, shook the legs of his jeans down over his work boots, and started toward the pasture fence. Wil was several inches taller than Ace, who topped the chart at five feet ten inches tall, making him the shortest of the five men who were fast friends. He had blond curly

hair that looked like he'd been dipped in a DNA pool
over in Africa. He wore it short and didn't attempt to
tame it other than slapping an old felt hat on his head
that made his head sweat in the summer and the curls
even tighter. His eyes were blue as a robin's egg and
he had a barbed wire tat around his upper left arm just
like Rye O'Donnell had.

Wil smiled when he thought about the tat. He and Rye
and Ace were finally all twenty-one years old. They'd
been to a rodeo down in Mesquite, Texas, and had far
too many shots with beer chasers after the dance at the
end of the rodeo that night. Rye was whining about his
woman running off and leaving him and how he'd never
trust another female. Ace was driving, even though he
couldn't have passed a Breathalyzer test from six feet
away. Wil was almost asleep when the truck stopped
dead and Ace told Rye to get out.

Wil had looked up to see the flashing neon sign of
a tattoo parlor and Ace telling Rye that he was tired of
listening to his bitchin'.

"We're goin' to go get us some barbed wire around
our arms. Our left arms," he'd said with a slur. "You
comin', Wil?"

Wil had asked them why they were getting a tattoo in
the middle of the night.

"Me and Rye ain't made for marryin'. We're goin' to
put a barbed wire tat on our left arm right up next to our
hearts and never let a woman get past it, ain't we, Rye?"

"Damn straight!" Rye'd said.

Now it was eleven years later. Rye was married and
he and Austin were happy as a couple of kittens in the
milk house. Ace still swore the tat was his guardian

angel and he'd never marry, not even if she was rich and beautiful.

Since Wil had met Pearl Richland, he wasn't so quick to vow that he wasn't interested in a long-term relationship, with or without barbed wire tattooed around his arm.

"On my way over to Wichita Falls to pick up a tractor part. Tryin' to get everything in workin' order before spring hits and we don't have time to breathe," Ace hollered as he made his way toward Wil.

"This'll be your first plantin' season without Gramps around. You'll miss him," Wil said when Ace propped a leg on the fence beside him.

"Already do. Old codger had to have his way about everything in the world and wouldn't change a thing. I kept thinkin' about how I'd do things when the ranch was mine and now that it is, be damned if I'm not gettin' more like him every day." Ace looked out over the cattle. "You might as well ride over to the big city with me and we'll get some dinner over there. I heard you been keepin' company with Austin's friend, Pearl. That so?"

"Guess I have," Wil said slowly.

"You got anything you have to be doin' this mornin'?" Ace asked.

"Jack is plowing up the west forty getting it ready for spring planting. I've been thinkin' about buyin' another tractor, so I could take a look at what the prices are if I go along." He thought aloud but didn't take his foot off the fence.

Ace nodded in agreement. "You need another tractor. One tractor ain't enough for a section."

"I might add another hand come spring. Been thinkin'

about building a bunkhouse out beyond the barns.
Maybe start off little with only three rooms and a small
den and kitchen all together, but make it so I can add on
later. I really hope to buy the farm next to me when it
comes up for sale and then I'll have to have more help."

Ace headed toward his truck.

Wil followed.

Red said she needed time to see if this was going to die
in its sleep, but he didn't want it to die. He wanted it to
survive and grow. It was time to stop worrying the whole
thing to death and begin feeding it. He flipped open his
phone and sent a text message to her cell: *I miss you, Red*.

Pearl was cleaning room number twenty-four and trying to figure out why the whole place felt as sinister as
if Lucifer had spent the night in it when her cell phone
set up a vibration in her hip pocket. She pulled it out
and read his message. Those few words sent a tingling
shiver down her spine almost as hot as when he touched
her skin. She sent a message back: *Me too*.

She'd dreamed about Wil again the night before. She
tried to remember the dream as she dusted, vacuumed,
and carried the towels and sheets out to the maid's cart,
but it wouldn't materialize. She just knew that she'd
dreamed about him and when she awoke she was scared
that he wouldn't go with her on Sunday. She'd be left
out in the cold holding the bag again just like she was
when Vince left.

The cell phone vibrated again. She pulled it out, expecting another message from Wil, but it was Jasmine:
On my way to see you.

Lucy stuck her head in the door. "I'm grabbing this laundry and it'll be the last load today. I thought I'd take the truck to the library when I'm finished. You need anything from town?"

Pearl shook her head. "My friend is on her way over here from Sherman to see me. Want to have a late lunch with us?"

Lucy's smile brightened the whole parking lot. "I'd love to. Where are we going?"

"Probably just the Dairy Queen. Jasmine loves a good hamburger."

"So do I," Lucy said and disappeared down the sidewalk pushing a cart in front of her.

Pearl had just put the finishing touches on the room when a small blue truck pulled up in front of the lobby. She recognized it immediately and waved at Jasmine when she stepped out and looked around.

"This is *Psycho*!" Jasmine yelled.

Pearl hurried across the lot and hugged her friend. "I told you so. Did you think I was exaggerating? Don't answer that."

"Does it have ghosts that haunt it at night?"

"If you'd have asked me that yesterday I'd have laughed at you, but today I'm not so sure."

Jasmine looped her arm through Pearl's. "I'm starving. Can we go eat?"

She was a couple of inches shorter than Pearl, tipping the height chart at just under five feet two inches. A brunette with a delicate, angular face, full mouth, and wide set light green eyes. She wore a red sweater, jeans, and red high-heeled shoes.

"Let me call Lucy and tell her to put the laundry on

hold. What is all that?" Pearl pointed at the suitcases in the back of the truck.

"My stuff. You said there was a café for sale. I'd like to look at it and then go to the bank if I like it. I've got my 401(k) money that I could use for a down payment. You said if I came to visit I could have a room." Jasmine talked too fast without catching her breath.

Pearl patted her arm. "What happened?"

"I need a change."

"What about your job at Texas Instruments?"

"I quit. Used my vacation time as notice time and quit. I've got to get out of Sherman and away from Eddie Jay and my momma who is driving me crazy."

Pearl led her inside the lobby. "It's just a little café with an apartment above it. It's been for sale for a year and no one has been interested. Serves breakfast and lunch, closes about two in the afternoon. Doesn't require much staff. The waitress might stay until you could get the hang of things, or you two might hit it off and she'll stay forever."

"You're not going to yell and scream at me for quitting a gravy job?" Jasmine asked.

"Not me! I run the *Psycho* motel. We are thirty. It's time to change or mold. I never did look good in the color of nasty old mold and neither did you. Pick out whichever room you want. You can have it as long as you want it."

"I'll clean or keep the lobby open or whatever to pay for it. I'll need everything I can scrape up to buy that café," Jasmine said.

"Lucy and I might take you up on that."

Pearl dialed the laundry room from the phone on the counter. Lucy picked up on the second ring.

"Jasmine is here and she gets cranky when she's hungry so leave the laundry until later and let's go get a hamburger."

"Do I need to change clothes?" Lucy asked.

"I'm not."

"Then I'm on my way."

Jasmine and Pearl were sitting in the recliners in the lobby when Lucy pushed through the door. They stood up at the same time and Lucy was amazed that Jasmine was even shorter than her or Pearl. From what she'd heard about the woman she expected her to be six feet tall, bulletproof, and maybe even clad in a red, white, and blue superwoman cape.

"What's the matter, Lucy?" Pearl asked.

"Nothing. I just wasn't expecting someone short like us."

Jasmine giggled. "I wasn't expecting you to be a small woman. From what Pearl has told me about you and your escape I kinda figured you for Wonder Woman."

Lucy's smile was slow but bright. "Guess we both had different ideas. I hear you like hamburgers?"

"My favorite food in the world. I'm a real cheap date. Hamburger, fries, and a chocolate malt and a man can topple me right into bed purring the whole way."

Lucy laughed. "Didn't work that way with Cleet, but I do like hamburgers."

Pearl locked the door and led the way back through her apartment. "We'll take the Caddy."

Jasmine cocked her head to one side. "Cadillac?"

"It's not what you think," Lucy said.

"Oh. My. Sweet. Lord," Jasmine said when the doors to the garage rolled up.

"Like it?" Pearl asked.

Jasmine opened the passenger door and crawled into the backseat. "Can I have it? I'll go beg my old job back and use my 401(k) to buy this if you'll sell it to me. Did it come with this motel?"

Lucy settled into the front seat. "It is one fancy thing, isn't it?"

Jasmine ran her hands over the leather seat. "It's beautiful."

"Wil already asked if he could buy it," Pearl said as she started up the engine.

"Well, he's not your friend. I am. And he only saved your life one time. I got you out of trouble that would have gotten you killed by your momma millions of times so I get first dibs when you sell it."

Pearl pondered over what her friend had said; Wil *was* her friend. No matter what happened lately she couldn't wait to talk to him on the phone or text a message to him to tell him all about it. They made beautiful love together and she loved him. But he was her friend, and that was important too.

"Your face got serious all of a sudden," Jasmine said.

"I'm hungry." It was the truth even if it wasn't the reason she'd gone quiet trying to sort out where Wil Marshall fit into her life.

"How far is it?" Jasmine asked.

"About five minutes," Lucy said. "Be glad the noon rush is over. When school lets out for noon there's not a place to park or to sit down in the Dairy Queen."

Pearl nosed the Caddy in between two Silverado pickup trucks and carefully opened the door. Aunt Pearlita would come back to life and haunt her if she was careless and banged up the doors to the car. Her phone rang and she flipped it open as she was getting out of the car.

"What's the matter?" Lucy asked.

"Nothing. Guess it was a wrong number. They hung up."

Lucy shivered. "That gives me creeps when that happens."

"Do-da-do-do," Jasmine made noises like a scary movie. "Tell me more. Am I going to have to chase ghosts away from the Longhorn Inn?"

Lucy giggled. "No! It's harmless."

"Who are you trying to convince, Lucy? Me or you?"

"Me, of course. I still have trouble going out the door without checking to see if Cleet's truck is out there in the lot."

Jasmine threw an arm around Lucy's shoulders and led the way into the Dairy Queen. "That sorry sumbitch pokes his head up out of the sand and us three women will take care of him in a hurry."

Lucy giggled. "Yes, we will."

They ordered hamburgers, fries, and malts at the counter and were on their way to sit down at a booth when Wil pushed his way inside. He got a cup of coffee at the counter and carried it to the booth where he slid in beside Pearl.

"Y'all havin' food or ice cream?" he asked.

"Food. Wil, meet my friend, Jasmine, who is going to stay a while at the motel and plans to look at the Chicken Fried to see if she wants to buy it," Pearl said. "And this is Wil, the infamous man you've all heard about. Who got rousted out of my motel on a trumped-up murder charge and then had to wake me up every hour all night after I tried to sprout wings and fly backwards down his stairs."

Wil smiled at the ladies across the booth from him. "Hello, Jasmine, and hi, Lucy."

"Hello, what are you having besides coffee?" Lucy asked.

"Ace and I had steaks over in Wichita Falls. Came home and had to do some book work and make a bank deposit. Saw your car out there and thought I'd stop in. I've got to get on home though. Jack has got plans so I need to do the night chores, and there's a cow in the barn that I'm probably going to have to spend the night with. It's her first calf." He brushed a kiss across her lips and said, "I'll call you later, Red."

He'd barely gotten outside when Jasmine grabbed her heart and fluttered her eyelids. "That is Wil? He's one damn hot cowboy. And how come he gets to call you Red when you'd tear the limbs off anyone else for even thinking that nickname?"

Lucy nodded seriously. "That *is* Wil and the stories will take all afternoon and most of the night if she hasn't kept you up-to-date on what's goin' on. He even cleans motel rooms and can match her in a shot challenge."

"You are shittin' me!" Jasmine gasped. "He didn't pass out before you?"

"I'm not sayin' a word," Pearl declared.

Jasmine looked at Lucy. "You tell me. I bet you know. You live there and see everything."

Lucy shook her head. "Can't tell what I don't know. If she gives you the details of what happened in the motel room you come on down to my room and tell me because I can't get her to tell nothin' about that part. Wake me up no matter what time of night it is. All I know is that on New Year's mornin' that room was already halfway clean when I got to it. Makes a body wonder what they were coverin' up, don't it?"

"Start talkin' right now. I can chew and listen," Jasmine said.

"I'll give you the short version," Pearl said.

"Before you start, explain to me why that sexy cowboy gets to call you Red," Jasmine said.

The waitress brought their food on a tray and set it in the middle of the table. "Anything else I can get you ladies?"

"More ketchup," Lucy said.

"Comin' right up," she said and pulled a full bottle from the booth behind them. "Holler right loud if you need anything more."

Lucy covered her fries with ketchup and picked up her burger. "He's got special privileges that only she knows about. I don't think me or you get to call her that, though."

"Hell, I wouldn't even try. Only fight we ever had was in kindergarten when I got mad at her and called her Red. She blacked both my eyes and bloodied my nose. We were best friends from that day on and I never called her that again," Jasmine said.

Lucy almost choked before she could swallow the bite of hamburger. "Did you really?"

Pearl grinned. "I did. Nobody in the whole school ever called me that again, either."

"I guess not," Lucy said. "Damn, I wish I'd been that spunky. If I had been I'd have never put up with Cleet."

"Why didn't you just beat the shit out of him? You could've waited until he was asleep and tied him up, then taught him a lesson," Jasmine said.

Lucy slowly shook her head. "I didn't ever have that kind of nerve. I dreamed about killin' him more than once, but dreamin' about it and doin' it is two different things."

"Why didn't you beat the shit out of Eddie Jay?" Pearl asked.

"Same reason Lucy didn't whoop her husband. We get comfortable in our rut and before long it's just life. It isn't right but it's what happens," Jasmine answered. "Now talk about what has been goin' on in this place since you took over that motel. I thought I was coming to a boring area, but I'm beginning to wish I'd quit my job weeks ago."

Pearl dipped fries in a pool of ketchup. "Most of the time it is kind of boring, isn't it, Lucy?"

"Not to me. I love it at the motel. I'm never leaving. It's the best thing that ever happened to me," Lucy declared.

"Okay, here goes," Pearl said.

They'd finished their late lunch and had had two cups of coffee each when she ended the story. School had let out for the day and the line of after-school traffic went from the counter to the door.

"Why haven't you branded him? You belong on a ranch. You were always happy when you were herding your daddy's cattle with a four-wheeler or throwin' hay in the barn," Jasmine said.

"I was not! I was happiest all dressed up and going out on dates. It was you who liked coming out to the ranch. We were switched at birth. I should've been your momma's kid because she likes big parties and having fun. And you should have belonged to my daddy," Pearl argued.

"You like to have fun, but your heart and soul is on a ranch. And you are avoiding my question about why in the hell you aren't already wearing an engagement ring?" Jasmine asked.

"Because I think we need a few days to let things simmer down, and because we haven't even gotten so far as to think that we're in a serious relationship. So we sure haven't discussed the *m*-word."

"Are you dumb-ass crazy? You can see him, can't you? You aren't blind. And he gets this dreamy look in his eyes when he looks at you like he could have you for breakfast, dinner, and supper and still be hungry. I damn sure wouldn't tell him to wait a week."

"Then you can have him," Pearl said shortly.

"I'd take him, but you don't mean that. Don't slam the door of opportunity. If you do it might not open when you decide you should've walked through it rather than shut it."

"Ah, Jasmine has put on her therapy hat."

"And I look beautiful in it, don't I, Lucy?"

Lucy looked from one to the other. "Don't get me in the middle of your fight. I'm the last person to judge whether a man is worth the bullet to shoot him or not."

"Let's go home and give those kids a place to sit," Pearl said.

"They look so young," Jasmine said.

"And they're looking at us and wondering why three old women are taking up space in their booth," Lucy said.

"I'm not an old woman!" Jasmine said.

"Remember when you were sixteen. How old was thirty?" Pearl asked.

Jasmine giggled. "Ancient."

"Right! Let's go home and get you settled into a room. Tomorrow we'll go over to the café and have lunch. Let you see if you even like the idea once you've eaten there," Pearl said.

Home! Pearl thought. *It had taken a while but Henrietta really was home.*

"What café?" Lucy asked.

"It's called Chicken Fried. It's south of Ringgold. Gemma O'Donnell has a beauty shop right next door to it and it's the only café in Ringgold and the only beauty shop. We'll all three go to lunch there," Pearl said. "But I'm tellin' you right now and straight up, Lucy is my help and you cannot coerce her into coming to work for you."

Lucy beamed. Nothing could take her away from the Longhorn Inn, but it was nice to be needed and wanted.

At eleven o'clock that night Pearl had filled fifteen rooms. She stepped outside for a breath of cold, fresh air and saw a thin beam of light filtering through the slim opening in Lucy's drapes. Evidently she was engrossed in a thick romance book. Jasmine had decided on the last room at the end of the east side of the motel. Everything was dark in that area so she had turned in for the night. The rest of the place was quiet so Pearl went back inside, flipped on the NO VACANCY sign, and headed back to her apartment.

The phone rang the minute she'd kicked off her shoes and she groaned. "Longhorn Inn, may I help you?" she answered on the third ring.

"Depends on what you mean by *help me*." Wil's deep voice sent a delicious tremble down her back. "What have you got in mind?"

"If you want phone sex you better call one of those 900 numbers that charge you seven ninety-five a minute."

"I don't want phone sex. I want the real thing. Can I come over?"

"Hell, no!"

He chuckled. "So now that we got that idea nixed, how was your day? Did you get Jasmine settled in and is she really interested in buying a café?"

"My day was busy. Yes, Jasmine is settled into the last room on the east wing and yes, she is interested in the café. She loves to cook. Always has. She should've been my momma's daughter instead of me."

"You can cook and do a damn fine job of it."

"Yes, I can cook. But I don't love it like she does. Where are you?"

"In the barn wrapped up in a quilt with an old pregnant cow that won't get on the ball and deliver her calf. Jack was wrong when he thought she'd calve tonight. Every song that played all day on the radio reminded me of you, Red. I miss you so bad. Are y'all really going to Chicken Fried tomorrow?"

"Yes, we are. For lunch. Why?"

"I've got to be over that way to see about a tractor. I might stop by for lunch just to see you since you won't let me come over and take a look at the little freckle on your fanny."

"Wilson Marshall!"

"Gotcha! Good night, Red. Sweet dreams."

Chapter 21

"I ALREADY LOVE IT," JASMINE SAID WHEN THEY PARKED IN front of the Chicken Fried café. It was a two-story white frame building that had started out as a home in the thirties for the family who owned a car dealership right next door. In the sixties a couple bought it and put in the 81 Diner. That folded in the early seventies and they rented it out as a home for ten years before selling it in 1981 to Dottie Jones who turned it into a café again. When her husband died in 2000, she had renovations done on the upstairs and created a living space. Now she was seventy and needed a hip replacement. The stairs were difficult for her to climb and she wanted to retire. But no one wanted to buy a café out in the middle of nowhere.

"It is cute, but I wouldn't want to cook for a living," Lucy said from the backseat of the Caddy. "Have you eaten here, Pearl?"

"Few times with Gemma. She's Rye's sister who owns that beauty shop." She pointed to the small building next door.

Jasmine beat them to the porch and sat down in one of the six white rocking chairs. "I like this idea. Sit and visit a spell instead of fast food and run. You got any idea what they're askin' for the place?"

Pearl shook her head. "It's been for sale for a long time so I'm sure it's negotiable. Dottie wants to move down to Beaumont and live close to her daughter and grandkids, so she might take a reasonable offer. And she needs hip surgery. She does the cookin' and hires a waitress."

"Would you change the name?" Lucy asked.

"No. I think Chicken Fried is cute. I even like the sign." Jasmine pointed to the stenciled letters on the plate glass window. She could see inside and there were only two tables left. A waitress hustled from the dining room to the kitchen but took time to stop and talk to the customers. The whole atmosphere was laid back and country.

"It'll be more work than making brownies in an Easy Bake Oven," Pearl said.

"Momma will hate it," Jasmine said.

Pearl led the way inside. "My momma hates the Longhorn Inn."

"Sit anywhere," the waitress called out. "Menu is on the table. I'll be right with you."

Covered with red and white checked oilcloth, each table had a lazy Susan with a sugar shaker, artificial sweetener, salt and pepper shakers, hot sauce, ketchup, and paper towel dispenser in the center. The laminated menu was printed on one sheet of paper and stuck between the hot sauce and sugar shaker.

Jasmine picked it up and studied it. Each day there was a lunch special. That day it was turkey and dressing, green beans, mashed potatoes, and choice of cranberry or tossed salad. If a person didn't want the plate special then they could order burgers, grilled cheese, or chicken fried steak, which came with a choice of mashed potatoes or fries, vegetable of the day, and a tossed salad.

She liked the setup but was already thinking about

what desserts she'd offer to go with the lunch special. Hot yeast rolls would be a given, so one day she'd make iced cinnamon rolls. Another she would offer a choice of three or four pies.

"I see wheels turning in your head," Lucy said.

"It's a perfect size. I'd just need one waitress and I'd do the cooking," she whispered.

They were so engrossed in the menu that they didn't see Martha Jane Marshall until she was standing right beside Pearl and said, "Hello, may I join you ladies?"

Pearl was so startled that she nodded.

Martha Jane wore jeans, a red sweater, and cowboy boots, and her hair had that fresh done look and smell. "I just came from Gemma's. Got a perm and my eyebrows waxed so that's why I look like I've been crying. Thought I'd stop in and have a hamburger since Jesse is off at a sale."

Pearl made introductions as Martha Jane settled into the fourth chair. "These are my friends. Lucy, who works at the Longhorn Inn and Jasmine, who might be interested in buying this place. This is Martha Jane, Wil's mother."

"I can see that," Lucy said. "He has your pretty brown eyes."

Martha Jane smiled. "Thank you. It's a pleasure to meet you. Pearl, I owe you an apology. I'm sorry for that comment that you heard as you were leaving the house the other day. I hope you don't hold it against me."

"Accepted, but what is it that you've got against red hair?" Pearl asked.

"It's something I never told anyone else. Even Jesse doesn't know part of it. But I wouldn't stand in the way of my son's happiness for anything in this world. Jesse was in love with a red-haired girl before I came into the picture. She taunted me horrible when me and Jesse started dating and said that she could have him back anytime she wanted. The day I married him she showed up at my house that morning and claimed that he slept with her the night before. After we were married she told everyone that the illegitimate son she bore was Jesse's child. She was a thorn in my side until she moved to California. I still pray every day that she never comes back to Texas."

"Wow! I wouldn't like redheads either," Pearl said.

"Thank you!"

"Why didn't you snatch her bald-headed and then slap her for not having any hair?" Pearl asked.

"I wasn't as brazen then as I am now."

"Too bad," Jasmine said.

The waitress stopped at their table with a pad and looked at Martha Jane first. "You decided?"

"Yes, I want a hamburger with mustard and no onions. Fries and Diet Coke. And I'll take the bill for this table today," Martha Jane said.

The waitress looked at Jasmine.

"Chicken fried steak, mashed potatoes, and sweet tea."

"I'll have the same," Lucy said.

"I want the lunch special. What's the vegetable of the day?" Pearl asked.

"Green beans with chunks of potatoes and ham."

"Sounds good. Sweet tea, please."

The waitress wrote the orders on her pad and disappeared toward the kitchen.

Pearl touched Martha's hand. "You don't have to pay for lunch."

Martha held up a palm. "My treat. I insist."

"You insist on what?" Wil asked from two feet away. He pulled a chair away from another table and pushed it up close to Pearl. "I didn't know you were having lunch with my mother."

"Neither did I."

Wil leaned across the space and kissed Pearl softly on the lips. "Hello, darlin'."

She always looked fantastic to him whether she was wearing jeans and a sweatshirt to clean motel rooms or all dolled up for a New Year's party, but that day looking at her made his mouth as dry as if he'd just crammed it full of sand. She wore faded jeans, a Western shirt with pearl snaps left open over a soft light green T-shirt. And she had on scuffed up cowboy boots. This was his favorite version of Red and he couldn't keep his eyes off her.

She reached under the tablecloth and squeezed his thigh.

He shot her a sexy grin.

"It wasn't planned. We just happened to be in the same place at the same time. What brings you to Ringgold today?" Martha asked.

"Chicken fried steak," he said.

The waitress came right over. "Your regular?"

He waved his hand around the whole table. "That's right. Put it all on one ticket and I'll take care of it."

"Thank you." Martha Jane smiled.

"But—" Pearl raised a hand and started to argue.

Wil grabbed her hand and held it tightly in his lap.

"So what is your first impression, Jasmine?" he asked.

"That I want to start to work tomorrow," she answered.

"It's gettin' up early and working hard," he said.

"Been doin' that my whole life at something I didn't even like. I'm goin' to talk to the owner after we eat and see if I can set up an appointment to go over the books and then I'm going to make an offer. My momma is going to pitch a fit but it's what I've always dreamed of doing."

"Why would your momma pitch a fit?" Martha Jane asked.

"Because her daughter wasn't supposed to be a cook," Jasmine said.

"Your momma disappointed in you?" Martha Jane looked at Pearl.

"Probably."

"How about you?" Martha Jane shifted her eyes to Lucy.

"My momma is so busy tryin' to take care of kids and grandkids that she don't have time to think about what I do for a livin'," Lucy said.

"Well, I wish I'd had all y'all's sass when I was your age," Martha Jane said.

The waitress brought a burger and fries on a heavy white stone plate in one hand and two chicken fried dinners lined up the other arm. She set them before Martha, Jasmine, and Lucy and went back to the kitchen for the other two plates which she set in front of Wil and Pearl. One more trip brought their drinks.

"Anything else I can get you folks?" she asked.

"We're good," Pearl said.

"Then I'll leave the ticket with this good lookin' cowboy and y'all can fight him over it." She handed it to Wil and was off to take orders from another couple who'd just arrived.

"God, this is good. Think she'll give me the secret

to making chicken fried like this?" Jasmine said between bites.

"Buttermilk," Lucy said.

Jasmine raised an eyebrow. "What?"

"Buttermilk. First you roll the steak in flour, then egg and buttermilk whipped together, and then back in flour. Then you get the grease really hot and only turn the steak one time. Turn it anymore and it'll be soggy. Trick is to fry it fast but get it done without losing the breading."

"You sure you don't want to work for me rather than clean rooms at the motel? I'll pay you more than Pearl pays you."

Pearl slapped Jasmine on the arm. "Some friend you are. Stay at my motel and steal my friend."

Lucy shook her head. "No, ma'am. I'm happy right where I am. I've had my share of hot kitchens and a man who didn't appreciate a single minute of all the hard work."

"Oh, you are divorced?" Martha Jane asked.

"You could say that," Lucy said softly.

"And you grew up with Pearl?" Martha Jane asked Jasmine.

"I did. My momma and hers are best friends. She is two months older than me. Her birthday is two days after Valentine's and I was born on Easter. Of course mine hasn't been on Easter but a few times, but we always had a big pink party on her birthday."

Wil had to let go of Pearl's hand to eat his lunch but he kept a thigh snug against hers. So her birthday was only three weeks away. He filed that information away. Later he'd plan something special for her birthday.

Maybe a quiet dinner for two with watermelon wine, rose petals, and satin sheets.

"I'm going over to Nocona to look at a good used tractor. Rancher over there has three for sale. I'm thinkin' about buyin' one. Want to go with me?" Wil asked Pearl.

"I'm driving," Pearl said.

"No, I am driving," he argued.

"I meant I drove over here in the Caddy."

"Go on. I'll drive the Caddy back to the Longhorn when I'm finished talking to the owner. I promise I won't hurt it," Jasmine said.

"And I'll tattle if she goes too fast or takes any stupid chances," Lucy said.

"I don't know much about tractors, except how to drive them," Pearl said.

Martha Jane turned her head so fast that her neck popped loudly. "You know how to drive a tractor?"

"Sure she does," Jasmine said. "Her father works at Texas Instruments, but he's also got this big old cattle ranch over south of Sherman. He made her plow fields every spring and summer. Her mother about died at the thought of her baby girl out there on a tractor but John said it was good for her. One summer he made both of us work a whole week in the fields as punishment."

"What did you do?" Lucy asked.

"We got into Daddy's good bourbon and then filled the bottle up with water so he wouldn't miss the liquor," Pearl said.

"John Richland is your father?" Martha Jane said slowly.

Pearl nodded. "Don't tar and feather me and run me out of town on a rail because of my heritage."

"He's bought cattle at our sale. Brought your mother to our sale last year. We had a very nice visit at the dinner afterwards. So you are her daughter. I would have never guessed."

"I look like an ancestor on Daddy's side and I'm afraid I got her quick temper, too. It's a sore spot with Momma who is a prim and proper southern lady," Pearl said.

Wil's dark eyebrows knit together in a solid line. "A southern lady?"

Pearl patted his arm. "You'll do fine when you meet her on Sunday. You aren't going to back out, are you?"

"I keep telling you that I'll be there," he said.

She nodded. It wasn't easy to believe him, but then he'd never lied to her. It was that niggling old thing from her past that kept raising its ugly head to torment her. Vince's mother hated her enough to send him away. Martha Jane apologized, but how would she really, really feel about a red-haired daughter-in-law?

Pearl nodded. "Just don't bring up great-granny Richland. She was a McDougal before she married and spoke with an Irish lilt. Daddy said she was wild Irish to the bone and had flaming red hair," Pearl said.

Wil polished off the last of his steak and pushed his plate back. "Okay, I'll remember that. You going with me to look at tractors?"

"I don't think so," Pearl said.

"Go on," Jasmine told her. "Lucy already said she'll keep me in line."

"Okay, but I need to be back in Henrietta by three for check-ins," she said.

"I can do that. You get her back by bedtime though," Lucy said.

—∿∿—

Wil kept time to the country music coming from the radio with his thumb on the steering wheel as they drove east. The sky was winter blue with only a few wispy clouds on the horizon.

"You think Jasmine will really buy that café?" he asked when they reached the outskirts of Nocona.

Pearl nodded.

"Think she'll get tired of it in six months and shut it down?"

Pearl shook her head.

"Not very talkative today, are you?"

"Well, you didn't set the cab on fire with conversation the whole way over here so don't blame me for the quietness. We're like a wildfire, Wil. It's hot as hell and destructive when it's burning, but it dies out pretty quick. It scares me that we might be just two people who've had a helluva lot of wild, hot sex and there's nothing left."

He turned right and stopped the truck after he crossed the cattle guard. "You really believe that?"

"I don't want to believe it but…" She let the sentence hang.

He pulled her across the seat to sit close to him, took her cheeks in his hands, and kissed her all over the face until she was giggling. The final kiss landed on her lips and there was no doubt between them that the fire was a helluva lot more than a flash in the pan. He drove on and parked the truck in front of a barn.

She let herself out of the truck and yelled at the elderly man coming out of the barn. "Hear you got some tractors for sale."

He pushed his sweat-stained old straw hat back on his head and grinned. "I got three for sale. How many you wantin' to drive home today, darlin'?"

His striped overalls were worn at the knees and hung on his lanky frame; his boots scuffed and down at the heels; his work jacket had patches on the elbows. He reminded Pearl of a scarecrow set out in the middle of a pumpkin patch to keep the birds from pecking holes in the pumpkins.

"Never know. If they are a buck ninety-nine a piece, I might just take them all three," she said.

"I reckon they'll be a sight higher than that but I bet me and you can reach some kind of agreement. You like John Deere?"

"Love that shade of green." She ran a hand over the biggest tractor like she was petting a horse. "Looks like you take care of your equipment."

"Honey, my wife, God rest her soul, told me when we married that if I kept my barn and equipment as clean as she kept her house and her cookstove we'd get along fine. We made it sixty years. I'm Farris Smith. Who are you?"

"I'm Pearl. Your wife was a wise woman. Interested in selling her cookstove?" Pearl hopped up in the seat and wrapped her hands around the steering wheel.

"No, honey. My daughter wants it."

"And I'm Wil Marshall, Mr. Smith." Wil extended his hand. "I'm the one who called about the tractors. You say you got three for sale?"

Farris had a firm handshake in spite of his bony, veined hands. "That's right. I'm sellin' off what I can and then I'm goin' to make the folks who bought the farm a deal on what's left over," he said.

Wil walked around the middle-sized tractor that was in mint condition. It wasn't new but it looked as if it had just rolled out of a display room.

"Why didn't they want it all?" he asked.

"Got their own equipment. Live right next door. That'd be two section lines down the road. I got two sections and they're makin' their place double in size," he explained. "Your wife is a pretty little thing. Bet she's hell on wheels. Can you keep up with her?"

Pearl hopped off the tractor and joined the two men. Wil pulled her tight against him and kissed her on the top of the head.

"It's tough but I manage. You know how these red-heads are. They got a temper and you got to stay a step ahead of 'em all the time."

Farris chuckled. "I sure do. My wife was a little short package like her. Didn't have red hair but had them same green eyes."

Pearl played along. "We got to have a temper or you old cowboys would run right over us."

"She even sounds like my wife. You take care of her, Wil. Them kind is hard to come by. Now about these here tractors. I've got each one of them priced separate, but if you was willin' to take all three I'd make you a mighty fine deal."

"I don't need but one. Maybe the middle-sized one," Wil said.

"How good of a deal you talkin' about?" Pearl asked.

"Tell you what. I ain't had my dinner yet so I'm goin' in the house and eat. Keys are in the tractors and there's forty acres behind the barn of nothin' but plowed up ground. Take them out there and run them around the field a few times. See which one you want and then we'll talk money." With a wave, he headed for the house, a gray frame ranch style place to the west of the barn.

Pearl shook loose from Wil and climbed up in the biggest tractor and looked down at him.

"You really know how to work the gears on that thing?" he asked.

She smiled at him, turned the key, and shut the door. She backed the tractor up, drove it around the barn and out into the field. It handled like a Caddy compared to the old worn out piece of crap her father had made her drive all week in the hay field that summer she and Jasmine got into trouble. It had a closed cab, air conditioning, and even a radio.

Wil folded his hands across his chest and leaned against the rough wood at the back of the barn. She didn't grind the gears a single time and the tractor purred like a kitten in her hands. When she reached the end of the field, she turned around without a hitch and drove it back to the barn.

She hopped down from the cab, landed square on her feet, and looked up at him. "Drives like a Caddy. Air conditioning and heat works fine. Radio picks up the country music station in Dallas loud and clear. Gears are tight. Cab is clean as the day it was bought. You can test this one while I see how the mid-sized one handles."

"Don't need to. I could see and hear it just fine. Take the next one around the field. It's the one I'm most interested in," Wil said.

"Don't get in a hurry about making up your mind. He might make you a deal you can't turn down on the whole lot of them. Bank would loan you the money on good equipment like this in a heartbeat," she said.

Wil bit back a grin. He didn't need to borrow money. He had cattle to outfit his ranch before he bought it and money left over after the sale from his rodeo days.

She drove the next tractor around the field and brought it back. "Just as well kept up as the bigger one. He's used this one more. Ask about how many hours are on each one. I'll bet this one has more than any of them because the seat is worn down more and the radio knob is looser."

When she'd driven the smaller one and parked it she said, "This is my favorite. I betcha his wife drove it because I can almost smell her perfume still lingering in there. It turns on a dime and if I had a ranch I'd buy it. Aren't you going to drive them?"

Wil shook his head. "He'll bring his books to show me how many hours they've been used and the upkeep. He looks honest. We'll see what his askin' price is on each one."

She bounced up on the tailgate of the pickup truck and swung her legs like a little girl. Driving the tractors had been fun. "So tell me, why are you buying more equipment?"

"I told you already. The ranch next to mine is going to be up for grabs before long and I'd like to expand. More land could run more cattle. The Lazy M takes care of itself, which means I raise my own feed for my cattle. So more cattle means more hay, which needs more land. I could use one more tractor right now. If I buy the land next to mine, I'll need at least two more and a bunkhouse so I can hire more help. Jack and I do fairly well but it stretches us pretty thin in the spring and summer."

"You like ranchin', don't you?"

He sat down beside her, his thigh tight against hers. "I love it. It's all I've ever known."

"You sound like my dad."

"Is that a good thing?"

"He says that his job gets in the way of his ranchin'."

"Guess it's a good thing, then."

"So which one are you going to buy and how much are you willin' to pay for it?" she asked.

"Depends on how many hours are on each one. I could use the big one but the middle-sized one is probably more in my price range," he said.

The back door of the house slammed and Farris took his time getting from the yard to the barn. He had a toothpick in the corner of his mouth and a quart jar of sweet tea in his hand.

"My wife woulda fussed at me for not offerin' y'all something to drink. You want some tea I'll go on back in the house and fix you up a jar full."

"We're good," Wil said. "You got some nice equipment here. Could I see the books to see how many hours are on each one?"

"Big boy there has three hundred. The middle one is the one I used the most and she's got four hundred and fifty. Little girl was Momma's tractor. She liked to get out in the field ever so often just to show me that she was still the boss. I hate to sell her but there ain't no way I need her where I'm goin'. She's got two hundred hours on her." Farris leaned on the fender of the truck and looked lovingly at the three tractors.

Pearl patted his hand. "Got lots of good memories in those green things, haven't you?"

Farris's voice quivered when he answered, "Yes, missy, I sure do. Me and Momma made us a deal when we married. We wouldn't never borrow no money for nothin' and we wouldn't buy on time. We saved a long time to buy our first tractor. It was a used John Deere and Momma worried that the mules we'd been plowin' with would get their feelin's hurt. We raised up four kids and times got hard sometimes, but we never went to the bank. I lost her three months ago. Ranch ain't the same without her."

"If the ranch don't produce it, you don't need it?" Pearl said.

"Don't never go against that and you'll be fine. I was askin' fifty-five for the big one, fifty for the middle one, and forty for the little girl. I'd made up my mind to take a hundred thirty for all three but if you kids want them, I'll take a hundred and twenty-five and be glad they're goin' to a good home. Crazy, ain't it, how you get attached to equipment just like they was animals."

"We'll take them," Pearl said without hesitating.

Wil's eyes widened. He'd been prepared to part with sixty thousand that day but not a hundred and twenty-five thousand.

"You don't think we'd better talk about it?" he asked Pearl in a tight-lipped, hoarse voice.

"No. It's a good deal and I like that little girl real well. I think I'll enjoy plowing up the fields with her and hookin' up a hay fork on the front to take the big round bales to the feed lot," she said. "You want to write Farris a check out of your account or should I?"

Wil almost swallowed his tongue. Was she willing to bankroll him?

"I'll write a check. I can probably get over here Saturday with a truck to take them out of your way," Wil said.

"That will work out just fine. Not that I don't trust you kids, but that way I'll be sure your check clears the bank by then."

"I understand." Wil reached for his checkbook inside his coat pocket. "I appreciate the good deal."

"You kids keep up that business about not goin' into debt and you'll do just fine. I'll go on in the house and bring the books out so you can see I'm not blowin' smoke up your under britches about the hours and the maintenance."

When he was in the house and the door was closed, Wil turned to Pearl. "Why did you do that?"

"Because it's a helluva deal. I was a loan officer at the bank in Durant. I know farm equipment. You should be dropping down on your knees and askin' for forgiveness for stealing those tractors from Farris. His kids may put out a contract on you when they find out that you rinky-dooed him right out of them."

"Maybe I didn't want to spend that much money today. Maybe I don't even have that much in my account," he said.

"Then I'll write half of it out of mine and claim the little girl as mine. I'll pay you room and board for her and come visit her when I get a hankering to drive around in the fields."

"Where did you get that much money?"

She pointed a long, slim finger at him. "Darlin', don't you worry about my bank account. If I wanted to buy those tractors and set them in the middle of the gravel parking lot at the Longhorn Inn just to look at, I could do it."

Farris returned with the paperwork all neatly filed in folders. "Momma took care of things proper."

He and Wil exchanged folders for a check.

"Thank you for doin' business with me. I think you'll be right happy with them and I feel like Momma is smiling down from heaven."

"I'm sure she is," Pearl said. "Let's go on home, darlin'. I can't wait to tell Lucy and Jasmine about the tractors."

"Them your daughters?" Farris asked.

"No, just my good friends," Pearl said.

"Well, you kids have a good day and I'll see y'all on Saturday." Farris put the check in his bibbed pocket and sauntered back toward the house.

Chapter 22

THE TEMPERATURE HOVERED AROUND ONE OR TWO degrees above freezing and it rained all day on Sunday. Three guests were all that checked into the Longhorn on Saturday night and they'd left early that morning, so Lucy and Pearl had the rooms cleaned by mid-morning. Jasmine had driven back to Sherman for the weekend to tell her mother that she was buying a café in Ringgold, Texas. Lucy had borrowed Delilah and gone to her room with a book for the rest of the day.

At noon Tess called the first time.

"Hello, Mother," Pearl said.

"You better start early because it's raining and the weatherman says it could freeze." Tess went right into the conversation without a hello.

"Mother, it's only rain. We'll be there in plenty of time. How's Aunt Kate?" Pearl said, but there was still a little doubt hiding in the back of her heart. One that said he'd change his mind at the last minute. He'd said they needed to slow the wagon down after that fantastic week of sex. Maybe after the week apart he'd put the brakes on the wagon and stop it completely.

When she tuned back into her mother's ranting Tess was saying, "Kate is cantankerous! She's trying to bully me into going to Savannah for a week with them. She's using the excuse that she and Mother shouldn't be traveling alone at their age, and please tell me that he's your boyfriend. It's bad enough that you spent the night at his ranch without a chaperone but if he's not your boyfriend that makes it even worse," Tess said.

"I don't know what he is right now." Pearl could see Tess going up like a bonfire if she knew about the week of sex every night.

Tess groaned. "I heard that you've had dinner with him and his family and then with his mother at the first of the week. That sounds serious to me. Did you shave your legs?"

"What?"

"Did you shave your legs and wear fancy underpants when you went to dinner with him?"

"What has that got to do with anything?"

Tess sighed. "You did, didn't you? I really, really did not want you to get mixed up with a rancher, but I suppose it's better than the alternative. Drive careful. I'll see you at cocktails."

"What's the alternative, Mother?"

"An ex-con biker who murdered his mother might be worse, but I'd have to think about it." She hung up, leaving only a guilt trip in her wake.

Pearl had talked to her mother six times by four thirty. She was about ready to sign the motel over to Lucy and run away to the Sahara Desert with nothing but a canteen. No cell phone. No computer and no way for her mother to get in touch with her. Lucy had the right idea when she faked her death and got the hell out of Dodge or Kentucky or wherever the hell it was. Would Wil leave his cows and ranch and go with her if she promised him wild sex every night?

She opened her closet doors and took out a pair of

skin-tight jeans, a Western cut lacy blouse that she'd worn to the rodeo the spring before, and her ivory eel cowboy boots. She chose a silver pendant with a crossed set of pistols over angel wings and snapped it onto a chunky necklace of graduated silver beads and went out into the lobby to see what Lucy had to say.

"Wow! You look like a cowgirl," Lucy said.

"I'm hoping my mother thinks the same thing. It's payback for her drivin' me crazy all afternoon," Pearl said.

"If that's payback, then what were you going to wear?"

"A green cocktail dress, but she has pestered the shit out of me all day so she gets the cowgirl me and she hates that."

"Why?"

"Because she wanted me to be Miss America. Beauty pageants, fluffy dresses, world peace, and flaming batons."

"What did you want to be?"

Pearl cocked her head to one side. "Did anyone ever tell you that you'd make a wonderful therapist?"

"Not me. I didn't even finish high school and them kind of people have to go to college. What did you want to be?"

"Truth?"

Lucy nodded.

"I wanted to be just like Aunt Pearlita. Be my own boss and do my own thing, say what I wanted and to hell with everyone else."

"Looks like you got your wish."

Pearl grinned. "I did, didn't I?"

Wil walked in and caught the last sentence. "You did what? You are stunning." He crossed the lobby in a few long strides, picked Pearl up, and swung her around several times. "I've missed you so bad."

"Thank you." Pearl blushed. "You look pretty damn good yourself and you are right. This separation shit is for the outhouse."

He tucked her arm into his.

"Don't wait up, Lucy. We might be late."

"No, we won't," Pearl said. "We'll be home by ten at the latest, maybe earlier."

Lucy waved them both off and went back to the computer where she was reading a Kentucky newspaper. Every day she checked to see if there was any more news about her, and every day she was relieved when nothing happened in her hometown.

Wil settled Pearl into the passenger's seat of his pickup and rounded the front end on his way to the driver's side. She stretched her neck to get a full view of him. Starched Wranglers that fit his sexy butt like a glove and stacked up over his shiny brown cowboy boots; chocolate-colored shirt that matched his eyes; and a deep brown Western cut corduroy jacket. His hair had been cut since they'd gone to Nocona to buy the tractors but it still looked like he'd combed it with his fingers into a devil-may-care look.

"Kiss me," she said.

He leaned across the seat and kissed her hard three times. "Don't be nervous. I promise not to eat with my fingers or pick my nose. Tell me about the folks I'm meeting tonight."

"Mother. Tess Landry Richland. The sweetheart of Savannah and runner-up for Miss Georgia when she was in college. The real deal with a singing voice from heaven and big blue eyes. If the other girl hadn't been a senator's daughter, Momma would have had the crown and it would be mounted on her tombstone when she dies."

Wil chuckled.

"It's the God's honest truth, Wil Marshall."

"Okay, now your father."

"Daddy is Texan. Cowboy boots. Tailor made Western cut clothes. Not as tall as you, more lanky. Good lookin' enough to make Momma move to Texas and bitch about it every day. She loves him but nobody is going to ever forget that she left her beloved Savannah for him."

Wil couldn't keep the grin off his face.

"And Granny who is visiting from Savannah. In the first five minutes she'll tell you that Momma was a runner-up for Miss Georgia and could have been Miss America. And that she comes to visit in the winter because the Texas heat in the summertime would melt her into her casket."

Wil laughed out loud.

"Don't laugh yet. There's still Aunt Kate. That's Granny's sister who was the wild one in the family. We think she's eighty-three because she's older than Granny and Granny is eighty-one. She will try to seduce you so get ready for it."

The laughter stopped. "You are shittin' me."

"Not even a little stink. She will and you'll have to play along or else she'll get her feelings hurt and I'll never hear the end of it. Tell her she's beautiful and flirt with her. Tell her that I saved your sorry ass from prison and you owe me for it."

"Prison! I thought this was all about thanking me for staying up all night with you."

"Well, there is that. Aunt Kate will want to really, really thank you."

Wil slowed down for the red light in Nocona. "Now you are scaring me."

She laughed. "I can't do it. I thought I could. Aunt Kate is very prim and proper. She really is over eighty and none of us will ever see her birth certificate, and we've been told that if we put her age in the newspaper obituary when she dies she will haunt us. But she won't make a play for you. She and Granny will bicker about how handsome you are right in front of you, but they are true blue old southern gals."

"You are wicked, Red. I believed you just like I did when you said your name was Minnie Pearl."

Pearl giggled and all the tension left her body. "Why don't you call me Minnie instead of Red all evening?"

"Because Red suits you better."

―――∞―――

Tess met them at the door and ushered them through the foyer into the living room of the long, low ranch house that looked like it sprawled on forever from the outside. The foyer with its gold gilt mirrors and Victorian settee and tables was the exact opposite of the living room done up in buttery soft leather sofas, a stone fireplace, and hardwood floors.

"They've arrived," Tess told everyone in the living room. "Pearl, darlin', introduce us, please."

"This is Wil Marshall. He's a rancher over in Henrietta and y'all know how we met. Wil, this is my mother, Tess; my father, John Richland; my granny, Miz Audry Landry; and her sister, Kate Fornell. Now that's done, Daddy, do you have Coors on ice?"

John nodded toward the bar.

"We are very pleased to meet you." Granny held out a blue veined hand. Her hair was still the same color as Tess's and her eyes as blue. Age had taken its toll on her face but her smile was breathtaking even at well past eighty. "We've heard so much about you and I do believe you are a Texan just like John. He stole my daughter away from Savannah and brought her down here to this hot country. I only visit in the winter because I'd suffocate and die in the summertime."

Wil brought Granny's hand to his lips and brushed a kiss across her fingertips. "It's all my pleasure, Miz Landry."

"You can call me Granny like Pearl does."

"Thank you," Wil said.

"And I'm Kate. I'm not as fragile as my sister." Kate held out a hand. Her hair was a shade darker than Audry's and there was a faint gray cast toward the roots. She was shorter and her sparkling eyes said that Pearl had told the truth when she said Kate had been the wild one. "I never had children so Pearl is my surrogate child. Thank you for taking care of her. She can be a handful, and she got that from me."

Wil kissed her fingertips. "Did she get her beauty from you as well?"

"He's too slick," Tess whispered to Pearl, but she held her hand out and smiled her brightest.

Wil kissed her fingertips. "I'm so pleased to meet you, but you all have to know that it was just precautionary that I stay up all night with her, and besides, she saved me before that."

John stuck out his hand. "I'm her father and I understand you run some cattle over in Henrietta. You any kin to Jesse Marshall from Bowie?" He was almost as tall as Wil but twenty pounds thinner. His face was angular and his eyes the same color as Pearl's. His dark hair had a heavy sprinkling of gray in the temples, and his skin looked like old leather from so many hours in the sun. He was slightly bowlegged from sitting a horse every evening and weekends, but he wore his Western cut dress slacks and shirt with style.

Wil shook John's hand firmly. "Jesse is my father. He taught me everything I know about ranching, sir. And I'm very glad to meet you. I understand you raise Angus?"

"That's right. What can I get you to drink?"

"Jack Daniel's. Two fingers. Neat."

"A man's drink. I like a shot of Jack before supper too. Gets a man ready to enjoy a good meal. Come on in the library and let me show you a picture of my prize Angus bull. He's throwin' big old calves that's got a jump on weight from birth. 'Course you got to have Angus heifers to breed him with or else the calves are too big for them to deliver."

"Cows, bulls, and ranchin'. God Almighty, John!" Tess said with a southern twang.

"Y'all can visit with Pearl. You been whinin' all week about how you never get an hour with her alone. Me and Wil don't need to hear about women things. Holler when supper is ready." John poured whiskey into two glasses, handed one to Wil, and then led the way through a door into the library.

"We'll keep him," Aunt Kate said the minute the door closed behind the men. "He's yummy. If I was thirty years younger I'd take him away from you."

"If you were thirty years younger, you'd still be old enough to be his mother," Granny huffed. "But he's a charmer, that one is, Pearl. And I like that in a man. That last one you had was a stuffed shirt. I didn't like him."

Pearl looked at her mother.

Tess picked up her margarita and downed half of it. "Don't expect me to open up both my arms because he kissed my fingers. He's another John Richland. You'd be getting your father in a younger form."

Pearl went to the bar and popped the lid off a bottle of Coors, tilted it back, and let the icy cold beer slide down her throat. "I'm not marrying the man tomorrow. I've only known him a few weeks. I just wanted you all to meet him so you would stop pestering me about him. Now you know he's a respectable man."

Aunt Kate laughed so hard that mint julep shot out her nose.

Granny shook a finger under Pearl's nose. "I swear you didn't get a bit of your mother's southern grace."

Tess did that thing with her chin that let Pearl know she'd been disgraced. "You might have done it, but you don't have to talk about it."

"Momma, it happened. We had a shot contest and I gave him a solid alibi and had a helluva hangover. He thought he could out-drink me on Jack and I proved him wrong."

Kate swallowed the mint julep quickly. "How many?"

"I think it was ten but it might have been eleven shots, but we were both still standing so I guess it was a tie."

"And he could still do it?" Kate asked.

"Kate!" Granny slapped her on the arm and then looked at Pearl. "Well, could he?"

Pearl held up three fingers.

"Holy shit! Don't you dare let him get away," Kate said.

Audry smoothed the front of her black velvet dress. "You should have stayed in Savannah, Tess. If you had, your daughter would not be running around like a hoyden sleeping with men she gets drunk with. You sound like Kate. She would've done something like that when she was thirty. Only difference is she wouldn't have owned up to it."

Kate shook her finger at Audry. "Tess married a man who adores her. She shouldn't have stayed in Savannah, Audry. She's right where she belongs. And Pearl, darlin', you be glad you live in an era when you can talk about whatever you want to. We fought long and hard for our women's rights."

Tess sighed. "I'm in the middle. Got a daughter who is more Texan than southern belle. A husband who *is* Texan, and then there's you two." She looked at her mother and aunt. "I think I'd rather join forces with Pearl."

Pearl jerked her head around to look at her mother. "What did you say?"

"Well, it's the truth. You're goin' to end up with that man in there and your father is going to be tickled to death with him. He's a rancher and they can talk cows and bulls and drink whiskey together. He'll be the son John never had. I'm glad you slept with him."

Pearl shook her head but the words didn't fly out her ears. "I can't believe you are saying that."

"I'm not an old fossil, darlin'. I know that today's woman is different than we were and I'm glad for it. But don't tell your father that you got drunk and slept with Wil. Let him think that you both passed out and slept in different beds. It's better that way." Tess patted Pearl on the arm. "Now, I'm going to tell the cook to put the food on the table and we're going to make those two ranchers come out and be nice to us. We are four beautiful women who deserve their attention."

"Momma, I might not end up with Wil."

"Bullshit!" Tess said.

"Double that," Kate said.

"Triple it," Granny said.

"You are all crazy as…" Pearl hesitated.

"We'll see." Tess smiled her brightest. "Maybe that bit of Indian in him will thin down Great-grandma's red hair and I'll get some dark-haired grandkids."

"Or maybe it'll be a throwback and I'll get a blond-haired great-granddaughter who'll be the next Miss Texas," Granny said.

"Y'all had better get on in to the supper table because you are on the verge of getting drunk," Pearl said.

"If we get drunk do we get to sleep with a Texas cowboy?" Kate whispered.

—◆◆◆—

The cook brought out hot yeast rolls and potato soup to start supper. It was one of Pearl's favorite soups, but she was so busy stealing glances at Wil that she hardly tasted it. He ate two rolls and every bit of his soup while telling the story of how Red had crawled right up on those tractors and sweet-talked Farris into a steal of a deal.

John smiled brightly and nodded at his daughter.

The next course was salad with homemade honey

mustard dressing and croutons made from day old garlic bread, toasted in the oven, and sprinkled with Parmesan cheese.

"This is really good," Wil said.

"Thank you," Tess said. "Mother taught me to make the croutons. They're the secret to a good salad."

"Tell me, how big is this property that you've got your eye on up there in Henrietta?" John asked.

"It'll double my ranch and I'll have to build a bunkhouse for extra help to run that many more cattle, but I think it would pay for itself in a few years."

John smiled and nodded. "Got a house on the property?"

"Just a small two-bedroom frame that needs repairs. Probably have to rewire it and run new plumbing lines. It's been there at least fifty years."

"Might be cheaper than building a bunkhouse and you could bring in help a lot quicker. That's all sayin' that it comes up for sale in the next year or two. Until then do you reckon you've got enough tractors to keep my daughter out of trouble?"

"I'm not sure there's enough John Deere tractors in north Texas to do that job," Wil said. He shifted in his chair until his thigh was tight against Pearl's. He didn't look at her but from her body language he was fully aware of the effect he had on her.

She finished her salad and dropped her hands into her lap, then very gently reached over and ran her fingertips up his thigh. When his muscles tightened, she squeezed. Two could play the game, and Wil Marshall had met his match in the dining room as well as in the whiskey contest.

The main course arrived: prime rib, mashed potatoes, and asparagus spears.

Wil took a bite and reached over to touch Pearl on the wrist. "Can you make this?"

"Of course she can. She was taught by experts," Granny said. "Tess has a cook but she can run that Rachael Ray on television some competition. And she taught Pearl. The girl knows her way around the kitchen as well as she does around a tractor."

"She didn't make supper for you yet?" Kate asked in mock horror.

"She made me cook," Wil said.

She squeezed his thigh a little higher up. "Tell them the rest of the story."

"What?" he asked.

"He does not allow women in his kitchen. Not to cook or to clean up. Want to tell them why?"

"Because the last woman who made a meal in my kitchen thought she could move into my house and tell me what to do, when to do it, and how to do it. She was ready to call in a decorator and take out all my furniture and put in black stuff from Japan," he explained.

"Man can't have that kind of heifer takin' over," John said with a grin.

Pearl gave Wil's leg another squeeze and he jumped.

"I never have liked that oriental stuff. Can't abide sitting on the floor in front of a little coffee table thing to eat my dinner. And I don't like sushi, either. In my world we call it bait," Wil went on.

"Amen!" John said with a booming voice.

"But I got to admit something. Red made lasagna and

hot bread sticks that was absolutely wonderful the other night," he said.

"You men are horrid. Little sushi never hurt no one. Why, me and Audry learned to really like it when we went on that Alaskan cruise last spring. It was real tasty so don't be putting something down until you've tried it," Kate said.

"You ready to eat a bait of calf fries?" John asked.

"I've never been hungry enough to eat bull balls," Kate said flatly.

"And I've never been hungry enough to eat raw fish. So I rest my case," John said.

"How about you? You eat calf fries?" Wil whispered to Pearl while Kate and John argued about sushi and calf fries.

"Love 'em. There's a place right across the river bridge in Terral called Doug's Peach Orchard that serves them. That's some good eatin' let me tell you. Austin and I meet over there once a month for a gab fest."

"I love that place. Want to run over there tomorrow night?" he asked.

She nodded.

"Why do you get to call her Red? She fought her cousins about that when she was little," Granny said.

Kate whispered in Granny's ear and she nodded. "Now I understand."

When the conversation went back to people he had no knowledge of, Wil leaned toward Pearl and whispered, "Understand what?"

"Aunt Kate said 'three times' in Granny's ear," she said softly.

"Three times. What's that got to do with... you told?"

"They were giving me fits about getting drunk and Aunt Kate asked if you could still do it after that many shots. She's very impressed."

It was the first time she'd ever seen Wil blush!

Chapter 23

MONDAY MORNING DAWNED WITH GRAY SKIES THAT looked like they could spit out a blizzard any minute. The wind barely stirred the bare tree limbs and the temperature hovered around the thirty-degree mark. Lucy and Pearl scurried from one warm room to the next, cleaning the twelve rooms that had had visitors the night before.

They'd have had one room each if the Wichita Falls shelter hadn't called at three in the afternoon and asked for ten rooms for a busload of women and children on their way to relocation south of Dallas. Pearl and Lucy had gone together to the grocery store a mile up the road and put together a food bag for each room. Luke signed a voucher and Pearl gave them the rooms for half price again.

After the women were settled in their rooms, Lucy offered Luke coffee and he told her that he'd be in Henrietta the next Wednesday.

"Reckon you could get away to go to a movie with me? Maybe we'd get some dinner beforehand?" he asked. She'd been walking on air all day and singing as she worked.

"There's a woman right here in Henrietta who should've been on that bus," Lucy said when she found Pearl in the laundry room.

"Oh?" Pearl raised an eyebrow.

"I see her at the library pretty often. I know the signs."

"What's her name?"

"Betsy Walton. She's beat down like I was and last week she had a nasty bruise on her cheek. I asked her about it and she said she fell down the porch steps. I've used that excuse lots of times. That and I walked into a cabinet door or else bumped my arm on the chicken coop."

"Lucy, next time you see her you tell her up-front that if she ever needs a place to hide to call you and you'll come get her. We'll put her up right here in the motel until she can get to a shelter."

"You'd do that? Run an underground for abused women?"

"Sure. But it's not just me who'd do it. You would help with it too."

"You are a good woman, Pearl."

"That's debatable, but you tell her. It might give her the courage to get out of that mess."

"I will and thank you."

Pearl's cell phone rang. She backed out the door, pulling a cart with one hand and answering the phone with the other.

"What's going on with you this morning?" Wil asked.

"I'm cleaning rooms. We had another busload of women who needed relocation last night. They're all gone and Lucy and I are working on rooms. You?"

"Just finished all my chores. Jack and I are about to get into the new tractors and do some plowing. Want to come run your little girl tractor over the ground this afternoon?"

"It'll take all afternoon to set things in order here."

"Then I'll see you this evening. Pick you up six thirty?"

"I'll be ready."

At six fifteen he called to tell her that Digger had been poisoned and he was at the vet's with him. "I'm sorry, Red. I'm taking him home but I have to give him medicine all night."

"Want me to come help out?" she asked.

"I'd love for you to, but there's no need in both of us losing sleep," he said.

"Who would have done such a thing?"

"Can't lay the blame on anyone. I caught him with a dead rat this morning. I never use poison to get rid of them but someone around here does. Digger goes out huntin' on his own. He might have run across it half dead from the poison and chased it down like a squirrel. Vet says he'll be fine but I'll have to watch him close tonight."

"Call me every hour with an update. I'd be worried sick if it was Delilah," she said.

"I will and I really, really am sorry."

"Me too," she admitted honestly.

On Tuesday he called at noon to tell her that Digger was begging for something other than water and the vet had said he could have dry food but no table scraps. "Poor old Digger thinks he's being punished. I told him to leave the rats alone from now on and he wouldn't be taken off his scraps."

"I'm glad to hear he's all right but you sound exhausted."

"I am. Jack is doing chores. I'm going to take a nap. Want to get some supper later this evening?"

"Can't. Lucy has a book thing at the library this evening. She's all excited about it and I wouldn't disappoint her for the moon. It's the first social thing she's done since she moved in a month ago."

He yawned. "I'd really like to talk longer but I'm brain-dead. I'll call soon as I wake up. Love you."

"Me too. I miss you."

"Fate is messin' with us, darlin'. But it'll get tired when it sees we mean business. And don't forget we've got a date Friday night to go to the Peach Orchard for supper."

She smiled. "Sleep tight."

Jasmine poked her head in the door of the room where Pearl was making beds. "I'm off to Chicken Fried to talk serious money. I've got enough for a down payment and I'm hoping the bank will finance the rest."

"Come in and help me make this bed while I talk. I've got an idea," she said.

Jasmine grabbed a fitted sheet from the maid's cart and stretched it over the side of the bed closest to the door. "Okay, talk."

Pearl worked the corners down over the mattress on her side of the bed. "How much you got to put down on this café?"

"Twenty percent. I think the bank needs at least that much, doesn't it?"

"That's right. But don't go to the bank for a loan. I'd like to invest in the café. Aunt Pearlita left me quite a bit of money. It's drawing savings account interest and I could loan you the eighty percent you need at one percent less than a small business loan. You'd have a deal and I'd be making twice as much as what I'm getting now on it. Interested?"

"Hell, yeah! How did she make that much money on a little bitty motel?"

"I don't think it all came from the motel. There was her husband's insurance money from the railroad and some wise investments on her part through the years. But when she thought she was nearing the end of her life she liquidated it all and put it in a simple savings account so I could get to it easily," Pearl answered.

"You got that much money and you're making beds?"

"Well, you're going to be making money hand over fist and you're going to be cooking."

Jasmine laughed. "Are we both crazy?"

"Probably. I'll call my lawyer and you tell them over at Chicken Fried that you're going to be ready to move in the apartment as soon as possible."

Jasmine hugged Pearl tightly. "I won't ever be late on a payment and you can eat there free anytime you want."

Pearl giggled. "No, I can't. That's no way to make money."

---m---

On Wednesday Wil called at six o'clock and woke her up. "Guess what? Austin is pregnant."

"What?" she asked groggily.

"Austin is pregnant. Rye is calling everyone he knows he's so excited. Aren't you happy?"

"I'm half-asleep and Austin is probably going to call me herself as soon as she gets off the phone with her mother and aunts."

"Well, go back to sleep, grumpy pants. I'll be happy enough for both of us."

The phone line went dead and she tossed her cell on the floor. Go back to sleep? Was he crazy? She had to get up, take care of check-outs, go to the bank with Jasmine who was moving in the apartment above the café over the weekend, talk to Lucy about how her book discussion went, and clean rooms.

"Go back to sleep indeed!" She fussed all the way to the bathroom. It was time for her and Wil to have a "sit-down," as her grandmother called it when she was a little girl and in trouble. No television. No sex. No kisses. Nothing but talk. She was in love but she didn't know where he stood. He'd said the words, but would he run away and leave her holding nothing but a fist full of memories and a broken heart? The Peach Orchard could wait. She and Wil were going to have a serious talk on Friday night. Saturday would bring one of two things: misery or happiness.

She heard from Austin that morning at nine when she was checking out the last customer. By then she'd had four cups of coffee, three donuts, and had worked up some excitement for her friend.

"I've been sick as a dog three mornings in a row but I thought I had the flu. The pregnancy test says different. Rye is dancing around like he did this all by himself, and the whole O'Donnell clan is ready to put a diamond crown on my head. It'll be the first grandchild. God, it's going to be spoiled," Austin bubbled on and on.

"Couldn't be any worse than we were."

"Your turn next."

"Bite your tongue, woman."

"I hear things are going well with you and Wil."

"Yes, it is, but that's hardly enough to make it my turn next. You'll have three and working on a fourth by the time I get around to kids."

"We'll see. Got a beep. It's Mother. She's already thinking pink nursery. This is the fifth time she has called this morning. She thinks I need to come to Tulsa for the next eight months and go to the specialists up there. Ain't that a hoot? I've got a ranch to help run and a watermelon crop to put in the ground in the spring. Pregnancy ain't goin' to slow me down one bit. See you later. Let's do lunch on Saturday."

Pearl laid the phone on the counter and looked up at Lucy, just coming in the door. "That was Austin. Everyone is walkin' around on clouds because she's pregnant."

"Must be nice. She and Rye been married long?" Lucy asked.

"Six months or so. She inherited her grandmother's watermelon farm. Came down to Terral from Tulsa. Tulsa is a huge place and Terral is smaller than Henrietta. She only meant to clean out the house and sell it but fell in love with the rancher across the street. He was in love from the minute he laid eyes on her and it didn't take her long to fall for him either."

Lucy leaned on the counter and braced her chin on her forearm. "Does he treat her right?"

"Like a queen," Pearl answered.

"That's wonderful. The world needs men like that. Betsy came to the book discussion last night. Her husband works nights so she was able to come without him knowing. We had a talk. I told her what you said. She thanked me but said he wasn't always mean. Just when he was upset. I've used that line before. She'll get tired of it one of these days."

"When she does, give her a room until we can find her a place. But for now you've got to get in my closet and find something spiffy to wear on your date with Luke. I'll polish your nails when we get done and you're going to knock his socks off."

Lucy giggled. "You think I could borrow that plaid skirt and the sweater? I'd feel real special in it."

"With your hair and eyes, it'll look better on you than it does on me. Luke won't be able to keep his eyes off you."

—*w*—

On Thursday Pearl and Jasmine spent most of the day with the bankers again. Then in the evening Lucy managed the lobby while she and Jasmine took both trucks to Sherman to load up the bare necessities for her to move into the apartment on Friday. It was past midnight when they got back to the motel and both of them had no trouble sleeping that night.

Pearl hit the floor running on Friday. They'd only had three guests the night before so Lucy took care of the rooms and check-outs while Jasmine and Pearl drove to Ringgold. The apartment had been emptied and cleaned so recently that it still smelled like disinfectant. They moved in a bed and Jasmine's clothing. The rest would be arriving in a moving van on Monday, the day that Jasmine officially took over the restaurant.

The sun was a thin glimmer on the west horizon when she drove into the parking lot at the Longhorn that evening. She dialed Wil's cell phone number and asked him if they could stay in that night. Maybe he could pick up hamburgers at the Sonic and bring them to her place because she wanted to talk.

"About what?" he asked cautiously.

"Us," she said.

"I guess we really should. Has the fire burned out?"

"We'll talk about it tonight. Don't forget the burgers and I don't want onions," she said.

"Yes, ma'am," he said. "Fries and a chocolate malt?"

"Yes, thank you."

"Six o'clock?"

"That's fine."

"Want to give me a hint?"

"No."

"Sounds serious," he said.

"It could be."

Wil showed up at five o'clock and slumped down in a recliner while she checked in guests. He looked at a magazine for a few minutes, then laid it aside and fell asleep, his head thrown back and his feet propped up.

After the guests were taken care of, Pearl sat down in the other recliner and watched him sleep. In that moment, sitting there beside him while he slept, she realized that she was truly in love with the cowboy. It wasn't a love like she'd had in high school with Vince and not even like what she'd thought she had with Marlin. And it damn sure wasn't like that rebound rebellion streak she had when she and Wyatt eloped on a whim after splitting a bottle of bourbon. It was a mature adult thing that consumed her body, soul, and mind. Parties didn't matter anymore. Dating wasn't so important. She wanted to wake up to this man's love forever.

He awoke with a start and grinned. "Did I snore?"

"No, but you did forget the hamburgers."

"Shit! I'll go get them."

"No, we can eat grilled cheese sandwiches and noodle soup out of a can. I'm turning on the NO VACANCY light and we're going to have—"

"A heart-to-heart?" he asked.

She nodded, stood up, and started across the floor with him right behind her.

"Do I go first or you?"

"I'm going first, Wil," she said.

He pulled out a kitchen chair and sat down. "If you are going to tell me to get lost, just spit it out before you make supper," he said.

"How would that make you feel?"

"Like shit. I told you I love you, Red. I don't say that when I don't mean it. But it scares the hell out of me. What if in ten years you get tired of me and want to go back to your parties and all those guy friends?"

"Let me tell you why I'm the way I am," she said as she heated soup and made sandwiches. She told him about Vince and how his mother had blamed her for Vince's rebellious streak. And how that she'd feared Wil's mother not liking her would cause the same problems.

"Darlin', Vince was eighteen and out sowing wild oats. I'm past thirty and I love my mother, but she doesn't have that kind of sway or control over my life. Besides, I think she's over her red-haired spell," he said. "Come here."

She put the sandwiches on a plate and carried them to the table. He pulled her down in his lap.

"I love you, Wil," she said.

He ran a rough hand down her cheekbone. "Forget the food. Let's make love. I've missed touching you and holding you. I even missed our afterglow."

She moistened her lips with the tip of her tongue and shut her eyes. He tangled his fingers in her red hair and pulled her closer to him. The kiss started off sweet and gentle but progressed into a hot desire that had to be fed with more and more passion. He stood up and she wrapped her legs around his waist. He carried her to the sofa and they tumbled down together without ever breaking the kisses.

"This sofa is too narrow but there's lots of floor," he muttered.

"There's a big bed right down the hall. Please stay with me tonight. Hold me all night and wake up with me tomorrow morning."

"Remember what you said about life being mostly chaos?" Wil said.

"I do, and the only time the world is right is when I'm in your arms."

He buried his face in her hair and said, "Me too."

He stopped at the bathroom, removed all her clothes as well as his, and opened the shower door for her. "I've been working most of the day and didn't take time for a shower. I was afraid you were going to tell me to 'hit the road, Jack' so I just came from work to the lobby. Before we go any further I need to clean up."

"Me too," she said.

The shower had not been built for two people but they managed, skin bumping skin, her butt arousing him to the ready stage when she backed up for him to wash her hair.

"I really do love you, Red," he whispered into her wet hair.

"And I love you," she said.

He finished soaping her whole body and rinsed her before shoving her out of the shower. "Wrap up in a towel. I'll be out in a second."

"Maybe I want to give you a bath," she said.

"Darlin', if you did, well, let's just say it would be fast food rather than grilled steak," he said.

She laughed and wrapped a towel around her body. By the time he finished and dried, she was in the bedroom, dressed in a black lace teddy complete with a thong to match.

His eyes widened.

"Do you like it?"

"Wow! Do I get to unwrap it like a present?"

"Depends on how fast you can unwrap a present. Just lookin' at you standing there like a marble God is making me hot as hell."

He swept her up and carried her to the bed and very, very slowly unwrapped his present. "I was so afraid you wanted to go back to your fast life," he mumbled.

"Fast food or grilled steak? Hmmm." She reached out and touched him.

He groaned.

"I'll take the grilled steak."

He slipped the thong down and stretched out on top of her, smothering her with kisses so hot that she felt as if she were the steak on the grill.

"I want some jalapeño poppers for an appetizer." She giggled.

He raised up and looked into her green eyes.

"That means fast and hot. Please make love to me. I've been ready ever since we stepped into the shower."

He kissed her and slipped inside her at the same time. Life would always be like a jalapeño pepper with Red.

She awoke at eight the next morning to the aroma of bacon and coffee wafting down the short hallway and through the crack in the bedroom door. Wil was gone and she was hugging a pillow, which wasn't nearly as comforting. She pushed back the covers, crawled out of bed, and padded barefoot to the small kitchen where she found him cooking breakfast.

"I was going to bring it to you in bed." He turned and kissed her on the forehead. "Did you sleep well?"

She wrapped her arms around him and snuggled up to his chest.

"Will you marry me?" he said quickly.

She gasped. "Say it again."

"Will you marry me? I don't have a ring but we can remedy that any time you want to go with me to a jewelry store."

"When?"

"Say yes and you can decide," he said.

"Yes," she whispered and wrapped her arms around his neck, pulled his lips to hers, and kissed him long and hard.

"Did you really say yes?" he murmured softly into her ear.

"I did. I love you, Wil Marshall. When I thought about talking to you seriously about us, I was scared to death you'd tell me that you weren't interested in a long-term relationship."

He tipped her chin back with his fist and kissed her with so much passion that she was convinced their love was much, much more than a flash in the pan.

Pearl didn't care that Valentine's Day was on Sunday. It was going to be her wedding day from the time that Wil proposed in her kitchen. So at a few minutes until two on Sunday afternoon she was settling a ring of white roses and lace around a burst of springy red curls on top of her head.

"I still wish you would have got a real wedding dress with a train from here to Savannah. This looks so plain," Tess fussed as she buttoned the sleeves of the ivory lace sheath dress with long fitted sleeves. "And what happened to my daughter being an entrepreneur who was going to turn that old motel into a work of beauty?"

"I'm still a businesswoman. Lucy is running the motel for me and we'll have weekly visits about things. But we've decided that the Longhorn Inn is already quaint and romantic just like it is, so we aren't making so many changes. And I've realized that I really miss ranchin', Momma. I miss driving a tractor and petting new baby calves and I miss—"

"Oh, hush! If your daddy hears you talkin' like that he'll never let me hear the end of it. But I really do wish you would've bought a nicer dress," Tess changed the subject.

"You got to have the wedding where you wanted, invite all the people you wanted, and do everything the way you wanted, Momma. You can overlook my dress."

"I think you are beautiful," Lucy said.

"And so are you," Pearl told her.

Lucy's wore a bright red velvet dress in the same style as Pearl's and carried white roses. Jasmine and Austin wore identical dresses and carried the same white rose nosegay bouquets.

The wedding planner stuck her head in the dressing

room and said, "Mrs. Richland, the usher is ready to seat you."

Tess kissed Pearl on the cheek. "That'll be one of Wil's handsome nephews. You really are beautiful, Katy Pearl, and I'm glad you are marrying Wil. He's a good man."

"Momma, I'm in love with him," Pearl said.

"I can see that, darlin'." She shut the door softly behind her, leaving Pearl with the girls.

Austin hugged her and said, "Jasmine is next. Maybe Ace?"

"Don't you be siccing cupid on me or Ace neither. After all those years with Eddie Jay, I may never get married. Lucy can be next."

"Hell, no!" Lucy said emphatically. "I'm going to run the Longhorn for Pearl and be happy dating Luke for a long, long time. I've inherited her apartment and Delilah is going to live with me. And I've hired Betsy to help me with cleaning. She's going to live in my old room. Her husband left her high and dry for another woman after he'd whooped on her for five years. I'm not about to be next in line. I've got it made at the Longhorn."

Pearl was still laughing over Lucy's newfound freedom of speech when the wedding planner brought her father into the room to escort her to the front of the church where Wil was already waiting with his groomsmen... Dewar, Rye, and Raylen.

"You are perfect today. I'm glad you didn't wear one of them big dresses. It wouldn't have been you," John said. "I have a little present for you from Wil."

He pulled a small velvet box from his pocket and removed a gold chain with a custom-made pendant of

Wil's ranch brand. He carefully fastened it around her neck.

"I can't even begin to tell you how happy I am that you are going to be a rancher, Katy Pearl."

"Thanks, Daddy." Her voice quivered.

"I'm glad you are marrying Wil. He's a good man and I'm glad to have him for a son."

Pearl swallowed a golf ball–sized lump. "You are going to make me cry."

"Can't have that, can we? It'll smear your eye makeup and your mother will never let either of us live that down. Let's go get this shindig over with so we can go to the reception and eat. If there's one thing Tess does well, it's throw a party." He laughed.

From the time Pearl met Wil's eyes there was no one else in the church. When her father put her hand in Wil's, that old familiar tingle glued her to the floor. When he said his vows and promised to love her not until death parted them but through eternity she didn't even hear Austin sigh. When the minister pronounced them man and wife and told Wil he could kiss her, she got ready for a shot of pure old steamy lust to shoot through her body.

She was not disappointed.

"I love you, Red," he whispered as he held her close after the kiss.

"I love you back."

The reception was elegant and lavish. Wil and Pearl danced their first dance as a married couple to an old George Jones tune, "I Always Get Lucky with You."

"I do," he said.

"Do what?"

"Get lucky with you," he answered.

"I thought you were a red-hot cowboy the first time I met you and I haven't changed my mind, so I guess I'm the lucky one," she said.

"I'm glad to be Red's hot cowboy."

She smiled up at him. "I didn't say it that way, but I like it. And don't you ever forget whose cowboy you are. I do not share!"

THE END

Acknowledgments

There are so many people I need to thank for making this series possible. My amazing publisher, Dominique Raccah, who continues to believe in me and my cowboy stories; my fabulous editor, Deb Werksman, who pushes me to write better and better books; Danielle Jackson, for whom there are not enough adjectives in the whole world, who takes care of blog tours, publicity, and a gazillion other things that keep my world going smoothly. Then there are all the folks at Sourcebooks whose names I don't even know but they take my books from manuscript to those beautiful things you see on the bookstore shelves. You are all wonderful!

I'd like to thank my agent, the great Erin Niumata of Folio Literary Management, for all she does and for always being there for me... even at midnight in London.

And once again my husband, Charles, who still drives me around to dozens of Texas towns until I find just the right one to set my books. He married this woman who cleaned his house, cooked his meals, and even tailor made his three-piece suits. Bless his heart, he now wears clothes right off the rack, eats fast food, and dust bunnies tell him bedtime stories while I finish one more chapter. And he hasn't visited a divorce lawyer one time in the forty-plus years we've been married... now that's a husband who truly understands having a writer for a spouse.

Then there are my kids, Lemar, Amy, and Ginny, who read my stories and tell me how wonderful I am; my sister who's always pushed me to write even when we were kids. And all you fantastic readers who read my books, take time from your busy schedules to write reviews, and send me notes.

And thanks to my fellow romance writer friends who are way, way too many to start naming.

Every one of you are truly the wind beneath my wings and I appreciate every single thing you do!

Carolyn Brown

About the Author

Carolyn Brown is an award-winning author with more than forty books published, and she credits her eclectic family for her humor and writing ideas. Her books include the cowboy trilogy *Lucky in Love, One Lucky Cowboy,* and *Getting Lucky;* the Honky Tonk series *I Love This Bar, Hell Yeah, Honky Tonk Christmas,* and *My Give a Damn's Busted*; and *Love Drunk Cowboy,* which kicked off the Spikes and Spurs series. She was born in Texas but grew up in southern Oklahoma where she and her husband, Charles, a retired English teacher, make their home. They have three grown children and enough grandchildren to keep them young.

Darn Good Cowboy Christmas

IT WAS JUST A WHITE FRAME HOUSE AT THE END OF A long lane.

But it did not have wheels.

Liz squinted against the sun sinking in the west and imagined it with multicolored Christmas lights strung all around the porch, the windows, even in the cedar tree off to the left side. In her vision, it was a Griswold house from *Christmas Vacation* that lit up the whole state of Texas. She hoped that when she flipped the switch she didn't cause a major blackout because in a few weeks it was going to look like the house on that old movie that she loved.

Now where was the cowboy to complete the package?

Christmas lights on a house without wheels and a cowboy in tight fittin' jeans and in boots—that's what she asked for every year when her mother asked for her Christmas list. She didn't remember the place being so big when she visited her uncle those two times. Once when she was ten and then again when she was fourteen. But both of those times she'd been quite taken with the young cowboy next door and didn't pay much attention to the house itself. The brisk Texas wind whipped around ferociously as if saying that it could send her right back to east Texas if she didn't change her mind about the house.

"I don't think so," she giggled. "I know a thing or two

about Texas wind, and it'd take more than a class five tornado to get rid of me. This is what I've wanted all my life, and I think it's the prettiest house in Montague County. It's sittin' on a foundation, and oh, my god, he's left Hooter and Blister for me. Uncle Haskell, I could kiss you!"

The wind pushed its way into the truck, bringing a few fall leaves with it when she opened the truck door. Aunt Tressa would say that was an omen; the place was welcoming her into its arms. Her mother would say that the wind was blowing her back to the carnival where she belonged.

The old dog, Hooter, slowly came down off the porch, head down, wagging his tail. Blister, the black and white cat, eyed her suspiciously from the ladder-back chair on the tiny porch.

Her high heels sunk into the soft earth, leaving holes as she rushed across the yard toward the yellow dog. She squatted down, hugged the big yellow mutt, and scratched his ears. "You beautiful old boy. You are the icing on the cake. Now I've got animals and a house. This is a damn fine night."

The key was under the chair, tucked away in a faded ceramic frog, just where her Uncle Haskell said it would be when she talked to him earlier that afternoon. But he hadn't mentioned leaving the two animals. She'd thank him for that surprise when she called him later on.

She opened the wooden screen door and was about to put the key in the lock when the door swung open. And there he was! Raylen O'Donnell, all grown up and even sexier than she remembered. Her heart thumped so hard she could feel it pushing against her bra. Her hands were shaky and her knees weak, but she took a deep breath, willed her hands to be still, and locked her knees in place.

"If it's religion you're sellin' or anything else, we're not interested," Raylen said in a deep Texas drawl. He'd been pouring a glass of tea in the kitchen when he heard a noise. Hooter hadn't barked, so he figured it was just the wind, but when he opened the door he'd been more shocked than the woman standing there with wide eyes and a spooked expression on her face.

She wore skin-tight black jeans that looked like they'd been spray painted on her slim frame. Without those spike heels she would've barely come to his shoulder, and Raylen was the shortest of the three O'Donnell brothers, tipping the chart at five feet ten inches. Her jet-black hair had been twisted up and clipped, but strands had escaped the shiny silver clasp and found their way to her shoulder. Her eyes were so dark brown that they looked ebony.

"Raylen?" she said.

Her voice was husky, with a touch of gravel, adding to her exotic looks. It made Raylen think of rye whiskey with a teaspoon of honey and a twist of lemon. He'd heard that voice before. It had been branded on his brain for eleven years, but she couldn't be Haskell's niece. Liz wasn't supposed to be there until the first of the week at the earliest.

"That's right. Who are you?" he asked cautiously.

"I happen to own this place," she said with a flick of her hand.

"Liz?" Raylen started at her toes and let his gaze travel slowly all the way to her eyebrows. She'd been a pretty teenager, but now she was a stunning woman.

"Surprise! I guess this chunk of Texas dirt now belongs to me. What are you doing here?" she asked.

Could Raylen really be the cowboy Santa was going to leave under her Christmas tree? He'd sure enough been the one she had in mind when she asked for a cowboy. She'd visualized him in tight fittin' jeans and boots when she was younger. Lately, she'd changed it to nothing but a Santa hat and the boots.

His hair was still a rich dark brown, almost black until the sunlight lit up the deep chestnut color. His eyes were exactly as she remembered: pale icy blue rimmed with dark brown lashes. It all added up to a heady combination, enough to make her want to tangle her hands up in all that dark hair and kiss him until she swooned like a heroine in one of those old castle romances she'd read since she was a teenager. Speaking of kissing, where in the hell was the mistletoe when a woman needed it, anyway?

Cowboys have roots, not wings. Don't get involved with one or you'll smother to death in a remote backwoods farm or else die of boredom. Her mother's voice whispered so close to her ear that she turned to make sure Marva Jo Hanson hadn't followed her to Ringgold, Texas.

Raylen stood to one side. "I came to feed and water Hooter and Blister. Haskell asked me to do that until you got here. We met when we were kids, remember?"

"I do," she said. How could she forget? She'd been in love with Raylen O'Donnell since she was fourteen years old.

"Haskell said that if you didn't like it here, he'd sell me your twenty acres." Now that was a helluva thing to blurt out, but he couldn't very well say that she'd grown up to be the most exotic creature he'd ever laid eyes on. That he'd thought she was cuter than any girl he'd ever seen when she was about fourteen or fifteen, but he hadn't realized that she'd only been the bud of the rose. The full-blown flower was standing before him right then, making him fidget like a little boy.

"I'm going to live here. Uncle Haskell said if I like it he'll deed the place over to me in the spring. The place isn't for sale and won't be," she said.

"And do what? Ringgold isn't very big."

She shrugged. "I don't know. Pet the cat. Feed the dog."

"That won't make a living, lady," Raylen said.

She popped both hands on her hips. "I don't reckon what I do for a living is one damn bit of your business, cowboy. Do you intend to let me come into my house?"

Why in the hell was he arguing with her? Never in all the scenarios that she'd imagined did he cross her. He'd kissed her. He'd swept her off her feet and carried her to a big white pickup truck and they'd driven off into the sunset. He'd smiled and said that he remembered her well and she'd grown up into a beautiful woman. But he hadn't argued.

Raylen motioned her into the house with a wave of his hand. She brushed across his chest as she entered the house and was acutely aware of the sparks dancing all over the room but attributed it to anger or disappointment, maybe even a bitter dose of both. She'd had Raylen on a pedestal for more than a decade and he didn't even recognize her. He was probably married and had three or four kids too. That was just her luck!

When she fanned past him he got a whiff of a

sensuous perfume that went with her dark, gypsy looks, and he wanted to follow after her like a lost puppy dog.

"I'll take over feeding the cat and dog," she said.

"Okay, then here's the key Haskell gave me." He dug into his pocket and handed her an old key ring with two keys on it. "Welcome to Ringgold, Liz. I still live on the ranch that surrounds this land. Haskell sold me most of his ranch six months ago, all but the part the house sits on."

"He told me."

Raylen headed for the door. "The O'Donnells are your closest neighbors. Come around to see us sometime. Be seein' you."

She wanted to say something; she really did. But not one word would come out of her mouth. Raylen in her living room, looking even sexier than he had when he was seventeen and exercising the horses. Raylen, all grown up, a man instead of a lanky teenager, talking to her... it was such a shock and a surprise that she was speechless. And that was strange territory for Lizelle Hanson.

"Dammit!" she swore.

The noise of the truck engine filled the house for a moment then faded. She'd been so stunned to see him that she couldn't think straight. She hadn't known what to expect, but it sure wasn't what she got. She fished a cell phone from her jacket pocket and punched a speed dial number.

"I'm here," she said when her mother answered.

"And?"

Liz giggled nervously. "It's bigger than I remembered, and there's a sexy cowboy who lives next door but he's probably married and has six kids because no guy that pretty isn't taken. I'd forgotten how big the house is after living in the carnie trailer."

"Have you unpacked? You can turn around and come back right now. You could be here in time to take your shift tomorrow night, and my brother can sell it to those horse ranchers next door to him."

"Not yet. I was on my way in the house when Raylen opened the door and scared the hell out of me. Hooter and Blister are still alive and well. I'm not ready to throw in the towel yet."

"Raylen?" Marva Jo asked.

"The sexy cowboy. I met him both times I came to visit Uncle Haskell. Remember when I told you about the boy that tried to beat me walkin' the fence when I was ten? That was Raylen."

"You are right. He's probably married and has a couple of kids. I was hoping the house would be butt ugly to you."

"No, ma'am. I squinted real hard and even imagined it with Christmas lights. Looked pretty damn fine," Liz said.

"We'll be in Bowie in a few weeks. By then you'll be sick to death of boredom. You were born for the carnie and travel," Marva said.

"I will have the Christmas lights on the house when you get here," Liz said.

"A house not on wheels with Christmas lights and a cowboy." Marva laughed. "Be careful that the latter doesn't cut off your beautiful wings, because that part of the country produces a crop of hot cowboys every generation."

"Good night, Momma. I love you," Liz said.

"Love you too, kid. Go prove me right about getting bored to tears. It's only half an hour until time to tell fortunes and I still have to get my makeup on. Does that make you miss me?"

"Not yet. I only saw you this morning. Hug Aunt Tressa and I'll see you in a few weeks."

—m—

Raylen drove down the lane and stopped. The left blinker was on, but he couldn't make himself pull out onto the highway. The whole incident at Haskell's place had been surreal. Haskell said his niece, Liz, was going to take over the property. He remembered Liz very well. She was the ten-year-old who'd walked the rail fence better than him even though he was thirteen. She was the fourteen-year-old who rested her elbows on the same rail fence and watched him exercise the horses. Now she was so pretty she sucked every sane thought out of his brain.

He finally pulled out on Highway 81 and headed north a mile, then turned left into the O'Donnell horse ranch. She'd find out pretty quick that a person couldn't make a living by petting the cat and feeding the dog, and when she did he intended to be the first in line to buy her twenty acres. It was the only property for a three-mile stretch down the highway that didn't belong to the O'Donnells.

He parked in the backyard, crawled out of the truck, and sat down on the porch step to his folks' house. Dewar drove up, parked next to him, hopped out of his truck, and swaggered to the porch. Just a year older than

Raylen, Dewar was taller by several inches. His hair was so black that it had a faint blue cast as the sunrays bounced off it. His eyes were a strange mossy shade of green and his face square. His Wranglers were tight and dusty; his boots were worn down at the heels and covered with mud.

"Y'all get those cattle worked at Rye's?" Raylen looked down at his own boots. They were just as worn down at the heels and covered with horseshit. His jeans had a hole in one knee and frayed hems on both pant legs. His shirt looked like it had been thrown out in the round horse corral for a solid week and then used for a dog bed a month after that. Damn it all to the devil and back again. He'd planned on at least meeting Liz the first time in clean duds, not looking like a bum off the streets.

"Yes, we did, and we would've got them done sooner if our younger brother would've helped," Dewar said.

"Aww, y'all didn't need me. And besides, if you worked harder and played with Rachel less, you'd get more done."

"Bullshit! You're just tryin' to find excuses." Dewar grinned.

Rachel was their oldest brother's new baby daughter, the first O'Donnell grandchild and only a few months old. Her father, Rye, was Raylen and Dewar's oldest brother. Her mother, Austin, had been a Tulsa socialite until she inherited a watermelon farm across the river in Terral, Oklahoma, and fell in love with Rye. Rachel was getting to know her two uncles and it was an ongoing battle about which one would be the favorite.

"Want a beer? I swear I'm spittin' dust and hot summer is long since past," Dewar said.

"I'd drink a beer with you," Raylen said.

Dewar disappeared into the house and brought out two longneck bottles of Coors, and he handed one to Raylen. "So you got the chores done around here or am I going to have to do those too?"

"All finished. Everything with four legs has been fed and watered. Horses are all exercised, and even Haskell's dog and cat are fed. His niece is over there now. She can take care of Hooter and Blister." He turned up the bottle and downed a fourth of it before coming up for air and a burp.

Dewar plopped down on the porch step beside Raylen. "Is she going to keep the place or do you have a chance at buying it?"

"Says she is going to keep it. I asked her what she was going to do to make a living in Ringgold, Texas, and she said she was going to feed the dog and pet the cat. Hell, if Haskell gives her his money as well as that twenty acres, she won't have to do nothing but feed a dog and pet a cat."

"What's she look like?"

"Damn fine. Not a thing like old Haskell. She's got jet-black hair and the blackest eyes you've ever seen, and her skin is this light toast color that says she's got some kind of exotic blood in her. Build like a red brick outhouse without a single brick out of place."

"You took with her?"

"Hell, no!" Raylen said too quickly.

COMING OCTOBER 2011
FROM SOURCEBOOKS CASABLANCA

MY
GIVE A DAMN'S
BUSTED

By Carolyn Brown

He's just doing his job...

If Hank Wells thinks he can dig up dirt on the new owner of the Honky Tonk beer joint for his employer, he's got no idea what kind of trouble he's courting...

She's not going down without a fight...

If any dime store cowboy thinks he's going to get the best of Larissa Morley—or her Honky Tonk—then he's got another think coming...

As secrets emerge, and passion vies with ulterior motives, it's winner takes all at the Honky Tonk...

Praise for *Lucky in Love:*

"A spit-and-vinegar heroine...and a hero who dances faster than she can shoot make a funny, fiery pair in this appealing novel."

—Booklist

"Carolyn Brown pens an exciting romance... This is one of those rare books where every person in it comes alive."

—The Romance Studio, *5/5*

978-1-4022-3928-1 • $7.99 U.S / £4.99 UK

HELL, YEAH

BY CAROLYN BROWN

She's finally found a place that feels like home...

When Cathy O'Dell buys the Honky Tonk, the nights of cowboys and country tunes come together to create the home she's always wanted. Then in walks a ruggedly handsome oil man who tempts her to trade in the happiness she's found at the Honky Tonk for a life on the road with him.

Gorgeous and rich, Travis Henry travels the country unearthing oil wells and then moving on. Then the beautiful blue-eyed new owner of the Honky Tonk beer joint becomes his best friend and so much more. When his job is done in Texas, how is he ever going to hit the road without her?

Praise for Carolyn Brown:

"Carolyn Brown takes her audience by storm... I was mesmerized." —The Romance Studio

"Carolyn Brown creates a bevy of delightful and believable characters." —The Long and Short of It Reviews

978-1-4022-3927-4 • $7.99 US / £4.99 UK

I LOVE THIS BAR

BY CAROLYN BROWN

Saddle up, cowboy…

She doesn't need anything but her bar…

Daisy O'Dell has her hands full with hotheads and thirsty ranchers until the day one damn fine cowboy walks in and throws her whole life into turmoil. Jarod McElroy is looking for a cold drink and a moment's peace, but instead he finds one red hot woman. She's just what he needs, if only he can convince her to come out from behind that bar, and come home with him…

Praise for *One Lucky Cowboy:*

"Jam-packed with cat fights, reluctant heroes, spirited old ladies and, of course, a chilling villain, Brown's plot-driven cowboy romance…will earn a spot on your keeper shelf."

—*Romantic Times*, 4 stars

"Sheer fun…filled with down-home humor, realistic characters, and pure romance."

—*Romance Reader at Heart*

978-1-4022-3926-7 • $7.99 US / £4.99 UK

GETTING Lucky

BY CAROLYN BROWN

Griffin Luckadeau is one stubborn cowboy...

And Julie Donovan is one hotheaded schoolteacher who doesn't let anybody push her around. When Griffin thinks his new neighbor is scheming to steal his ranch out from under him, he's more than willing to cross horns. Their look-alike daughters may be best friends, but until these two Texas hotheads admit it's fate that brought them together, running from the inevitable is only going to bring them a double dose of miserable...

Praise for Carolyn Brown:

"*A delight to read.*" —Booklist

"*Engaging characters, humorous situations, and a bumpy romance... Carolyn Brown will keep you reading until the very last page.*" —Romantic Times

"*Carolyn Brown's rollicking sense of humor asserts itself on every page.*" —Scribes World

---

978-1-4022-2436-2 • $7.99 U.S. / £4.99 UK

ONE *Lucky* COWBOY

By Carolyn Brown

No big blond cowboy is going to intimidate this spitfire!

If Slade Luckadeau thinks he can run Jane Day off his ranch, he's got cow chips for brains. She's winning every argument, and he's running out of fights to pick. But when trouble with a capital "T" threatens Jane *and* the Double L Ranch, suddenly it's Slade's heart that's in the most danger of all.

Praise for *Lucky in Love*:

"I enjoyed this book so much that I plan to rope myself some more of Carolyn Brown and her books. Lucky in Love *is a must read!"* —Cheryl's Book Nook

"This is one of those rare books where every person in it comes alive… as they share wit, wisdom, and love." —The Romance Studio

978-1-4022-2437-9 • $7.99 U.S. / £4.99 UK

Lucky IN LOVE

By Carolyn Brown

BEAU HASN'T GOT A LICK OF SENSE WHEN IT COMES TO WOMEN

Everything hunky rancher "Lucky" Beau Luckadeau touches turns to gold—except relationships. Spitfire Milli Torres can mend a fence, pull a calf, or shoot a rattlesnake between the eyes. When Milli shows up to help out at the Lazy Z ranch, she's horrified to find that Beau's her nearest neighbor—the very man she'd hoped never to lay eyes on again. If Beau ever figures out what really happened on that steamy Louisiana night when they first met, there'll be the devil to pay…

Praise for Carolyn Brown:

"Engaging characters, humorous situations, and a bumpy romance… Carolyn Brown will keep you reading until the very last page." —Romantic Times

"Carolyn Brown's rollicking sense of humor asserts itself on every page." —Scribes World

978-1-4022-2435-5 • $7.99 U.S. / £4.99 UK

One Fine
COWBOY

BY JOANNE KENNEDY

The last thing she expects is a lesson in romance...

Graduate student Charlie Banks came to a Wyoming ranch for a seminar on horse communication, but when she meets ruggedly handsome "Horse Whisperer" Nate Shawcross, she starts to fantasize about another connection entirely...

Nate needs to stay focused if he's going to save his ranch from foreclosure, but he can't help being distracted by sexy and brainy Charlie. Could it be that after all this time Nate has finally found the one woman who can tame his wild heart?

Praise for *Cowboy Trouble:*

"A fresh take on the traditional contemporary Western... There's plenty of wacky humor and audacious wit in this mystery-laced escapade." —*Library Journal*

"Contemporary Western fans will enjoy this one!" —*Romantic Times*

"A fun and delicious romantic romp... If you love cowboys, you won't want to miss this one! Romance, mystery, and spurs! Yum!" —*Wendy's Minding Spot*

978-1-4022-3670-9 • $6.99 U.S. / £4.99 UK